STRAIGHT SHOT

JACK LIVELY

GENERAL PROJECTS

For Elsa

CHAPTER ONE

A MAN WAS WALKING the platform, scanning the train as it crept into Alencourt station. I was sitting at the window, watching him as we got closer. The brakes shrieked. The guy moved slow and stiff, his head swiveling like a searchlight as the train inched past. Looking for someone. He walked against the train's direction, while his head rotated back with it, holding each window in place as his eyes examined it, then circling back to scan again, as the next car came abreast.

The train approached; we got closer. I could see his eyes darting around, the head tracked smoothly. Then the eyes found me, but settled below my eye line. Like he wasn't interested in my face. Then the guy lifted his gaze to mine and we were looking directly at each other, engaged. The train was moving painfully slow, so there was plenty of time to get a good look.

Looked like he had recognized me, but I didn't know him.

Then the train stopped with a delayed lurch, and I saw him back off and disengage. Around me passengers were already dragging their bags and children off luggage racks and train seats. Soon they were flooding the platform and the guy was gone.

I was halfway to the entrance hall before I saw him again, over by the ticket desk, trying not to stare at me. He was maybe nineteen or twenty. Close small eyes and a tiny chin, like a rat. Dark hair buzzed to a number two, stripes shaved into one side. Like the Adidas logo. I went over to the information board and examined him in the glass reflection. He couldn't stop himself from looking at me. Not a professional. Some kind of petty criminal maybe.

I looked up at the clock over the information booth. Quarter to noon, Saturday, June 23rd. It was my first time in France.

The station was busy. People dragged wheeled suitcases around, ran for trains. Footsteps slapped on the concrete, echoing around the big hall. Mothers and fathers pulled their kids. The rat-faced guy I'd never seen before was just standing there looking at my back. I supposed he was planning to mug me.

The entrance to the street was a wide stone arch leading to two-way traffic and a park on the other side. There was a kiosk in the park with newspapers and magazines, and a big coffee cup on the roof. I figured I could cross through the traffic and wait to see if the guy came after me. On top of that I could get a cup of coffee.

I jogged across, weaving between taxis.

I ordered coffee at the kiosk and watched the entrance to the train station. Nobody came, nothing happened. I stretched out and yawned. My joints cracked. Twelve hours on the train. The coffee was dark and bitter. It came in a small paper cup. I drank it in two sips, crushed the cup in my fist and threw it into a garbage can. I didn't see anyone coming after me.

The weather was gray and so was the town. Gray stone. Gray poured concrete fixtures. Warm droplets of moisture hung in the air, threatening rain.

I noticed the second guy right off the bat. He must have circled around the park to flank me. This guy was bigger than rat-face and wore jeans with a thin leather jacket. He looked like a young thug. Same age as the first guy. The second one had wet-looking hair combed in a side part.

So I figured the first guy would be coming up behind me. They had wanted me to notice the second one. That was the strategy, distract, induce panic, come at me from both sides. I'd been out of the military for only a week. Their little strategy wasn't going to work.

The park was carved up into little walk-ways. I went off the footpath and cut across the lawn. Using peripheral vision, I clocked rat-face coming off the street and passing the kiosk. He and his leather jacket buddy were moving in sync, wedging me in. Dense evergreens crowded the path where it sunk down in a dip a dozen yards away. The dip would do. I figured less than twenty seconds casual walking.

Laurel bushes blocked out the light. The dip was an intersection. A spider web of narrow walkways converged in its hollow. But the two guys were gone. I stayed there for a couple of minutes to see if they would come. Maybe they were waiting me out. But nobody waits more than a minute. A minute's a long time if you're waiting. Young thugs in particular are impatient, nervous and jumpy. You can always wait them out. The two guys didn't show.

I exited the park and crossed over to the sidewalk. The town center was old and busy. The kind of old that gets preserved by committee. Busy with regular people doing regular things that hadn't changed all that much in a couple hundred years.

Twelve hours on the train made me want to stretch out. To walk. To loosen the hips and the knees and ankles. But first I wanted to stop by the town hall, see if I could find any record of my mother's family. She had been French and spent her summers in Alencourt. I was curious about that side of my family because as far as I knew, my mother hadn't ever come back to France after moving to the United States.

The center of town was a big old medieval square with an ancient church right in the middle of it. The town hall was on the edge of the square. I told the old mustachioed guy at reception what I was looking for and he pointed across the square. He had to push his glasses down off his forehead to look at me. Blue eyes magnified and focused. He said that records were kept in the library, which was on the other side of the church. The old guy looked at his watch and shook his head; chances were the library was already closed for lunch.

But it wasn't quite closed. I got in the door. A young woman wearing a floral print dress was turning over the sign at the front desk, from open to closed. I made it to the counter a split second before the sign flipped and put my hand next to it. Which made her look up. I gave a winning American smile. The librarian was in her twenties, strawberry-blonde hair, long nose, high cheekbones, slim.

I said, "You're closing for lunch."

"Yes, monsieur."

"Can I bother you for half a minute?" I smiled.

"You can bother me for half a minute." She smiled back.

So I told her about my mother and how she had spent summers with family in town. I asked the librarian where I could look if I wanted to find traces that her family might have left.

"Your family."

"Excuse me?"

"You said you wanted to find traces of your mother's family, but it's your family as well."

Which was true, and maybe a better way of putting it. The librarian asked me to write down my mother's name and date of birth. She told me to stop by in the afternoon, say five. She said she'd see what she could dig up. But there were no guarantees. Some traces remained over time, others got wiped away. Depended on a lot of things.

I wrote the name down, *Delphine Vaugeois*, and the date of birth. Then I thanked the librarian and walked out.

Five hours. Enough time to have lunch, check out the town, take a walk, stop by the library, and then get the late train out. Maybe there was a sleeper. I was headed south. Spain or Portugal and the beach. Figured I'd stay there for a month or a year, or however long it took to get bored of the beach. For the moment I was thinking about food and more coffee. Otherwise I felt good.

Off the church square, I turned into a series of narrow, crowded streets. The old town. Shoppers jostled in line for the butcher or the baker. The scent of fresh bread and coffee had settled. I squeezed through a knot of people outside the bakery and felt a push from behind. Turned to look. It was the second guy, with the leather jacket and the wet-looking side part. I could smell the stuff in his hair.

So these clowns had waited for me. I had to give them points for persistence. But, what made them think I was a good mark?

Up ahead on the left was a little side-street entrance, even narrower than the one I was on. I looked to the right, across the street. A new guy. Same age as rat-face, similar style. The local young thug look, but this time with longer hair in a ponytail and a manicured stubble beard. These guys were easy to spot because the rest of the crowd was older and dressed conservatively. The ponytail guy was dressed in a track suit like the rat-faced guy from the train platform.

So now there were three. The first guy with the rat-face and Adidas stripe shaved into his head, leather jacket side-part from the park, and ponytail with the facial hair.

Their plan was simple.

Leather jacket side-part was pushing up behind me so I'd move forward, out of the bakery crowd. The new guy with the ponytail was there to push me left, into the side street. I figured rat-face would be waiting there. So that was their plan. They would pen me in and try to rob me. I thought, *welcome to France*.

I stopped abruptly and let leather jacket side-part guy walk into me belly-first. I felt him grab my shirt above the waist. Which was a mistake, because I used his grab to pull him closer than he wanted. I stomped on his foot with my left heel and crushed his instep. The guy grunted, surprised. The stomp made him lean forward and I whipped my right arm back and nailed him in the nuts with the heel of my hand. I pulled away from his grab and felt the back of my shirt tear as he bent over and fell.

Which pissed me off somewhat. The shirt was new.

The third guy was moving from my right, trying to corral me towards the side street. His ponytail was pulled back tight. His little stubbly beard was carved into a thin shape on a weak face, but he had stunning bright blue eyes highlighted by dark eyelashes, like a male model. He was reaching into his pocket with his left hand, and I was on him in two steps, shutting him down. His right fist came up in a wild flail with no momentum. I stepped into the swing and at the same time transferred body weight from rear to front leg. I bent the knees, sinking low. Moved in close and punched my right elbow into his solar plexus.

The tip of the elbow made contact with a click. He went down in a sprawl.

The solar plexus is a bundle of nerves right above the abdomen, where it meets the chest. It's nearly impossible to actually hit the solar plexus because it sits too deep inside. But, if you get low and aim up, kind of diagonal, you can impact the nerves enough to fire off impulses to the target's diaphragm. When you get it right, the shocked nerves over-stimulate the diaphragm, which contracts. The target thinks that they are suffocating.

Which is what happened to the ponytail guy. I didn't swing my elbow in, I punched it out. The pointy part hit him right in the chest hollow. I followed through like he was made of paper. He hit the ground and started to spasm and gasp. He'd survive. In a few minutes the diaphragm would relax. But he'd get all clammy with cold sweat for at least an hour.

Two down, one to go.

I turned left to face the side street. I was right about the rat-faced guy, the number two haircut man with the Adidas stripe and small, close set eyes. He was coming out of the side street in short steps. This was someone who didn't do enough walking. Too much sitting around playing video games. I detected hesitation. His plan wasn't working out. He hadn't wanted to do it in a crowd.

He had a knife in his right hand. The blade was a Spyderco one-handed opener. All steel. Pretty nasty. But the steel handle isn't much good because it gets slippery when wet. And if you're not plan-ning on getting a knife wet, you shouldn't be taking out a knife. I stepped in quick and caught him off-balance. He found himself too close-in to use the blade. I could feel the guy's breath on my face, onions and spice. He had a panicky expression, lips drawn back in a distorted scowl. People aren't generally comfortable with getting up close and personal.

I took control of his knife hand and bent the wrist hard. Living beings move away from pain. So the guy tried to get away, but I kept the pressure on, pushing him back towards the side street. He groaned. His eyes rolled back in small sockets. The Spyderco clattered to the street. I adjusted my body weight and twisted quickly, pushing the trapped hand back towards the arm and up. The little scaphoid bone in his wrist snapped like a dry chopstick. He gave a little shriek.

Shouldn't have taken the knife out.

There was another high-pitched shriek from my left. Which turned out to be a uniformed policewoman blowing on a whistle. We made eye contact. Hers were hazel with green flecks. She had a police cap on. Her ponytail came out the back. She had little stud earrings, made a couple of steps towards me and grabbed my shirt. "Stay there."

I relaxed and let my hands hang down, unthreatening.

CHAPTER TWO

THE POLICEWOMAN WAS TOO close for her own safety. I could have done anything. I had total freedom of action. French cops use a Sig-Pro. Polymer grip. 9mm Parabellum. It's alright. Decent bang for the buck. The gun was tucked away in a leather holster at her waist. Although a little thumb snap over the grip made sure she'd never be able to pull it in a hurry.

She dropped the whistle on its lanyard. Her fist clenched my shirt at chest level. Her hair smelled clean and good. She pulled a tactical radio from her shoulder and called backup. Then she looked at me, unflinching. She was way too close.

The policewoman wore a blue polo shirt with a name tag sewed in above her right breast. It said, 'Nazari.' The top button was undone. Officer Nazari was in her late twenties, early thirties. She had been in the sun recently. Her skin was gold with freckles below the throat. I looked back at her. She blushed.

I said, "What did you see?"

"I saw you injure two men in an unprovoked attack."

"Which men?"

She darted her eyes over, but the thugs were gone. The people in line for the bakery gawked at us.

"There were three guys. One of them had a knife. They tried to rob me. Now they've gotten away. But it's not your fault."

She looked uncertain. I got it. From her point of view I had attacked a couple of guys. She hadn't seen the knife. Hadn't seen the leather jacket guy in the crowd. Just the two out in the street.

I said, "It's alright. Do what you have to do. You can let go of me, I'm not going to run away."

Nazari relaxed, but she didn't let go. I liked her. I started feeling the adrenaline afterglow. My hands shook and I felt cold. I said, "Can I take off the backpack?"

She released her grip. I took off my pack and felt the back of my shirt. The tear in the shirt was vertical, all the way up to the shoulder blade. I could feel the air coming through it.

"I liked this shirt. Got it yesterday."

She looked at the shirt. Sky blue cotton with a nautical wheel logo, embroidered in gold.

She said, "It's too preppy for you."

"That's what I liked about it."

"You heard the one about putting lipstick on a pig?" I smiled. I could feel her heat. One human being to another. We looked at each other for a while.

Another cop arrived, running. He was tall, and older. Late forties, early fifties. Distinguished-looking, like he might be comfortable in a command position, or sitting in an executive chair. He had good salt and pepper hair with a complete hairline, intact after running for a couple of minutes. The guy was tanned and had deep lines creasing a handsome face. His name tag read, 'Bonnet'.

He came to a stop in front of me. He was staring me up and down. He said, "Who the hell are you?"

It was a weird question, considering the situation. I answered, "I'm the little guy you're supposed to be protecting."

Bonnet barked an abrupt laugh and glanced quickly towards Nazari, then back at me. He was looking at my shirt and I figured he was concerned about the tear. I said, "It got torn by one of the attackers."

Interest draining from his eyes, he turned to Nazari. "What's going on?"

"Attempted aggression. This man is going to make a complaint."

The two cops had the same insignia, which didn't have very many stripes. Two relative rookies. C-class officers on a beat patrol.

Nazari stepped back. The heat went with her. She let her older colleague take over, but not in a way that indicated deferral. More like she was letting Bonnet do the boring work. Nazari picked at her fingernails while the cop questioned me. I told him what had happened. Three young guys. Scouted me coming off the train. And then this. He asked for ID. I showed him my US passport. He wrote the number down. He drew out my name. "Mister Tom Keeler." Wrote it down.

The street carried on bustling around us. There were more important things than two beat cops talking to a big American guy with a torn shirt. There was fresh bread to secure before it ran out. Flowers for the table. Meat from the butcher. People were doing their Saturday morning routine.

The cop explained to me that there had been an uptick in mugging attacks. He almost apologized. He asked to see my train ticket. I handed it over. He wrote something down. Bonnet asked about the muggers. What they looked like. I described them. Young, military-aged males, late teens or early twenties.

Bonnet repeated laboriously. "Pulled-back ponytail, well-trimmed beard." I nodded. "Dark hair?" I nodded again.

The policewoman looked up from her fingernails. "Why did you say 'military-aged males'?"

They both looked at me with interest.

I said, "Habit. I just received my discharge from the military."

She said, "You've just got that little bag?"

"I have family here."

Nazari nodded. "Is that why you speak French?"

"My mother was French." It was like we were on a first date. Nazari was still messing around with her nails and sneaking glances at me.

Bonnet broke it up. "How can we get in touch with you, Mister Keeler?"

I shrugged. "I don't know."

There was a dead silence for a moment. Nazari said, "Phone?"

"Nope." They both looked at me like I was from another planet.

Bonnet made a puffing sound with his mouth. "*Bon*, ok."

The policeman looked at his watch. He said, "Twelve thirty-two" and looked at Nazari. She flicked something off her nail and looked up. Bonnet wrote down the time. He wrapped up the little notebook and put the pen away. Then he took a phone from his pocket, walked away a couple of steps and turned his back on us. Nazari looked at him for a second or two. She turned to me. "Need anything?"

A couple of women walked by, arm in arm. One of them gave me a disapproving look. She actually shook her head at me. I was about to take it personally when I saw that her friend was looking at my shirt. I guess the torn shirt made me look like riff-raff, roused by the police.

Nazari saw them looking, and looked at her watch. "Maybe you want to go get a new shirt."

I said, "Ok, where do I get a new shirt."

Bonnet had finished texting his wife, or whatever it was and was stepping back towards us. I looked at him. He shrugged his shoulders and blew out air. He said, "I don't do the shopping."

Nazari was more helpful. She said, "Go to Fanny's. Everything else will be closing for lunch now." She stepped out into the street and pointed away from town. "Maybe a five-minute walk to the departmental road, then you make a right."

Bonnet turned to his colleague. "Let's go back."

She ignored him, said, "Will you be ok?"

I liked that she cared. It was professional.

CHAPTER THREE

Fanny's was a tiny store on a country road. Cars whizzed by once in a while. Across the road were small fields and then a little river. A sandwich board sign out front had a picture of a fox and the words 'Fanny's Friperie'. I opened the door and a little bell rang. The door closed and with it the fresh air. I was hit by the stink of old clothes. Like being suffocated by a stuffed bear.

A cheery voice called out from the back. "*Bonjour.*"

There was hardly any space to move. On one side, wool dresses and thick coats were packed tight on hanging rods. I waded through. On the other side, cotton and polyester dresses hung in thick clusters. They smelled of bleach and floral-scented steam water. A large flat wooden counter sectioned off the back of the store. A sewing machine sat idle. Scissors and other paraphernalia littered the surface.

A big woman in her fifties with a mass of red curls was removing clothes from donation bags and sorting them into piles. I figured she was Fanny. Behind her was a young girl with short black hair. She was bent over a black garbage bag, pulling clothes out. It looked like a struggle. Fanny took a look at me and pointed to the other side. "Men over there".

Aside from a limp tux, the mens was all hunting gear. There were enough used camouflage shirts, coats, jackets, trousers, and hats to trouble duck and deer for years. I said, "I'm looking for a shirt." I showed her the tear in the back of mine.

Fanny came up to the counter and put her hands on her hips, inspecting me. "Big strong guy like you needs size large or extra large." There was a wonderful mischief in her eyes that I liked immediately.

I said, "What do you have?"

Fanny clucked her tongue. "What do we have? What do you want?"

"A replacement. I'm not picky. As long as it's comfortable. That's my only criteria. After this I'm giving up on trying to be fancy."

She hunted through the back. Came out with a brown shirt in packaging. "Never been worn. New ten years ago. Try it on."

I pulled off the torn shirt. The brown one fit fine. Fanny looked satisfied. She inspected the torn blue shirt with the little nautical logo at the breast. Like a ship's wheel. Fanny held it up. She said, "Good brand. Expensive. What a pity."

I'd bought the shirt in Berlin the day before. Some store in the train station. I was walking around waiting for a connecting train. It was a designer brand apparently.

I asked her, "Where do you get these clothes from?"

"People die. We get their wardrobe." Fanny laughed. "Not to worry, I'm joking. Well, sort of. Donations, a lot of donations." She looked back at the girl, still struggling with the garbage bag. "Right, Miriam? A lot of donations."

The girl came up. She had eyebrows straight as rulers. She said, "A lot of donations. Yes."

Fanny stepped up and straightened the collar of my new brown shirt. "There. You look fine, for an American."

I said, "My accent."

She said, "Good French. American accent. You are on vacation?"

"My mother spent summers around here. I wanted to see it."

Fanny perked up. She said, "What's the family name?"

I said, "Vaugeois. Her name was Delphine Vaugeois. But that was a long time ago. I just wanted to see the place."

"Vaugeois." Fanny widened her eyes. She looked thoughtful, but stayed quiet. I paid for the brown shirt and thanked her. She responded politely and said goodbye. I squeezed my way out of the shop. I had my hand on the door when Fanny's voice stopped me. "You know ..." she said. I turned. "There is still a Vaugeois or two in Alencourt, at least partly here. Simone and Gilles."

"Is that right?"

Fanny nodded solemnly, like she was letting me in on a secret. "There's a house. Brumaire." She pointed through the door. "Over the bridge. You'll find it. Say hello from Fanny."

Brumaire. Why not? I thanked Fanny and went out the door. The little bell tinkled.

The wind blew. The air was warm. A little white Citroen sped by. The cloud cover was impenetrable, silver. Across the fields the river was silent. I crossed the road. Walked down to the water. Yellow gravel and clay crunched underfoot. I sat on a bench. Nothing was going on there. The water was faster than it looked from the road. I noticed a heron standing on one leg. Gray. Perfectly hidden against the river bank. Judging by the heron's position the water was shallow. A willow leaned thirstily. I felt myself winding down.

The incident with the muggers had been distracting. The guy had spotted me when I was still on the train. Maybe I looked like a tourist.

As far as I knew, my mother had left her homeland as an eighteen-year-old and never looked back. Like a lot of Americans. Maybe she had played here on the river bank, or sat on this bench as a teenager, looking out at the water, thinking about life. The country air was good to breathe after the train ride. It smelled clean.

I decided to check out the house, Brumaire. I would still have time to catch an overnight train out of Alencourt before dark. I like trains. I stretched out again. Cracking joints.

From downriver a barely perceptible whining sound had become the annoying buzz of a modified motorcycle engine. A couple of teenagers were cruising up along the little river tow path. Destroying the peace. Stirring the fish. The guy in front revved his engine. It was a derestricted 125 cc trail bike. They modify them to go faster than the law permits. These kids were being annoying on purpose. That was fine, I can be extraordinarily patient.

The rider in back held on to the seat bars behind him. He looked at me through the full-faced helmet visor. Just a set of eyes looking. I looked back. The bike fishtailed before it got to the bench. Swerved around and behind me. The machine veered fast in front of me. I didn't pull in my legs and the driver had to react quickly to avoid hitting me. The rider laughed and yelled something to his friend, which I didn't pick up.

Then, the driver hit the throttle and launched into a little grassy field back towards the road. He braked and kicked up dirt. Throttled again. The bike went into a doughnut spin, shredding grass and dirt all over. A cloud of fumes drifted slowly on the river wind. They did three doughnuts and sped off.

A minute later all that remained was a pall of engine fumes hanging in the air. The heron was gone. I listened to the river come back to life after the disturbance. A ripple broke the surface, a fish or something else.

CHAPTER FOUR

THE BRIDGE WAS NARROW. There wasn't a car in sight. A little sidewalk hugged the edge. I could see the algae on the river bed. Shallow water. Trees swayed in the wind. The opposite bank was hillside and then forest. I followed the road for a while until it met an unpaved driveway on the left. A little hand-painted metal sign hung on a tree, off to the side. Brumaire.

A murder of crows rose out of the yellowed field to my right. Screaming.

I crunched over clean gravel. On the right side of the drive a gate-keeper's cottage was pushed into the woods. Alongside was an old Renault hatchback in dark green. Past that, Brumaire came into sight straight up ahead. The house was an antique stone villa. Three stories tall with smaller windows on the third floor, presumably old servant quarters. Wide and squat with a zinc roof. It sat square against a limestone cliff face.

I walked up rounded stone steps. The terrace floor was ceramic-tiled in black and white checkerboard. A decorative iron balustrade spun around the house. Wisteria vines crept and twisted over the iron. I knocked on the door. No answer. I waited a while. Birds swooped playfully. The gray sky was lowering. Looked like it was going to rain. Shutters were closed in the downstairs windows. Behind the house was a field with a single tree in the middle of it. A rocking chair was positioned to look at the tree. I put my backpack down on the terrace. Put myself in the chair. I looked at the tree for a while.

Nothing else was happening. Just the tree swaying in the humid breeze. The grass grew. I closed my eyes.

When I opened them again a man stood looking at me. He was on the other side of the iron balustrade. The man wore gardening clothes and frayed leather gloves. A wheelbarrow at his feet, filled with stones. A rake balanced over the top of the wheelbarrow. The gardener must have already spoken because he wore the impatient look of someone forced to repeat themselves.

"Bonjour Monsieur."

I acknowledged him politely, *"Bonjour Monsieur."*

The guy was compact and muscular, in his mid-forties with a full head of brown hair, falling like a mop over a wide forehead. Around five foot eight with ropey and thick muscle on his arms.

"Are you looking for Madame Vaugeois?"

I said I was. The man nodded. He had the wary look of someone who doesn't often run into strangers. He said, "Madame is aware of your visit." It wasn't really a question.

I said, "No."

He blinked. "You are waiting for her?"

"That's right."

"But she is unaware that you are waiting."

"Correct. I haven't met Madame Vaugeois yet." The guy just looked at me, didn't understand. I said, "Madame Vaugeois doesn't know me. I don't know her. And I'm going to wait for her until she gets here."

The gardener hesitated for a moment. He was sizing up the situation. I could almost hear the wheels turning over in his head. Like a mechanical clock.

Tick.

I didn't look or sound like a salesman.

Tock.

I had no car.

Tick.

I spoke with an American accent.

Tock.

Was I a thief?

Tick.

Unlikely.

Tock.

He did the right thing. Took his eyes off me, picked up the wheelbarrow and rolled it down towards the garden. I appreciate that kind of thinking. Run through the options, make a decision. I watched the gardener move down towards the gatekeeper's house. His back was ramrod straight, even accounting for the weight he carried. He guided the wheelbarrow carefully along the edge of the drive, keeping the fat front tire aligned.

A big black Mercedes cruised up the drive, sweeping past the wheelbarrow. The car was a huge S-class, at least a few decades old. I made it an S-600 V12 with six liter engine. The tires clipped the lawn, spraying gravel. Brakes creaked to a halt.

Eventually the door opened and a suede slipper emerged. The toe stretched out tentatively searching for the gravel surface and, finding it, settled. Heel followed. Once the foot was stable, the rest of her was ready to get off the seat and contemplate standing up. When that had been accomplished she eased herself out of the Mercedes.

Simone Vaugeois was an elegantly dressed woman in her seventies. She had expensively dyed brown hair with red highlights. Large opaque sunglasses clipped to her face. She wore a silver pant suit.

"Ahhh," she breathed. It meant, back home. Finally.

The passenger door opened on the other side of the Mercedes. Vaugeois said, "I think it's going to rain, Maria."

A voice chirped rhythmically, "It's what they said on television this morning, madame. Rain in the afternoon."

"Good for the garden, bad for the spirit," said Madame Vaugeois.

I had remained silent for long enough. To observe further would be intrusive. I coughed and stepped towards the entrance. She didn't notice, so I coughed again. "Bonjour, Madame."

She turned abruptly, disoriented. She noticed me. Took down her sunglasses. I regretted not coming out faster, but I had been deep in the terrace. She instantly assumed a formal, questioning tone. "Monsieur? Bonjour."

She struck out towards me. Chin jutting forwards. Called over her shoulder to Maria. "Maria, put the tart in the kitchen. And don't forget the potatoes."

"Yes, Madame." I could only see the top of Maria's head past the car. Apparently she was petite.

We met in the middle of the steps. Madame Vaugeois had her hand extended in the French manner and I took it. Hers was dry and cold. I could feel bones moving around inside loose skin. A gold chain hung on her wrist. Two rings were snug around long fingers. A diamond-studded wedding band and a solid gold family crest on the pinky. Her nails were burgundy and freshly painted. She looked at me questioningly. As if my presence must have had a quick and uncomplicated explanation.

But family is complicated.

I said, "I am sorry to surprise you unannounced. I am Delphine Vaugeois' son. Tom Keeler."

Simone Vaugeois's eyes were blue and watery. She wore copious amounts of eye-liner, shadow, and mascara. I thought it strange that she would get herself dolled up like this for a trip to town. She glanced about her. Maria carried a flat package from the patisserie towards the side of the house. She appraised me. "You said, Delphine?"

Vaugeois pronounced my mother's name differently than I had ever heard it. In French it sounded lighter, more airy than I was used to. To me, my mother's name had always been business-like and tough. Feminine, but hard-edged. Delphine on Vaugeois' lips made it elegant and soft.

"Yes. I'm Tom Keeler." I grinned at her, hoping to lower her defenses. "I'm sorry to barge in on you like this, ma'am. I was traveling through the region and thought I'd stop for a few hours. My mother told me so much about Alencourt."

"Your mother told you about us?"

Strictly speaking, my mother had never spoken specifically about anyone. So I said, "Mom had good memories of her summers in Alencourt."

"It is beautiful here." She had a low voice. Gravelly. She had smoked many cigarettes in her time. She was distracted, looked over my shoulder, and said, "Did you meet Daniel?"

I followed her gaze. The gardener was cleaning the rake out front of the gatekeeper's house. He was pulling off the dead leaves and dry grass. So his name was Daniel.

"Daniel, yes."

I saw her making up her mind. Something clicked and she went into a different mode of hospitality. "What an amazing coincidence. I wasn't always a Vaugeois." She showed me the ring. "I married Gilles Vaugeois. So, I wouldn't have known your mother." Her mouth turned down. "Gilles is poorly at the moment. You'll forgive me, but he is probably best left alone." She placed her hands on my shoulders. "But you stay for lunch. You will meet the priest. I must prepare. Please come in. Father Bousquet will be arriving. I'm sure he will be happy to speak with you. Come."

I retrieved my backpack from over by the rocking chair. Vaugeois saw it. "Are you staying?"

"No. I've got a train to catch tonight."

She relaxed. "Bon. We will send you away with a very nice lunch." A modest white Volkswagen pulled up behind the Mercedes. She lifted up on her toes and back. "Voila. The priest."

~

FATHER BOUSQUET STABBED at a roasted potato. He was tall and broad and around Simone's age. He had a full head of white hair and a wild look, subdued by the years. He was dressed casually in a blue shirt and slacks. He was scrupulously clean-shaven.

Madame Vaugeois said, "Father Bousquet visits every week. He likes to look in on us."

Bousquet said, "I enjoy your company, madame, that's all."

Vaugeois said, "And to make sure I'm still around."

"Not at all."

Simone had already put down quite a few glasses of red. She turned to me, happy to explain things. "Father Bousquet and I have a special project. Don't we, Father?"

Bousquet put down his fork and looked up from the plate. "We organize a small charity for the migrants up north. Madame Vaugeois is a most important supporter. Many people from the southern countries are currently attempting to reach the United Kingdom. They cannot easily cross the Channel and we end up with large amounts of refugees in makeshift camps and rather terrible conditions. I'm sure you have heard."

I said, "Alencourt is pretty far from the coast."

"A few hundred kilometers. But the train station here is a hub for the region. We often have people passing through. Quite a few of them migrants."

Simone Vaugeois waved a silver-plated fork in the air. "It's a human tragedy. The tragedy of our time. We already have enough of them here and no one knows what to do with the new ones."

I said, "You have migrants in Alencourt?"

Father Bousquet shook his head. "No, we don't have camps here."

Simone Vaugeois said, "I hate to say it but the *cité* is not far from being a migrant camp."

Bousquet turned to me. "Madame Vaugeois is provocatively referring to the public housing projects. Previous generations of immigrants have been housed by the government in large buildings that we call the *cité*. Every decent-sized French town has their *cités*." He turned to Madame Vaugeois. "Simone, of course it's not the same thing. You can't just lump all people together and complicate things."

"For me, as a French person, the *cité* is another kind of migrant camp. It is Calais, but worse because it's permanent. It's a huge mistake that we'll never be able to put right. Before the *cité* we never had much crime. It's an insult to everyone, including the poor people who live there."

Father Bousquet didn't respond to Madame Vaugeois. He ate for a while. Drank the wine. Complimented the chef. Vaugeois was content to let it lie.

After lining up his silverware on the plate, Bousquet turned to me. "We have a complex of *cités*, to the north of town. Three big buildings. The complex is called *Les Brosses*. Approximately three thousand residents. There is some crime. They are less-privileged, for the most part. It is difficult for even second generation immigrants to find work. And they are discriminated against." Bousquet waved his hand in the air. "Enough of our problems. Tell us about yourself. You are a cousin of the Vaugeois?"

"My mother was a Vaugeois, Delphine."

"I take it she emigrated?"

I said, "Yes. She left France before I was born."

The priest nodded, "Before my time."

Madame Vaugeois clapped her hands together. "I must get the family tree."

CHAPTER FIVE

MADAME VAUGEOIS RETURNED with two heavy and unruly binders held together with twine. I stood and helped her with them. The covers were red cardboard, faded with age. In between the cardboard was paper. Old paper.

Bousquet and I watched as she spread the pages around the table. Scribbled lines and arrows connected boxes with scribbled old family names. Birth certificates were mixed up with property documents and hospital records from other centuries. She hunted around for a while and Father Bousquet did his best to help her.

There was a Delphine eventually, somewhere down the line, at approximately the right year. In the end they both concluded that Gilles and Delphine Vaugeois were distant relations through a thick web of marriages. What had endured between them, genealogically speaking, was the name Vaugeois. She said, "Let's just say that we are cousins," and poured herself more wine.

She and Bousquet packed the papers back together between the red cardboard covers and tied the twine around. The things held together okay and the priest put them both to the side. Simone Vaugeois stood up to remove the plates. I rose to help, but she dismissed me. "No, it is impossible. You're a guest. But I wouldn't mind if you carried these back to Gille's library. I think I've damaged my knees carrying them."

"Of course, ma'am."

She pointed and explained how to get there. I picked up the binders and tucked each of them under an arm.

The library was upstairs and down a hallway and then around a corner. The door was open at the end of the corridor and I could see the bookshelves. The room was large with high ceilings. A country gentleman's library with wood-paneled walls. Books from floor to ceiling, a big old desk with a leather blotter, and leather armchairs with appropriate reading lights. I set the binders down on the desk, careful not to disturb several framed photographs.

I recognized Simone Vaugeois in a few of the photos, all at least two decades old. I figured that the guy next to her was Gilles. They looked happy and healthy. Gilles was slim and a careful dresser, with a shock of brown hair. He wore a shirt and tie in all the photos. He was also interested in maps. That much was obvious. But not only maps, an entire bookshelf was taken up by technical publications relating to land and property. Old ordnance surveys were stacked from left to right. A large map of the region hung framed on the wall.

I went back down.

Bousquet was sitting alone at the big table. "Find it okay?" I nodded.

"A lot of maps."

"Oh yes. Gilles liked maps. All kinds of things like that, he was a very interesting man. Which makes all of this so sad actually. But maps are a local sport." Bousquet looked at me. "You see, we're fascinated by the land under our feet. Thousands of years of history all around us. It's the difference between Europeans and Americans. You can start over, it's much harder for us."

"Is he sick?"

"Your cousin was the victim of an attack. He suffered blows to the head." Bousquet let that sink in. "Madame Vaugeois can explain it to you better than me. I don't know the details like she does. There have been doctors and operations and hospitals involved. I think it's complicated." He changed the subject. "You are traveling around Europe now? Is it a holiday?"

I told him that I'd received my discharge from the military a week earlier. I was planning to roam around the world for a while. Not exactly a holiday, more like a ramble.

Bousquet said, "The American military. Did you serve anywhere *interesting?*"

"Depends upon what you mean by interesting."

"Hot. Difficult. Tough. The American military is not exactly a peace time force these days, *n'est ce pas?*"

"Correct."

Father Bousquet gave me an appraising look. He said, "I take it that you were an officer, a professional soldier?" I didn't say anything. He continued, "I only say this because of your age."

I said, "I served out my first contract and then went for officer."

Bousquet nodded seriously. "I was never in the military. I avoided conscription."

The phone rang somewhere in the house. Three rings and then stopped. Bousquet poured himself a little red wine. He tapped his glass to mine. "I sense a peach tart coming."

He must have been clairvoyant because sure enough, Madame Vaugeois entered the dining room with a large peach tart. She set it down with an exhaled, *"Voila!"*

Maria set a pile of small plates down on the table. "Should I reserve a portion for Monsieur Vaugeois?"

Simone said, "Yes please, Maria."

Father Bousquet had his head down, studiously engaged with his slice of pie. Madame Vaugeois looked at me curiously. She said, "You are already well known in Alencourt. There has been a phone call for you. The police would like to interview you at the station." She paused for effect. "They have assured me that you are not in any trouble. They ask that you make a formal statement. Apparently there has been an incident?"

Bousquet looked up. "And how did they know that Monsieur Keeler is here?" He looked at me wisely. "I didn't know that foreigners were obliged to report their whereabouts in this country, at least since 1945."

"An attempted mugging this morning. I reported it to the police. My shirt was torn during the attack and a police officer recommended that I buy another one at Fanny's Friperie. So I guess that's how they knew I was here. Must have asked at the Friperie."

Vaugeois gave a short cry. "Fanny's. Just across the river."

I nodded. "She's the one who told me that a Vaugeois was still living in Alencourt. Otherwise I wouldn't have come to your house. She sent her regards."

"You know that Gilles was violently attacked and robbed. Gilles, my husband and your cousin."

Bousquet concentrated on his dessert. I followed his lead and didn't press. I asked if he was still at the house.

She said, "Gilles is resting. In any case, I have told the police that we are having peach tart for dessert. They can wait."

Father Bousquet was reflective. He meticulously cut a piece of tart with the edge of his spoon. "And there is Benoit Houdin, of course. It's been a violent year."

Vaugeois nodded. "Monstrous."

I said, "Benoit Houdin?"

Bousquet finished off a mouthful. "The town treasurer. A very close friend of the mayor. He was murdered with his family. A home invasion. Police investigators from the BRI came down from Amiens up north. The BRI is our version of your FBI." Bousquet paused, thinking. "For the second time, because they came for Gilles also. They don't seem to have any leads. Houdin's murder happened a few weeks ago in fact."

Simone Vaugeois let her spoon fall on the plate. "Big city problems have arrived in Alencourt. None of this would have happened even ten years ago. The world is going to hell!"

Father Bousquet wiped his lips with the cloth napkin. "I don't know. Things are changing, that's for sure. But they always change, don't they, Monsieur Keeler?"

"I guess they do."

Vaugeois smiled. "Anyway, I'm sure none of our problems will prevent you from enjoying yourself."

I thanked her for taking the call from the police. "I am sorry if this causes you any distress."

Madame Vaugeois waved me away. Father Bousquet said that he'd drive me to the police station.

CHAPTER SIX

BOUSQUET DIDN'T END up giving me a ride into town.

An unmarked black BMW pulled up just as we were saying goodbye to madame. Bousquet and I watched as the car stopped behind his Volks. A muscular plainclothes cop in the passenger seat got out and loped over. He wore an orange police armband over a brown leather jacket. He had a shaved and tanned head. He was around my height, in his mid-thirties and moved like an athlete. The driver stayed in the car.

"Monsieur Keeler?" I nodded. He didn't look at me directly, rather scanned the area. He took in madame and Father Bousquet. The house. He looked up at the roof. Scanned the cliff ridge line above Brumaire. The cop turned his attentions back down to me. He saw my bag and said, "Is that everything?"

I didn't like how he eyeballed everything except the person he was talking to. So I ignored the question and asked my own. "Want to show me your identification?" The cop looked at me directly then. First with open hostility, then he sniggered and brought out a leather badge wallet and flashed it quickly. I said, "I'd like to look at that if you don't mind." He shook his head in disbelief and handed it over.

The badge was in French. It looked like a badge. The bald cop's name was Grouse. He was a big guy, and held the rank of sergeant. I said, "What kind of a name is Grouse?"

Grouse looked as mean as he could manage. "Give me back the badge."

I tossed it to him short so he had to snatch for it, then turned towards the house. Madame Vaugeois was smoking on the terrace. She had the cigarette in her mouth, while her hands were busy pushing a lighter into the pack. I went back to the steps and thanked her for lunch. She kissed me on both cheeks. I told her that it had been really good to meet another Vaugeois. She was pleased at that. A little unsteady on her feet. She called me 'cousin' and said that I should come back anytime. I told her that I'd most likely go straight to the train station after speaking with the police.

FATHER BOUSQUET SHOOK hands with a firm dry grip. His hand was large. It was a little like holding onto the blunt end of a baseball bat. An old one, like the bat Babe Ruth might have discarded after hitting a home run. A bat that was nicked and scarred. He gave the waiting cops a look. "If you need anything don't hesitate to be in touch with Madame Vaugeois. She knows where to reach me. Not that I am difficult to find. I enjoyed meeting you."

I said likewise, and meant it.

Grouse was tapping his finger on the car door. He was impatient, holding it open for me. His other hand rested at his waist. I saw the bulge of a service weapon beneath the leather jacket. The policeman looked at my canvas backpack and said again, "Is that all your stuff?"

I ignored him and climbed into the back seat and closed the door. Grouse got into the front. The driver gripped the passenger seat headrest and twisted around, reversing the car down the drive. He had light, short hair, was bearded, and smelled like stale tobacco. I said, "Grouse, you haven't introduced me to your buddy." Neither of them responded.

Brumaire retreated through the windshield. Madame Vaugeois stood a couple of steps above Father Bousquet. They were in conversation. I glanced at the gatekeeper's house as we passed by. Daniel was stacking large stones from the wheelbarrow alongside the little cottage. I yawned, felt real sleepy all of a sudden. Must have been the wine. The car smelled like aloe-vera moisturizer. I figured it was what Grouse used to shine his head.

The bearded cop made a right after the bridge. We drove along the river for a while. The water was calm, like before. The sky was really threatening to rain. On the other side of the river I saw a large villa. Most of it was protected from view, but the roof and some of the top floor was visible. The house looked even more impressive than Brumaire. I estimated that it was geographically behind the Vaugeois house, maybe half a mile through the woods, on the same side of the river.

I leaned back and closed my eyes. A habit I'd picked up in the military. Concentrated on relaxing all my muscles. From the head down to the end of my toes and back up again. Any kind of travel, plane, train, automobile, you will find me sleeping. I once fell asleep sixteen hours into a forced march at five thousand feet. I just slept and walked. I have a recurring dream. It's real simple. I'm in free fall. There is nothing around me, just air. No ground below. No sky above. I'm in free fall. Tumbling and getting nowhere. Takes some getting used to.

The station was modern and small. Two municipal police cars were parked out front at a diagonal. The gray cloud was pressing down and darkening in places. Grouse looked at the sky for a while as we drove in. He didn't say anything.

The bearded cop parked in the visitor spot. My door was locked from the outside. So I waited for the bald guy to open it for me. He took his time. I didn't think that was nice. But I didn't fuss. I slung the pack over my shoulder and headed into the station.

It's hard to remember sometimes that cops are people too, and not just cops. The same is true for military service men and women. In the end they are men and women, people. Just like everyone else. Once you've experienced combat, the distinction is even simpler. Combatant or not. That is if you can tell the difference. The real trouble starts when you can't.

The cops escorted me through the door. People lingered in the lobby. They waited around the coin-operated coffee machine, reclined on chairs lined up along the front window, and mostly stared into their phones. There was a desk manned by a uniformed officer. There was a plant in the waiting area. A spiky thing with a reptilian trunk. Looked like it had been chosen for its resilience and autonomy. There wasn't a lot of noise. Just the murmur of nervous voices. Grouse looped an identification lanyard over his neck. He nodded to the cop behind the counter, who buzzed us through.

We entered the working part of the station. Uniformed police huddled around desks. There was a better-looking coffee machine and a water dispenser with small cone-shaped cups. The uniforms were 'Municipal Police'. The plainclothes men took me up a flight of stairs. Black steel handrails and white concrete. The steps had tiny smooth stones set into them. In through another door. Down a corridor. Offices either side. No more uniforms.

We walked into an interview room. A big glass window faced out to an empty and large open-plan area with desks. It was a squad room, and looked like it had never been used. A big table was in the direct center of the interview room. Chairs around it. Grouse motioned me to give him my bag. I didn't give it to him. I said, "Grouse, you're rubbing me the wrong way. I'm taking a disliking to you already and we just met. Let's start over by you trying out the word 'please'."

Grouse said, "Please."

So I gave it to him.

He dumped out the contents of my pack on the table. He went through it systematically. Torn blue designer shirt, Gore-Tex jacket. Toothbrush. Toothpaste. US Passport. Two pairs of underwear briefs. Two extra t-shirts. Four pairs of socks. No junk, nothing extraneous.

He looked at me suspiciously, said, "Where are the rest of your possessions?" I didn't answer. Just locked eyes with him. The bearded cop whispered in his ear. Grouse broke the eye contact, said, "Please wait here." They walked out of the room and closed the door.

I sat down in a chair facing the big window. I looked through it into the squad room and saw Grouse and the beard reappear there. The beard stepped through a doorway off to the side. He came back out with two new plainclothes cops and a uniformed officer. The plainclothes were an older woman and an enormous man around my age.

CHAPTER SEVEN

THE UNIFORMED GUY entered the interview room first. Up close he was all prim and proper with an erect posture and tightly knotted tie. I smelled French aftershave. He held out a hand and I took it. "Alain Rigalle, Director of the Municipal Police." Rigalle had a dry and firm grip. His wrist was encircled by an expensive-looking watch. The plainclothes cops lurked behind him. The woman had a grim smile, the giant's mouth hung slack.

Rigalle was the type who made a point of staring into your eyes. Like he'd read about that as a technique. I met his gaze. "Thank you for coming in, Monsieur Keeler. We take these kinds of inquiries extremely seriously. In particular, my colleagues here are investigating recent acts of violence in and around Alencourt. Unlike some other communities we are not habituated to violent attacks on our streets. I would appreciate if you could take the time to confirm some details with these investigators. We don't know if the episode this morning is connected to other ongoing investigations, but it is possible."

I nodded. He stepped back and made space for the other two. The woman extended a hand. "Inspector Martaud. Research and

Intervention police." I shook it. The giant just stood behind her. Martaud was tall and thin and had a lined face, gray hair and steel-gray eyes. She was a striking woman and resembled a bird of prey. The guy with her was a giant. A muscular beast with a mop of blond hair He wore a bulging polo shirt and very tight jeans. Martaud carried a file folder. She smiled at me. "This is Caro."

The big guy called Caro put a laptop on the table and then sat down. As if he'd done enough standing for the day. He barely fit in the office chair. Rigalle pulled a chair back into the corner, like an observer.

Martaud was still on her feet. "I'm sorry that we had to disturb you. I'd just like to ask you a few questions if you don't mind. And we will take your formal statement." Martaud put the file down on the table and took a chair. She looked at me and something occurred to her. "Just to be clear. You're not accused of anything. This has to do with the incident this morning."

"Did someone die?" I asked.

She looked up from the file. "Why do you ask that?"

"No reason really."

"I'm not at liberty to release potentially sensitive information because the investigation is open, but it has to do with the report that you gave to the municipal police earlier. If you just answer a few questions, that will be all that is required and you will be on your way." She put her hands on the table and examined my stuff. She looked thoughtful. "Let's put your belongings back."

I thought Martaud was offering to do it for me, but I was wrong. She looked at me. The giant was squeezed into his chair behind her and to the side. I didn't fuss. Just put my stuff back. Brought the pack around to my side of the table. She said, "According to the notes, this morning, you claimed to have successfully repelled an attack by three men."

"Lucky I guess."

Martaud gave a cynical laugh. "Yes, very lucky, as according to your report one of them was armed with a bladed weapon."

"Correct."

She said, "Are you trained to deal with three attackers, Monsieur Keeler?"

"I've had military training."

Martaud shook her head as if this were a miracle. Looked at the other guy. "Military training." Caro the giant nodded in mock gravity. She leaned back in her chair and said, "The *American* military." The municipal police director, Rigalle, had a pained expression on his face as he ran fingers through his mustache.

"That's correct."

Rigalle leaned forward. "In what capacity did you serve, Mister Keeler?"

"322nd Special Tactics Squadron out of Mildenhall, UK."

"What does a special tactics squadron do exactly?"

I shrugged. "You know, stuff that we can't talk about mostly."

The BRI people sat there looking at me blankly while they digested what I'd just said. Rigalle was looking at me curiously. I guess he was trying to decide what exactly I was, to him.

Then Martaud started again. "*Bon*, can you tell me what it is that brings you to Alencourt?"

"My mother spent time here as a kid."

"Staying with family, the Vaugeois."

"That's right."

"Regarding the attack, do you see a connection to your military service perhaps?"

"There is no connection to my service."

She thought for a moment. "How long do you intend to stay?"

"I have no specific plans. Maybe a month, might be a year. Depends."

Rigalle laughed. "Depends upon what, Monsieur Keeler?" Martaud glanced back at the uniformed cop.

"On how I feel."

Martaud turned to the big guy behind her and nodded. Caro shuffled his chair forward, made it to the table and opened up the laptop. When he spoke, his voice was low-pitched and hoarse. Which is just one side-effect of steroid use. "Can you please repeat what you told the municipal police this morning?"

I repeated the story. He stabbed at the keys with two massive fingers. Then excused himself from the room. Martaud opened up her file folder. She slid a mug shot towards me. "Recognize him?" I didn't, and said so. She kept on going. All young men in their late teens and early twenties. Most looked like they had North African ethnic origins. I kept on rejecting the mug shots. She kept on sliding more at me. None of them matched. We did that for a while, around forty mug shots. She didn't look happy or unhappy. Just going through the motions.

The giant came back in with a sheet of paper. Passed it over to Martaud, who read it over.

"Alright that's fine. If you would sign this declaration form we can make your statement official." I took the sheet from her. My French conversation was a lot better than my reading. But I got by, more or less. Martaud passed a pen over. I signed. Gave the pen and the document back to her.

"Thank you, Monsieur Keeler. I hope that this does not come as a shock to you, but there has been another robbery using a bladed weapon in the same area today."

"Let me guess, the victim didn't make it."

"I'm afraid not. Stabbed in the heart. The victim died at the scene."

I chewed on that for a moment. I felt terrible suddenly. I had pulled my punches with the muggers this morning. I should have gone all in. Now someone was dead. Maybe a good guy. It wasn't my fault, but that didn't make me feel any better.

"I'm sorry to hear that. Do you have any leads?"

Martaud put the documents back in the file folder. "Only the descriptions you gave."

I said nothing. She extended her hand and began to stand. I said,

"I understand that there was an attack on my cousin, Gilles Vaugeois, a while back. Are you investigating that?"

Rigalle coughed and spoke from the back. "Do you have any new information?"

"I don't, no."

Martaud was looking at the municipal police director and shifted her gaze over to me. "We can't comment on open investigations I'm afraid." She stood up. I joined her and we shook hands. Martaud said, "Thank you for your time. I wish you a very pleasant and safe stay in Alencourt and in France. Caro will show you out. Goodbye."

On my way out I passed Rigalle standing stiffly by the door. Engulfed in a cloud of cologne, the Director of Municipal Police smiled warmly.

CHAPTER EIGHT

It was raining by the time I got out of the station. Fat drops plunged to the ground, splashing off the concrete surfaces of Alencourt. The police station's walls were dirty up close. As if no amount of cleaning could scrub off the grime. I put on my Gore-Tex jacket and looked out from under the awning. A cop was huddled outside, smoking. I asked him the way to the train station. He jerked his chin to the left. Rain drops hurtled through the air. Pools of water had formed in uneven parts of the road and sidewalk and were peppered with falling rain. A constant surface disruption. I walked away.

I figured that was it, I was done with the place. I thought I'd get to the train station and board anything going south. The rain made that an easy decision. I'd never visited, but figured there wasn't much bad weather in Spain this time of year. I was glad to walk.

Why had it been necessary for Police Chief Rigalle to sit in on a routine interview? Why couldn't they have just brought the mug shots with them to Brumaire? Would have saved a lot of trouble.

There was a two-finger whistle from the road. A police Peugeot 308 was trailing my four o'clock. I hadn't noticed it because of the hood I was wearing. I kept walking. The car was creeping, real slow. I sped up the pace. The police car followed. The two-finger whistle again. Coming from the passenger side. I looked closer at the car. Windshield wipers and rain obscured the interior.

The driver's side window came down. The uniformed policeman from earlier was at the wheel. The distinguished-looking Bonnet, of the little notebook. I looked across and saw the policewoman in the passenger seat. Nazari, the one with the hazel and green eyes. With the sun freckles at the hollow of her throat. She'd been the one whistling. Nazari gave me a little wave. I walked over. When I got closer Bonnet said, "Want a ride?"

I got in the back. Sat behind the driver. He looked at me in the mirror, said, "Where to?"

"Train station."

The windshield wipers squeaked. Bonnet put the car into gear. Nazari turned around and extended her hand. "Cecile Nazari."

I said, "It's written on your shirt." I took the hand. Strong and warm. "Tom Keeler."

Nazari said, "Yes, I know." She indicated the driver. "That's Bonnet. But you know already because it's written on his shirt."

Bonnet made eye contact and nodded.

Nazari was still smiling. She said, "You know this is a police vehicle, Monsieur Keeler. No door handles on the inside. We might have to hold you for a while."

Bonnet caught my eye in the mirror. He said, "She's kidding."

She said, "I'm kidding. Leaving us already?"

I said, "Somewhere it's not raining."

She laughed and examined her fingernails. Shaking her head. She said, "Have to do my nails again."

I said, "You have plans tonight?"

She said, "I do actually."

Bonnet said, "What did the assholes want with you at the station?"

"Assholes?"

Nazari said, "Research and Intervention police. The BRI. We call them 'assholes' for short."

"Asked me to give a formal statement."

Bonnet asked, "Rigalle there?"

"The police director. Yes."

"They tell you about the new victim?"

I nodded. "Correct."

We drove for a little while. The scenery rolled by. The wipers squeaked.

Nazari said, "I guess you got lucky. Seeing how it turned out for the second victim."

"Maybe."

Bonnet glanced at me in the rear view. "Trust me, you got lucky."

We were already in the town center, the historical part near the station. I said, "Here already."

Nazari said, "We don't have much else. It's a train station town."

Bonnet was slowing down to pull over. Nazari turned around to look at me again. She said, "Did they show you pictures of the crime scene?"

I said, "No."

"Me and Antoine were first responders." She pulled out her phone and tapped it a few times. Passed it to me. "Something for you to remember us by," she said.

Bonnet was alarmed, but spoke quietly. "Cecile."

Nazari said, "Chill out, Antoine."

Bonnet was shaking his head. As if to suggest that she shouldn't be showing those photos to civilians. But I'd seen enough death that I understood the fascination it held. Her screen was filled with a photo of a recently deceased man lying in a pool of blood. He looked like other dead human beings that I had seen. Maybe some people die peacefully in bed, or in an armchair. Maybe those bodies look composed and calm. As if they just fell asleep. The hectic desperation of sudden violent death leaves the body ungainly, limbs splayed out in the wrong way. No knifed or shot person looks like they're asleep. Depending upon the ordinance, they might not even look human anymore. This guy was lying on his side, curled protectively around the knife entry wound to his chest. His eyes were open. He looked like a lifeless thing, strange and uncanny.

"Who's the victim?"

Nazari said, "Afghan documents. Name of Gulam Qayoumi. Legally registered as an asylum seeker in France. Probably on his way up north."

Bonnet said, "Not his lucky day."

I flipped through the pictures. There were multiple angles and multiple distances. Nazari had covered the scene pretty well. Close-up shots and medium shots. Wide-angle shots to show context. Like a textbook exercise in crime scene photography, except for the last shots. Because the photos also told a chronological story, like a movie made up of still frames. The last photo looked like it was taken with the phone held down low, as if in secret. It was a shot of the crime scene after the BRI investigators had arrived. Inspector Martaud was standing over the body. Behind her I made out Caro's enormous silhouette. Bonnet had his back to the camera and was turned at a three-quarters angle towards Martaud and the body. I could make out his face.

The victim, Qayoumi, had made it to his fifties. His head was matted with dense, curly hair that was still mostly dark with a scattering of grey. He wore a collared sky blue shirt and jeans and ankle-length black leather boots. His left arm was pinned beneath him. The right arm ended in a hand placed protectively near the wound area. Qayoumi's sleeve was pushed up, exposing a tattoo on the inside of his wrist, visible in the close-up shots. Three words, and above the words, a line and three dots above the line. The dots were in a row. I figured the words said something profound in Dari or Pashto, the two main languages in Afghanistan. I spread my fingers on Nazari's phone screen and enlarged one of the photos with a good angle on the wound.

There was something that Nazari and Bonnet had missed. Something important. I understood why they hadn't noticed it, because they were municipal cops and it was probably the first time they'd seen a violent death. The eye just goes to the wound and misses anything else.

Qayoumi had been knifed in the heart. The blade had made a neat hole in his blue shirt, just below a nautical logo. Like a ship's wheel. It was the same brand designer shirt as I had been wearing and the same sky blue color.

Which meant two things. First, that they had mistaken me for this guy, Gulam Qayoumi. But they had realized their mistake and found him, and then killed him. Second, they hadn't known what he looked like, just that he would be wearing a specific shirt. I remembered the way rat-face had looked at me below the eye line. He'd recognized the shirt first, then looked at my face.

I handed back the phone to Nazari. Bonnet was looking at me in the rear view.

CHAPTER NINE

Nazari climbed out of the car after me. "I'll make sure you get on your train."

I almost protested, but changed my mind. "Sure."

She bent down to speak with Bonnet through the driver's side window. He said, "Where are you headed?"

"Parts unknown. I'll see when I get to the ticket office."

"Well don't forget to send us a postcard."

He drove off. Nazari stood up. She looked great. The blue uniform hugged her body. She rested a hand on the holstered Sig-Pro. We walked into the station. She pointed to the departure board. It was about twenty yards in. We strolled over. I looked at her silhouette a couple of times. She was tall and in shape. She wasn't afraid to eat, but did some kind of regular exercise. Early morning runs and light calisthenics. Maybe a habit formed in the academy. A dedicated young professional. When she got to the departure board she said, "Somewhere with no rain."

"No rain, good food, beach, sun."

"You forgot beautiful women. That's usually on the male fantasy bucket list."

"No need to travel. We've got that right here."

She blushed. We were both in a high state of distraction. We were standing close and I could smell her hair. It was not the right place or time. She got it together first and pointed at the departure board. "You have a train leaving for Tours. That's south. From there you can do what you want."

"Out of your jurisdiction."

"Out of sight, out of mind."

"That'll be fine. Thanks for chaperoning me."

"Train leaves in half an hour. Want to get a coffee?"

We sipped small paper cups of coffee at a little table. The seating area was inside the train terminal. Blocked off by poles and a fabric banner with the coffee shop's logo. All around us the train station was buzzing with activity. A regional hub in a small town. People disembarked at Alencourt. They got off their train and went over to the departure board. Then they got back on to trains going other places. Most of them didn't even get out of the train station. I thought about the dead guy with the shirt. Qayoumi. An asylum seeker from Afghanistan. I said, "What do they do with the body?"

"What body?"

"The dead guy today. Qayoumi."

"I'm not totally sure. He's registered with the state as an asylum seeker. So the state might pay for a burial. Also, he has a name, which is a good thing."

"Everyone has a name."

"Many people travel through here unregistered and without documents. So if they are found dead they just get buried with a number."

"But if they have a name," I said, "I guess someone in some office somewhere does a search before they bury them."

"I suppose they do, sometimes. But, if the name is common the search won't yield much."

"Why's that?"

"For one thing he'll be in the French system as Gulam Qayoumi, so they'll track those records easily enough. If he had registered at the time he entered Europe, most likely in Greece or Italy, he could be tracked there as well. But because Qayoumi registered as an asylum seeker in France, the trail ends here."

"That's already a trail."

"True," Nazari said. "But it's unlikely that Qayoumi arrived in France first. More likely he was illegal from his point of arrival to the moment he registered in France."

"You said, 'for one thing'. What's the other thing?"

Nazari adjusted the brim of her hat. "The translation from the original language to French usually makes it difficult to continue the search in the country of origin, using the documents that we have."

"The Afghan script or whatever."

"Right. There are many ways to do transliteration. Let's say Qayoumi speaks zero French. The official asks him to spell his name in French, well he can't. So the official just writes it as it sounds to him."

"And maybe the next official decides it's got a U in the name, QU in Qayoumi."

"Or a Y at the end instead of an I at the end," Nazari agreed.

"So tracing him is a mess."

"Yes. Precisely."

"And why would he register in France if it's not the point of entry into Europe?"

"The way it works is that once an asylum seeker is registered in Europe, the country in which they first register is considered to be responsible for them. So, if Qayoumi were registered in Bulgaria and then caught by the authorities in France, he would be sent back to Bulgaria and they'd deal with him there. Many of them prefer France, Germany, or the UK to countries like Slovakia, Bulgaria, Greece, and Italy."

"He registers in France because it's better to be an asylum seeker here than in some other places."

Nazari gave a wry smile. "Not great, but yes, better than some other places. Maybe. I'm not an expert."

"Looking at the photos I'd say he's a pretty well-dressed asylum seeker."

"Hmmm I hadn't noticed that." Nazari pulled out her phone and flipped through the images.

I said, "Look at the boots for one thing."

She showed me the photo. Ankle boots in leather. Zip-ups. I said, "Sixty euros minimum."

"Twenty or thirty if they're fake leather."

"Still expensive for an asylum seeker."

"That's possible."

"Look at the shirt," I said. "The close-up shot on the knife entry that you took."

She flipped to the photo. Saw the nautical symbol. A ship's wheel. "Designer brand. But I'm not convinced that he's some kind of rich asylum seeker."

I said, "Ok, forget that. You remember this morning? My shirt was torn and you gave me directions to replace it."

"Fanny's Friperie," she said. "Did you find something you liked?"

I unzipped my Gore-Tex jacket and showed Nazari the brown shirt underneath. "It's fine. Do you remember the old shirt?"

She shook her head. "Sorry I wasn't paying attention to your shirt."

I said, "You were grabbing me by the shirt."

She laughed and turned a darker color. "I remember the grabbing part."

I picked up my backpack and fished out the torn shirt. I showed her the logo with the nautical wheel. "It was the same shirt."

Nazari looked at the shirt, then looked at the photo on her phone. "Same shirt."

"Yes. The very same shirt. Even the same color."

"You're suggesting that the attacker thought you were Qayoumi? In which case it isn't a robbery, more like an assassination."

"Mistaken identity. He didn't know what the target looked like, just knew what shirt he was wearing."

"Did you tell the BRI assholes?"

"No. I didn't realize until you showed me your pictures."

"So you repelled the attackers and then they went and found someone else with the same shirt."

"They regrouped after attacking me, got fresh orders, and went back out. The thing was a targeted operation and the shirt was the target."

"Maybe you should go back and tell the BRI assholes."

I said, "Maybe you should. I'm getting on a train."

Cecile Nazari's hands were playing with the coffee cup. Crumpling it and unfolding the cardboard. They were good strong hands. Capable hands. "Where did you learn to defend yourself like that?"

"All over, but they tied the bow on it in Texas."

She crushed the paper cup again. "Anyway you're leaving. Which is probably a good thing. Who knows, maybe you were the target and Qayoumi was the mistake?"

I shook my head. "Not likely."

Nazari angled her head, as if nothing were impossible. We were avoiding eye contact. She was looking around, anywhere but me. I did the same. For a while we didn't talk. Just looked around at the train station. The station was covered by a large shed roof. It had iron rafters from long ago. The roof itself was wood.

I said, "Did you show your photos to the investigators?"

Nazari was distracted, thinking. She muttered, "They take their own. But I can mention your theory to them. If I see them." We watched a group of teenagers crossing the train station noisily. She said, "You should get a ticket now."

I refocused. "That would be a good idea, yes."

We stood up. She said, "Ticket office is over there."

I put on my backpack. We walked slowly across the cold wet floor of the train station. "You were here to see family." She asked, "Did you?"

That reminded me of Simone Vaugeois' husband, Gilles, who I hadn't met. I nodded. "Ended up meeting a cousin, or something. Distant."

"Sometimes distant relatives are best."

I asked, "Did you hear about an attack a couple of months ago? Old guy hit on the head?"

"Sure, that's what Bonnet was talking about when he told you about an uptick in muggings."

I said, "Otherwise you don't get a lot of muggings."

"No. It's a quiet town." She stopped herself. "Well it's normally a quiet town. We had a murder three weeks ago in fact. An entire family chopped up. What do they call it, a home invasion."

"Benoit Houdin."

"Correct. Town treasurer."

"Chopped up, means?"

"Axe murder. The family was killed and then dismembered. Limb for limb. Then they piled all the pieces in the living room. Like something out of a horror movie. The whole thing was incredibly gruesome."

"The old guy that got attacked is my relative. Gilles Vaugeois."

She turned to look at me. "Seriously?" She got a distant look in her eyes, looked away from me for a second, then looked right back.

I nodded. "Never met him before. Didn't even know that he existed. What happened?"

She said, "Happened almost six months ago. In fact it was the reason the BRI assholes showed up in the first place. Then the Houdin thing, and now they've become a regular feature. Anyway, Gilles Vaugeois, massive trauma to the head. Couple of weeks in a coma. I'm not sure that he's eating solid food now."

I remembered the dessert portion Maria had reserved for him. "I think he can eat."

"He must have severe cognitive impairments, given the injuries."

"Vaugeois said he was hit on the head."

"Weapon was a screwdriver. I believe penetration of the skull.

Depressed skull fracture followed by intracerebral haematoma in the right frontal lobe with an overlying skull vault fracture."

That was a precise description for a young municipal police officer. I said, "How do you know that?"

"I'm preparing the exam to join the BRI. I've done theoretical forensics. You get used to the terminology. I'm interested in the autopsy reports. It's rare that we get an autopsy in Alencourt and I'm friends with the medical examiner."

"You'll become an asshole."

"Better than an idiot."

I said, "Can you break it down for an idiot?"

She smiled. "Someone stabbed Gilles Vaugeois with a screwdriver. Left it in his head. The tip of the screwdriver went into his brain. Your old cousin almost certainly has permanent functional deficits."

"They got leads?"

She shook her head. "No prints on the weapon. No good physical evidence at the crime scene. Just a screwdriver in the poor old guy's head. Unprovoked attack."

I said, "Wallet stolen?"

Nazari said, "He was out for a walk. It happened a few hundred yards from his house. Wasn't carrying anything."

"Guy gets a screwdriver in the head six months ago, and a local big shot gets chopped up by an axe murderer a few weeks ago. Now the dead Afghan asylum seeker. Charming little town you've got here."

She wanted to respond, maybe defend her town, but a group of teenagers swarmed around us noisily on their way to a train. We didn't even try to talk until they had passed. She said, "I guess you should get a ticket now."

We had drifted close to the ticket office, stood there awkwardly for a while. She was a fine-looking woman and smart and competent. And she seemed to like me, which was a bonus. There was definitely a sense of something unfinished. I didn't want whatever that was to get old and rotten, like some bad aftertaste. Apparently neither did Nazari because she looked at me with those clear hazel and green eyes and said, "Goodbye, Tom Keeler," and walked cleanly away. I watched her go across the station. Kept looking at her until she passed through a set of doors at the other side.

I went to the ticket office. Bought a one-way trip to Tours. They had a big map of the French rail network up on the wall. The line went to Tours and then forked off towards Bordeaux and connected straight to Spain. I heard there was good surfing in Spain. I don't surf, but where there's surf there's beach. And I sure as hell beach.

The train was waiting on the platform. I got on the first carriage and walked through looking for a good place to sit. There weren't many people on the train just yet. Fifteen minutes or so remained before the departure time.

I pushed through the doors separating carriages. After a while I came to a rail car of old-style seating compartments. Each compartment had two rows of seats facing each other and a glass door to the corridor. Both the door and the outside window could be covered with curtains. I found an empty compartment and went in. I drew the curtains closed and sat down in the corner, all alone and peaceful.

Cecile Nazari was a missed opportunity. But missed opportunities happen all the time. No regrets. It is what it is. On the other hand, Mom's distant relatives. The lunch with Simone Vaugeois had been okay. No regrets there. Good peach tart.

The compartment door rattled. I parted my eyelids halfway. A small boy was looking at me through a crack in the door. He was having a hard time opening it. I pretended to be asleep. Hoped that he would go away. An adult hand reached in to unlock the door. It slid open with a bang. A woman and two kids spilled inside. They began to settle themselves in the carriage. The boy was bouncing on the seat opposite. The baby was beginning to cry. I didn't feel qualified to help. She was also dealing with a big suitcase. That was it. I opened my eyes.

"Can I help you?"

She needed the help. The suitcase was heavy. I threw it up on a rack above the seats. The woman began to unwrap an evening picnic. The woman offered me a Tupperware box filled with red cherry tomatoes. I declined politely.

The little family unit made me think. My family had been small, just me, my sister, Mom and Dad. Mom had died pretty early, and Dad wasn't very family oriented. So it had been us kids, pretty much. Which is one reason why I didn't think about family that often. But here I'd been gifted with another shot at family. Gilles, Mom's distant cousin, who I hadn't even met. I wondered if they had known each other growing up. They weren't all that far apart in age.

I had never even intended to meet family in Alencourt. Hadn't known that any existed. But now I did. That was a fact I couldn't go back on. Maybe the librarian in the floral dress had something to tell me. I'd straight-up forgotten about her. But most importantly, I hadn't even seen my cousin, Gilles Vaugeois, who'd been injured in a violent attack. Didn't I have a burden of duty to at least lay my eyes on him?

A train crew member passed through the carriage. He was warning friends and family members of passengers that the train was about to depart. Telling people to get off the train if they didn't have a ticket. The boy was excited that the train was leaving. Maybe they were traveling to meet up with Dad.

I stood up. Put on the backpack. The woman was feeding her baby. She looked up at me in dismay. "I hope we're not disturbing you. I'm sorry for the noise."

I reassured her, "Not at all. I've just realized that I left something behind. I have to go back."

She looked at me strangely. But she didn't argue. Ultimately she was pleased to have the carriage to herself. I stepped off the train. Whatever, I wasn't done with Alencourt.

CHAPTER TEN

The rain had stopped and a breeze was blowing through town. I got something to eat and then found a hotel. Paid in full and got a keycard for both the room and the front door, which the guy at the counter said was locked after ten. The room had a window, a bed, a chair, and a flat screen TV bolted to the wall at an unusable angle. I threw my backpack on the chair and sat on the bed. It was good enough.

I opened the window to let some air in. The evening wind was fresh and easy, riding the cusp between late spring and early summer. I lay fully clothed on the bed. Alencourt was quiet for a Saturday night. Nothing happening outside. No noise really. A couple of cars once in a while. Not a party town. I was beat. The hotel was old. I considered going out for a beer. But the establishment would be small. Locals would know each other. I would attract attention. I didn't want to attract attention.

I visualized.

The kid with the Adidas stripe in his head. I'd broken his wrist. So he'd be wearing a bandage or a cast now. Then the second one. Side part gelled hair and leather jacket. A case of bruised testicles possible. Finally the ponytail guy with the manicured beard, a sore chest, injured pride. Three of them. Footsoldiers of some kind. Curious.

I hadn't planned on coming to Alencourt until the day before. Bought the train ticket on a whim. It was totally random. There was another question: had Qayoumi been on the same train as me? The guy with the broken wrist had been scouting the train. He saw me first and stopped looking.

The blue shirt with the nautical logo.

The Afghan guy Qayoumi was a target. Why? The footsoldiers had messed it up by attacking me. Some kind of gang conflict over trafficking maybe. I'd done tours in Afghanistan. They grow a lot of drugs over there.

I figured Qayoumi had been on the same train, got overlooked because of me, and then got picked up later on, once they'd realized the mistake. Which meant there were more people involved. Including someone running surveillance and scouting wherever Qayoumi had boarded the train. The one to send the message, *The blue shirt with the nautical logo.*

But then there would be other, more important operators. Commanders who gave orders and let footsoldiers take the punishment. Interesting.

I was feeling confined in the hotel room. Felt like maybe going out for a prowl. If there's a chance to be out there in the world, I'll take it. When you're in the field, on your own or with your team, you've got options either way. They can change, you can rework the options if someone's closing them down. My job had been to close off the other guy's options in a major way. Felt weird to just sit around on my ass after contact with an enemy. My instinct was to get closer, not further away.

But, on the other hand, I was a civilian now. I needed to readapt to regular life. Whatever that means.

I stared up at the ceiling. A thousand miles from sleep. *Call it tourism*, I thought. Be a good civilian. Go out there for a prowl. Call it a healthy walk. Then, come back to the hotel and sleep when you're done. Go back to see the Vaugeois cousins in the morning, meet Gilles, regardless of his current disability. Finish up the project, complete the mission.

I swung up to a seated position. Feet on the floor. Stretched out. Yawned. Cracked my joints. Time to go prowling.

The hotel lobby had maps of the town nicely folded in a rack for tourists. I opened a map and looked at it for a minute. It gave me a sense of orientation. I memorized the map and left it there. Walked ten minutes away from the hotel in a random direction and found a French fast food joint. They hadn't yet caught on to the burger thing. So I ordered a kebab and a soda. There were a bunch of delivery guys on scooters out front. They were sitting on their bikes with helmets half off. Looking at their phones and talking. A lot of them looked like their parents or grandparents might have come over from Algeria, Tunisia, Morocco, or any number of French ex-colonies.

Father Bousquet and Simone Vaugeois had spoken about the *cité*. Social housing with people crammed in tight. First, second, and third generation immigrants living cheek by jowl. Bousquet had called it *Les Brosses*. That was the name of the place. The word meant The Brushes.

I thought again about the guy with the broken wrist. The one who had scouted the train and found me instead of the Afghan. Him and his buddies had looked like these delivery guys. Same style of clothing, same style of haircut. That's where they would be. The rat-faced guy would be easy to spot. Find the guy with the broken wrist and see what happens from there. Watch him. See what he does and who he talks to. If I don't see him, no biggie.

I asked one of the delivery guys directions for *Les Brosses*. The guy was eating potato chips out of a bag. Didn't seem to want to bother with talking, so he just pointed west. Said something like, "There." I left the kebab shop and pulled the Gore-Tex jacket's hood up. Dumped the food.

I slipped like a ghost through empty streets.

The old town faded away. I entered a light industrial area. Warehouses and low buildings with fenced-off yards. Sodium lights spilled weak orange around hard shadows. Trucks parked for the night behind wire. I was wearing a pair of hiking boots I'd had for a few years. They were quiet for boots. There were a couple of torched cars up on the sidewalk.

The railway was a perpendicular line. North to south. It ran through the place like an obstacle. The tracks were elevated by a massive berm and protected by a high fence. The road turned north running alongside the tracks. After a while there was a turn under the railroad. Then, the street cut hard to the south, running back along the rail line.

Straight ahead a footpath curved through a grassy area beneath a highway overpass. The highway itself was high up and inaccessible. Present only as a single sound, like a weird electrical hum. The terrain was bleak and man-made. Grass areas sectioned with concrete walkways. Sharp-angled terra-formed berms edging the highway and railroad. This place was definitely cut off from town. Once out from under the highway overpass, the footpath broke into a residential area. Until then, I hadn't seen a living soul. Now, in the distance, human figures moved. Beyond them *Les Brosses*.

CHAPTER ELEVEN

EACH OF THE three buildings of *Les Brosses* was a replica of the others. A grassy park surrounded the housing complex. Footpaths were laid in, running through bushy landscaped areas and terraformed bumps. Vapor light posts were distributed around the grounds. The lights were head-height and the effect was modern. There were benches. A few of them occupied by couples. The place wasn't ugly either.

Les Brosses was situated with its back to the train tracks and highway. On the other side were cars and a road that ran right alongside all three buildings. I figured the backside was used by people walking into town, while the front accessed public transportation and personal vehicles.

I circled around. Spiraling closer to the buildings. There was nothing special going on. The park was well tended and the damp grass, herbs, and flowers smelled nice. A couple kissed on a bench. They didn't even look up at me, which meant they felt safe. The buildings loomed closer. I cut over to the north side and then circled around to the edge of the last building. I watched some kids kicking a ball around. It was that time when parents and old people call it a night. The front door is locked. Children are put to bed. Stories are told, if the kids are lucky. Dishes are washed and put out to drain. TV sets blink on. Faces reflect the shimmer of moving images and light.

None of the kids kicking the ball had a broken wrist. They all had perfectly healthy bones.

So I moved on. Hoisted myself up into the plant bed and stepped through to a footpath. The middle building was set at a forty-five degree angle from the road, which was lifeless and lined with parked cars. More people were gathered close to the building. I sat down on a bench and watched. Thirty yards distant. Kids in several clusters. Talking with each other. Laughing, passing stuff around, like cigarettes and joints and cans of beer and a ball. I counted nineteen individuals. All military-aged. Adolescent or early twenties. Fifteen male and four female.

I waited. Maybe half an hour. Nothing happened. A few kids showed up, a few kids left. The group size stayed about the same. The voices grew louder. Those standing began to lean. Some sat down on a poured concrete bench. I watched.

To wait and be unseen requires the operator to blend into the picture, as if he'd always been a part of it. The two things that attract attention are unexpected movement patterns and new objects in the picture. I was only a new object for a moment, since the average human attention span is less than twelve seconds. An operator gets used to waiting. I can wait for hours. Days. Infinite waiting ability. When I want to. But I didn't want to.

I approached the mezzanine from the south. The concrete stairs were wide and angled at forty-five degrees to the facade. The mezzanine extended across the entire front. It accessed residential apartments and corridors that plunged deeper into the building. Halfway down, two figures reclined against the balcony wall, deep in the shadow. The glow of a cigarette tip gave it away, then the tinny sound of music from a phone.

Then, the high-pitched whine of derestricted trail bike engines cut the night.

I could make out light and shadow down the south side of *Les Brosses*. I walked across the mezzanine. Past the couple sharing a cigarette, entwined in darkness. From the mezzanine I could make out a basketball court, fenced in on all sides, screened by a stand of trees. Through the trees, trail bike headlights swung erratically within the caged court.

I came down the stairs. Stayed close to the buildings and then moved off the path into the stand of pine trees. I leaned back against one of them and slowly sank into a crouch, like I was tying my shoe, but I stayed down.

They were playing a game. Each bike had a driver and a rider. Until five or six hundred years ago, knights on horseback would joust, maybe on this very spot. They galloped at each other and tried to throw the other guy off with a lance. The bike guys were doing something similar, like jousting on horseback, but with trail bikes in a basketball court. Maybe it was post-modern.

The riders worked the throttles, red-lining the engines. Then, at the same time, they each dumped the clutch, unloading the power straight to the wheel. They were separated by a distance of around eighty feet. The bikes leapt at each other like fighting dogs. One of them was red, the other white. When they came together the passengers tried to knock each other off. It was pretty brutal and looked like a lot of fun.

The riders had discipline. They didn't clutch at each other. They kept fingers safe by punching or pushing. The goal was to throw the other rider off. I could hear them laughing and cursing at each other. But it was amiable. They were buddies in a tough neighborhood.

The white bike went down, skidding out. The rider got it back up fast, but the passenger was thrown. He had to walk back to his seat. The red bike was in position by then, engine revving. The red bike's rider shouted something in a derisive tone. He wore a white helmet with flames up the middle, like a mohawk haircut. The white bike squealed around in a rubber-burning doughnut and got back in position. Then they did it again.

This time the mohawk helmet guy went down. Passengers were taking a beating. After a while they got tired of it. The white bike did a full screaming circle of the basketball court and rocketed out. The entrance was facing me. The bike braked hard at the footpath and peeled off away from *Les Brosses*. I saw that the red bike was getting set to do the same. So I moved.

I stepped across to the footpath just as the bike was revving to leave the court, moving towards the entrance, blocking the way. The rider opened up the throttle and lurched forward, keeping a tight rein on the gearbox. I stayed put. They could go through me. But they'd need to be prepared for pain. They couldn't see my face because of the hood and the lighting. The bike approached slowly in fits and starts. The modified motor had an unpleasant sound, a little too frantic and anxious. I figured these guys would be the same. Frantic and anxious. When the bike got close I put my hands out and approached.

"Can I ask you a question?" This wasn't acknowledged. So I asked again, "I just have a little question for you. I'm looking for a friend of mine with a broken wrist." I mimed a broken wrist. "He's probably got a bandage on. Very short hair with stripes on the side. It happened today. Do you know him?"

I couldn't make out the faces behind their helmet masks. It was dark. The trail bike made an aggressive high idling sound. There was a minute of frozen time. I figured the rider was trying to calculate, gauging if knocking me over was going to be worth it. Anyway, my goal was to provoke them and if these guys knew the rat-face with the broken wrist, he'd find out about it.

I stepped back and gave them an exit. The rider snapped it into first and hit the throttle. As they passed me, I locked eyes with the rider sitting in the back with the flaming mohawk helmet. We looked at each other for a split second, but it was enough. The guy's eyes were bright blue, rimmed with dark lashes, like a male model. It was the ponytail guy from earlier. The rat-faced guy's buddy who I'd put down. But it was too late to grab him.

The bike veered through a plant bed and onto the path. They took off and bumped down from the curb to the street and away. The derestricted engine's scream echoed off the buildings until it was a distant noise. Like a mosquito.

After a while the regular sounds came back. Cars, insects, the occasional voice, a dog. I sat on a bench and counted five minutes before heading out.

Les Brosses turned into an area of fenced-off wasteland and junkyards. Stuff you find outside of any town center. There was a railroad crossing. Then residential streets started up again. Houses, one after the other, in a line, dimly lit in the night. French houses don't have yards, they're closed in with walls. They plant bushes and trees to block off the view from the road. Once in a while a ground floor window was visible. Sometimes lit. Mostly I got the impression that people turned in early on a Saturday night.

A car turned the corner. The headlights washed over me as it straightened up and then drove past. It was a blue Opel Corsa. There were two silhouettes in the front. Other than that I couldn't see. The Corsa continued on for a block and then made a left. Red tail lights faded off.

I caught sight of a couple of people out walking. Going from some place to another place. Or maybe just walking in circles. I crossed an intersection. An old guy on a pushbike rode through. I got closer to town. A couple stood watching a small white dog piss against a tree. They had a plastic cone over the dog's head. Maybe he was a biter. They didn't speak and I passed them silently.

I walked for about a quarter of an hour more in almost total silence until I got to the hotel. The keycard for the hotel door caught in a pocket fold, so I had to disentangle it. While I was doing that, headlight beams glinted off of a parked car and I looked around.

A blue Opel Corsa came past. Same registration plates as before. Two silhouettes in the front.

I had last seen the car about fifteen minutes earlier. If I walked briskly at around five miles per hour, fifteen minutes of walking would be just over a mile, which was a decent pace for a person. But for a car, five miles per hour is unacceptably slow, which meant that they had either stopped and waited, or had gone somewhere else and come back.

I don't like having my sleep interrupted, and you never really know. So I went up to the room. I brushed my teeth. Then packed and put my backpack on. I went downstairs. The lobby was dark. I left the keycard on the desk. Stood still and listened. Nothing was happening in the hotel. Except for sleep. And mechanical things, like the ticking of a clock, or the mechanism in the refrigerator under the bar in the breakfast room. I went down a little corridor behind the desk. Found the kitchen and a back door. There was no alarm. The back door locked behind me.

A little alley led out to another street lined with closed establishments and apartment buildings, shuttered stores and bolted doors. It was too late to find another room. I walked north-east for twenty minutes and found the river.

I lay down in a copse of trees protected by bushes. I had the backpack for a pillow. It took a minute or two to settle. Then I could hear the water moving along the river bank, over rocks and around branches. I could smell the vegetation and the moist soil.

And across the water came another sound. Familiar music drifted through the trees, skipping over the gently flowing river. I nailed it. Stevie Nicks singing 'Sara'. 1979. Vintage Fleetwood Mac. 'Drowning in the sea of love. Where everyone would love to drown.' And along with Stevie's sweet voice I began to make out the tinkling of glasses, the light laughter of a man or a woman. The sounds of a Saturday evening. And the low gravelly chuckle of Simone Vaugeois floated in the crisp evening breeze.

CHAPTER TWELVE

WHEN I TURNED up the driveway to Brumaire, Stevie Nicks was howling the last of her sweet song. Sara wasn't going to change or stop, but Stevie would be there for her. Forever. The drive was packed with cars. A woman was smoking a cigarette on the terrace steps and looking at her phone. Beside her was a half-glass of champagne.

I nodded politely, "*Bonsoir* madame," and kept moving.

Two tables had been set out on the terrace. A bunch of well-dressed people lounged around the table to my right. I didn't know them from Adam, but I know how to walk into a party uninvited. First thing. You don't make eye contact. Second. You smile and keep moving. You act like you have always just recognized someone who's just a little bit beyond. This gets you through the outer layers. Before some guy asks if he can help you.

You keep moving. *Not too fast, not too slow.* Then you do what you have to do. You take them out, or whatever. I wasn't planning on hurting anyone. But I did want to meet my cousin, Gilles Vaugeois.

A couple of the gentlemen wore suits. The ladies wore dresses and tasteful make-up. The men smoked cigars. Their voices were lyrical and low. Like aging Latin lovers. They sipped amber liquid from heavy crystal glass.

Behind the terrace, two sets of double French doors had been unlatched on either side. The wisteria was in bloom, exuding a musky scent. The tinkle of crystal drew me through the open front door. The corridor went back to a massive curving staircase. I recognized Maria, the maid, walking straight towards me carrying a tray of empty glasses. She looked surprised. "Monsieur."

"*Bonsoir.*" Kept moving. *Not too fast, not too slow.*

To the right was a drawing room. To the left was a dining room. Lunch with Simone and Bousquet had been in the room on the left. The drawing room on the right contained a pool table. A couple of guys were playing. Cognac glasses rested on marble surfaces. The room was stuffy with cigar smoke.

Maria went into the room on the left. I went after her. I spotted Simone before she saw me. She was multi-tasking her party, chatting to two older ladies while supervising Daniel, the gardener, who was fiddling with a champagne bucket. Daniel was better-dressed than earlier, looking uncomfortable in a collared shirt.

She saw me and put her hand to her mouth, settling her weight back on high heels.

"Tom!" She pronounced my name like comb, or dome, or Tome. "Tom, what are you doing here?"

She approached and looked up at me. I said, "Couldn't sleep."

She looked around for her champagne glass and found it. Grabbed the glass, sipped from it, then smiled, as if what I had said was a joke. "We're not sleeping here either, Tom. As you can see." She searched around again with her eyes. Found Daniel. "Daniel, please pour Tom a glass of champagne."

Daniel nodded seriously and began to open a fresh bottle. His shirt was starched and looked weird on him, as if his sun-blasted face didn't belong sticking out of that collar. He flashed eye contact and went back to unwrapping foil from the champagne bottle.

She looked up at me and grinned. "How did you know?"

I shrugged, "Sometimes, you know."

She was already nodding. "Exactly. That's precisely how it works."

I took a glass of champagne from Daniel and thanked him. Simone put a hand on my shoulder and introduced me as her cousin to the ladies with whom she had been conversing, Nicole and Claire. She took my backpack. "I'll put this in your room." I didn't complain.

The women seemed amused. Nicole and Claire had silver hair cut above the shoulders. Both asked me about my connection to Simone. I answered their questions. Gilles wasn't in the room. I thought he might be upstairs in bed, or in a wheelchair somewhere. After a while I excused myself.

The house was built around the central stairwell, which climbed up to a skylight several flights above. The stairs curved away from the middle, hugged the wall, then turned back to the center of the house. They were carpeted in deep emerald velvet with brass rods. The wooden balustrade was ancient oak. Smoothed by the passage of hands. Paintings of unsmiling people were set on the wall as the steps rose. It occurred to me that these might be my ancestors. The thought was ridiculous. I felt about as French as a Maine lobster roll or a Winchester Model Seventy.

Upstairs I figured there would be a series of bedrooms. I walked along the corridor. Looked left, looked right. Fancy bedrooms, a large bathroom suite. At the end of the corridor was a closed door. I listened. Heard murmuring within, like low conversation. I was trying to make out who or what, when loud footsteps approached the door from inside. I stepped back. The knob turned and there was Simone, surprised to see me for the third time that day.

She stood in the doorway in an exaggerated pose. "Tom. You are going to bed?"

"I was looking for the bathroom."

She looked up into my face. Her eyes were searching, grasping for what she might hold on to. "This is your room, Tom." She indicated the empty bedroom that she had just been preparing. "You like two pillows, yes?"

"Yes. Thank you, ma'am." I figured that she must have been talking to herself in the room.

She took my arm. "Come. I will show you the toilet and the bathroom. These are not the same thing."

As we walked, I concluded that she was very drunk, but surviving. She was that kind of hardened party survivor. A professional. Anything involving hospitality was a breeze for her, provided it fell within acceptable parameters. And within those, she was untouchable. Would never make an error. Madame Vaugeois guided me towards one of the bathroom suites.

She said, "When you come down I will introduce you to the mayor," and pirouetted faultlessly on one of her high heels.

CHAPTER THIRTEEN

I WALKED BACK into the room while the mayor was shooting pool. But it wasn't exactly pool, it was French billiards. There were only three balls and no pockets.

The mayor was a tall man in his sixties with a full head of casually cut white hair and a perma-tan that looked real. The man was tall and obese. It was the mayor's shot. The stick looked puny in his hands, fleshy slabs that swallowed up the pale wood. His opponent stood with his back to me. The cue hit the white ball, which hit other balls, which rolled around and bounced off the banks and each other. It seemed pointless. I couldn't see where the balls were trying to go.

The mayor sank into the velvet cushions of an expensive-looking antique armchair. He retrieved the butt of his cigar from a crystal ashtray and set about lighting it. The other guy walked around the table to take his shot. When I saw his profile I recognized the cop from earlier that day, Antoine Bonnet. Bonnet observed the table, then looked up and saw me. There was a flash of recognition and surprise before he suppressed it, concentrating on the table. He shifted over and I saw the Police Chief Rigalle, across the green surface of the billiard table. Rigalle was lighting the mayor's cigar and speaking in his ear, the mustache moving up and down.

Bonnet took his shot and missed the balls completely. He shrugged and came around the table.

"Keeler, you surprised me. I thought you had left us. Could have sworn that I dropped you off at the train station, and that you had actually boarded a train." Bonnet extended his hand and I shook it enthusiastically. The cop looked good. An athletic late forties. Fresh in a pink collared shirt and dark blue slacks. I couldn't help looking at his shoes, suede loafers in burgundy. Bonnet laughed. "You're looking at my shoes?"

"Shoes make the man."

He looked at mine, hiking boots with complicated-looking cross-hatching of canvas, fake suede, and boot lace. Like an ugly overgrown sneaker. Bonnet said, "I don't even know how I would describe your shoes."

"In that case it's probably not worth trying."

"You must be right."

I shrugged. "Looks like I've got family here in town."

He looked amused. "Is that right, you're a Vaugeois?"

"In some form, yes."

Simone Vaugeois tugged at my arm. "Come on, I want to introduce you to the mayor."

Bonnet said, "I'll catch you later, Keeler."

I nodded at him, thought he was a pretty decent guy. Simone led me to the other side of the room. The mayor was lining up his shot. The police chief stood up cordially as the madame approached. "Monsieur Keeler."

Madame Vaugeois said, "He has returned to the bosom of his French family."

Rigalle found that amusing. "And it's quite a family indeed." He turned back to me. "Are you a billiards player?"

"Not really my thing. I can't work out what it is they're doing."

"This is the real thing, Monsieur Keeler, it's not eight ball."

"It doesn't make any sense to me. The balls bounce around and they hit each other. Looks to me like they have nowhere to go, but I'll take your word for it."

"There's a quote that I love, 'Show me a good pool player and I'll show you a misspent youth.' Mark Twain. Do you know it?"

"W.C. Fields, I think."

Rigalle's face reddened. "I'm happy to be corrected by a true American *soldier*."

The mayor had taken his shot. A couple of balls had bounced around with nowhere to go. Looked random to me. Bonnet was examining his options. The mayor put a thick arm around Bonnet, distracting his concentration no doubt. He had a massive gold ring on one of his fingers. The mayor addressed Madame Vaugeois and me. "If you think Antoine's good at billiards you should see him play tennis." He squeezed Bonnet, who winced and smiled grimly. I didn't blame him for feeling uncomfortable. The mayor grinned and looked the cop up and down. "This one is definitely going places."

Simone Vaugeois coughed. I could see her preparing to impose herself on the conversation. She addressed the mayor with the kind of formal determination a hostess can pull off. She said, "Monsieur the mayor, may I present Tom Keeler, a lost Vaugeois from America."

The mayor smiled and leaned his cue up against an antique cabinet. His blue eyes were exceptionally light colored. They flicked between Vaugeois, myself, Rigalle, and Bonnet, gauging the audience and their various needs and demands. The mayor was a large and commanding presence. He extended a hand. "Jean-Baptiste Marbot." I took it. The hand almost completely enclosed mine, thick as a rib steak.

The mayor didn't let go. His other hand waved the cigar around while talking. He looked me in the eyes and said, "There are no lost persons in Alencourt, monsieur. And certainly no lost Vaugeois. Your relations are my closest and dearest neighbors." He looked at

Madame. "The only house in town nicer than Brumaire is mine. Isn't that so?"

Simone Vaugeois smiled and shrugged. "A very nice house, Monsieur the Mayor."

I remembered the house across the river, when I'd been riding in the back of the unmarked police car. I could imagine Marbot there, maybe eating a cake on the terrace.

I looked down at my hand, encased in what is known as a *power grip*. Rigalle was at the mayor's shoulder, smirking, his face red with drink. I looked at Mayor Marbot, who was trying to do some kind of forceful trick with his eyes, while trying to strengthen his grip on my hand. The mayor held the look a little too long, and in his eyes I saw indifference, like that of a predatory animal.

Marbot's eyes flicked around like pale pins, agitated and calculating. Probing the room. Taking its temperature. He pulled me in towards him. It was one of those classic politician power moves, playing to the bleachers, the well-off men and women in the room, by demonstrating physical domination. I saw Bonnet standing off to the side and watching, thoughtfully. I met his eye for a moment, then turned back to the mayor.

The entourage laughed. Simone Vaugeois stood smiling, oblivious.

I allowed the mayor to pull me in a little tighter. Enough so that our clasped hands were hidden by my body. With my thumb I traced the web of skin on the mayor's hand where thumb and forefinger meet. This is a pressure point, usually used to relieve pain. A couple of millimeters away is a point where a thick blood vessel runs over bone. Marbot's hands were encased in a thick layer of fat, so I had to work hard. I fastened down on that blood vessel with my thumb, using brute force to work through the fat and crush it quickly into the bone. The pain is sharp. I locked my thumb down and kept it there, constricting blood flow. Marbot instinctively pulled his hand away, but because he had already pulled me in, he had no leverage, no place to go. I stepped into his personal space and further reduced his ability to move, trapping the mayor between the antique cabinet and my body. Nowhere to go, only pain.

I released him and said, "Nice to meet you, mister mayor."

Rigalle was standing at the mayor's shoulder, transfixed by what had just occurred, most of it hidden by our bodies, hands tucked in between us. The police chief had noticed, as had Bonnet. The cop turned back to the billiard table. The mayor smiled weakly and rubbed his hand. He glanced at me like a reprimanded cat. He said, "I hope you enjoy yourself, monsieur, our town is one of the most beautiful in France," and turned away towards the elegant men and women of Alencourt.

A red-faced man in an impeccable suit raised a cognac glass. "Here's to poor old Houdin!" I figured he was referring to Benoit Houdin, town treasurer and axe-murder victim.

Simone said, "And Julie, and the kids."

The red-faced man had tears running down his cheeks. He made no attempt to wipe them. The mayor bowed his head and assumed a sorrowful look. Rigalle echoed his boss. Marbot's eyes searched for a glass and the police director followed his look and found one for the great man. The mayor announced, "To Benoit, Julie. The Houdin family. To a true friend."

There was a moment of silence. Everyone wet their lips with cognac or champagne. Then Madame Vaugeois and the mayor launched into a conversation about quality of life certifications for towns and villages in France. Rigalle pulled me away by the elbow. "Come, let's have a drink. I'd like to hear about your military service. I myself served in the French army. Nothing interesting, you know that conscription was compulsory until only recently."

There was almost nothing I wanted to avoid more than discussing military life with the police director of Alencourt. But he drew me out of the billiard room, which was open to another large room, deeper into the house. Several younger people stood around a marble chimney mantlepiece. They were laughing and animated, except for one.

Officer Nazari stood looking at me as if she'd seen a ghost. Rigalle saw her and was confused for a moment, before realizing. "Of course, you two have already met."

CHAPTER FOURTEEN

I FELT my face become hot. Nazari was blushing. She was wearing tight new denim pants and a frilled white cotton blouse that hugged her form and came up high at the neck. It had the effect of perfectly accentuating her most important lines. Her hair was up in a side bun with most of it popping out carelessly.

She was very good-looking.

Rigalle was talking my ear off about his military service, which had apparently been spent in various air conditioned venues across the diminishing sphere of French influence. I had worked with the French. There were good ones and there were bad ones. Rigalle struck me as one of those networker types who land the top jobs, but not altogether a bad guy. More like a guy with his nose to the wind, which is to say, a guy without strong opinions one way or the other.

Nazari broke from the group as we approached. Flashed me a look. She wore eye make-up, blue lines and dark shades. She went quickly out of the room. Rigalle noticed. I said, "Excuse me," and followed her. I didn't pay much attention to the director of municipal police just then, but I did see a flash of anger as I left him standing.

Nazari was at the bottom of the big stairwell. She was all red. "You came back for me."

"I did?" I was unsure on that account, but it might have been true.

"You did."

She grabbed me by the hand and pulled me past the stairwell towards the back of the house. The corridor darkened as we moved away from the festivities. There was a turn and then a door off to the right. Nazari opened it. A dark room. She pulled me in and shut the door.

Pitch black. Couldn't see a thing. She reached up and put her arms around my neck. I could smell her fragrance and I felt her breath and strands of her wild hair on my face just moments before her lips made contact with mine. We came together. Every part of us searching out the parts of the other one and getting rid of any distance between them. Our fingers probed and caressed. We stayed like that for a long time. Until she pulled her lips away from mine and said, "Do you hear that?"

I said, "Hear what?"

She said, "Nothing," and came at me again. As if the brief separation had been such a bad idea that we had to make up for it in spades. We were really getting into it when she pulled her head back and said, "Wait, listen."

I had already heard it and ignored it. There was some kind of mechanical hiss on the other side of the room.

I could tell that the room was big. Just in the way sound moved around between the walls. Now that we'd been there a while, my eyes had adjusted somewhat to the darkness. I could make out a bed, and a shape on it. Heavy drapes were drawn across windows on the other side of it. There had been a medicinal smell in the room. Like a balm made from roots and herbs. It was mixed with the odor of hygiene products, like anti-bacterial soap and rubbing alcohol.

I took Nazari's hand and went to the window, drew the drapes back a touch. Moonlight got through. Gilles Vaugeois was a lump in the bed. He looked asleep. At least unconscious. He had a nasal cannula pushing oxygen into each nostril. Like a drip irrigation system for the brain. The tank was right next to Vaugeois' bed, emitting a hiss as the gas was released to his nose.

Nazari cursed and stood tight against me from behind. She pushed her fingers into my front pocket and held me like that. We looked at Gilles for a while. I could see the scar on the right side of his forehead. There's almost no part of the human body more difficult to penetrate than the forehead.

I thought of putting a screwdriver in there. Doable, but tough. It's the last place any trained operator would choose. Even if you weren't going for a precise target, artery or organ, you'd want to go somewhere soft. Which meant that the attacker was both careless and extremely strong. We stood there looking at him for a minute or two. It made sense that he was on the ground floor. Nazari said, "Do you think he can hear?"

"I don't know." I stood over him. His eyes were closed. The eyelids quivered. Ragged breathing made his chest rise and fall. I said, "Probably not."

Nazari said, "I have to go."

I turned and we kissed more. After a while we disentangled. She stood close to the door and tucked herself back together again. I put back the drapes and walked through darkness to her. Found her. She was soft and firm and smelled good.

She began to open the door, but I stopped her. There were voices on the other side. I figured she would want to be discreet. I brushed past her. Gently twisted the knob and got the door open a crack. It was just enough to make out Daniel the gardener and Maria the house-keeper. They were having a heated argument in whispers. I tried to figure out what they were saying, but realized they were speaking in Portuguese. It was the argument of a married couple.

Maria was pushing her point of view and Daniel was not liking it. At least that was my interpretation of their mime show. They were beside a half-open door. Daniel closed it and locked it. He gave the key to Maria, who hadn't stopped whispering. Nazari and I waited a while in the dark. She leaned her head into my chest. Traced her fingers across it. I curled her hair in my fingers and watched Daniel and Maria. They came to some kind of conclusion eventually and left.

We got out of Gilles Vaugeois' room and closed the door. Nazari faced me. "I look okay?"

"You look perfect."

"That's not what I meant."

I pushed a couple of hairs into place. I looked at where Daniel and Maria had been arguing. The door was shorter than the others on that corridor. Maybe a cellar. She said, "I have to go. I didn't come here alone."

"You came with your partner?"

"Antoine? No, I came with the other cop."

"The chief?"

"Yes, Alain." She read my look, smiled and said, "Yeah, but it's not like that."

"What's it like?"

"The party's a benefit for the foundation and Rigalle's on the board. He's my boss. He asked, so I came."

"But he thinks you came for him, right?"

She shrugged. "It's possible, in the weird fantasies of a man like Rigalle." She gave what I thought was a very French shrug. "Look, the guy's married with kids. I'm friends with them."

It was my turn to shrug. "Hey, relax, it's your life, but married with kids means exactly nothing right?"

"Yeah, I know. Whatever. Who knows what men think? Or if they actually think."

"What about your partner, the older guy. He's involved too?"

"Antoine? He's old friends with Mayor Marbot and Rigalle."

"High flying for a beat cop. Fraternizing up the chain of command."

"I was in the academy with Bonnet. It's his second career. He'd been a big city banker. Hated it and switched, but he knows everyone in town."

"Middle-aged crisis or something like that."

"Something like that. They're probably looking for me." She kissed me. "I have to go."

I said, "Will you look up a car plate registration for me? Can you do that?"

"Maybe. Why?"

"Humor me and I'll tell you later." I gave her the blue Opel Corsa plate number I'd memorized. "Think you can remember that?"

She nodded. "Got it." Pulled away from me. "You'll find me?"

I said I would. She smiled. "Unless I find you first," and disappeared down the corridor. I counted three minutes waiting outside the cellar door.

When I came out again the party was pretty much over. The mayor had already gone and the remaining guests were saying their goodbyes. Police Chief Rigalle avoided me completely. Nazari left with him and shot me a slow look as they went down the stairs.

Back inside, Nazari's partner Bonnet had hung back. He waved me over to the marble mantlepiece where he was nursing a cognac.

Bonnet poured me a couple of fingers. I sipped at it and said, "Nice party."

"It's a decent cause."

I agreed with that. "No harm in helping other people, that's for sure."

"So what made you come back?"

"I guess it was my cousin. I didn't actually get to meet him earlier on. So I came back to do that."

"And you met old Gilles tonight? I didn't see him around, exactly."

I said, "Your partner introduced us."

Bonnet coughed, surprised. "Cecile? Introduced you tonight?"

I kept a straight face and looked him in the eye. "Yes, very pleasant."

He smiled. "Right, pleasant. Screwdriver in the head. Pretty unfortunate thing to happen."

"Unfortunate is for an accident, or a coincidence. I'd say this was quite a bit more than unfortunate."

"Maybe terrible is a better word then."

"That begins to describe it, yeah. And there are other issues now."

"Other issues. So what, you're planning on staying?"

I looked at him; he seemed like a decent enough guy. "Are you suggesting that I shouldn't?"

Bonnet widened his eyes. "Not at all. I'm happy for you to stay. It's a free world isn't that so?"

"Well that's an aspiration that I tend to favor. It's a free world some places, not all. Certainly should be a free world as far as I'm concerned."

"On that we can agree." He raised his cognac glass, we clinked. "And I'm sure we agree on a lot more."

"No doubt."

Bonnet downed his cognac and set the glass down. "Look, Keeler. If there's any way that I can help you, or your family here. You let me know."

I told him that I appreciated the offer and that I was sure that he was already doing everything he could as a member of Alencourt's finest. Bonnet seemed satisfied at that, and genuinely concerned.

I walked him to the terrace and we shook hands.

CHAPTER FIFTEEN

MARIA AND DANIEL were efficiently putting everything away. I sat down on the terrace with Madame Vaugeois. She lit her cigarette with a fancy lighter and took a drag and let out a stream of smoke and a sigh, "Ah." Then she looked at me square and said, "Bon. That was a success."

"I'm glad to hear it."

She shifted in her seat and flicked the ash into a bronze ashtray. "No, I mean it. I told you about the *Fondation D'Accueil*. It's the purpose of the evening."

Fondation D'Accueil translated as 'Welcome Foundation'. I recalled Simone Vaugeois statements on migrants from earlier. I said, "I wasn't sure that you looked very charitably on migrants."

She dismissed me with a wave of her cigarette. "That's not true at all. I don't see any contradiction. It's true that I don't want them to stay; that would be the end of France. But they are human beings no? Of course it is our duty to help them." She looked at me funny. "It's not only for Father Bousquet and the church."

"That's why the mayor and police director were here."

Vaugeois agreed. "We have good civic engagement from the municipality. Thanks to me perhaps." She looked satisfied.

I said nothing.

She took a hard pull on her cigarette and breathed out between her teeth. "Gilles and Benoit were close, you know. Gilles wasn't an important man, like Benoit, but they were both interested in local history and that kind of thing."

It took me a second to remember that *Benoit* was Benoit Houdin, the guy who had been murdered along with his family a couple of weeks ago. We'd toasted his memory earlier, with Mayor Marbot.

"What kind of local history?"

"Oh I don't know, the things they spoke about in Gilles' study. You know men, they're always going on about history and archaeology. It's very significant to them. And some of it is interesting. It's important to know where we come from."

She stopped talking then. As if some kind of a switch and been flipped. She kissed me on both cheeks and excused herself. I sat on the terrace for a minute and went upstairs to the room she had prepared for me.

Which was spacious. The bed was a single. Like a kid's bed, which I figured it had been. There was a sink in the corner, blocked off by a wooden folding partition with painted oriental designs. She had even put a towel there for me. I brushed my teeth and switched off the light. Got into the bed and lay in it. I could hear the sounds of Brumaire finally winding down for the night. I estimated the time at a quarter to two in the morning.

I slept like a baby, but briefly.

A sharp sound woke me before dawn. I opened my eyes and lay still. Faint blue light rimmed the curtain's edge. I heard the sound a second time. A human voice. A cry or a gasp. A voice without words. I waited and listened. A minute or two later there was a dull bang and a raucous clatter. Like something breaking, or many things falling all over a polished wood floor.

I swiveled out of bed. Dressed. Slipped out of the room. I crept along the corridor on bare feet. It was quiet in the house. Someone had made a noise and was now keeping still. Maybe waiting to see if anyone had been roused. The floorboards were creaky. Old house.

I kept to the edges near the wall. The joists would be stronger and more firmly attached. Joists are usually spaced forty or sixty centimeters apart. I wasn't worried about someone hearing me. I just wanted to hear them first. So I placed my feet carefully, sliding them forward until I found solid footing. I made it to the stairwell without a sound. Thick green carpeting allowed me to bound soundlessly in three or four leaps. Landed like a cat.

I stood there a couple of beats, listening. I could hear breathing coming from the dining room. I walked over and turned the corner.

Gilles Vaugeois was sprawled across a drawer full of spilled silverware.

The old guy was dressed in classic blue stripe pajamas. He must have noticed me because he started moaning and gasping. He was bald with a thin puff of white hair awry above his pink liver-spotted head. The screwdriver scar looked angry and swollen. He had a long nose, dripping with moisture. His neck was scrawny and barely held up the head, bent into his chest. I went to him. Supported him under the arms from behind.

"Let's get you back to your room."

He moaned and gasped. Not like he was trying to say words, more like an animal discomfort. A line of spit traced from the corner of his mouth to the front of his pajamas. He was light and I lifted him without trouble. His bare feet scrambled for purchase and eventually settled. I took the weight. Slung his arm over my shoulder and held his wrist. I had him around the waist with the other arm. He was skin and bones, it was like carrying a classroom skeleton in a cloth bag.

I guided him out of the dining room and into the corridor. His head brushed against the side of my face. Halfway down the corridor he started to fret. He tried to pull away, but I held him firmly. I said, "We're just gonna get you back to bed, buddy."

The old guy moaned and struggled some but quickly got docile.

The door at the end of the hallway was cracked open. I pushed it with my foot. The curtains were drawn and the room was pitch black. Dawn light was filtering through the rest of the house. It spilled into the room through the open door like a gray ghost. Simone was curled up on her side in the bed. She had a sleep mask on and was snoring lightly. I noticed an orange foam plug sticking out of her ear.

I was kind of surprised to find they still slept in the same bed. I'd figured that she would be sleeping in her own room, given her husband's condition. Then I wondered how she could have slept through her husband's agitation without waking up. Then I noticed prescription bottles crowding the bedside table. Looked like they were both on a decent daily cocktail of pills. Plus she wasn't shy with the wine glass.

I got Gilles around to the other side of the bed. The covers had been thrown back. The oxygen pump had been switched off. I settled him into bed. Pulled the sheets over the bony body. He groaned and made incoherent sounds but didn't try to get up again when I closed the door.

One wall of the dining room was taken up by a massive antique sideboard. It was a glossy oak piece with a patina of age and class. Gilles had pulled a silverware drawer. It had fallen to the floor, along with the heavy knives, forks, and spoons. I picked up the cutlery and put it back in the drawer. Each piece had a different little section to go into. I had to stack them neatly for it all to fit. The utensils were substantial, solid silver. Probably worth a bundle.

By the time I got it in order, the drawer was pretty heavy. It made me less surprised that Gilles Vaugeois, a frail and unwell old man, had dropped it. The drawer was an old and stiff system of wood grooves and sliders. Took me a while to get it back in, but after a couple of tries I slid it flush.

It made me wonder why he had taken the drawer out all the way in the first place, since it was so difficult to operate. If he were looking for a spoon or something, he'd have pulled the thing open just enough to get it. Why bother with pulling it out all the way?

I eased the drawer out again and put it on top of the sideboard. Then I got down and peered into the cavity. There wasn't enough light to see inside, so I stuck my hand into the hole and felt around for a while. A groove was carved into the back. I ran my finger across it horizontally and bumped into a strip of tape holding something in. I peeled the tape off with my nail and pulled it out carefully.

It was a section of duct tape. I turned it over and examined the adhesive side. In the center of the strip was a small skeleton key. The kind of key that unlocks a jewelry box or something of that nature. Perhaps a wardrobe, but not a big one.

I stuck the key back onto the adhesive, reached into the drawer cavity and pressed the tape where I had taken it. Found the grooves for the drawer and slid it home. Went back up the stairs. In the room I opened the curtains, undressed again and got back to bed.

CHAPTER SIXTEEN

I WOKE for the second time that morning, rested and clear-headed. It took me a while, but eventually I found a good reason to get out of bed. That reason was the smell emanating from the kitchen. Like an alley cat, I found myself sauntering down through the heart of Brumaire into the kitchen.

Maria was pleased to see me. Madame had asked her to prepare a petit déjeuner américain. She made scrambled eggs and bacon and while that was going, squeezed a couple of oranges into a glass. That was accompanied by a big chrome carafe of strong black coffee, and amazingly, a tall stack of pancakes appeared. Maria apologized for the fact that maple syrup wasn't available but would local honey do? Sure it would. She even had some strawberries cut up and decorating the pancakes along with a dusting of fine sugar. Maria put it all in front of me on the big farmhouse table. I organized from left to right and started taking care of everything nice and easy.

Turned out to be after ten in the morning. Whatever, I had no special place to be, no particular time to be there. I ate nice and slow. Everything was wonderful and even better than it smelled. I polished it all off and then got to work on the second part of the coffee pot.

About that time Simone came bustling into the kitchen. She was all dressed up in a bright purple power suit and matching heels and carrying a large quantity of flowers threatening to overwhelm her. Maria clucked. I stood up to help.

"Tom!" She set the flowers in a big pile on the table. Kissed me on both cheeks and waved me back to the chair. I thanked her and Maria for the breakfast and made some joke about French hospitality. Simone laughed. She and Maria divided the flowers into several bouquets. Each went into its own vase.

Simone ticked off the various parts of the house that the flowers were supposed to end up in. Maria had suggestions of her own. They were like an old couple. I figured it was a Sunday ritual. Church and then flowers. I asked again if I could help and they both waved me away. So I nursed my coffee cup.

Madame Vaugeois finished with her flowers and sat across from me at the big table. "Tom," she said. "You can help me with one thing, if you agree."

"Sure I can. Anything you need, ma'am." I said.

"Bon. Thank you. I would normally ask Daniel to help but he's taken the Renault and won't be back until the afternoon."

She led me up a narrow flight of stairs to the top floor of the house. This had been the old servants' quarters. There were about six or seven little rooms up there. Now they'd been stuffed with old junk that the Vaugeois hadn't wanted to throw out. One little room was full of black garbage bags, each bag stuffed with clothing.

Vaugeois said, "I've decided to give it away. I was going to wait for Father Bousquet to arrange something, but since you're here I thought we could just get it done. What do you think? They're doing a donation trip today and we can load these in."

Truth is I'm always interested in a little manual labour to polish up my genetic inheritance. I lifted a couple of bags and figured they weighed something like twenty pounds each. Two-handed that made forty pounds. There were around twenty of them. Which made ten trips up and down two flights of stairs, give or take a couple. No problem.

I took my time. Simone had backed the big S-600 Mercedes up to the house. She'd opened the trunk and the back doors. I started loading the bags in. The trunk had a nifty organizer with emergency triangle, rope, and a high visibility vest. Probably had a flashlight in there as well. I pushed that back to make room for the black bags.

The bags filled up the trunk and the entire back seat. I was still in bare feet. She inspected me. "Why don't you take a shower and then you can help me take all this over to Fanny's, if you don't mind." I didn't. I went upstairs. Found the shower and took a long and hot one. Felt great after the little run up and down the stairs.

She drove. I sat in the passenger seat, well-fed, well-rested, and clean. Truth be told, I was still buzzing from the kiss with Nazari. A happy man.

The car was big and luxurious. Leather seats and dash. Glossy oak paneling inside. Simone slipped on a pair of large sunglasses. Which made her look like a purple bug. She rolled the big car down the gravel drive. I pushed a button and the window descended smoothly. Little servo motors hummed in perfect synchronicity. The sound of the tires moving across the driveway pebbles was louder than the massive engine, a soft and reassuring twelve cylinder purr in the background.

Madame Vaugeois made a right turn and gave the engine a touch more gas. The Mercedes growled a little. It was a great day. Sunny and clear and dry. The trees on either side of the road still had the fresh green of late spring, before the summer starts getting old. I let the slipstream wash over my hand. She looked at me and smiled. She said, "Tom."

I said, "Yes, ma'am."

Then we heard the whine of a trail bike engine revving. It was like the sound of a chain saw. But more annoying. We were almost at the bridge. I looked through the trees and could see a white bike moving along a parallel dirt trail. Keeping pace with the car. She said, "Pests."

I said, "You see them a lot?"

She laughed. "They ride along the trails next to the river."

"Who are they?"

She was irritated. Flung her hands in the air. "Them. I don't know. Teenagers." She turned east after we hit the main road. She glanced at me. "Noise pollution. They should be banned."

The ponytail guy with the blue eyes was one of these trail bike kids. I figured the trail bikes were popular sport for the kids cooped up in *Les Brosses*. Then I thought about the attack on Gilles Vaugeois, the screwdriver to the head. Getting through that skull would have been tough. Certainly for someone using muscle power. But it occurred to me that, with engine power, the attack made more sense. Then I pictured the scene, one of those kids on the back of a trail bike, plunging the screwdriver into old Gilles.

"Why do they ride here?"

She looked at me. "It's public space. Forest with trails along the river. I imagine they don't have many other places to go."

"You can call the police to report a nuisance."

Vaugeois laughed. "That would only make it worse. Imagine if they knew it was me calling the police!"

I tried to imagine what would be worse than a screwdriver in the head. I said, "I could have a word with them if you like."

"With the police?"

"No. With the kids on the bike. I'll ask them not to buzz too close to the house, if it disturbs you."

She glanced over at me with wide eyes. "Tom, is that safe?"

"I think so. They have no reason to hurt me. I'll just speak with them and see if we can come to an agreement."

"You would do that?"

"Sure. I'll do it later."

Up ahead was Fanny's Friperie.

Simone said, "Voila. We're here," and pulled up behind a white

Dacia van in front of Fanny's and honked the horn. "Maybe we'll get some help." She put the Mercedes in park and killed the ignition switch.

The young girl with short dark hair came out of Fanny's. "Bonjour, madame," she said politely. "Can I help you?"

"Bonjour, Miriam," said Simone. "Do you know my nephew, Tom?" Now I was her nephew.

Miriam smiled shyly at me. Simone stood still in her sunglasses and purple power suit. It took me a moment to recognize that she was soaking in the rays. I said, "Sun feels good, right, ma'am?"

"I love the sun, Tom."

Miriam helped carry the bags. We unloaded the Mercedes into the front of the store. One of the bags in the back seat had come open. Simone climbed onto the seat and tried to put everything back in. She held a brightly patterned scarf out the door. "Hermes! Now that's refugee chic."

I didn't comment and neither did Miriam. Simone tied off the bag and handed it out of the car to Miriam, who took it inside. Then, she came out and asked if we would like tea or coffee. Simone took Miriam's arm and said, "That is exactly what I would like, darling. I haven't had coffee today. I start with tea and then I need a coffee around eleven in the morning."

The store was dark and empty and smelled like old clothes and garment cleaning supplies. But laughter and voices could be heard from the back, like contented bubbles in a bathtub. Behind the counter a door opened to a large kitchen extension. Unlike the shop, the kitchen was full of light, almost like a greenhouse. Through the wall of windows, a vegetable garden was visible in the back.

Fanny was doing something complicated with a pitcher of milk. She looked healthy and alert, a big woman with a mass of red hair to suit. In the light I could see streaks of gray. She had it all piled up and pinned with a pencil. I could easily imagine her in the vegetable plot trimming tomato plants and runner beans.

Father Bousquet was seated at the table. "Monsieur Keeler. Still in town I see."

Fanny said, "He's getting to know his French family."

I smiled and nodded. Caught Simone's eye. Accepted a biscuit from Fanny. "*Oui* that's right," I said in an exaggerated American accent.

Simone quipped, "He's very happy eating American food. And lots of it."

"That's true, ma'am. But I don't discriminate. Any kind of food will do, as long as it doesn't come out of a plastic bag, or a can."

Fanny was putting the milk in a little fridge. She sized me up. "The shirt fits well, monsieur."

I said, "Call me Tom. The shirt's fine."

Fanny poured coffee for Madame Vaugeois and me. Simone sat down and gossiped with Father Bousquet. Until he looked at his watch and said, "Time to go. Miriam?" Miriam hadn't said a word the whole time. Just helped out with the coffee arrangements. Bousquet looked at me and said, "Miriam and I are taking a load of donations up to Calais." The priest stood up. He was broad-shouldered. With both of us standing, the kitchen became small. I stepped out of the way. Bousquet moved past me. "Every Sunday. Right, Miriam?"

Miriam blushed. She was petite and boyish. With a shock of very dark hair covering her forehead. She wore a dark shirt and jeans. An upside-down silver hand pendant with an eye in its palm hung from her neck on a chain. "Yes."

The Dacia was already half full with boxes. I helped Father Bousquet and Miriam load the clothes into the back. There were the bags from Brumaire, plus three times as much from Fanny's. Fanny said, "Now that's a load."

I said, "What's in the boxes?"

"I don't know."

Bousquet said, "Food. Dry goods and some boxes of nutritional supplements."

The priest went back into Fanny's to use the bathroom.

I asked Fanny, "Don't priests wear a collar?"

"Right, but he's a Jesuit."

"They don't wear collars?"

"Father Bousquet doesn't have a specific church."

Simone broke in, "The world is his church."

Fanny said, "I've seen him wear his cassock with the collar and everything."

"When he met the Imam?"

"Yes. Exactly."

Simone turned to me. "He wears it on special occasions."

The trail bike from across the river started up again, cutting into the conversation like a neighbor's lawn mower, but worse. Simone closed her mouth. Fanny shouted above the noise, "He probably thinks it's pretentious. He's a real worker-type priest of the old school."

Simone continued, "I was going to say, a few times a year. Father Bousquet puts on his collar a few times a year."

The bike crossed the river. Then turned away from us, motoring down the road. The annoying whine tailed off. Bousquet came out of the store. He was wearing jeans and a blue and black flannel shirt. His big red hands hung like slabs of meat. He was almost my height.

"Come with us to Calais, Keeler. I'm sure you'll find the trip interesting."

I looked at Madame Vaugeois, who shrugged. I couldn't think of any reason not to go, so I went.

CHAPTER SEVENTEEN

MIRIAM DROVE THE DACIA. Father Bousquet sat in the middle and I was squeezed between him and the passenger door. We got out of Alencourt. Which meant winding up the valley road to a plateau. The landscape thereafter was a featureless blur of wheat fields and rapeseed. The rapeseed flowering in bright yellow. Yellow as far as the eye could see. Punctuated by spiny black electricity towers slinging power lines across the fields. Occasionally the van passed through a patch of forest. Like a train going through a tunnel. Then we shot out again into the bright yellow. Half an hour in, Father Bousquet's head dropped to his chest. His breathing got regular and slow.

I looked at Miriam. Miriam looked at me.

I said, "Does he always fall asleep when you drive?"

She bobbled her head. "Every time. Half an hour, like clockwork."

"It's a healthy habit."

"Father Bousquet likes to sleep."

"How long have you worked with him?"

She nodded. "For the last two years. He sponsors me."

"Sponsors how?"

"I came from Afghanistan. I have an asylum registration. Father Bousquet sponsors my citizenship application."

I said, "Did you learn to drive in Afghanistan?"

She shook her head and looked at me as if I were ignorant. "No. Of course not. I learned to drive here."

I let her drive. Which she did competently. Miriam and I didn't speak for about an hour. She was probably just fine not talking at all.

I was thinking about the 'Welcome Foundation'. The mayor was involved, helping to get the city machinery mobilized. The guy had seemed like too much of a prick to be charitable. But then again, maybe guys like that get involved with charity to look good. To cover up their greed and self-interest. Hiding the warts. Like putting lipstick on a pig.

"Are you the only one sponsored by Father Bousquet?"

Miriam had been thinking about something. She didn't begrudge my intrusion. "No the foundation currently sponsors a few hundred applications. I'm one of the lucky ones."

"Must be a pretty tough selection."

"Yes, the board reviews the candidates on a rolling basis. And selects only as many as the foundation can support."

"How do they choose?"

"I was interviewed by the board."

"Like an audition. People sitting behind a big table asking you questions."

"Sort of. They do it once every couple of months."

"Who's on the board?"

"I don't know all of them. Father Bousquet, Madame Vaugeois, because she's a big financial backer, the mayor. A couple of other people I didn't know."

"And what's your role specifically?"

"Me? I help out with the odd thing, here and there. Like today."

"And preparing the clothes at Fanny's yesterday. That was part of your 'Welcome Foundation' activity right?"

"That's right. This is outreach, to migrants in the field."

"You like it?"

"I like helping. I like to help people the way that others have helped me."

"You got family in Afghanistan?"

"My parents. If I can get citizenship they'll be able to come here. I hope."

I detected a sadness in the way that Miriam spoke. I've been to Afghanistan several times. Most families have tragic stories. I said, "You had other family members?"

Her brow was knotted, lips pursed. I watched her struggle to get her emotions in order. It didn't take long. That was one strong girl.

Miriam looked at me with brimming eyes. "Sorry, it's not easy to talk about."

"You don't have to talk about it."

"I had two older brothers. They were beheaded in front of us as an example. My father was a librarian and my mother writes. Apparently there was an issue with my mother writing, being a woman and all. My father read the wrong kind of books. So that didn't help."

No self pity there. Plenty of anger.

"I'm sorry to hear that. I hope you get your parents out of there."

She said, "Thanks".

"Are there many Afghan asylum seekers here?"

"There are some, not many. But there are plenty who pretend to be Afghan."

"Why would they do that?"

"The state recognizes Afghanistan as a place that people need asylum from. So Afghans get asylum seeker status pretty easily once they get here. Syrians too. But not Libyans, Iraqis, or Pakistanis or Jordanians, for example."

"Like a hierarchy of pity."

Miriam glanced at me. "That's one way to think about it."

"So people falsify papers. To make it look like they're Afghans or Syrians."

"Yes. That's right."

Miriam concentrated on the driving. I let her stay in the zone. I was looking out the window while thinking about that and noticed something that I could have easily seen and not registered. But I caught it. A lucky thing, part of my lizard brain ticking away behind the scenes. I was looking at a blue van, and not really seeing it. Just looking in the general direction of the van and thinking about Miriam and our conversation.

But then I saw it.

Specifically I was looking to my right at a blue Mercedes Sprinter van, at the driver of the van. The driver whose head was buzzed in a number two and had an Adidas stripe pattern shaved into the left side. We were a couple of yards behind the Sprinter, but closing. I kept watching as we drew level. Then we were alongside the blue Sprinter. I was looking at the guy's face. Which I recognized. And across his body, resting on the steering wheel, the right arm was splinted and bandaged. I turned my head away, didn't want the rat-face guy to recognize me.

After a while Miriam had pulled the Dacia far enough ahead that I could resume my position. I adjusted the side mirror to see behind us. The Sprinter was falling back. The rat-faced guy was driving slow. Slow for a guy with an Adidas logo shaved into his head. I thought, 'small town'.

Miriam gave me a *'what are you doing'* look when I adjusted the mirror. I said, "Are we getting close?"

"Next exit."

"Calais?"

"It's not exactly Calais. The authorities don't let them get that close to the crossing. They camp out a mile or two from the tunnel."

I looked in the mirror. The blue Sprinter was further away now. Miriam flashed her indicators and was pulling into the right lane. There was a traffic circle at the end of the ramp, about 500 yards off. I lost the Sprinter in the mirror when we turned off the highway to the ramp. Father Bousquet snorted loudly and opened his eyes. "Ah, bon. We're here."

The traffic circle was a round grassy island. Miriam took the second exit. There were no more rapeseed fields up here. The fields were dull green. I'm not very familiar with farming, but those might have been potatoes or cabbage, or something like that. Sturdy crops that grow in adverse windy and cold conditions. Miriam drove on a small departmental road for a few minutes.

Then we entered a sparsely wooded coastal forest. Pine trees. Sandy soil. Miriam slowed down, because now there were people around. Walking along the side of the road in pairs, or in groups of four or six. They walked slowly, like they had nowhere special to go. Then there were people squatting in the bushes. Tending to small fires and camping stoves. Hanging laundry on trees. Then there were tents. Some small, others large. Some new, others old and patched. I could see people lying in them reading books and looking at phones and talking and sleeping. There were tents that stretched the definition of a tent. Tarps were draped over frames made from tree branches and miscellaneous junk. There was a lot of garbage lying around. Mainly plastic water bottles and plastic carrier bags, and fast food packaging.

Miriam brought the Dacia to a stop near a wood-framed cabin with tarps for walls and a roof. It was large and relatively sturdy. There was a big banner on it that read; *Fondation D'Accueil*. Next to the cabin was a large water container. People crouched to fill their bottles and move on, others took their place. The line was about twenty deep.

We got out of the van. A tall skinny bearded guy with glasses and an elegant blonde woman came out of the Welcome Foundation cabin. They greeted Father Bousquet and Miriam like old friends. The blonde woman nodded to me. She was pleased with the haul. They helped us unload.

When we were done, the woman rested a hand on Father Bousquet's arm. She wore a shawl and sturdy hiking boots. She said,

"Father, you look like you could use a coffee." She turned to me, Miriam and the skinny bearded guy, whose name was Greg. "The youngsters can take this to the distribution center and come back for their reward."

I didn't mind being called a youngster, although Miriam and Greg were easily ten years younger than me. We piled everything up on two hand trailers. Rolled it through the forest for a while. People were everywhere. Mostly men, but not exclusively. Some small children were playing with a ball in a muddy clearing. Smoke from cooking fires was pervasive.

We arrived at a cluster of corrugated steel-roofed structures. Not exactly buildings, but not tents either. This was the distribution center. Greg explained it to me. He said the camp had a hierarchy. There were a couple of leaders and the rest did what they said. Greg said it was like wolves and sheep.

"No, it's not like wolves and sheep."

Greg looked at me, but I didn't say anything else. Wolves and sheep are complicated, like an ecosystem. Like predators and prey, but complicated. This was simple, like abuse and domination, and underserved status.

The Welcome Foundation had to hook up with the leaders. Who were older men, or else nothing got done. Which meant the food and water and clothes wouldn't reach the people that needed it most. So the old men chiefs had to be kept happy and respected. I knew the drill. Been there, done that. Same in every refugee camp from Iraq and Syria to the Congo. Want to help a woman and her kid? Got to grease the palm of a man. Tradition must be respected.

A couple of the old guys were sitting around smoking cigarettes and drinking tea. They didn't bother to stand when we showed up. But they waved and smiled and indicated where the donations should go. Greg had a grin pasted on his face. He went over and shook hands, doing the rounds, obsequious. We unloaded the clothing and supplies into a tent with corrugated steel roofing. Nobody seemed too excited by the arrival of clothes, dry goods and nutritional supplements. Even in emergency situations there is business as usual. As I walked out of the tent, my eye was attracted by a blur of motion.

The blue Mercedes Sprinter van was moving through the forest, maybe a hundred yards away.

They must have taken another access road. I turned to Miriam and Greg. Said I'd meet them back at HQ shortly. Said that I wanted to take a piss.

CHAPTER EIGHTEEN

I walked to the back of the distribution center until I was out of sight.

Then I sprinted in the direction the blue van had gone. I ran hard, making up for lost time. I wanted to see what the rat-faced guy with the broken wrist was doing. No camp-dweller was bothered by me running. They were doing other things. Probably had seen worse, or more bizarre. Probably were getting used to the occasional violent outburst. Par for the course in transient communities.

The blue Mercedes Sprinter was parked on a sandy trail alongside a cluster of cheap one, or two-man camping tents. A red cord had been strung up between trees, several sleeping bags were hung from it, airing out I guessed. The back of the van was open and guys were getting out in torn-up athletic shoes or plastic shower slippers. Their feet were covered in a lighter color dust or sand that was leaving traces on the darker trail.

The migrants looked as if they hadn't seen daylight in a while. They gazed around bewildered and bleary-eyed in dusty clothes. They were mostly young, but not exclusively so. They were exclusively male. I was looking at a human trafficking operation. This was the culmination of an epic journey, or at least an important point on that journey.

The guys were brushing themselves off. A light cloud of dust, like fine cake flour, hung in the air. They were getting oriented to their new surroundings. The forest, the garbage, the other people making camp with them. The tents and sleeping bags must have been part of the deal; passage to the camp, inclusive of tent. I stayed back far enough to observe without being seen. Figured I'd wait a while.

Rat-face from the train station was sipping out of a tall energy-drink can. He held a cigarette in his wounded hand and alternated between cigarette and can. He was talking to a couple of guys dressed, like him, in branded sportswear. Rat-face said something quick and then turned and walked off.

I figured they had a toilet facility of some kind. Even ant colonies arrange separate living, waste and burial areas. I decided that I was going to have a conversation with him, so I followed.

The guy walked stiffly, making short little steps. I tracked him for a few minutes, screened by trees. He was absorbed by the sweet drink and his cigarette. Up ahead, a large wooden shack. At least a couple of hundred yards from the nearest tent. I could smell it and it smelled bad.

As he approached, rat-face dropped his cigarette into the can, then chucked the can idly onto the ground. Which erased any residual sympathy I might have had for him. Given that he was a mugger, possible accessory to murder, and a human trafficker. Now add littering slob. He began loosening his waistband before entering the shack.

There was nothing going on around the outhouse, which was isolated for good reason. Still, I didn't want to draw attention. So I figured I'd do it inside. Which wouldn't smell good. But wouldn't take long, given I had no sympathy for the guy, wounded or not. I walked around the other side and looked in through a space between wood slats. He was the only customer. I saw him squatting at the hole. I had my own sanitary considerations. So I counted to thirty in my head, to let him get the job done. Then I walked back around to the entrance and into the squalid room.

There were four holes in the ground. They were connected by a trench. That was it. Flies buzzed around incessantly. The guy was squatting over one of the holes. He was vulnerable, holding up his pants carefully. I said, "Remember me?" And kicked him in the face.

The top of my hiking boot connected with his nose at an awkward angle. Which sent him over onto his back, where his first instinct was to pull up his pants, even before attending to his broken nose. By the time the guy's hands flew to his face, my boot was on his neck. I applied a little weight. He gurgled. I said, "Whatever else you do, don't touch me." Blood flowed down and mixed with the gunk on the ground. It was too late for him to keep his clothes clean. But it wasn't too late for me. I said, "If I get dirty you're going to drown in that hole. You might drown in that hole anyway. But if I get even a single drop of shit on me it's a certainty."

The guy was only now beginning to register who I was. Back somewhere in the far reaches of his brain was a memory of my face, associated with the sharp pain and humiliation of his wrist being snapped. It was a distant memory to be sure. But he made the connection. His eyes darted left and right, which was like a tell. The wheels and cogs in his mind were turning over. Pulleys and axle rods were getting into gear and sending messages to his mouth.

He managed to shake his head left to right under the boot. "Oh no man, it was a mistake. It wasn't supposed to be you."

"I'm not too sore about it and you've already been punished."

"So what do you want?"

"Let's start with this. What is this?"

"What do you mean, this?"

"The migrants."

He spit blood to the side. "You don't want to mess with this. Just leave it alone."

I pushed the boot into the soft part of his throat. He struggled to breathe. Veins stuck out. I released a little. "How often do you make the run?"

"Every other day. Sometimes once a week. Depends."

"Depends on what?"

"On when they call me, man. I just do delivery."

"Where do they get the migrants from?"

"Listen, I'm sorry about yesterday. I promise it was a mistake. Please, just leave it all alone. This is bigger than you or me. This is a tiny part of something that's bigger than anyone. They'll erase you and me like ants. Just let it go."

"Just answer the question. Where do they get the migrants?"

"As far as I know they just come, eagerly, with pleasure. And they are happy to pay."

"Who sent you to take out the guy with the blue shirt?"

Rat-face began to tear up. "You have to understand. They might still kill me for the mistake."

"Who sent you?"

He cried real tears. "I can't tell you because they would know that I had, and then it wouldn't be just me, but my sister and my parents and maybe even cousins. They won't stop." I could see the resolve on his face. Which told me that there were worse things than drowning in a shit-filled hole in the ground. My boot pushed his neck into the dirt. I could have broken his neck if I had pushed any harder but I was feeling sorry for him. All that talk of his sister and parents and cousins had humanized rat-face.

"Empty your pockets."

The guy choked and turned red. He looked horrified. I let up the pressure a little. He squeaked, "What?"

"Empty your pockets. Right there on the ground."

He removed a money clip and a phone from his pocket. I took the money clip. About a hundred in cash and a neat little stack of business cards. They were the same card in multiples. Le Foxy Kebab.

"What's Le Foxy Kebab."

"Restaurant I work for."

"Doing what?"

"I told you. Deliveries."

"Deliveries in the blue van?"

"Motorbike. The van isn't mine. I deliver with a bike."

"You ever ride in the woods by the river?"

"Sure, everyone does."

I put the cash and a business card in my pocket. Took my foot off his neck. The guy shook his head and spit blood. He looked at me with a good measure of hatred. I said, "And by the way, littering is an offense." And dropped the phone and the money clip into a hole and walked out. I could hear him cursing as I took great big gulps of wonderful fresh air.

Away from the outhouse things were happening. People were organizing their meager belongings into some form of order. Migrants like these were the survivors, the strong ones who got through the sudden hell of war and breakdown. Which didn't mean that they were well-meaning, or book smart, or community-minded. Just indicated creative pragmatism.

Guys like me are trained survivors. Million dollar products of the most sophisticated war machine ever known to the human species. Looking around the forest camp I didn't see trained survivors, I saw born survivors.

I drove on the way back. Father Bousquet snored. Miriam closed her eyes. Maybe she slept, maybe not. Either way, she didn't make a sound. It was strange getting back on the road after the migrant camp.

I thought about Gilles Vaugeois. What had he gotten himself involved with? Whatever it was seemed unresolved. I figured I was now the one to resolve it. Like a family affair. First I had to understand what it was. But I'm not an investigator. That's not my skill. The only way I know how to operate is directly and with extreme prejudice. Which isn't to say I'm a blunt instrument, I'm a sharp one.

CHAPTER NINETEEN

It was late in the afternoon by the time we got back to Alencourt. Father Bousquet and Miriam were awake.

We bumped over the bridge. The sun was still high and the river looked beautiful. I looked across the cab and into the forest. The high whining of a trail bike had started up. They dropped me off at the driveway. When the van cleared off, I stood still and listened to the forest sounds. The trail bike was somewhere near the bridge.

I figured that in France it made some sense to live by Napoleon's maxim: '*First I get involved, then I see.*'

Simone was having coffee in the drawing room on the right. With her was an older lady named Odile. Odile was very nice and even stood up for me when I came in. I shook her hand and dutifully sipped coffee and ate a piece of cake.

After enough time had passed I said, "Ma'am, do you mind if I take the car?"

Simone touched my arm. "Are you going to talk to the boys on the motor bike, Tom?" She looked spacey, like she'd taken a happy pill before her friend came over.

"Yes," I said. "I'll just have a little chat."

Simone Vaugeois had a big grin on her face.

Odile was perched on the edge of a fancy old chair. "Do you know the speed limit? The police are very strict."

"Yes, ma'am." Simone fetched me the keys. I said, "I'll be back in ten or fifteen minutes."

She said, "Be careful, Tom. And please be gentle with my car. I even have a name for her."

I said, "Of course. What's the name?"

Simone said, "I call her Bertha."

It was Sunday, no-one was out. Nothing was happening. Presumably people were in their houses getting ready for dinner, or doing whatever they do on a Sunday. I slowed down for the bridge approach. A few seconds later, I saw the flash of white through the trees. The bike wasn't moving. They were parked by the river.

The dirt trail turned off just before the bridge. I stopped the car on the edge of the road and rolled the window down. The guys had their helmets half up on their heads. They were smoking and lounging around. One of them was sitting backwards on the bike. He had a ponytail flapping around behind his head. The other leaning against a tree. The ponytail guy looked at me. I looked at him. The thought crossed my mind again, 'small town'.

I didn't want to scratch Bertha. So I rolled the car over the lip from road to dirt trail. I let her go nice and careful down the incline. Ahead of me I could see the guys getting on the bike, fastening helmets. They hadn't expected the big car to come down the dirt road. It never had before. Now they were scrambling.

The driver revved the little trail bike motor. The ponytail guy jumped on behind him and the driver let out the clutch. The rear wheel chewed dirt and spat it out in a long arc. I watched through the windscreen, bearing down on them. The bike leapt forward alongside the river. I could see what he was going for. A hundred yards downriver, the trail went tight. Trees closed in. The Mercedes would never make it through that. I hit the gas and got right up on their tail in half a second.

The little bike looked puny from where I sat, like a flea or a mosquito.

The rider looked back at me. The same blue eyes and the helmet. White with a red and orange flame up the front. Like a mohawk haircut. I thought, 'My man'.

'Tactical contact' is the art of knocking over a bike without hurting the riders too bad. The world is full of cheap little motorcycles, and military-aged males tend to enjoy riding them for all kinds of reasons. That's why I was trained to knock over guys like that without killing them. It's easier to kill, but the dead don't talk.

The driver cut across the track wildly, veering from right to left and back. I didn't know why he did that. Maybe he'd seen it in a movie, on his little phone screen. Once he got where I wanted him, I touched the gas. Bertha responded. I kept the pressure on. Relentless. The Mercedes barely made a sound. The trail bike's engine was going full-bore. Like a stone cutting saw. But it was a small 125 cc engine against twelve cylinders of German power. The left side of my bumper touched the bike and it went over. Easy as that.

Tactical contact. They spilled off to the left. I didn't have to worry about running over them because of the angle. I stopped the car, put it into park, turned off the ignition and got out. Now that the bike was down, the river was quiet and pleasant again.

The driver was up and running. I didn't bother chasing him, the ponytail guy was enough. It was even better not having to worry about two of them. The driver looked comical running flat out with his helmet on. I wondered if he might just bump into a tree and knock himself out, like in a cartoon.

The rider was pinned by the bike. He was trying to get out from under it. I pulled it off and threw it to the side. Grabbed the guy by his mohawk flame helmet like a handle and dragged him back to the Mercedes. He flailed around and made it a little more difficult than I liked. So I kicked him where it counts. He moaned and tightened up. Which made dragging him easier.

I dumped him by the car and put my boot hard on his chest. He was breathing heavily through the mouth guard. His eyes flashed wildly. I looked around nice and calm. It was a pleasantly wooded spot near the riverbank, with enough trees and brush to prevent a nosy onlooker from seeing anything from the other side. I opened the trunk. Got out the rope from the emergency kit. I dragged the guy up the little grassy incline to a more secluded spot. Unsnapped and pulled off his helmet. He looked terrified.

He spit at me. I punched him in the mouth and caved in a front tooth. After that he went limp. Simone's emergency kit had just about enough rope to hog-tie him. Hog tying is a method by which one takes a single rope length and ties another person's hands to their feet, and the feet to their neck. This interconnected binding is a wonderful restraining technique because when the subject struggles with either hands, feet, or both, they strangle themselves.

When I got the guy fixed, I went back to the Mercedes for a rag. Nothing in the trunk. I rummaged around under the seats and found one of Simone's fancy silk Hermes scarves, spilled from her donation bags. While I walked back up, I opened the scarf and looked at it.

The silk was light blue bordered by navy. It felt really soft and at the same time durable, a high quality textile, that's for sure. There was a complicated design with theatrical masks and gold-colored ancient guitars or lutes. I thought, *everyday luxury*.

CHAPTER TWENTY

I BALLED the beautiful scarf up and stuffed it into the guy's mouth. He tried to spit it out but I punched him in the nose, fracturing it clean at the bridge. He moaned and I pushed the scarf all the way in until he gagged on blood and silk and was forced to try and breathe through the broken nose. He was having some trouble so I leaned in and straightened the fracture.

I said, "Breathe through the nose." He looked at me wildly with those bright blue eyes, but started passing air through his nostrils. There was a slight whistle around the crushed cartilage but the air passed. "That's better. Stay calm and relaxed and you'll be alright. I keep bumping into you and your friends."

He tried to speak through the scarf in his mouth. I shook my head. "Not yet."

I searched his jacket pockets and his pants pockets. In his pants there was nothing but loose pocket change and a house key. I made that into a little pile at the base of a tree. In the jacket I found a burner phone. I pocketed the phone. Then I put my knee on the guy's chest and let the weight come down.

"I'm going to ask you questions. Are you going to talk to me? Just nod or shake your head." He wasn't cooperative. Maybe just too damn scared to cooperate. I got down really close to him and said, "I'm not interested in hurting you. Just nod if you understand what I'm saying."

The guy nodded. I said, "Good. So will you talk to me if I take that thing out of your mouth?" He was blowing air in and out through his nose and moved his head up and down vigorously. I took the scarf out of his mouth. The guy got his breath back and said something extremely rude to me. It was about my mother. I put the scarf back in.

I was beginning to be annoyed. First, I was feeling bad about letting the rat-faced guy go without telling me anything. Now I had another chance. Second, Simone might want to take Bertha out again, so I didn't have all day to mess around with him. Bad luck for the guy, but then again he'd been the one to take that Spyderco knife out in the first place.

I picked up the mohawk helmet and went down to the river and took my time filling it with water. The guy was watching me as I came back. He must have realized what was happening because he went bug-eyed and started huffing and puffing and wriggling all over the place.

I took his feet and dragged him around until his head was positioned downhill and the feet were pointing up a fifteen or twenty degree incline. I soaked the Hermes scarf and put it over his mouth and nose. He struggled, so I knelt over him and used my knees to pin his head like a vice. I slowly poured water from the helmet on to the scarf. Soon the Hermes silk was thoroughly soaked and the guy struggled to breathe through it. Luxury waterboarding.

I stopped pouring. "I'm going to sort of kill you, but not quite. Then we'll talk."

He wriggled. I poured slowly. Waterboarding simulates drowning. Because of the incline, the technique doesn't actually get water into the lungs and so doesn't asphyxiate the subject. It just fills up the head and neck with water so they think they're drowning. We had it done to us in training so we'd know how it felt when we did it to someone else. I lasted longer than most. Around twenty seconds. I never saw anyone beat twenty-five.

A professional athlete or a trained operative can exhale out the nose slowly for around fourteen seconds. After that, they've got to inhale, to get oxygen to the brain. When they try to inhale through a wet cloth they're sucking in water because the wet cloth is a one-way valve. You can exhale through it, but you can't inhale through it. The cloth sucks into your mouth and you start to panic. That's understandable when you've got collapsed lungs that can't fill up with air.

This is precisely what was going on at that very moment. The ponytail guy's lungs were collapsed and he was unable to refill them. He was panicking and convulsing, like a rigid muscle. His neck was thick-veined and red with the struggle to get air pumping into his lungs again. I stopped pouring. He'd lasted a little over ten seconds, which I didn't think was too bad, given the circumstances.

I removed the scarf and turned him over so the water could pour out of his head. He collapsed into a blubbering mess. Spitting and choking and heaving as his oxygen-starved body convulsed involuntarily. When he was done getting back to life, I turned him onto his back again. He was truly frightened. I figured I might get an answer or two out of him before he got his wits back together.

I said, "Can you hear me?"

His chest heaved. He nodded enthusiastically. "What do you want?"

"I'm just wondering, out of curiosity, who sent you to take out the Afghan guy?"

He looked away from me. "They'll kill me."

"I'll kill you first."

The kid was streetwise and not that stupid. He eyed me. I could see that cognition was beginning to happen in his brain. The oxygen had returned and he was thinking quick. On the one hand he didn't want to be waterboarded again, even with a silk Hermes scarf. On the other hand he had other people to worry about. So, the question on his mind was which was the least of two evils, me or them.

He said, "I don't know what you mean. I'm just a delivery guy."

I said, "You and everyone else in this town."

The kid wasn't half bad as a young and dumb soldier. He'd gone from blubbering mess to clamming up in about ten seconds. He needed to come close to death again. I put the Hermes scarf back over his mouth and nose. He wriggled around some. So I vice-gripped his head with my knees again. I poured river water from the helmet over the scarf, slowly. He lasted five seconds before I had to resuscitate him. When he'd gotten the water out of his head and neck the kid lay there spitting and blowing. He was saying something. I had to lean down to hear it.

"Le Bucheron," which translates as The Woodcutter.

"Uh huh. The Woodcutter."

The kid spit to the side and repeated himself. "The Woodcutter."

"Where does one find The Woodcutter?"

"Le Foxy Kebab."

I said, "If I have to come back and find you I'm going to kill you."

"Go to Le Foxy Kebab. They'll cut your head off, but be my guest."

I ignored that. "What does *Le Bucheron* look like?"

"Fat and bald."

I said, "Do you take clients up to Calais?"

"I haven't been up there."

"Dangerous line of work."

He looked at the river, sullen.

I bent down to the trail bike, took out the key and threw it out into the middle of the river, then went back to the guy and untied him. When the rope got loose from his neck and hands and feet he lay there on his side gasping. I pushed him with my toe. "Put the rope back in the trunk of the car." He looked at me weirdly. "Go ahead. Just do it. Put it back neat."

While he did that I inspected the car. A little scratch on the front bumper, but hardly visible. I wiped it down with the Hermes scarf. Rinsed the scarf in the river and wrung it out a few times. I left the scarf under the passenger seat. Silk dries fast. I turned the Mercedes around. Rolled gently up the dirt track to the road. I looked in the side mirror, the guy was already gone.

There was something that I'd forgotten. I stopped the car. Put it in reverse. Rolled the Mercedes back down the incline until I came up alongside the trail bike. I got out of the car and went over to the bike. I popped the seat up and looked inside the little storage area. A pack of cigarettes, and a bundle wrapped in a rag. I unwrapped the bundle. Three screwdrivers. Good ones with slotted cushion grips. I selected the biggest one of them and tested the blade. The flathead was wide, shaped like a snake head. The tip had been sharpened to a razor edge. So the kid wasn't innocent. As the rider, he would have been the one to lean over and stab Gilles Vaugeois in the forehead. At speed, with the derestricted trail bike engine, he would have managed enough kinetic energy to put that thing into the skull.

I wrapped the big screwdriver in the rag, took it back with me to the Mercedes, and placed it on the passenger seat.

When I rolled back up the incline, and came over the top, a Municipal Police Peugeot 308 was blocking the road entrance.

The words 'Police Municipale' were painted on the hood in boxy block letters. The same words were boxed into a horizontal blue stripe running across the two doors. The sun reflected off the windshield, making it impossible to see inside. I accelerated slowly to beat the glare and the cruiser responded, rolling over the dirt and gravel like a mirror image of what Bertha the Mercedes was doing. Pretty soon we were forming up into the classic police cruiser conversation configuration, the cop sixty-nine. The driver's side window rolled down and Bonnet was looking at me with a little smile on his face. All that was missing was a sack of doughnuts.

Bonnet took down his sunglasses. "Keeler. I was wondering what old Madame Vaugeois was doing down by the river in her big Mercedes. Had me concerned that she'd gotten stuck." He looked down the hill behind me. I was sure he was able to see the trail bike.

Maybe he'd already seen it. Maybe he'd seen everything. "Everything ok? What's going on?"

"I was admiring the river. It's a lovely day."

He was looking at the trail bike. "Yeah, beautiful isn't it? You have any trouble with that?" Bonnet pointed down the hill.

"No trouble really. Just a little thing."

He was nodding his head. "Yes. That is a thing, isn't it? Hard to be patient sometimes."

"I'm an exceedingly patient guy."

"But even so, sometimes even the most patient of guys run out of patience. Like there's a tank of patience and it gets used up. Nobody's infinitely patient."

"That's the truth. You're a perceptive guy, Bonnet."

"Thank you for the compliment. I aim to serve." Bonnet admired the view for a while. Then he said, "Keeler, if I go down there right now, what do I find?"

"You find a trail bike without a key."

"Key got misplaced."

"The guy misplaced his key. I discussed that with him for a while. Then, he went to find a replacement key."

"So in a way, you came down here to help out. You saw someone who was stuck and you came down, like a helpful tourist or something."

"That's right, something like that. The guy had a problem and I helped him make a plan."

"So the guy's gone. But he'll come back."

"Should come back for the bike, if I were him."

"Maybe when he's sure that nobody is here."

"The guy wouldn't want to disturb anyone, or be a public nuisance, I discussed that with him. Those bikes can be a problem. That's for sure. At this point he'd want to take his bike and leave discreetly."

Bonnet was nodding again. He was a good-looking guy, and easy going. The kind of guy that is easy to like. I was liking him. He said,

"Well Keeler, looks like you're a helpful type of person. We need helpful people like you around, maybe you should consider staying, putting down roots." I didn't say anything. Bonnet continued, "Anything I can do to help here?"

"Would be good if there was more of a police presence along the river. Maybe a couple of extra patrols, on top of what you already have. Some of the older residents are concerned."

"I'll tell the chief. We're stretched pretty thin, but I'll let him know your concern."

"I appreciate that."

"My pleasure. I hope to see you around."

Bonnet slid the sunglasses onto his face, nodded to me, and turned to the wheel. I'd kept the big Mercedes in gear and eased down on the gas to accelerate slowly up to the road. Behind me, the cruiser continued forward in its arc, making a perfect u-turn. I turned right on the road, towards Brumaire, in my rear view I caught Bonnet's Peugeot 308 turning the other way, towards the bridge.

CHAPTER TWENTY-ONE

I PARKED in front of Brumaire. Got out and stretched. I tucked the
sharpened screwdriver bundle into the waistband at the small of my
back. My hand ached a little from punching the kid in the mouth. I'd
hit his front tooth and had the mark to prove it. A little red dent in the
knuckle. The cliff loomed above the house. Its limestone face, white
and chalky and picturesque. Madame Vaugeois was out on the
terrace. She inhaled deeply. "Tom. What a beautiful day!"

"Bertha's a wonderful car." I handed her the keys.

"And the motorbike?"

"They agreed to go elsewhere, ma'am. They were very polite and
reasonable. I'm willing to bet that they'll leave you in peace for a
while."

She was agog, mouth open. "Really?"

I nodded and smiled. She reached up and put a hand on my
shoulder and then pecked me on the cheek and then the other cheek.
"Thank you for helping me today, and for helping Father Bousquet
and Miriam. You're a welcome guest."

"My pleasure, ma'am."

"Any plans for today?"

The weather was excellent. It was late afternoon and the sun was still up and shining. I'd eventually go and check out Le Foxy Kebab, but it was too nice out to be overly ambitious. "Honestly, I don't have any plans. I'll just let things happen."

Vaugeois liked that. "Like a free man, Tom?"

"Just like that, ma'am."

I went for a swim in the river. Simone showed me the way. She also gave me a pair of Gille's shorts and a towel. I followed a path from the back of the garden, winding downhill towards the river. The woods were dotted with stone ruins, walls, and ancient farm structures. The light cut through the trees at an oblique, late afternoon angle. At the end of it was a shady cove of fine grained sand.

The water was clean and cold, and perfect.

After the swim I lay down on the towel. Let the residual sun warm me and dry my skin. I thought of my mother swimming there, many decades before. Not with Simone Vaugeois, but maybe with Gilles. It was strange to think of Mom and Gilles as cousins, as children.

The footpath wound away from the bottom of the river valley and back up towards the rolling hills above.

Brumaire was located at the point where the incline sharpened. I figured the location had been chosen against the possibility of the river flooding. After a few minutes walking I noticed an overgrown mound off the footpath. I'd observed it on the way to the river, but from the other direction I could clearly see an opening.

I went through. Three paces in it began getting dark. The air completely changed, suddenly humid and smelling of mold. I felt the wall. Damp limestone. I kept going. The tunnel descended gently into the darkness. I stepped carefully and soon ran into crumbled rock and soil. This had been blocked for a long time. There was no way to continue. So I turned around.

When I got near enough to see Brumaire through the trees I went off the footpath. Bushwhacked through the forest. I skirted the house and climbed a steep incline overgrown with brambles. I could have taken an easier route, but going straight up was more efficient and I didn't mind the exercise. After a couple minutes climbing and getting scratched, I arrived at the cliff top overlooking the house. I lay the towel down and got on my belly to have a look-see.

The cliff towered over Brumaire. I was almost looking straight down at the house. The layout was spread before me. Driveway winding north-west to the road. The cliff I perched on hugged the eastern side of the house. Directly west on the other side was a large field bordered by a stone wall, maybe one hundred yards out. The sun was going down on the other side of the trees there. South was another field with a small apple orchard and then a stone wall approximately three hundred yards out. It was a large property. All together a difficult position to defend without a decent-sized team. An easy position to attack. There were multiple entrance points. The house was so big that you'd need at least five operators to cover the attack surface. So if it got to that I'd need to figure something out.

Nothing was going on. I started to dread getting dragged into a lengthy French dinner with Madame Vaugeois. So I tried to think of ways to avoid it. Couldn't really think of an excuse and figured I'd just face it. A silver Peugeot 206 cruised up the driveway. Came to a halt next to the Mercedes.

Then the burner phone rang in my pocket. The one I'd taken from the ponytail guy earlier.

I pulled it out and pressed the green talk button. Put the phone to my ear. Down below, Cecile Nazari stepped out of the Peugeot. She was looking trim and fit in jeans, gray t-shirt and a pair of aviator sunglasses and light athletic shoes.

The phone said nothing for a moment.

Then a male voice, "You've committed suicide, it just hasn't happened yet."

I didn't say anything. I admired Nazari walking towards the house.

The voice said, "I can never understand why people put themselves into situations that have nothing to do with them. Why would someone do that? Can you explain that to me?"

Nazari disappeared: I guessed she was going up to the terrace. I hoped she was looking for me.

I said, "Nobody lives forever," and hung up the phone.

CHAPTER TWENTY-TWO

By the time I got to the bottom of the cliff I was hot and scratched all over from the prickly bushes. As I came around to the front I ran into Daniel. The gardener was on his knees weeding a bed of flowers. I wanted to ask him about the overgrown tunnel entrance, but also wanted to pre-empt any possible dinner plans at Brumaire. So I said a curt *bonjour* in passing. "Bonjour Monsieur," Daniel responded stiffly.

Nazari was on the terrace. Her eyes flicked over me, took in the scratches and the swim shorts. "Better get changed, I'm rescuing you."

"Yup. I'll be two minutes."

Ran up the stairs. Changed back into my clothes. Hung the towel to dry. Got back down in two minutes. She was still on the terrace. I said, "Where's Madame?"

"In the kitchen. You're safe. I told her."

"Excellent. Let's go."

We got in the 206. Nazari put it in gear, reversed back down the drive. The car whined. She put it into first and did a K-Turn out of there. I put my head out the window and whooped at the setting sun.

She smiled real wide. Her ponytail was blowing around with the wind. Her arms were tanned and strong. I couldn't help noticing the way her legs moved when she switched up the gears. She looked great. I said, "Where are we going?"

"My place. I'm putting you under house arrest."

I was okay with that.

We made it through the door to Nazari's little house with our clothes intact. After that things got wild. We were like two energized magnets bouncing between the walls. Her body was long and lean and full and round in all the places where I hoped it would be. At one point she rose above me. Her arms were up and she was pulling her hair loose from the ponytail. We were locked together otherwise and all that mattered was contact and texture. Our nervous systems were synchronized and compatible. She was generous and willing and adventurous in equal measure. After a couple of bouts we lay on her living room floor, temporarily emptied. I traced a line of sweat at the hollow of Nazari's throat. She turned on her side to face me. Her hazel and green eyes were sated and gleaming, like a satisfied puma.

She ran a finger over a pattern of scarring on my shoulder. "How'd you get that?"

I said, "That one might have been Morocco or maybe Mauritania, I never really figured out which side of the border we were on."

"I didn't know that the USA was at war with Morocco or Mauritania."

"Yeah, I don't know either. They don't tell us the big picture, just the gory details."

"What were you doing there?"

"If I remember correctly, I was upside-down holding onto a rope in a phosphate mine and someone decided to fire a rocket-propelled grenade at me."

"You fell?"

"I was attached to the rope. They pulled me out."

"But what were you supposed to be doing?"

"Rescuing a bunch of French guys, as a matter of fact."

"A real Francophile."

"You bet."

Then we went back into it for a couple of rounds. We ended up on her bed lying on our backs looking at the ceiling. It was a creme-colored ceiling with a red Chinese paper lantern hanging from it in the middle. I complimented her on the lamp. My fingers went into her hair and her hands went for me. We tousled around again, but by then we were lazy. I ended up on my side looking at her, my hand playing with the little curve at the small of her back. She had her head on her folded arms, contented.

Nazari said, "I checked on the vehicle registration number you gave me last night."

I was making slow and lazy circles on her back. "The Opel Corsa."

"That's really nice. I like that." She wiggled slowly. Mumbled, "Yes. Blue Opel Corsa, just as you asked."

"What did you find?"

"It's a rental. Pegasus Auto Leasing in Lille."

"Where's that exactly?"

"It's a city up north. East of Calais, on the Belgian border."

"Thanks for checking. I guess I could go up and find out about that in Lille. Is it far?"

"Not very far. Care to say why you wanted me to check on that registration?"

"I thought I was being followed. Couldn't be sure."

"Kind of paranoid are we?"

"I'm making the transition to civilian life. It requires an extensive program of mental and physical rehabilitation." I drew a line up her body with the palm of my hand. She wiggled.

"I can help with that. We must begin with a large dose of physical therapy." We moved together exactly enough to kiss, but no more. She broke away, about a millimeter. "You were in the army a long time ago?"

"Air Force. I just got out a week ago."

She turned over on her back. Lay a hand on my hip. "Living the easy life now."

"What can I say? I'm enjoying the freedom to do what I want, when I want. Can't get enough of it."

"Nothing to hold you down. Like in an American rock and roll song or something."

I said, "That's right."

"Air Force." She rolled onto her side; her fingers traced a line up my chest. She put her lips together and made a propeller sound, her free hand flying around in the air.

I said, "I was search and rescue. We get people out of bad situations."

She said, "Which explains the paranoia."

"I'm a trained and experienced paranoiac."

"I can respect that. I'm a cop."

She stood up from the bed. "I'm going to take a shower." The bathroom was adjoining. She strode proudly naked, upright and beautiful. When she got there she turned to me. "Coming?"

We took a long shower together. There were interruptions. Afterwards we were back on the bed, still naked but with wet towels bunched up around us. She said, "The bed's wet now. Look what you have done, Keeler."

I said, "You ever hear of someone called *Le Bucheron*?"

"The Woodcutter."

"Right. Maybe some kind of a criminal figure here in town."

Nazari started to retrieve our clothes. "Never heard of *Le Bucheron*. Why do you ask?"

I delivered a discreet flow of information. Controlled and limited by requirements, considering that she was on the police force. She stopped getting dressed while I spoke and listened intently, which suited me fine. I told her about the trail bike kids. I gave her a non-detailed account of my conversation with the mohawk helmeted guy with the ponytail and that I had confiscated his burner phone. The key terms were The Woodcutter and Le Foxy Kebab. I withheld the screwdriver and much else besides.

She got back to her clothes. "The Woodcutter." She looked at me curiously. "Good name for a gangster. What's he supposed to look like?"

"Fat and bald. I'm imagining the Buddha."

She was putting on a clean pair of white cotton panties. It was distracting.

When we were fully dressed, I said, "We going somewhere?"

"I'm starving." She took out her phone and pecked and tapped and swiped for a while. She looked at me with a little smile. "I hear Le Foxy Kebab is highly rated and open on Sundays."

CHAPTER TWENTY-THREE

NAZARI'S HOUSE was on a little road that forked off a two-lane departmental road running along the river, the equivalent of a county road back home. Hers was a reconstructed outbuilding from what used to be a farm estate. Which is why the exterior was all ancient stone from the original farm. Neighboring houses had been part of the same estate. Otherwise the view was a mix of open fields and groomed parcels from the old farm. I waited outside for her to get ready. It was a beautiful and warm evening. The moon was big and rising. The landscape glowed. Pale lunar light kicked off the stone masonry, the river water, and the tree tops.

Between her house and her closest neighbor was a slight incline. The remnants of ancient farm walls were like lumps in the dark. I recognized the shape of a mound, not unlike the one I had found on the way back to Brumaire from swimming in the river.

Nazari came out of her house and locked the door. I asked her about the mound. She said, "They're everywhere around here. It's all about the limestone. People used to dig it out wherever they needed to build." She indicated the mound. "Most of them are blocked. My neighbor cleared that one and made it into a wine-tasting room."

She turned her Peugeot right at the departmental road, back towards town. A blue van was coming the other way, slowly, as if looking for an address. The driver and passenger were both scanning the landscape. They looked like lost delivery drivers, or utility workers. Lost and searching for a landmark. They were like twins with identical facial structures and narrow eyes. The van passed by.

I watched her drive. She was humming to herself. A little smile was playing out and then tapering off to a more reflective look. A lot of people hunch up when they drive. Nazari wasn't hunched, she had good relaxed posture. She looked like someone who knew what she wanted. I figured that was to get into the research and intervention brigade, BRI. That's what she'd said. I asked her, "When's the exam?"

She had been thinking about something else. "What?"

"When's the exam?"

"Oh. For the BRI." She glanced at me. "September."

"You'll get in."

"It's a tough exam."

"You'll make it."

She laughed. "How the hell do you know if I'll get in?" I tried to think of something intelligent to say, but didn't manage. She said, "As a matter of fact I'm pretty sure I will."

Sunday night. Nothing going on, no one out. Couple of cars on the road. Everyone else home watching TV. I started to recognize the scenery. Half a mile away the three residential towers of *Les Brosses* rose above. Nazari slowed the car into a parallel parking lane out front of Le Foxy Kebab. The restaurant occupied the bottom floor of a three or four-story mixed-use building.

It was a cramped walk-in with booths lined up on either side and a counter in the back. The menu was posted on a board above the counter. The kitchen was visible from the front through steel service shelving. To the right side of the counter was a door with a toilet sign screwed into it.

Two of the booths were occupied. A family with young children and a party of thirteen or fourteen-year-old teenagers eating French fries with ketchup and grilled meat on sticks. A guy wearing a baseball cap was seated on a stool at the counter. He too was chewing on a kebab. Holding the stick with one hand and idly nibbling.

The special was Le Foxy Burger, so I ordered it. She ordered a salad. I paid in cash at the counter and then we waited in our booth nursing cans of Coke. There was no fat bald guy, just two men working the kitchen, while the guy out front watched the game on TV. When the food was ready I went up and fetched the tray from the counter.

The burger was serviceable. Like a burger, but with spices. Like a kebab, but on a bun.

"Good?" She asked.

"Works. You?"

"Nothing special." She pushed the remains of her salad away.

I studied the remains of my Le Foxy Burger. It wasn't gourmet, but I'd had much worse, often and for extended periods of time. I wasn't complaining. She was looking at me. I said, "Whatever."

She looked around Le Foxy Kebab. "You see a fat bald guy?"

"Nope."

"Have you got the phone?"

I pulled out the burner phone. Slid it across the table. Nazari flipped through it. Thumbed some keys and buttons. "Call list only has one number." She looked at me. "Shall we give The Woodcutter a call?"

"He already called. But he didn't have anything interesting to say."

"Maybe if I could hear his voice, as a native French speaker, it might shake something loose."

"Is that what they teach you in the textbooks?"

"Yeah, it is. You get them talking and something shakes loose eventually."

"Such as?"

"Accent, intonation, emotional state, physical condition. For example a fat person might speak differently than a skinny person.

She'll have a fuller acoustic cavity. A person with allergies or with a cold will also speak in a particular fashion. There's always something. On top of that people generally like to be listened to."

I said, "Let me do it. You shouldn't get involved."

She slid the phone back to me. "Put it on speaker."

I selected the number and found the button to put it on speaker. Dial tone chimed from the little phone.

It rang for a while.

Then someone picked up. "Yes." Same voice as before. Male, and deep, like from a large body.

I said, "This is Keeler." Nazari and I had our heads together over the phone, which was on the table between us. She shot me a look.

The voice said, "The dead man walking."

I said, "Aren't we all dead men walking?"

The voice said, "Thank you."

The phone clicked off.

Nazari said, "Why did you tell him your name?"

"Why not? It won't matter in the end. Did you get anything?"

"French guy, no noticeable accent."

"I think he's a big man. Physically. Any way of tracing the call?"

"No. Even if I wanted to and I don't. We would need to have an open investigation approved by a magistrate. But there is nothing here that would interest a magistrate. Just a phone that you illegally took off some kid you mugged."

"Alright let's get out of this place."

We sat in her car.

I said, "Ever have complaints about the kids on trail bikes?"

She placed her hands on the wheel, looking at her nails. "Sure, we get complaints about them all the time. Harassment, disorderly conduct, noise. They're what we have for local hooligans."

"Do they all come from *Les Brosses*?"

"Depending upon who you talk to, all of France's social issues come from places like *Les Brosses*." She turned her big and beautiful eyes on me. "But look on the bright side, I come from *Les Brosses*."

"It's just a place right?"

"It's just a place that has more than its share of poverty. But more than its share of hope and aspiration as well."

I told her about the migrant trafficking I had witnessed earlier. She wasn't surprised. "Any time someone wants something badly, there will be more than enough people willing to take advantage of their situation." She looked up at some movement in a residential block window. "The situation with migrants is spawning an underground economy. You've got smugglers of all kinds either exploiting migrants to carry drugs, exploiting female migrants, or exploiting migrants who want to get into hard to reach places."

"Like the UK."

"Right."

"Why do they want to get to the UK?"

"Perceived opportunities, linguistic and economic, I guess. Or they may have family there already."

"So trafficking in migrants wouldn't surprise anyone."

"Nobody would be surprised. The BRI is heavily involved in those kinds of operations. The municipal police doesn't deal with it directly. It's out of our jurisdiction because by its nature, smuggling and migration crosses national boundaries."

"Is it illegal to extract money from migrants in exchange for transport?"

"If they are illegal migrants, yes. There are occasional prosecutions. Usually when political will shifts in that direction. Temporarily."

"I think Gilles Vaugeois was caught up in something tangentially related to this. Would the police be interested in the connection?"

"Frankly, you would need to come up with something more than 'I think'."

"What would happen then?"

"Municipal Police don't handle investigations. Rigalle just hands over anything we've got to regional agencies, like the BRI."

"Rigalle makes those decisions."

"The mayor signs it. Rigalle's the commanding officer, but he answers to the mayor. All Municipal Police in France are under the direct command of local mayors."

I had been toying with the phone and accidentally hit the call button. I pressed stop when I realized what I had done. The phone was ringing the same number as before. Then it stopped. She said, "Hold on. Call that again." I pressed the call button again and waited.

The phone rang. "Now be quiet," she said.

The phone rang. "You hear that?"

"What do I hear?"

Nazari put her hand on my arm. "Listen."

Then I heard a distant ring-tone. A tropical rhythm. Maybe samba. It was coming from Le Foxy Kebab.

"It's not from the restaurant." She looked at me. "It's from above it."

We sat in silence and heard the distant tropical rhythm again. Looked at each other.

I pressed stop and the tropical ring-tone stopped abruptly.

Nazari said, "The Woodcutter."

I said, "An office above the restaurant. Nobody's there, or else he would have picked up."

"He must have just left."

I scanned the area because you never know. No fat and bald men. No fat or bald men. Only skinny men with hair, and women and children.

CHAPTER TWENTY-FOUR

I said, "I'll check it out."

"I'm coming with you." She opened the driver side door.

I put my right hand on her left. "Not a good idea. You're a cop, off duty. I don't know what I'm going to do or who I'm going to run into. This is reaching into the unknown. You could lose your job."

"You need backup."

The street was dark and empty. Except for the light spilling out of Le Foxy Kebab. And the orange vapor lamps that lined the sidewalks. A cat huddled underneath a parked car and then dashed across the street.

I squeezed her hand. "What I need is for you to stay in the car and keep a look out. Use the phone. He might have gone out for cigarettes. Might be on his way back right now."

I looked at the restaurant. The view would have been better if the Peugeot was reversed a couple of yards, but that wasn't possible because there was a car right behind us. "Get in the backseat. It's got a better view. Call me if you see someone going to the toilet who is not already a paying customer. The stairs are accessed from that door."

I called her phone with the burner, so she had the number. We set the phones to vibrate, not ring. She climbed into the back seat of her Peugeot. I got out of the car and closed the door. I had the burner in my front pocket. I crossed over to Le Foxy Kebab and waited outside.

The family with young children were gone. Their table was a mess. The teenagers were drinking soda and finishing off French fries, no doubt cold at that point. Another booth was occupied by three young men who hadn't been there earlier. They had their heads down over dripping kebab wraps. I waited. I could see Nazari's shadow in the backseat. Two big women in tight jeans walked into Le Foxy Kebab. I stepped to the side and counted two minutes. One to get comfortable at the counter and the attention of the baseball hat guy. Another minute to start ordering.

The traffic circle was over to my right. Beyond it I could make out the street lights. On the other side, to my left, was *Les Brosses*. But there were buildings in the way and I couldn't see the towers. I just knew they were there. I looked straight ahead at the Peugeot. Nazari's head was in shadow, upright, alert and watching.

Two minutes. I turned and walked into the restaurant.

The three young men had the look, branded sportswear, short buzzed haircuts. They were occupied with their kebab wraps, juices dripping through paper, flowing over hands and fingers and onto plastic plates in front of them. I ignored the teenagers. The women were standing at the counter tapping impatient fingernails on plastic. I went past, screened by their bodies. The baseball hat counter guy was turned towards the kitchen, fixing an order slip to the steel shelving unit. I opened the toilet door and slipped in. Closed it behind me.

The corridor was dark, illuminated only by an unseen window. So I waited for my eyes to adjust. To the left, the corridor stepped down and continued into greater darkness. A toilet sign was fixed to the wall. A finger pointed. To my right were stairs, as I'd guessed there would be. I climbed up to a landing, where the window was located. The stairs switched back to the second floor corridor. Here, the floor was tiled and the walls were bare except for a framed photograph of a Mediterranean beach. Opposite the photo was a door.

I tried the handle but it was locked.

I pulled the burner phone and called The Woodcutter's number. The tropical disco beat sounded off above me, through the ceiling. I stopped the call. Retraced my steps out of the office and closed the door behind me. I walked back to the stairwell and heard the door open from the restaurant down below. I stopped moving. Waited to hear breathing, or footsteps coming up the stairs, or away, to the toilet. The only thing I could hear was noise from Le Foxy Kebab.

If Nazari was watching and had a good view of the door, she would have seen a person entering. The door must have just popped open. A faulty latch mechanism would explain it. I hadn't noticed either way. The door had latched just fine before. I took the stairs to the third floor. The corridor was the same as the second. Tile floor. Bare walls. No photograph. The third floor office door was directly above the second floor office door.

I tried the knob. The third floor office door was unlocked. Which made me pause because maybe there was someone in there. And if there were, that someone might have seen the doorknob twisting. In which case they might be carefully and quietly retrieving a weapon from the desk drawer and then checking the load, and racking a round into the chamber. If there was a safety they would be quietly clicking it off with a thumb. Then the front sights would be trained on the door around chest height.

But people don't actually fire weapons blind, into the dark. Who knows? It could be a little old lady looking for the bathroom. I stepped to the side, twisted the doorknob and pushed it open. I let the door swing by itself. The hinges made very little noise, just the swish of lubricated metal on metal. Nothing happened. There was no sound, other than the door on its hinges and muffled Middle Eastern music from the restaurant. The office was dark. I looked in. There was nobody there, only the sparse outlines of a desk. I walked inside and closed the door.

The office had a window out to the street, through which electric light entered. There was a single desk in the middle of the room. On the desk was a laptop computer and a burner phone, identical to the one I had in my pocket. A chair was tucked under the desk. The chair, a desk, a laptop computer and a burner phone. There was nothing else in the room. No shelves, no pictures, no lamp, no plants. The room smelled of fresh paint.

There was a small bathroom off the main office. I flipped the light switch. Porcelain sink, no soap, chrome faucets, white plastic garbage can, porcelain toilet, pink toilet roll on a white plastic holder screwed into the wall. The screws had been painted over, white. I picked up the garbage can. I pulled off the lid. No bag inside. I was setting it down again when I noticed a small thing at the bottom. I pulled out a balled up paper pellet. Like from a tiny piece of paper or the wrapper of a drinking straw. I pulled it out and put the can down. I unfolded the paper. A basic receipt from a cash register. Crumpled and with tiny printed characters. I folded the receipt in quarters and slipped it into the little change pocket of my pants. I turned off the light.

The office was clean and white and sanitary. Which meant that the occupants were careful and discreet people. The phone and the laptop were rectangular black shapes on a white rectangular desk. I used my knuckle to press the green call button on the front of the tropical disco burner. The display lit up and showed the most recent incoming call, the phone in my pocket. The tropical disco burner was The Woodcutter's phone.

A door opened down the hall. And with it, the sound of conversation leaked out into the corridor. Two or three people talking. Footsteps approached the office where I stood. I backed behind the door. The burner phone's display was still illuminated from when I had pressed the button. It would automatically shut off after a certain amount of time, depending on how it had been set. Thirty seconds, a minute, ten seconds, it was impossible to know.

CHAPTER TWENTY-FIVE

THE DISPLAY GAVE off a sickly white glow, it was relentless, maybe permanent.

The knob turned and the door swung easily, toward me. I held up my hand and used my fingertips to stop it hitting my face. I took a chance and peered around the door. A tall thin man stepped to the desk and stopped, looking at the lit up display. He wore a sports track suit in light blue. A white racing stripe ran vertically down both sides. The guy had the temples and back of his head shaved clean and a thin manicured beard, no more than a line along his chin. I couldn't see his face. The display switched off and the room went back to being lit by street vapor light through the window. The guy stepped to the desk and reached for the laptop and the phone. When he began to turn around I went back behind the door. He then left, leaving me standing alone in the room again. A key turned and locked the door from the outside.

The desk was now empty. I tested the door knob. It was locked and I was stuck inside with nothing to show for my efforts. The office was three stories up from the street. I figured the window would be too risky. I was more concerned with being seen from the street than falling. Calling Nazari for help was out of the question, too risky for her. Kicking the door in would attract attention from the people who were evidently just down the hall.

I examined the door jamb. The device had an automatic safety feature when locked by a key. The mechanism featured a curved and sprung bolt that snapped into place when the open door is pulled shut. A simple credit card can be slid between door and jamb. My bank card and identity documents were in Brumaire.

I took out the burner phone and examined the back. It was the kind of phone where the SIM card goes under the battery. The back slid off with a little push from my thumb. The battery tumbled out, and I caught it before it hit the floor. I stuffed the battery and phone into my front pocket. The back piece was thin plastic, but slightly curved all the way around its edges. I tested the way it bent and figured it was rigid enough to break if I did it right. I bent the plastic back hard and fast. The top quarter snapped off with a click.

There were a few millimeters of air between the door and frame. The locking bolt was barely visible as a shadow in the gap. I slid the plastic piece into the space above the bolt. It fit there with a small amount of play, maybe a millimeter. I eased the shim down and worked it where I thought the angled part of the locking bolt would be. Nothing happened.

I realized it was the wrong side of the bolt. So I pushed the phone piece out as far as I could through the gap and then pulled it back at the same time as I pushed down with force. The pressure compressed the spring and moved the bolt back into the door. I blocked the door jamb with the phone back and turned the knob. The door opened. The locking bolt sprung into its extended lock position. I put the broken plastic in my pocket.

I stuck my head out into the corridor. Silence. Nothing was happening, except for faint noise from Le Foxy Kebab, two stories down. I left the room. Closed the door and locked it by pushing gently until the spring was compressed and then released into the door jamb. It made a solid click. The third floor corridor had an extra dimension that the second did not. Another office down the hall where the stairwell would be if there had been a fourth floor. I walked over to the office door. Which was sound-proofed, evidently, because I couldn't hear anything and no light leaked from underneath. Inside the door was the Woodcutter, whoever that was.

I weighed the options. I could feasibly break the door down and try to kill everyone inside. But it was risky, because I didn't know who or what was in there. One fat and bald Woodcutter, maybe, if all of that Woodcutter nonsense could be believed. One tall and skinny guy, who had taken the laptop and phone, almost certainly. The other unknowns remained unknowns. Could be three in there, could be five. I'd heard two voices at least, but maybe there was an army of mutes. Second, even if I did succeed in killing everyone in the room, Nazari would be on the hook, which is what decided the question. I'd have to come back, and next time I'd at least bring a screwdriver.

I walked down the stairs to the ground floor. The restaurant's bathroom access door had been closed in the meantime. I opened it a crack. The baseball hat counter guy wasn't there. I walked into Le Foxy Kebab. The teenagers had gone and had left their booth a mess of ketchup. It looked like a murder scene. The two women were eating kebab wraps held gingerly in front of them by long nail extensions. They ate clean. No drip, no mess, no fuss. Acrylic fingernails punctured the wraps like talons dug into prey. The three young guys were slumped into their booth enraptured by their phones. They didn't bother looking up as I walked out of Le Foxy Kebab.

Nazari's Peugeot 206 was gone, replaced by an empty parking spot.

I glanced around for a few seconds but knew that I hadn't mistaken the parking spot, her car was gone. Then I remembered the battery had come out of the phone when I'd used it to get out of the locked office. I pulled the burner phone and the loose battery from my pocket. Slid the battery into place and pressed the little power button on top. After a while the phone powered on. I saw five missed calls from Nazari, ten seconds apart.

There was one text message, '*Tried calling. At the police station.*'

CHAPTER TWENTY-SIX

It was well after midnight by the time I paid off the taxi and was standing across the street from the police station, which looked even smaller and dirtier in the dark. I spotted Nazari's silver Peugeot 206 among the cars. The double glass doors parted automatically when I approached.

The station was deserted. Two empty coffee cups occupied a lonely corner of the front desk. Nothing moved, nobody spoke. Not a whisper. The coin-operated coffee machine stood all on its own. A plastic cup forgotten beneath the spout. Now half-full and cold.

Left behind in the panic.

No coffee drinkers were slumped in the chairs lining the front window. Now just empty blue plastic bucket seats and a lone sweat-shirt. As if someone had got up and left, quickly, without looking back.

Left behind in the panic.

The desk was unmanned. A beige battery-operated doorbell ringer was Scotch taped to the surface. I pressed the gray button in the middle. And was rewarded by a ding-dong sound from behind a two-way mirror. A fit man in his seventies came out of the office. He wore civilian clothes. A silver brush mustache structured his upper lip. "Monsieur, if you don't have an emergency, I'd appreciate if you could come back tomorrow morning. We are operating a skeleton crew tonight."

"Did something happen?"

"You could say that. There's been a serious incident and we're short-staffed for the moment."

"I get it. They called you in to man the desk. All hands on deck."

"You got it." He looked proud but not vain. This was a man who showed up when he was needed.

"Can you tell me what happened?"

"No can do."

"I'm waiting for a friend. She's a cop. Mind if I wait here?"

"Go ahead. Let me know if you need change for the coffee machine. You might have to wait a while."

The man returned to the office behind the two-way mirror. I could picture him operating a secure radio rig. Directing communications between the dozen or so Municipal Police officers. I sat down on one of the blue bucket seats in the waiting area. Sent Nazari a text message from the burner phone. '*At the station.*'

There was no reply. I dug out change from my pocket and put it in the coffee machine. There were two choices. Espresso coffee and Oolong tea. I chose Espresso. Which came out in a thin liquid stream, which was at least warm, if meager. I nursed it as long as possible. Then I just waited.

I thought through the sequence of events between the time I had arrived at the train station Saturday morning and now. I did it slow and easy. Putting events and people and things into place in my mind. The initial violence of the attempted mugging and then the actual murder of the Afghan. These events seemed to connect to the trail bike kids and the migrant trafficking operation that I had witnessed. It seemed credible that the trail led to the office above Le Foxy Kebab, and The Woodcutter. The Gilles Vaugeois connection looked tenuous. But all of it slotted in somehow.

One hour.

I remembered the receipt that I had found in the bathroom garbage can above Le Foxy Kebab. Pulled it out of my little change pocket. It was a small quartered square of paper. I unfolded it. The electronic printing was dark violet on white. There were five items purchased. There were no actual words anywhere on the receipt. Just codes and prices in euros and centimes.

Three items for five euros and sixty-nine centimes. One for thirteen twenty-eight, and another for thirty-two eighty-seven. Which made sixty-three euros and twenty-two centimes in total, not including tax. The three items for five sixty-nine had the same code. Same item. I played with the prices in my head. Five sixty-nine's not a big amount, but it's not a bag of potato chips either. The ticket wasn't from a supermarket, it had no logo or store name. A mom and pop store maybe. A DIY hardware type of shop possibly. Tools. Maybe a place that only took cash. I didn't have any way of knowing.

I had found the receipt balled up in the garbage can. I ran through the motions. Items bought in a store. Receipt gets balled up but there's no place to throw it away. So you shove it in your change pocket. Then later, you're cleaning up in the bathroom. You pull it out of your pocket and pitch it into the can. No brainer. But the profile is specific. This isn't someone who litters. This isn't a teenager. It's an adult with responsibilities. A grown-up. Which didn't exactly get me anywhere. So I folded the receipt back into quarters and stuck it back into my change pocket.

I got up and stretched. Walked over to the coffee machine and watched the plastic spout divulge another thin stream of something they called espresso.

Two hours.

The phone vibrated after three hours. A text message. '*On my way.*'

Twelve minutes later a Municipal Police car drove up. Nazari and three men got out. Only one of them in full duty uniform. Nazari wore a police jacket over the clothes she had on before. The other two men took off their police arm bands and walked towards separate parked cars, presumably going home. The uniformed cop and Nazari came into the station lobby. She reached behind her back and unclipped a holster from her belt. It was a Sig-Pro service piece. She saw me sitting in the waiting area and held up a finger like, one minute. The uniform buzzed them into the station offices.

A couple of minutes later she came out and walked over to me. Without the Sig-Pro, which I figured got registered back into the station armory. She looked beat. She said, "Will you come home with me?"

"Of course. What happened."

"I'll tell you in the car. I don't want to talk here."

We walked out of the station. And got into her Peugeot. Closed the doors. She turned to me. Her eyes were rimmed red.

She said, "It's Rigalle, the chief. You remember him?"

CHAPTER TWENTY-SEVEN

I SAID, "Yes of course, director of municipal police."

"He's dead." She spoke deliberately, as if each word were precious.

"What happened?"

"I received an emergency text when I was in the car, waiting for you." She rubbed her eye with a fist. "I tried calling you a few times, but I had to go."

"I understand. You got the call and had to go."

She nodded. "I was the last to respond. They even called in reserves."

"I noticed."

"So after I got my weapon I went to the scene. I got to the location and it was Alain's house, which I know pretty well. I assumed that it was bad, but nobody had told me what I was going to find in there." She started bawling. I let her. She wept in gusts and bursts, with violence. Then she stopped. "My colleagues were canvassing neighbors and the job was to set up a clean perimeter so that the investigators could have a decent crime scene, you know."

I nodded. "Go on."

"But I had to see, of course." She looked at me. "How could I not, right?"

"Right."

"So I go into the house, through the tape and everything. With the plastic boots on because I needed, really needed, to see. But Tom, there were only pieces left. There wasn't a whole person. It was disgusting and it smelled terrible by then. And I was walking through it, getting my feet bloody, messing up the scene; at that point I was beyond caring or knowing. Because I was confused. There were too many arms, too many legs, too many pieces. I didn't get it, didn't understand. All of the limbs and pieces had been piled onto the living room carpet, a Persian carpet. Which I remembered well, because I was there when Clotilde bought it." She looked at me again. "But then I realized and understood that it wasn't just Alain piled up there, but the whole family. Clotilde, little Anne, Benny, and the chief. Together." Nazari stared out the front of the car into the nothingness. She blinked, as if she'd forgotten anything that had happened before the call. "I'm sorry I had to leave you, it was an emergency. A cop thing."

"I understand completely. The phone was off, I had the battery out. You did what you could to alert me."

Nazari lowered her chin and put her hands over her eyes. She leaned against the steering wheel. I put a hand on the back of her neck, to comfort her. Then she suddenly swept her hair back with two hands, fingers raking the wayward curls. She tied it all together with a hairband from her wrist. She looked at me hard. "They were murdered with an axe. All of them mixed up and lying there in pieces on the floor." She stared out at the darkness through the windshield, shaking her head. "We've got to get this bastard and make him pay." She looked at me. "Make him pay, Keeler, make him pay."

I said, "An axe killing, like Benoit Houdin."

"An axe, or multiple. Unclear at the moment. Yes. The same signature as the Houdin family. Whoever did that is back, never went away in fact."

"Why do they think it's an axe?"

"Force of the blows. Trauma of entry wounds. Secondary marks on the walls and furniture. Dents and cleave marks that conform to the shape and size of an axe blade."

"The follow through, from the blows."

"Correct. The murderer strapped them to the dining room table and hacked their limbs. One by one. While the other family members must have been watching. I can't imagine what that was like."

"Strapped how?"

"The kind of strap you use to tie things down to a car roof rack. That's the preliminary opinion, based upon marks found on the body parts. The kind of straps that you tighten with a ratchet."

I nodded. "Ratchet straps. I imagine they would have been incapacitated first, before being tied down. Particularly a strong guy like Rigalle."

"Clotilde, his wife, she wouldn't have gone easily either." She looked up at me with the hazel and green eyes. A roving headlight beam flashed over them, picking up the color and enhancing. "The table was hacked up of course. By the axe. Raw splintered wood. Like the devil's dinner or something. It was crazy."

"Dismembered bodies."

"Didn't even look real, to be honest." Nazari laughed bitterly. "Luckily at some point you stop thinking of them as human. Just a pile of remains. Fresh meat and blood."

She cried some.

I put a hand on her shoulder and turned her towards me. "Listen. They were already gone when the bad stuff happened. The bad stuff wasn't for them. It was for you, for us. For those who would find the bodies."

She spoke softly. "How do you know that? How can you say that with such certainty?"

"I know. I've seen it, more than once. People respond differently to killing. Most do it reluctantly. They need to be convinced that it's the only possible solution to the problem, whatever the problem is. So they harden themselves to the necessity and do it. But they make it as clean and fast as possible. Then there are a small percentage of people who get off on committing violence. Not only criminals but cops and soldiers as well. And when the killing starts these people reveal themselves. Whoever did this is one of those. A pure psychopath. Criminal psychologists have studied them. It's a performance. They do it for others to see. For those who find the bodies."

I pulled her towards me and her head fell onto my chest. I put my hand in her hair and held her there. She was crying softly into my shirt. After a while she stopped crying and just leaned against me.

Two cars pulled into the police station parking lot, a black BMW and a marked police car. From where I sat, I could make out the bearded plainclothes cop behind the wheel of the first car, the unmarked black BMW. Grouse jumped out the passenger side. He looked agitated and impatient. Bouncing on the balls of his feet while his partner rolled up the windows and dealt with the ignition key.

I said, "Here come the BRI."

Nazari looked up and took a moment. "The assholes from Amiens."

I said, "Do all BRI investigators look so intellectual?"

She laughed. "Did you meet the boss, Martaud? She's probably overseeing the crime scene."

"I did. And her sidekick, Caro."

"Martaud's more like the profile I'd expect. The others I don't know. I guess they have qualities."

"You knew them before all of this?" I asked.

"No. Never saw them before this started."

The driver of the cop car killed the ignition. The front passenger door opened and Antoine Bonnet stepped out. Bonnet opened the rear door, and held it, like a valet parking attendant. It took a while, but eventually a passenger emerged from the rear seat. It was Mayor Marbot. Which explained the delay; he'd been squeezed in back there and had taken some time to shift his bulk around.

I said, "Your partner Bonnet, tight with the mayor."

"Antoine. The mayor moved him to interim chief, now that Rigalle's dead."

"Is he the most qualified, in the hierarchy?"

"Maybe the mayor wanted someone he could trust, given the uncertainty. They already know each other, so Bonnet's a known quantity, given the urgency."

"Maybe."

Bonnet was walking alongside the mayor. They were speaking, a serious conversation. Calm and detached, but serious. Bonnet did most of the listening, Mayor Marbot did most of the talking. Terse, quick sentences. The BRI guys were waiting for them. Bonnet saw us, probably recognized Nazari's car. He motioned to the BRI guys and the mayor, a hand signal that said, 'hold on a second'. Then he jogged smoothly across the street.

I said, "He moves pretty well for his age."

Nazari was watching him with me. "Antoine's a serious tennis player."

Bonnet reached the car and Nazari rolled down the window. He bent down and looked at me, then looked back at her.

"You okay?"

"Yeah, thanks. You?"

"I'm okay." Bonnet spoke across Nazari to me, sitting in the passenger seat. "Keeler."

"Sorry about your loss."

"Thanks." He looked back at Nazari, "I've got a lot to do now."

She said, "I know, go and do it. Find those bastards."

"We're going to find them, no doubt." He looked over at me again. "You take care of her."

"I doubt she needs help."

"Probably not, but just the same."

"No problem."

Bonnet nodded and jogged back across the street. He rejoined the little power group of cops and the mayor. Then, all together, they walked into the police station. The automatic doors opened and sucked them in. A minute and a half later the light went on in the second floor squad room window.

I said, "So the BRI guys just come and help themselves to the second floor squad room."

Nazari was organizing her hair. "That's right. Because it's a small station we keep space open for outside investigators." She pulled her seat belt on and clicked it in. Reached into her pocket for the car key. "I don't know if you're aware of the police structure in France."

"Not very."

"Municipal Police are the lowest form of cop. In most towns Municipal cops don't carry guns. It's entirely up to the mayor if we're armed or not. Our mayor said we should be, so we are."

"Ever use it?"

"The service weapon? Only at the range."

"And you told me that it's the mayor who calls in the outside investigators from the BRI."

"Correct, the mayor and the chief." Nazari turned the engine over and started it. "Now I just want to go home. Take a shower. Sleep." She looked at me. "With you."

"Sounds good to me. Tough night."

We passed through the empty and still town. Empty of people and animals and vehicles. Just vapor lamps that shone a light for absent observers. Unless it was for us, speeding through the blank streets. We didn't speak during the ride. Nazari pulled the Peugeot into the little overgrown driveway of her house.

By then the moon was low and not quite as bright. She took my hand and led me down the stone path towards her front door. She said, "I love the way the river looks from up here at night."

She stifled a yawn. And then I felt her hand tighten its grip on mine until her fingernails bit into my skin hard enough to leave marks. She froze where she was on the path, looking directly at the front door. I had to step around her to see what it was that had captured her attention.

The front door of her house was ajar. In the dim light I could make out shredded wood around the door jamb.

She stepped back and whispered, "I left my weapon at the station."

I took a couple of steps to the door and looked in. "I don't think anyone is here. No car and I doubt they came on foot. Most likely they've been and gone. You ever clear a house?"

"No."

"Go back to the car. Call in to your colleagues and report the break-in."

"Okay." She went quietly towards the car.

I walked to the front window. Squatted down on my heels and listened. I waited more than two minutes. There were no sounds other than those that could be expected in a rural location in early summer. I pulled the door open. The lock had been jimmied by a crow bar. One big pull. Long crow bar. Splintered wood. I entered the kitchen, left of the front door. I pulled a mid-length blade from a counter-top knife block.

Then I cleared the house, room by room. Nobody was there. The house was intact, just as we had left it, as far as I could tell. I left the knife on the counter, leaned out the door and gave a two-fingered whistle.

Nazari came into the house hugging herself and shivering. "What do you think he wanted?"

"Can't know for sure, but I don't have the best feeling about this."

"So just say it. I'm thinking the same thing."

"They came for you or me, possibly for both of us."

"To kill. Like he killed Rigalle and his family and the Houdin family. He would have succeeded if we hadn't been out to dinner." Nazari's eyes were wide and rimmed in dark circles. She was losing it.

I said, "Not he, they. One person couldn't have done that to the Rigalle family and the Houdins. Not alone. There were at least three perpetrators." She was looking away, distracted. I said, "Look at me now." She looked at me. I came closer and put my hand on her shoulders, "They won't succeed because I'm between them and you. I won't let that happen."

"How can you take on three killers?"

"I can take three guys."

She looked at me for a long moment. "I didn't call the police station."

"Why not?"

She reached in her pocket and withdrew a folded slip of paper. "I found this in my locker. It's from Alain. I found it just now, at the station. He must have put it in there today, while I was with you." She handed the folded sheet of office paper to me. I unfolded it.

The sheet was regular office printer paper. In the middle of the page was a rectangular wide-angle photograph of Nazari, taken by one of those tiny cameras built into computers. She was looking into the computer monitor. Beneath the rectangular photo was a scribbled note in ball-point pen, '*This is dangerous. We need to talk. Face to face, no phones, no computers. Come to the house. Don't speak to anyone about it. - Alain*'

I looked at her for an explanation. She said, "When I told you that I checked the blue Opel registration, it wasn't that simple. I'm not an investigator yet, so I don't have my own computer. This morning I went by the station. I knew that Alain wouldn't be at work and I used the computer in his office to do the registration look-up." She looked up at me. "And now he's dead, and they've broken into my place as well."

"In that case, you did the right thing not calling the station. No phones no computers, that means the lines of communication are compromised." I handed the note back to her and she started folding it.

Nazari nodded, as if she already knew that, which she probably did. She said, "You never said why you wanted me to look up that plate registration."

"I did. I thought I was being followed the other night. Two guys in a blue Opel Corsa."

"So maybe you were being followed."

"Yeah, maybe I was."

Then, swiftly, she crushed herself to my chest, gripping me with all her strength. Pulling my shirt towards her hard. She let out a suppressed scream. It was rage, more than fear. I felt her hot breath against my chest, pulled her tight, looking over her head through the living room window. The moon was down, just above the valley.

CHAPTER TWENTY-EIGHT

WE HIT the road and got out of town. I drove. South, away from
Alencourt. I didn't have enough information yet, only disconnected
fragments. Which meant that I didn't know who was what or where
they were coming from. So we needed operational distance. A chance
to get oriented and make decisions.

Nazari sat in the passenger seat, staring out the side window. I
couldn't see her face. I rolled down my window and tossed the burner
phone into a field. Those things can be tracked, which is why you
burn them. We drove for an hour without saying a word. Then she
started talking as if nothing had happened. Whatever it was she was
processing, she'd worked some of it through her system and was
dealing with the rest.

We found a motel with a twenty-four-hour desk. I stayed in the
car while she registered. We showered and that took some time.
There were more distractions. It ended up being a slow shower. So it
was close to dawn by the time I crawled under the covers. I was tired,
but not that tired. She got into bed after me and smelled good. Clean,
like soap and musk. The sheets felt light and cottony. Her body was

real and firm and soft and warm and above all alive. She was insistent and strong. We made love fiercely, with intent.

And slept for exactly two hours and ten minutes.

Then we got up. Fully alert, no fuss. She had to go to work. She'd wanted to call in sick but I vetoed that. We had to act like we weren't concerned. Had to push back by being reactive and capable.

There was a French version of a diner attached to the motel. They agreed to do eggs. I figured they'd seen tourists before, so were open to negotiation. No bacon, just ham, which wasn't a problem. No hash browns, so we had toast, which was fine since they had coffee. We sat in a booth and the waiter brought two cups of it.

Nazari said, "Let's run through it out loud."

"Is that what they teach in the BRI investigator course?"

"Yes. You talk it out, like a narrative. You have to tell the story, see how it fits together. Eventually it makes sense. They call it a *fact-pattern*."

"Where do you want to start?"

"We start with the headline."

"Rigalle's murder."

"I found Alain's note after he was murdered, but he wrote it before, obviously."

I sipped coffee, swallowed and spoke. "Rigalle finds out that you looked up the blue Opel registration and wants to speak to you, writes a note about it, and is then murdered with his family. A public execution."

"Because someone thinks that it was him snooping, not me?"

"Maybe."

Nazari said, "In addition to that, the murderers pay a visit to my house."

I said, "Which would indicate that they knew you had done the registration lookup, not Rigalle."

"Which indicates that they had access to the camera feed on the police chief's computer."

"That looks likely."

"Fine." Nazari sipped from her coffee cup. "Now that links the Rigalle family murders back to me, possibly to you, and according to Alain's note, to the police station."

I said, "Therefore, we assume that the police station is an unsafe operational environment."

"Maybe a bent cop. Someone on the take."

I layered raspberry jam on a piece of buttered toast. "I haven't told you what happened last night, above Le Foxy Kebab."

I told Nazari about the room with the laptop and phone and about the other office down the hall. I showed her the receipt I'd found at the bottom of the bathroom garbage can. I told her about the guy whose wrist I had broken on Saturday and whose face I had kicked in on Sunday. The guy with the Adidas stripes in his head. How I had seen him up at the migrant camp near Calais. She knew about the ponytail guy down by the river. She didn't know that these were two of the guys who attacked me in town. So I told her, and how I thought it was all connected.

"YOU ATTACK the Adidas-striped guy up there after you've already broken his wrist the day before, and then you attack the other guy by the river." She shook her head with a wry smile. "Not bad for your first two days in France."

"There were sharp instruments involved." She smiled. I said, "I operate with extreme prejudice. It's going to get worse. The instruments are sharper and heavier now."

I was thinking about the axe.

Nazari waved away the prevarications. "So there's a connection with migrant trafficking, which makes sense. It's big business these days."

"There's something else that I didn't mention before, about the mohawk bike kid. I found a sharpened screwdriver under the bike seat, three of them."

Nazari looked daggers at me. "And what did you do with them?"

"This isn't going to be resolved in court."

Nazari shook her head. "That links the Vaugeois attack to the trail bikes and The Woodcutter, and therefore to migrant trafficking and the killing of the Afghan."

"Correct."

"But that has no connection to the fact-pattern we have built up around the Houdin and Rigalle murders."

I popped a toast triangle into my mouth and chewed for several seconds. "Another thing. You know that the link to the Houdin family requires another look at Houdin. What was he, the treasurer?"

Nazari said, "The money guy. Not a politician. He managed all the town finances. Houdin was one of the golden boys. Handsome guy from a rich traditional family. Big house. Local roots. In the mayor's clique."

"He and Rigalle knew each other?"

"Sure. Small town, similar age, same social class."

The waiter approached with a pot of coffee and we stopped talking. He left the pot. She said, "They're warning off others. Butchering the Rigalle family was all about sending a message."

"I think so. And there's another thing."

"What's that?"

"Cop killing. That isn't done lightly. There are usually consequences."

Nazari looked into her coffee.

I BUTTERED a fresh piece of toast. The bread was good. I said, "Killing cops usually aggravates any given situation. So now the situation is aggravated." What I was thinking was *weapons*, and the fact that I didn't have any. I figured I'd get my hands on a piece pretty soon, either way.

Nazari asked the waiter for a pen. She unfolded a napkin. "Look, here's how we're supposed to think about this. A fact-pattern is like a constellation in the sky, the Big Dipper or something." She drew a bunch of stars, then she started connecting them with lines. "The facts are stars, and when they connect to each other they make a pattern right, like the Big Dipper and Orion."

"What's Orion, I only know the Big Dipper."

"Orion's a hunter with a club and shield."

I nodded, "So far so good."

"So we've got Orion and the Big Dipper, but they don't connect. So we need a plan to connect the constellations."

I said, "The Afghan dead guy on one side, with the trail bike kids, Woodcutter, and a tangential relation to Vaugeois." I poked her drawing. "And on the other side the Houdin and Rigalle killings." I circled the two constellations with my finger. "Is that what you mean?"

"That's what I mean."

I finished a cup of coffee and poured another. I said, "Here's the plan. You're going to work. If anyone's paying attention, it looks like you're just doing what you always do, being a cop. But today I'm coming with you, at least initially. I want to be seen at the station."

"And then what?"

"Then I will leave and walk around town. See if someone picks up my tail. If there is a bent cop at the station, there is a chance that I'll be followed. And if I am, then I'll do my thing."

"What do I do?"

"Go to work as usual. Keep the routine."

"You're using yourself as bait, Keeler. Is that wise?"

"Probably better to think of me as a carnivorous plant with legs. If they're wise, they'll just give up now, immediately. At least they'll have a chance of staying alive."

"After the station?"

"I'll pass by Le Foxy Kebab, not for the food. I'll go back upstairs, see what happens. By the end of the day we should have a couple of new facts."

"A clearer *fact-pattern*, Keeler. Connected constellations."

CHAPTER TWENTY-NINE

The drive back to Alencourt took over an hour. We entered along the river, from the south. A low fog hung across the water. The mist had already burned off the shallows but lingered where the river was deepest. It was still early Monday morning and the sun glanced off the water and made the trees glow from underneath. Traffic wasn't bad and Nazari parked the car at a quarter to eight in the morning.

I got out and stretched. Cracked my knuckles and arched my back a couple of times, cracking joints there as well. I felt good. Pampered and rested after only a couple hours sleep. Ready for anything.

She locked the car. She was looking at me with a smile on her face. I said, "What are you smiling at?"

"You. You look amped. As if you're excited about the prospect of someone coming after you."

She was right. I was excited about that prospect. "I won't lie. I feel good. Feel like cracking heads. But, it's not like I'm impatient or anything. Don't forget, I've got experience in this department."

"The cracking heads department?"

"That's right."

I followed her into the police station, which was open for business as usual. The desk officer was back at his post. I waited while she figured out a visitor badge for me. The coffee machine hummed with potential. The spiky plant had closed for the day, maybe digesting whatever unlucky creatures had tried to settle during the night.

NAZARI BUZZED us into the working part of the police station. She left me by the better coffee machine while she went to the staff lockers to get changed. A couple of uniformed officers looked at me, but left me alone. The visitor pass hung around my neck on a blue lanyard. I filled a small paper cone with water and drank it.

The room was arranged around a grid of four desks, three of them empty. One desk was occupied by an older man in Municipal Police uniform. Three younger uniformed officers were gathered around in a cozy huddle drinking better coffee and speaking quietly. All four officers were male and armed with Sig-Pros in identical holsters. I figured they were the day shift waiting for the late night shift to come in from the field.

Nazari had disappeared down a corridor in the back. I walked over to look into it. There were offices and an armory, a bathroom, and evidently the changing rooms. Maybe they had a holding cell. Nazari's old partner, and new interim director of police stepped out of the bathroom, brushing his sleeves and fixing his cuffs. Bonnet saw me looking through the door. He smiled, beckoned me in.

He was wearing his old uniform, but with new shoulder stripes. As a military man I notice these things. The old ones were a couple of chevrons, the new ones were four stripes. "Keeler," he extended a hand. I took it.

I was looking at the stripes and Bonnet shrugged. "Yes, strange."

"I bet it's a tough job. A lot of responsibility all of a sudden."

"I won't be able to fill Rigalle's shoes, but I'll try and do a decent enough job until they find someone to take over."

"I'm sure you'll do better than that."

"We'll see." He pointed to a doorway. "I've got an office now, come and sit down."

We went into the office. The desk was positioned facing the door, with three standard seats. On the wall behind were framed pictures of the dead police director with older and rounder fellows in uniform. Looked like someone had already boxed Rigalle's stuff, outgoing. There were a couple of boxes with what looked like Bonnet's stuff, incoming. Some of it already unpacked, like a line of silver plaques with his name on them. Looked like Bonnet had won the local tournament a couple years in a row. I said, "Tennis champ."

He smiled. "I've had my day. Nothing too flashy, just the local tennis club. I suppose I'm what you call *competitive*." He pointed to a plaque. "That one was doubles, I won it with Alain Rigalle. Couple of years ago. He was also a fierce competitor." Bonnet's eyes reddened and went moist. "Did you know that we were friends before I joined the force?"

"I didn't know that."

"He was a hell of a guy. Someone with true values who wanted to make a difference."

"Did he?"

"Did he what?"

"Did he make a difference?"

Bonnet looked for a moment like he'd swallowed a ping pong ball. He coughed. "Of course he did. Every cop makes a difference every single day." Standard response. He drew a tissue from a box on the desk and wiped his eyes. "Now we have our work cut out." Bonnet looked up at me. "You're here with Cecile?"

I didn't say anything. He nodded. "She's a good woman. Is she helping you with that problem at the Vaugeois house?"

"What problem is that?"

Bonnet rolled his eyes. "C'mon, we're friends here. We already talked about it. Gilles was attacked, you were concerned about it. Plus what happened to you when you first got here. I get it."

"I figure you have bigger things to worry about now."

"Listen, Keeler. Normally, I shouldn't be discussing police matters with a civilian. But, given what happened to you." He made a shrugging gesture and sighed. "We have big problems in this town. I've had to step up here. If there is anything that you have discovered, anything that might help the investigation, I'd appreciate you telling me."

I said nothing.

Bonnet pressed on, "I saw you yesterday. What you did with that kid. You and me, we're on the same side here. We want the same thing. Justice and resolution."

I said, "Maybe."

"Maybe?" Bonnet's face went blank, like he was deflated, disappointed, or both. If it was an act it was a pretty good one. I didn't trust the mayor, and Bonnet was the mayor's man. But, it was wiser to conceal my suspicions.

I said, "The kid on the bike was one of the guys who attacked me in town. I'm not a cop, I'm just a guy who doesn't like to be threatened."

"So you wanted to teach him a lesson."

"Something like that."

Bonnet picked up a tennis racket and examined the strings. "I don't know if those kids are capable of learning lessons, if you know what I mean."

I said, "You're probably right. But I don't see it as my business if the kid doesn't know how to learn. Then he just gets the pain without the lesson."

Bonnet laughed. "That's a good way to put it, Keeler. The pain without the lesson."

"Maybe I should have been a poet."

He said, "Well, if there's any way I can help you, just let me know. My door is always open."

There were three new tennis ball cans on the edge of his desk. They had the word 'pro' on the label, which was gold.

I stood up. "Good to see you."

We shook hands across the desk.

A glass door on the other side of the police station led to stairs. These wound up and back to the squad room, currently being used by the Research and Intervention team from the bigger town up north, the BRI unit. I walked through the glass door and climbed the stairs. Then up the switch-back to the second floor. The door to the squad room was on my left and the interview room straight ahead. I used my visitor ID to buzz into the squad room and was mildly surprised when it worked.

Caro and the bearded cop were chewing croissants and drinking coffee. They had feet up on a big table. A paper bag was torn open revealing a clutch of French pastries. I figured that was the local equivalent of the doughnut. White paper coffee cups were lined up next to a pile of black plastic burner phones. Caro was perusing a stack of eight by tens. The photographs looked tiny in his massive hands. As I came in he handed one to the beard. Caro saw me first and visibly flinched.

Flinched like he hadn't been expecting me. Like he wouldn't have flinched for anyone else. It was a little moment, but in my experience little moments give big insights. It was fast and instinctive, but I made a flash decision to be aggressive. It's the training. Like Napoleon said, *first I get involved, then I see.*

I walked nice and easy towards them and smiled broadly. "At ease, gentlemen. No reason to stand for me." The eight by tens went face-down. I snatched one up from the table. Carnage. The Rigalle family in a mixed-up pile on the living room rug. Like a butcher's table after they'd got done taking care of a new delivery of slaughtered pigs. I said, "Reading the funny papers, I see."

The beard eased his legs off the table, but didn't get up. He said, "Those are police property."

I flipped the photo back at Caro and picked up another one. The beard sighed and shook his head. The second eight by ten was a close-up shot of Rigalle's severed head. The eyes were closed and the face was barely recognizable. Puffy and white after the blood had drained. The head rested upright on a coffee table. I slid the photo back.

The beard smiled. "If you have to puke, do it in the bathroom, or better yet, downstairs with the uniforms."

Caro stood and glowered. His biceps were the diameter of medium watermelons, thighs like beer kegs. His voice was a hoarse, barely articulate growl. "What are you doing here?"

I stepped into his personal space and clapped him on the shoulder. I was in there before he could react. Sluggish reflexes. But it was like slapping a stone wall. "It's only been two days and your voice has gotten worse. You should take a break from the juice, big guy."

Caro croaked defensively, "It's worse in the morning." He stepped back and ran into his chair, almost knocking it over.

I said, "Easy now." The big man scooped up the eight by tens, turned around and fled the squad room.

The beard looked up at me. "It isn't safe to antagonize Caro."

"I don't do safe."

The beard was languid. I wondered what his pupils looked like behind the sunglasses he still wore. "In that case what is it that you do?"

"You really want to know?"

He popped his feet back up on the desk. "Sure."

"To be honest, I'm only good at one thing really."

"What's that?"

"Seek and destroy. I'm not much of a cultivator. I was never the guy to go in last and do the first-aid, more like the one to go in first and do the damage. I let other people clean it up."

The beard gave a short, uneasy laugh. Martaud walked in with the bald cop, Grouse, following. Caro lurked in the back. Martaud said, "Those are fascinating attributes, Monsieur Keeler, but I fail to see how they would be usefully applied here in Alencourt."

"You'd be surprised."

"I already am." Martaud appraised me. "Just curious, where were you yesterday afternoon?"

"With a friend."

"The friend have a name?"

"None of your business."

Martaud flipped a look to the beard and he started collecting the burner phones from the table. I counted five or six of them.

"I thought you were leaving Alencourt. Why are you still here?"

"I met someone."

Martaud's eyes had gone from gunmetal gray to pale gray, the way skies can change on a windy ocean day. "You were in the military, Keeler. Maybe you've read the various theories about friends and enemies."

Caro had kept in step with Martaud, like a giant shadow.

I said, "I was never much of a reader. But I'll tell you something for free. I've worked with the best investigative units in the world, and they don't look like you. Not a bit."

"What do they look like?"

"They look busy."

"We have our own methods in France. We don't compare ourselves to other forces."

"Yeah sure."

Martaud said, "Well anyway. The theory of friends and enemies is simple. Either you're a friend or an enemy."

It was meant to sound profound but fell flat because just at the end of her sentence Nazari walked into the squad room. All eyes shifted. She was wearing her blue Municipal Police uniform and ball cap, along with a Sig-Pro pistol holstered at the hip. She came up behind me. I didn't turn away from the investigators. Nazari said, "I was looking for you, Tom. Let's go downstairs."

Grouse, the bald cop said, "Oh, now it's Tom." His eyes gleamed and he made an obscene gesture.

I spoke to Martaud. "You might want to keep this one on a leash, for his own health and safety." I didn't look at Grouse, but I knew that he was chomping at the bit.

Martaud said, "Aggressive energy is expected and encouraged in an operational unit."

Nazari stepped up. "What's going on?"

I said, "Nothing, we were just getting reacquainted." I turned to Grouse. "And I'm looking forward to the next reunion."

We walked out the squad room and into the corridor. Then down the stairs. On the stairwell landing, Nazari stopped. "What the hell was that all about?"

"No idea. I guess I provoked them a little."

"Is that what you wanted?"

"I was improvising, but they really rose to it."

"I already told you they were assholes."

She had to go out with her colleagues. The beat cop routine, walking around in pairs looking for whatever cops look for. Maintaining a presence for the citizens to feel safe. I told her that I'd pick her up at six, when her shift ended.

I took another tour of the downstairs police station rooms, just to make sure that everyone had taken a good look at me. I figured if one of them was on the take, they'd be alert. If a call was to be made, it either already had been, or was in process.

CHAPTER THIRTY

For search and rescue, the mission is to save lives. *That others may live,* is the motto.

After a recruit passes the candidate course, he undergoes two years of training. Airborne school, Combat Diver school, Underwater Egress, Air Force Basic Survival, Free-fall Parachute, six months of Spec-Ops Combat Medic Training and another half year of Specialist Training.

The Specialist Training part is where it gets interesting. The vast majority specialize in combat arena operations. Your classic war zone. A few young highly trained but relatively unsophisticated and inexperienced killers—are siphoned off to the spooks. Because, even spooks need rescuing. They get the war zone stuff plus a little extra on the side. Among the dark arts that the young operator learns in spook rescue school, one of them is covert street surveillance and counter surveillance. I was one of those spook-trained operators.

A built-up area with stores provides excellent opportunities for counter surveillance. I stopped twice for coffee. Tied my shoe laces several times. Flashed glances in reflective store windows. And took advantage of every possible choke point I could find. I made a mental catalogue of each human being encountered in a 150 yard radius around my mobile body. I categorized hair color, clothing type and color, skin tone, age, gender and outfit. These attributes were collated to time and geography.

It is almost impossible to follow a trained operative alone. He will eventually make you because you can only change outfits so many times. If, at the beginning of my walk I had noticed someone and then half an hour later seen the same person in a different outfit, they'd be blown.

Which is why I had walked for so long and for so far. The mantra is to hope for the best and plan for the worst. The plan was to string out any surveillance team so that they would have to double up eventually. I hadn't seen a thing. Not a single repeat over five miles by my count. So I figured I wasn't being followed.

Half an hour after arriving at that conclusion, I was sitting in a cafe across the street from Le Foxy Kebab. Folks were drinking small cups of French coffee and eating croissants at the cafe bar. It was a warm and sunny day and the street side of the cafe was open to the sidewalk. Small round cafe tables were spread out. I was sitting three tables back, just inside the restaurant. Consequently, I had a good view of the front of Le Foxy Kebab. I couldn't be observed from the second or third floors. I sat there for thirty minutes, just watching and waiting. Soaking in the situation until I became part of it.

The morning trade was mostly workmen. A sky blue cleaners van was parked right next to Le Foxy Kebab. The side of the van was a logo in soap bubbles and an aspirational image of a resolute man in blue uniform with a baseball cap, holding a mop. Nothing happened that was in any way remarkable. Twenty minutes later a couple of young men strutted into Le Foxy Kebab. They walked up to the counter and ordered. Then they took seats in a booth. A refrigerated meat truck partially blocked my view.

I paid. I hadn't noticed any access to the building besides the bathroom door from Le Foxy Kebab. But that didn't make sense for a mixed-use building with offices above. I did a walk by. There was a door in-between Le Foxy Kebab and the next commercial property over, an outfit selling insurance. The door would lead to a stairwell with direct access to the upper floors. So there were at least two ways of getting upstairs, that and the bathroom entrance from the restaurant.

I kept going. Walked around the block and turned onto the street behind Le Foxy Kebab. It was residential. The row of houses backed onto small fenced gardens. I figured there was the same on the commercial side. A garden backing onto another garden. If that was the case then there would be a back door. There was also the window from the half-landing of the stairwell. I retreated to a small park and found a bench to sit on. The bench faced towards a large fenced-in auto-repair shop's yard. A couple of mechanics were busy pulling apart engines.

I reflected on the situation.

The target was the second office, third floor. I didn't know what I was going to find there. Whatever it was, I didn't want to be seen entering, and climbing around looking for an open window in broad daylight isn't very subtle. Climbing over fences and through back yards didn't seem any better. The direct approach was best. In through the front door.

The bathroom door of Le Foxy Kebab had worked once so why wouldn't it work again?

The counter was empty. Only one guy working. Double duty, counter service and kitchen. The two young guys at the booth didn't even look up at me. So I walked straight through to the bathroom door and turned the knob, which was locked.

A voice called from the kitchen. "Hey!" The guy was looking at me. "Hold on!" I waited. He came out of the kitchen. "I locked the door because the cleaners came." He held out a key on a cheap plastic tab and a length of old string. "Be careful. The floor might be wet."

I shrugged. "Thanks, pal."

"No problem."

CHAPTER THIRTY-ONE

THE FLOOR WAS NOT WET. I walked up the stairs. The window was open on the half-landing. I kept on going. Second floor, the door across from the Mediterranean beach photo was exactly as I had left it. No one had come to work yet. Monday mornings are tough. I walked across the hall to the stairwell and continued up. A stout young guy in a bulky blue uniform and cap was mopping the stairs. He wore thin disposable sanitary booties over his shoes and blue latex gloves.

The guy jumped to the side when he saw me. "Excuse me, sir."

I nodded politely in return. "Thanks," and brushed past him.

As I walked up to the third floor the cleaner called from below. He had a strong accent that I wasn't able to place. "Sir. Excuse me, sir."

I waited at the top of the stairs. He stopped just below me. "Please be careful the floor is wet." The man had blue eyes and a Slavic or Caucasian facial structure. High cheekbones and narrow eyes.

I said, "I'll be careful," and turned back up the stairs.

The third floor was wet. I looked down at the footprints my boots made on the tiles. They were clear and well defined. I might as well have stepped in black forensic ink. Which didn't make me very happy. I heard the sound of a vacuum cleaner.

The office door where I'd gotten stuck the night before was locked. Across from the door, a mop bucket, and a carrier box filled with tidily organized cleaning products were lined up against the wall. I walked down the hall to the second office door, from which I'd heard voices. The door was wide open and I walked in. The office was sparse. There was a cabinet along one wall, a desk and chair in the middle. Against the other wall another cleaning guy in blue uniform and cap was standing on a sofa.

The cleaner was balancing himself with difficulty and wore the same blue plastic sanitary booties over his shoes as his colleague. The guy was about the same height and body shape, short and stocky. And therefore this one was having a hard time reaching the top of the wall with the vacuum cleaner hose. He was trying to reach the corner where the wall meets the ceiling. Like his colleague, he wore blue latex gloves.

The guy noticed me out of his peripheral vision and turned. Narrow blue eyes in a Slavic or Caucasian face.

He switched the vacuum cleaner off and stepped down from the sofa. He was relaxed, friendly and smiling. Same accent as the other guy. "Bonjour, monsieur. Can I help you?"

I recognized him and my blood chilled quick. Not so much the face, but the eyes and the fact that there were two of them. I had seen him and his twin in their blue van when we were driving out of Nazari's place the night before. They had been searching for something. I had figured they were lost, but now I realized that they were looking for Nazari's house. I figured they had planned a cleaning operation there, but we hadn't been in.

The guy didn't move. The smile on his face was fixed. I was too far from him. He would have time to draw a weapon. I had none. I figured fifty-fifty I'd get out of the room alive.

I said, "Sorry about the footprints."

He looked at my boots, shrugged and indicated the sanitary booties. "It's why we wear these. So I don't have to worry about footprints when I clean."

"I'm looking for the travel office. Did they move?"

The guy's face didn't change. "I don't know, sir. The landlord wants the place clean is all."

"New tenants?"

He shrugged and smiled. "I don't really know. We just do what's asked. Maybe he just likes it clean."

The cleaner watched me with a half smile. He had dropped the vacuum cleaner hose on to the sofa. I realized that he was seconds away from pulling a weapon. Probably tucked into the waistband of his pants.

"Sure. Thanks." I turned around and walked out, waiting for the bullet in the back.

It didn't come. I wasn't on their list, or they didn't know what I looked like, which was a shocking omission. Which meant all kinds of things, like it was Nazari they'd come for the other night, not me. The vacuum started up again behind me, swallowing up the sound of my boots stepping across the damp floor.

Down the hall towards the stairwell. The first cleaner was standing by the stairs. The mop was leaning against the wall. The cleaner stood easy and relaxed with a nice wide and stable stance. His arms were ready and loose. He was thickly muscled. A trained and experienced killer. I smiled and spoke loudly against the noise from the vacuum cleaner. "It's hard to keep up with friends these days. The world changes so fast. Makes the head spin."

He nodded. "Yes, sir."

I brushed past him and started down the stairs. I counted four steps down, then turned and grabbed the guy's ankle with both hands and pulled hard. He lost his footing and grunted. Used all of his reaction time groping with his hands to avoid hitting his head on the stair, which left me an opening to grab his head with two hands and smash it hard against the edge of the second stair. The impact stunned him.

I didn't take any chances and did it again fast, twice, as hard as I could. The guy went limp. I came up with a Beretta 9mm, tucked into his waist at the back.

The Beretta had a long and thick suppression barrel screwed into the muzzle. I slid open the action, one in the chamber. Let the clip drop heavy in my hand. Decent load. Snapped it back in. I thumbed the safety horizontal and put the barrel behind his ear. I lay down on the stair, below his lower body, so that only my hand and the Beretta were at the level of his head. I shot him once from five inches. His brains and skull and blood painted a thick arc where the wall and stairs met. Some of it got on my hand, but otherwise I was clean. I wiped my hand carefully on the back of his blue uniform. The gun as well.

The suppressed Beretta had made a loud popping sound, nowhere near silenced. But the vacuum cleaner hadn't stopped working. I looked over toward the second office, barrel up. Fully expecting the other cleaner to have heard the shot or the sound of the guy falling. Maybe not. I moved in a crouch towards the office, two arms extended loosely, eyes roaming. *Not too fast, not too slow.*

The cleaner was still up on the sofa with his back to the door, on his tip-toes, stretching his stout and tough body for a hard to reach spot. He was sucking up dust from the corner with his right hand, while holding himself against the wall with his left. Then he switched hands and steadied himself, using the free hand to shake out a shoulder cramp. I stepped into the room, took up a firing position and shot him once in the back. The guy tumbled off the sofa with a loud thud. I pulled him by the foot and rotated the body away from the cloth-covered furniture. Then I stepped back about three yards and aimed at the back of his head. The Beretta made two loud pops and the cleaner's face exploded out along the floor.

I thought, Monday morning is not the right time to clean. That's Friday night.

CHAPTER THIRTY-TWO

THE SECOND CLEANER had an identical weapon. I wiped them both and hid one of them in the bottom of the carrier box. The other went into my waistband, in the back, with a round in the chamber. Then I hunted down the four casings. One for the first cleaner and three for his buddy. The first one was all the way down the stairs in a corner. The casings went into the carrier box with the gun.

The first cleaner's body had slipped down several steps. I took both of his wrists and pulled him up. Then dragged him along the hallway and into the second office. The mop was still leaning against the wall where he had left it. The carrier box contained plenty of cloth wipes, a roll of white garbage bags, a box of latex gloves, a box of plastic sanitary booties and assorted spray bottles and containers of cleaning product. I pulled out a pair of latex gloves and put them on. Then put a pair of blue sanitary booties over my hiking boots. Tight fit, but they didn't tear.

I cleaned my way backwards, from the stairwell, down the corridor and into the office. I used a combination of paper towels to pick up the big stuff, anti-bacterial spray bottle and wipes to clean off the residue, and a good old fashioned mop and bucket to finish off. I cleaned blood, brains, skull fragments, hair, and my footprints. Neatly removed all traces from the corridor and packed the cleaning tools into the office. Then I closed the office door. Now I wanted to know where the other bodies were. That is, the Woodcutter and his friends.

I thought, secondary staircase.

At the end of the hall, past the first office, was a long, steep staircase that switched back twice, directly down to the street. There were no bodies. I opened the door and looked out. The cleaning van was parked to the right and the refrigerated meat truck was just in front of the door. There were no windows to the back of the cleaning van. I went up to the third floor.

The dead cleaners looked like twins lying side by side on their backs. Two similar bodies without faces. Actually, the first one still had a bit of face left. Enough to see the faint curl of a smile. I figured Chechnyans or Dagestanis. B-grade freelancers. Experienced, brutal and effective, canny and resilient, but not known for subtlety. I turned their pockets. One car key and nothing else. No wallets, no identification, no phones. The key was for a Ford. The cleaning van.

I opened the back of the Ford. The doors swung out. On either side of the interior was custom-built storage for cleaning supplies. Rolls of plastic sheeting in two different grades. Another shelf was stocked with all kinds of spray bottle products. I closed the door.

The refrigerated meat truck was parked just in front of the stairwell. I had overlooked it, which made sense because it was parked in front of a kebab restaurant. There was no one in the cab. A clean and new truck. Maybe a Chinese brand. It was a modern meat truck. No refrigeration box sticking up from the top, everything built-in and streamlined. I peered into Le Foxy Kebab on the off chance that the driver was eating after delivery. The young guys from before had gone. The restaurant was empty.

I approached the refrigerated meat truck with curiosity bordering on morbid fascination. I could hear a faint hum from inside. The refrigerated section had a side hatch with two large clasp handles. I

saw then that the truck had been parked so that when the refrigeration unit hatch was open, it made a perfect connection with the stairwell leading up to the third floor. It would only take a few seconds to
move bodies from the staircase and into the truck. The gap between
truck and building was sheltered from sight. I took the Beretta from
my waist and thumbed off the safety.

But I needed two hands for the clasp handles of the refrigeration
hatch, so I reset the safety and tucked the Beretta back into my waistband. I swung the handles open and the hatch popped out, releasing
a short hiss of fog, which cleared quickly to reveal a guy working a
saw back and forth across meat. He was getting good leverage, poised
in mid-sawing motion. He looked up at me.

I got the Beretta out and in front with the safety off. The guy was
dressed in a hazard suit, the kind of head-to-toe, hooded gloved and
booted gear that you see in disaster footage. He would have been
right at home in a movie about Chernobyl, or a chemical spill, or an
alien invasion. Except there he was crouched in the back of a refrigerated truck sawing off someone's leg. All I could make out were two
narrow blue eyes through the glass lens of his chemical protection
hood. I put a round between them, which spidered the glass around
the bullet hole. The shell casing popped up and clinked underneath
the truck. I managed to get a foot on it before it rolled away.

In the back of the cleaning van I found a roll of thick plastic
sheeting, duct tape, and a cutting knife in a handy tool caddy. I cut
two big lengths of plastic. Back in the office, I rolled each cleaner into
a section of plastic sheeting. It was the thick polymer kind that you
struggle to puncture with a thumb. I lifted the plastic-wrapped and
taped bodies over my shoulder and down the hall one at a time, then
did a controlled slide down the stairs for each. Opened the door to
check. Shifted the corpse to the refrigerated section. Repeat.

I took everything out of the office. The cleaning supplies and the
bodies. Supplies went into the Ford, bodies got refrigerated. The guy
in the hazard suit had a key ring in his pocket. It held a bronze
skeleton key, a regular door key, and a black plastic fob for the meat

truck. I locked the meat truck and jumped into the cleaning van and took a look around. Old Ford van, everything manual. Manual gear shift and a manual radio with an old cassette player. There was no tape. There was nothing in the back except cleaning stuff. Nothing on the dash. Nothing in the fold-out ashtray. Nothing in the glove compartment. Nothing on the floor, or under the front seat. Nothing under the floor mats. Nothing under the visors. It was clean.

I drove the Ford around the corner and pulled into the auto-repair yard. I left the key in the ignition and stepped out. A big dog was chained to an engine block. He was a sleepy-looking mutt. I looked around for the boss. A guy with both hands deep into a wheel well used his chin to point. I followed his chin and found a small dark wiry guy with pens in his dirty overall pockets.

He asked what he could do me for. I told him I wanted a full transmission replacement, that I wasn't happy with the clutch link-age, and that he could take his time doing it because I was going on vacation for a week. He said six grand. I said that was fine and invented a phone number on the spot. He wrote it down without batting an eyelid. We didn't shake hands.

CHAPTER THIRTY-THREE

THE REFRIGERATED meat truck was a marvel of technology. The shift was automatic and the dashboard had a big black screen with the word 'smart' just below it in rounded letters. The truck started up without a key, just the push of a button. It was enough to have the black plastic fob in my pocket. It was so quiet, I almost didn't notice the motor, humming along in the background. The black screen lit up and showed an engine and a battery in some kind of cyclic relationship. I figured that was because it was a *hybrid* vehicle. Half electric, half gas, or something of that nature. The other half of the black screen was filled with numbers and symbols that related to the refrigerator behind me.

I drove the Chinese meat truck east and found a highway after ten minutes. The highway wasn't busy. Midday traffic on a Monday. I cruised for forty minutes and then looked for an exit. After a half-hour of driving around I found what I was looking for, a moderately large light industrial area. Looked like the French urban planners kept things organized. The dedicated industrial area had warehouses, depots, factories, and all manner of large open parking lots and storage yards. I parked behind an enormous flat building that advertised winter storage for RVs. The back fence looked out on train tracks. I figured June was about as far away from winter as anyone could hope for. Then I opened the hatch.

The fridge was cold.

The bodies were wrapped up in the heavy polymer sheeting. And not all in pieces yet. I figured the hazard suit guy was getting a head start while his buddies cleaned upstairs. There were four victims, not including the guy in the hazard suit and the two cleaners, which brought the count up to seven in total.

One fat bald guy, The Woodcutter. Shot point-blank in the forehead, flash burns from the muzzle blast all around the entry wound. The tall skinny guy from the night before with the light blue tracksuit and thin line of a beard along his jaw. Shot in the neck and the eye. The rat-faced guy. Gaping neck wound. Artery severed, head hanging loose on what remained of his neck. Spinal cord visible. I thought, axe attack, single blow.

The last body was the ponytail guy with the bright blue eyes. I couldn't find any external wounds. I didn't imagine that the freelancers were subtle killers so I dug my thumb and index finger into the area just above the kid's throat and behind the chin. The hyoid bone holds up the tongue. I felt around for it until I got it and pushed. It was broken in at least one place, which is a sign of violent asphyxiation.

No bruising on the neck. Probably a plastic bag.

I searched the truck and found a clean hand axe and a pair of red ratchet straps behind the front bench, which was confirmation enough that I had found the psychopath responsible for the axe murders of Houdin and Rigalle. The axe was new and barely used, the price sticker still on the handle, which accounted for the blade's factory sharpness. It had a decent heft and I could imagine swinging it in a controlled manner. I looked out the windshield at the bleak industrial landscape. A huge tractor trailer drove by, no doubt looking to unload and then move on, or else to load up and move out.

I recreated the scene.

The rat-faced guy was an example; he'd messed up. Didn't deserve the bullet, so he got the axe. The hazard suit guy was the axe man. He probably did the ponytail as well. Put a plastic bag over his head and held him there while the others watched, probably did him or rat-face first.

The cleaners allowed the meat man the examples. He was a full-blown psychopath. They allowed him the examples so that he didn't take it out on them. The meat man had been useful in some ways.

Benoit Houdin and Alain Rigalle were public examples. Which meant that quite a lot of people were in on whatever was going on. They needed to be kept quiet. I wondered if Nazari and I were to be examples and figured that no, we would have just been disappeared in the meat truck. The Woodcutter and the tall thin guy were not dead because of anything they had done wrong. They were dead because they were loose ends that needed to be cleaned up. Evidently by the cleaners, professionals hired by a third party.

Which begged the question of who the third party was. Whoever they were, I was moving up the chain of command.

The truck was otherwise empty. Nothing in the glove compartment and nothing else under or behind the bench seat. I had an idea. It was a modern truck, and modern things have computers in them, and computers are like little snitches that keep track of everything you do with them.

The black screen on the dash came to life when I pressed the fob. I flicked around and pushed icons until I found the GPS navigation. It showed where I was and asked where I wanted to go. On the bottom of the screen was a row of symbols. I pressed one and got a list of popular destinations around me. Which included a train station. I memorized the route. Looked like it was a couple of miles away.

Then I hit the other symbols and after some trial and error found a list of previous destinations. There were two basic categories of previous destinations. Destinations that the meat truck guy had entered into the computer, and destinations that the computer had remembered without anyone asking for it. Useful, and potentially dangerous.

The meat truck psycho hadn't asked the computer to register anything in the first category. But regardless of that, the computer had memorized everything for the second category. The only thing I knew about computers was that they don't make any sense to me, but that doesn't mean that they don't make sense. They've got their own logic. There were quite a few destinations. But there was one destination that the truck kept returning to, an address on the outskirts of Alencourt.

I wiped down the Berettas and left them in the truck, along with everything else. It was too risky to walk around with guns, and suicidal to walk around with guns that had just been used in several killings. I locked the vehicle. Then I started walking toward the train station.

It was coming up on two o'clock in the afternoon. Nazari got off work at six. As I hiked along the road, I tossed the Chinese meat truck fob into a little pond. It sank with barely a ripple on the surface. I found the key to Le Foxy Kebab's bathroom and tossed that in as well. I kept the skeleton key and the door key that I'd found on the meat truck guy.

It took a while to hike to the train station. Then I had a long wait for the train back to Alencourt. The address logged by the Chinese meat truck's GPS was a small house in a working class district.

By then it was Monday at quarter to four, the time of day when people at work begin thinking about leaving, and people left at home begin thinking about taking a nap. So there's no one around. Nobody driving, nobody walking. No helicopters picking up accident victims on the highway. Nothing and no one, just a weird silence punctuated every ten minutes by an airplane cruising at thirty thousand feet. A forty-year-old woman leaned out the window of an apartment building across the street and pegged socks to a laundry line. Then she went back inside. The front door had two locks. I knocked first and wasn't surprised when nobody answered. I used the keys and entered the house.

The cleaners had lived like pigs. The furnished house was made up of a living room, kitchen, and two small bedrooms with a small toilet and a shower closet. The living room, kitchen and bedrooms were overflowing with take-out food containers and empty beer bottles and cans. Crushed boxes of cheap cigarettes had been tossed willy-nilly around the place. Any available receptacle had been used as an ashtray.

In the kitchen, a burner phone rested on the counter. A black charging cable fed it juice from the wall plug. I pressed buttons and found the call history log. It was empty. Looked as if the cleaners had been more careful than their meat truck colleague, and routinely deleted any incriminating logs as soon as they finished a call. I pocketed the phone.

One of the bedrooms was shared. Two suitcases were pushed under the single beds that lined up on either side of the room. The cleaners, brothers or cousins. I found French passports in the suitcases with French names. False identities no doubt. They also had back-up guns. Identical Berettas with boxes of 9mm ammunition. I wrapped the weapons in a clean towel from the bathroom closet. Stuffed the package into a backpack I found on the bed, alongside the two boxes of ammunition.

The other bedroom was a single. Just one bed and one suitcase. The passport was French and so was the false name given to the meat truck psychopath. His suitcase contained a collection of two hand axes and a large fireman's axe. Charming guy.

I estimated by the garbage and the state of the toilet that they'd been in the house for a month. Which gave the whole situation a time span. A month ago, three freelance professionals had been brought into town for some cleaning and public butchering. Which was by any measure an extreme step.

But, instead of getting out after the first killing, they'd stuck around, on call. Shacked up in the house. Playing cards, ordering take-out and drinking beer. Until the next assignment. Which meant they hadn't been afraid of getting caught. Which meant they'd felt safe and protected. Until I showed up.

I found it highly unusual that a bunch of cop-killing murderers roamed safe and free, rampaging for a month without fear. If I were in their place I'd be on a different continent by now. Therefore I had to assume they'd been hired and protected by someone, or a group of people.

And furthermore that these were people capable of offering protection from the investigating authorities. Sounded more like Iraq than France.

CHAPTER THIRTY-FOUR

THE POLICE STATION was another hike. But I like walking and thinking.

I walked and I ruminated. And after walking for the better part of an hour, I arrived in front of the police station. I had a bunch of questions and ideas that I wanted to test out. But I didn't want to test them out there; I wanted to get far away from there.

Because inside the police station was at least one bent cop who had been more than willing to feed Police Chief Rigalle to the axe man.

I WALKED in the front door of the little Alencourt police station at six pm. I asked for Nazari at the reception desk. A big guy was sitting on the blue bucket seats. Seats, plural, because he was spread out across three or four of them. The guy was speaking Spanish into a cell phone. I didn't want to stare, so I looked at the carnivorous plant.

A couple minutes later, Nazari came out. I said, "Let's get out of here, but keep the uniform."

"Why? I usually get changed."

"I'll tell you why later, but we need you to look like a cop."

"I see." She patted the butt of her Sig-Pro. "I need to check the weapon. I'll be back in a minute." She went inside the station.

She came back in uniform but without the gun. "Where are we going?"

I said, "One hundred yard rule."

"What's that?"

"Let's get a hundred yards from here before we talk."

She quit speaking and we walked to her car. She started the engine and backed out of the parking spot. She kept the car in reverse and backed all the way to a spot on the side of the road, about a hundred yards from the station. She looked at me. "Okay. So tell me what happened."

I gave her a recap of the day. Minus the part where we had passed the cleaners on our way out of her place the night before. I felt that was a little too close to home and fanning the flames of fear wasn't what I had in mind. Quite the opposite. I wanted her to feel safe and confident, able to think clearly and rationally. I also withheld the part about the two Berettas I was carrying in the backpack. She was still a cop. I didn't tell her where I'd parked the refrigerated meat truck and she didn't ask.

She looked at me for a while, then looked out the windshield, absorbing the information. Her eyes widened and then came back to normal.

She shook her head, as if to clear it. "Let's update the *fact-pattern*. Have we made it clearer?"

"We've linked the Vaugeois attack to the Houdin and Rigalle killings, through the cleaners."

"Therefore both link back to whoever it was that hired the cleaners in the first place."

"Correct."

"And we find them how?"

"I don't know." I patted my pocket and brought out the burner phone from the cleaner's house. "I'm assuming this is how they got in touch. Call history has been erased."

"So, you're hoping someone calls."

"Something like that."

"And the Afghan?"

"Linked tangentially through the Woodcutter and his crew."

Nazari thought about this for a moment. She said, "What now?"

I said, "Your house isn't safe, you can't stay there."

"I'm with you on that, a hundred percent. Too isolated. I need to stop by the house so I can pack a bag."

"Of course."

"So why the uniform?"

"We're going to talk to Simone Vaugeois. I thought we could impress her with a uniformed police officer."

Nazari looked at me. "It's going to get worse, isn't it?"

"It's going to escalate, because that's the direction it's been going, escalation."

"Once they figure out that the freelancers aren't coming back they'll call someone else."

"That's highly likely."

"And that 'someone else' will be better."

"They might be, but not as good as me."

She smacked the wheel. "Did you get the registration numbers?"

"Which registration numbers."

"The vehicles that you dumped. The cleaner's van and the meat truck."

I nodded. "Of course."

"Then we need to run them, right now."

"Is that safe?"

She smiled. "At this point, what is safe supposed to look like?"

She had a point. "How soon do you get results when you do the look-up?"

She started the car and got it in gear. "Immediately. I'll be a couple of minutes max."

She drove one hundred yards to the police station. I reeled off the cleaner's van and the refrigerated meat truck numbers that I'd memorized.

I waited in the car. Ten minutes later she came back out of the station with several printouts.

She tossed them at me. "Read it out loud."

I examined the printouts while she drove. The cleaning van and refrigerated meat trucks were both registered to private companies. "Argo Enterprises. That's the cleaning van. Meat truck is registered to a company called Gilbert and Sons. Both companies have a postal code starting with the numbers seven and five."

"That's Paris. They give specific addresses?"

"Just the code."

Nazari whistled. "That'll take some leg work."

I said, "I think we're at the leg work stage. We'll need to find out who rented the Opel Corsa from that place."

"Pegasus Auto Leasing in Lille."

"That's the one."

She turned the wheel. "Too late now to make the calls, but I'll start calling around tomorrow. You said you saw two people in the Opel."

"Correct. Is that meaningful in any way? Is it unusual to rent a car in Lille and drive down here?"

She shook her head. "On its own, no, it isn't unusual. Let's just say that at the moment it's a fact to add into the fact-pattern."

"I can live with that."

We drove for a while without speaking. Then she turned to me and asked, "How did you kill them?"

"Cleanly with the least amount of fuss, given the circumstances."

"Did they deserve to die?"

"Most definitely. They would have done the same to us, with the maximum amount of fuss."

She nodded to herself, as if resolving something. "They would have made us suffer."

"They would have done terrible things."

"So it was justified, even though it was outside of the law."

I said, "They put themselves above the law. It was their choice, not ours."

She nodded. "They *tried* to put themselves beyond the law."

"Anyway," I said, "I'm not a lawyer. I don't know much about the civilized kind of law. I'm more comfortable with the laws of physics. Not in a technical way, but experiential. Ballistics, inertia, friction, gravity. I know about that kind of thing."

She shot me a look with those hazel and green eyes. "I can vouch for your command over the laws of physics. You do gravity and friction pretty well."

"Thanks, but it takes two to tango."

"We can do that again, soon."

"I very much hope so."

"Good, so do I."

CHAPTER THIRTY-FIVE

SHE DROVE and I looked out the window. Her house was past Brumaire. Farther out along the river and up into the valley. After a while we passed Fanny's Friperie, which was closed. And I found myself thinking about the Afghan knifing victim, Qayoumi. Moreover, I was thinking of Nazari's photo of Qayoumi's tattoo. Some word in Dari or Pashto. Maybe Miriam could read it. Maybe it meant something.

Since it was Nazari who had initially pointed the way to Fanny's Friperie, the day I'd arrived in town, I asked her if she knew Miriam. She did. I said, "Remember the tattoo on the Afghan victim's hand, on his wrist? Maybe we could get Miriam to read it."

Nazari didn't remember seeing the tattoo. She dug her phone out of her pocket and multi-tasked, driving and thumbing through the photos. She glanced at it and passed the phone to me. "This one."

I examined the photo.

She had centered the camera on Qayoumi's fatal knife wound. The tattoo was on the inside of his wrist. Three groups of letters, which I figured were three words. And below the words, a line with three dots above it. I turned the phone to see it better. Not that I could read the words anyway, but I wanted a closer look. The whole picture rotated in response, so that I was looking at an even worse angle. I said, "I hate these phones."

"Can you read Arabic?"

"No. But I doubt that this is Arabic. The guy's from Afghanistan. They speak Dari or Pashto or something, some kind of Persian-related language."

"Pass it over, I'll try to read it. They all use the same Arabic alphabet and there are commonalities."

"They do? How do you know?"

"My parents are Egyptian."

I looked at her in surprise. "And you read Arabic?"

"Of course."

"Why didn't you read it before?"

"Didn't see it, or if I did, didn't think it was important and the thing rotates whenever you try and read the words."

I handed the phone back to her. "Try and read it now."

Nazari multi-tasked. She manipulated the phone with a lot more precision than I had managed and drove at the same time. She figured the phone out. "It's just Arabic, not Dari or Pashto. The words say, 'Unity, Liberty, Socialism'."

She handed the phone back.

I looked at the picture. It rotated back and the letters were vertical, not that I could read them anyway. "You sure it's Arabic? It looks the same as Dari or Pashto to me."

"One hundred percent. It's Arabic. Every country has their own dialect, but there's a standard written Arabic for religious texts and more formal stuff."

"You don't say."

"Anyway, we're here." She was pulling into the old farmhouse estate.

She parked and got out. "I'm going to pack a bag, give me a couple of minutes."

I stayed in the driveway, looking at the landscape. Down-river, the sun was still high. The trees and far-away hilltops blocked some of the light, making shadows on the water, which, seen from a distance looked like animal shapes.

The old farmhouse estate was on a gentle hill, sloping down toward the river. Across from her cottage was a neighboring property and I spotted a mound that looked a lot like the cavern entrance I'd seen in the forest outside the Vaugeois house. I walked over to it and looked in. Unlike the tunnel entrance at Brumaire, this one was well maintained. I walked through the stone archway into the cool dark tunnel. After twenty yards I came to a locked door. The air in the closed tunnel was already musky and humid. I heard Nazari's voice from above, and turned around.

Her bag wasn't that big, a medium-sized duffel. I said, "You got everything you need there?"

"You think all this is going to take a long time?"

"No, it's going to be over real soon."

"So ..."

I nodded. "Right."

We got back into her car and back on the road. Then I felt the cleaner's phone vibrate in my pocket. The one the killers had used to communicate with whoever it was gave them orders.

I pulled it out. A missed call. I had been underground. The screen said 'Unknown Number'.

CHAPTER THIRTY-SIX

I asked Nazari, "How do they get an unknown number?"

"In France you can dial a blocking code. Three six five one."

"You learn that studying for the investigations unit exam?"

"Yes I did."

"You're an exceptional student."

"Thank you."

I put my hand out the window and let the breeze pass over my skin. It felt good.

"Which reminds me. About the Afghan guy, Qayoumi, did they do an autopsy?"

Nazari said, "Because it was a murder the body is automatically referred to the medical examiner. So yes, he would be autopsied."

"And?"

"And I don't know."

"Can you find out?"

She looked at me. "Actually I can, since I know the medical examiner personally." She pulled out her phone and multi-tasked. "The advantage of small towns."

From my point of view it was a one-sided conversation. Because all I heard was Nazari's voice. Which was a fine -sounding voice. Smooth and throaty, all at the same time. Neither high nor low, but right in the middle, flowing calmly, a good voice. She was apologizing. She was sorry for the hour, and for the call in general. But then she asked the question, and after that she was listening for a spell. The guy spoke and I heard crackling sounds from the speaker that was held up to her ear. She nodded and made the kind of sounds you make, so that the other guy knows you're listening. Afterwards she thanked the guy and said good night.

"He was eating dinner with his family."

"Sounded to me like he spoke a lot."

"He was talkative. The guy loves his job. He said the Afghan was referred. He got Qayoumi on the table."

"And found what?"

"Well that's the thing, they only did an external examination. Cause of death was already determined so no reason to open up the body. That's the law. No reason to do an internal if cause of death is determined prior."

"What does external consist of?"

"Check the surface area. Anything on the skin gets bagged and examined. Hairs, paint, cosmetics, sand, jewelry. Whatever they find they examine. Then they do an ultra-violet scan for anything not visible to the human eye, which is a lot. You wouldn't believe the stuff that exists that we can't even see."

"What happens to that stuff?"

"They have a special vacuum cleaner. Sanitized hosing and everything, sucks it straight into a hygienic bag."

"So no incision, no electric saw, no examination of vital organs, nothing of that nature."

"Nothing like in the movies, no. They just skipped that part and went straight to the paperwork."

"Anything unusual?"

"Apparently not. The knife was inserted into Qayoumi's thorax and penetrated the heart. End of story."

"Good aim."

"Not only that, the blade length was perfect. Knife went to the hilt, right between the ribs."

I thought for a bit. An Afghan with the words 'Unity, Liberty, Socialism' tattooed on his arm. I said, "You know anything about Afghan history?"

"Pretty much nothing, no."

"I don't know much. But I've been there a bunch of times, in various capacities, for assorted reasons. So, you pick up some information here and there, from locals usually. They had a communist government. But that was a long time ago. Qayoumi looks like he's in his fifties right?"

"Sure. Late forties, early fifties in my view."

"Before we went in, the Russians were there. The Russians lost and left. Far as I know, the war against the Russians effectively killed any kind of Afghan socialism by the mid-eighties. That would have been what, thirty or forty years ago, depending. Even if Qayoumi was the last socialist left in Afghanistan, he would have been thirteen or something when the commie dream finally died, maybe younger even. Why would a ten-year-old get a tattoo like that?"

"He wouldn't."

"Right. He wouldn't. But if he did, what would that tattoo look like forty years later?"

"Stretched and faded because the kid's grown."

"Correct. Look at the photo."

Nazari got the photo back up on her phone and multi-tasked again.

I said, "Stretched and faded?"

"Negative. Not exactly crisp and clear, but easy to read and not distorted. Tattoo looks good."

"Which means that the guy was a fully grown adult when he got inked."

"Right."

"And the tattoo isn't in any kind of Afghan language."

"So maybe he's not an Afghan."

"So maybe he's not."

Nazari said, "What are you thinking?"

I looked over at her. "I'm going to make a call. Can we stop?"

"Why can't you call from the car?"

"It's not that kind of a call."

"What kind of a call is it?"

"It's a stand and concentrate kind of a call. It's a make sure the reception is good kind of a call."

She nodded. "Okay. No problem."

A couple of vehicles whizzed by going the other direction. We were passing through a residential area near the river and closer to the town center. We were coming up on a little grassy recreation spot with picnic benches by the river. I said, "Pull in over there."

She pulled the car over, parked and said, "So make the call."

I got out of the car and made the call. I used the cleaner's burner and dialed a number that's accessible and free from anywhere in the world. A female voice answered after three rings. "Yes?" I repeated a string of numbers a couple of letters and then some more numbers. There was a pause on the other end. Then, "Code?"

I spoke a long combination of letters and numbers.

"Who's speaking?"

"Captain Keeler."

"*Retired* Captain Keeler."

"Correct."

"Why am I speaking to a *retired* Captain Tom Keeler?"

"I need to speak with Blomstein."

"I don't know a Blomstein."

"Yes you do. He's sitting right next to you. Just transfer the call."

There was a longer pause. Then the call transferred and was picked up. "Keeler."

"Blomstein."

"You're bored already. You regret everything."

"Not bored. No regrets."

"So why are you calling me?"

"I'm going to send you a picture. I need to know if we've got anything on a guy. And I need to know what it is if we do."

"You're retired."

"Correct."

There was a long pause. "I guess it takes getting used to."

"No. I'm used to it already. I was used to the idea of it a year and one week ago. I have no problems being retired, Blomstein. I've just got a little issue with a face is all. It's not complicated."

Blomstein chuckled, and he said, "Alright. You get last licks. Send it to the usual address."

"Will do. You'll get the face in a couple of minutes."

I killed the line.

Nazari was waiting in the car. I said, "I need you to send your pics of the dead Afghan to a guy I know. If Qayoumi's an Afghan, chances are he's in a database and we'll have something on him. If not, we'll see."

"Who's the guy?"

"He's just a guy."

I wasn't going to tell her that Blomstein was a US special operations intelligence officer based out of RAF Mildenhall, England. Nazari made no fuss. I gave her the electronic address, which was a combination of numbers and dots and a couple of letters, lower case and upper case, with a hyphen here and an underscore there. Her phone made a swishing sound when she pressed the button to send.

I hoped we wouldn't get to Brumaire while Madame Vaugeois was having dinner. I figured she might consider that rude.

In the event, we arrived right on time. The days are long in June and the French eat late. Nazari pulled the little Peugeot up behind Simone Vaugeois' big Mercedes S-600. The musky scent of wisteria wafted through the open passenger side window. The limestone cliff loomed above. The white rock-face was lit up by a couple of spotlights on the roof of the house. The effect wasn't bad. It made the place look like a museum or something classy like that.

We got out of the car and approached the stone steps. Gilles was sitting on the terrace in the rocking chair. Maria had her hand on the chair back and was giving it a little tug and a push every other time it fell back on the rockers. She was singing a song in Portuguese. Sounded pretty sad and sweet, but she stopped when we came up the steps. "Bonsoir, Monsieur-Dame."

I bid Maria a good evening. Gilles was slumped in the chair. His face slack, but the faint outlines of a smile were present in the turn of his mouth. As if he had enjoyed the rocking motion. The scar on his forehead bulged, purple and angry. Nazari said hello but he didn't respond. She turned to Maria. "Does he understand what we say?"

"The doctor says no, but I'm sure he does, mademoiselle. One hundred percent." Maria paused and looked at me.

I said, "Doctors don't know anything. Like trained mice in a maze."

Maria nodded profusely. "That's true. She turned to Nazari. "He never responds." She looked at Gilles as if trying to elicit a response. Then back to us. "But I'm sure he will. One day he will."

I said, "I hope so." Which was the truth. There was a lot that Gilles could tell us. Didn't look like it was going to happen today though.

Maria said, "Are you staying for dinner?"

"If that's okay with Madame Vaugeois."

Maria nodded. "Madame will be happy that you are back." She said to Gilles, "I'll only be a minute. Don't move."

Gilles twitched an eyelid and the side of his mouth curled up slightly, maybe half a millimeter. Or maybe one of those micro-measurements, like a nano-meter. Whatever it was it would have been imperceptible to most people. Maria disappeared into the house. I squatted down so my head was level with his. Looked him in the eye. Vaugeois' eyeballs were still and the eyes unblinking. I figured they were working okay. I said, "You recognize me?"

No response at all. Not a quiver, not a ripple. His eyelid didn't move and his lips had shut.

But he was breathing faster.

CHAPTER THIRTY-SEVEN

We took Simone inside and sat her down on her favorite sofa. Nazari stayed within touching distance. The uniform worked as a pacifier. Older people can often be reassured by a uniform. As the world becomes stranger and more out of their control, the forces of order increase in importance. We told her about the suspected link between the attack on Gilles and the trail bike thugs. Nazari put a hand on her shoulder and the shoulder softened and visibly relaxed. Madame had no problem with Nazari staying over. I framed it as a safety precaution. We didn't try to pretend that the police were officially involved, but the uniform helped.

The other thing was that Simone wasn't fazed that Nazari and I were together. I told her in a matter-of-fact way and asked if she had a room with a bigger bed. Vaugeois swept her gaze back and forth between Nazari and me like a searchlight. She looked pleased. "Of course I have a proper bed for you." She got practical. She was concerned with dinner. Everything else could wait until after dinner. The menu was complicated. There was a duck involved.

At the table, I struggled with the duck. It was like arm wrestling an anaconda. Neither Simone or Nazari had any issues with it and I figured it was something you had to learn as a child. Like tap-dancing or the piano or riding a unicycle, or like people who walk around with things balanced on their heads. Luckily it came with potatoes, which I know how to eat.

I asked Simone about her husband Gilles' hobbies and interests. "Ma'am, you had mentioned his interest in local history."

"Oh yes. Gilles was endlessly interested in the history of our region and this town." She shot me a benevolent look, and daintily forked a morsel of pink duck flesh into her mouth.

"What kind of things was he interested in?"

"It changed all the time. You have to understand, we're not in America, Tom. Human beings have lived in Europe for more than forty thousand years. This is what Gilles was always saying. He would say that written history is just the tip of the iceberg."

But in any case, what I was trying to achieve was a sort of profile of Gilles Vaugeois before the sharpened tip of a screwdriver had entered the frontal lobe of his brain. Because, there must have been a reason why Vaugeois was a threat to whoever was behind all of this, and I didn't know what it was. So I was interested to know what Vaugeois was into, what he was known for and what had made him a person of interest within the community. And everything that I was hearing pointed to Gilles being a kind of brain. An academically inclined smart guy with the right social background for hobnobbing alongside the likes of the mayor and his cronies.

I said, "I'm trying to build up a mental image, ma'am. You said something about archeology."

"Did I? Why don't you look in his library?"

After dinner, Nazari and I helped clean up the table. Then we did the dishes together while Simone excused herself to prepare a room for us. Nazari rinsed and scrubbed, and I dried and set the plates and cooking equipment in a drying rack.

Nazari said, "So what do you think the perpetrators are thinking right now?"

"I figure the person who called the cleaner's phone is wondering where the cleaners are because they didn't call in. They must have had some kind of a system. Like they were supposed to call in or message when the job was done."

"But the cleaners did their job. The Woodcutter and his people are gone. Wiped off the planet in a way."

"Correct. They did their job, but they weren't clear and away yet. I got to them in the final phase so I doubt they called it in."

"Calling it in at that stage would be presumptuous."

"You call it in when it's done, not while you're cleaning it up."

"Ok, I get that. It makes sense."

"Which is why the client, perpetrator or whatever you want to call them, is asking the question but not yet panicking. Maybe they've done a drive-by of Le Foxy Kebab. Found nothing. I figure they'll wait until tomorrow before getting worried. At most they're pissed off."

"But not anxious."

"I wouldn't think so. Not yet, but soon."

"At which point they'll call in someone else."

"That's a good possibility."

She yawned. It was late.

The new bedroom was next door to my old one. The room was bigger. It had two single beds pushed together with a double bed sheet over the twin mattresses. We didn't mind. Nazari was wearing her cop uniform. The French care about their tailoring. Which was one reason why peeling off her uniform was so enjoyable. I did it carefully, and took my time. It started off with me sitting on the edge of the bed and admiring her. She stood confidently, watching me watching her. Maybe she liked what she saw. Then she came close enough for me to reach out and connect.

Each little section of her uniform that I unbuttoned and peeled away revealed new and wonderful territories to explore. And each time I peeled away the blue cotton, the remaining uniform hugged her body even closer and more perfectly than it had before. The other reason it was so enjoyable would be Nazari herself, who played the role for keeps and might have arrested me if I had stopped for too long.

In the end I managed to get her uniform off entirely. And by then we were horizontal on the two beds. In the low light of a small lamp her skin was gold. I explored the surface of her body, marking first the peripheral points and then exploring important sites in the interior. For her part she was doing something similar. We got up to all kinds of things in all kinds of different and interesting positions. It was like we were effortlessly tumbling down a slide of mutual sensation. After a while the light went off and it was all texture, smell, sound, but no visuals. Except for the shapes and things that we saw in the dark. If it was possible to top the last time, we did it.

Until we fell asleep.

I slept for a couple of hours and then opened my eyes. Wide awake and restless. Nazari purred softly beside me. I slipped out of bed and pulled my clothes on. I needed to be outside. I felt closed in. I felt like I needed a prowl. I figured, maybe a tour of the perimeter. Get into the trees a little and feel the dirt under my feet.

I retrieved one of the Berettas from the bag and stuck it in my waistband at the back.

CHAPTER THIRTY-EIGHT

THE BIG HOUSE wasn't silent. It made all kinds of little night time noises. Once in a while there was a gurgle. Wood joints creaked together. The house was speaking, in its way. I crept through it on my bare feet, listening to what Brumaire had to say. Either Madame Vaugeois or Maria had locked the front door. They'd left the key hanging from the inside, so I was able to open it with minimal fuss. I stepped out.

The night air was cool on the terrace and there was enough light to see the open spaces pretty well. Night animals had gone quiet and I waited for them to pick up again.

When the low hooting of an owl and the scraping of a million insect wings resumed, I padded down the terrace stairs and onto grass, which was cool and damp beneath my bare feet. I started with the cliff side, creeping between the house and the limestone face. Then I cleared the corner and looked out in the dark towards the end of the walled garden and the place where the path broke towards the river.

I explored the far end of the garden and prowled close to a wood pile. The forest looked back at me, dark and unknowable. The dark and the dirt made me feel free and easy. The smell of the forest and the outdoors was good. So I looked into the night and put my mind into another gear.

Tactical thinking. Defense in depth.

The driveway passed the gatekeeper's house, which meant that it wasn't the most advantageous entry point for a home invasion. Far better to avoid that obstacle and come in from other directions. The cliff was an obstacle, but had advantages for the attacker, height and observational view. If it were me, I'd put someone up there to spot and snipe. Then two clean attack vectors. One corridor from the garden gate, where the path to the river began. Second over the stone wall from the road. Just across from the big house. Then I visualized, played it out like a video game in my mind.

I may have fallen asleep, or maybe not. One moment I was sitting there thinking, and in the next moment something had changed. It was the night creatures. They had stopped again, but it wasn't me who had stopped them. There was something else out there. I stayed like that, leaned up against the tree, until I heard a faint noise from down below, toward the driveway. Then I stood up nice and slow, careful not to move my feet.

I shifted between trees, aware and heedful to keep an obstacle between myself and the source of the noise. Which was coming more often. Crunching and scraping. Someone was moving out there. For all I knew there was a team, dressed in black, equipped with night vision gear and noise suppressed weapons, keeping radio silence and creeping through the trees.

I could hear movement, so I figured they didn't know I was there yet. I had the Beretta out and in hand.

I crept between trees, one stride at a time. Hug the tree, wait and listen. I heard two distinct footsteps coming from down near the gatekeeper's house. Couldn't have been anything else. I listened hard, another step. I heard no more than one or two people, maybe coming up from the driveway. I decided to flank them and come in from the rear. I waited to hear another step, then I got low and moved laterally and slightly downhill. Five paces, each pace measured to land with a tree between myself and the intruders.

I was slightly behind them and it was time to look. I moved my head laterally around a thick trunk. Daniel the gardener was urinating on a tree fifteen feet from my position. I pushed the gun back into my waistband.

And then the phone in my pocket started vibrating.

Which would have been okay on a city street. Nobody would have heard it. But out there in the woods at night the vibration was loud as a ship's horn. I pressed a button on the side of the phone, through my pants. The vibrating stopped.

I stepped around the tree and into the moonlight. Daniel the gardener was standing still, zipping up his fly.

I said, "Evening."

"Evening."

"Fresh air's good."

Daniel nodded. "Sometimes I can't sleep."

"Same."

"Pissing on a tree beats the porcelain anytime."

"Agreed."

"And the flush is too loud in our house. Maria wakes up. She's anxious, you know."

"I wouldn't know it by looking at her."

He nodded once. "Good night."

"Good night."

Daniel went inside the gatekeeper's house, quietly.

I crept back to Brumaire, mounted the steps and re-entered, quietly.

CHAPTER THIRTY-NINE

I WENT up the stairs to Gilles' library on the second floor.

The door creaked open on heavy old hinges. I closed it and stood for a moment in the pitch dark. I had already traced the path from door to desk in my mind. So I walked it and flipped on the desk lamp without a fumble. The room glowed in polished wood paneled glory.

Like his house, his wife, his car and his pajamas, Gilles' library was a classic. The wood paneling was of another era, a time when craftsmanship was available and quality was expected. A time of artisans who had learned from their fathers, and father's fathers, and so on. The woodwork emanated pride, pride of the craftsman, and pride of the intellect that demanded a special place for special works of the mind.

All of that was expected, in a house like Brumaire, for the social class that Gilles and Simone were a part of. It came part and parcel of a world in which the higher classes felt special, by dint of being born to wealth. But what wasn't expected was that Gilles Vaugeois hadn't filled his library with the usual highbrow literary works that nobody ever read, but that everyone knew they were supposed to read. He had filled the library with the fruits of his mental labor and research, with a little wink to entertainment and nostalgia on the side.

One of the walls was taken up by windows. So there were three wall-sized bookshelves. Standing just inside the door, I was looking at Gilles Vaugeois' desk. A massive oak object set in the center of the room. I went around the desk and sat down in Gilles' chair. The leather and oak had been brought together by a serious artisan, maybe a long time ago. The cushioned chair was firm and pleasant to sit in. It took my body, without calling attention to itself like a so-called ergonomic chair.

I pulled out the top desk drawer. A sparse collection of objects were neatly squared away. A notepad with a sharpened pencil. A shallow tray of paper clips. A mini-mag flashlight. An Opinel pocket knife with wooden clasp handle. I fingered the knife and then put it back. Flipped through the notepad, it was blank. There were two larger drawers, either side of the desk. The first was empty. In the second I found a cigar humidor and paraphernalia.

Behind the desk was the first wall of books, and enough space to walk around and look at them. There were all kinds of books. Old leather bound tomes, frayed fabric-bound hardbacks, ratty paperbacks and clean paperbacks, magazines, loose-leaf maps and sheafs of notation held together by fold-back paper-clips.

I pulled out a couple of them and flipped through pages in no particular order. Maps and notations. Comments on mapping techniques, topographical maps of the area. Farmland parcels. There were books filled with historical maps that told stories of the area. Agricultural information maps which showed how farming had changed. One year wheat was in; a hundred years later it was rapeseed for cooking-oil.

It occurred to me that there was no organizing principle to the bookshelf, it wasn't in alphabetical order, nor was it by author. But from what I'd seen, Gilles had been an obsessive organizer. So there must be a rhyme and reason to the order of books. I stepped back all the way to the desk and leaned on it, and noticed the framed map hung just to the left of the floor-to-ceiling bookshelf.

I examined the map up close. It was of the local area, what the French call a *department*. Alencourt was directly in the center of the department, but all around were other towns, villages and communes. Like Gravins, Lascombe, and Sevenans. The river was named *Le Menthon*, and flowed through the department in a diagonal line from north-east to south-west. Vaugeois had made little marks around the map. Circles were drawn in colored pencil.

I stepped all the way back to the desk again and got the big picture. The bookshelf itself was a map of the local department. In the middle of it were documents and texts relating to Alencourt. Then the river areas continued on either side, top-right and bottom-left. Top and bottom were books and documents relating to the north and south of the department, and so on. The bookshelf was a map. Maps within a map.

To my left, another wall of books. Legal texts, all of them. Vaugeois had been a lawyer, so that made sense. Lawyers have to memorize stuff, that's their job. The law is written down, it's a book. Lawyers need to know that book by heart. The best lawyers can memorize and think at the same time, the worst lawyers can only memorize and repeat.

I turned left again, like a compass needle, and found myself facing the door. The bookshelf was narrower, accommodating the doorframe, but still ran from floor to ceiling. It was a collection of books from a series. The spines were all the same width. Multi-colored volumes in bright hues. I tilted my head sideways. It was an adventure book series from the nineteen-fifties and early sixties. Explorers and train robbers, spies and crooks. This was Gilles' collection of nostalgic books from his childhood.

I inserted my finger on top of a red book spine, so as to pull the book out by tilting it towards me. Instead of one book tilting down, the entire central section came out. Because they weren't actually books, it was a hidden panel made of fake book spines that came down on well-oiled hinges and laid flat against the wall, revealing a heavy safe with a dial set in the middle of it. The safe was a *Fichet-Bauche*. Old and sturdy French strong box, all steel and painted glossy gunmetal gray. The dial was made of the same material, painted black with shiny metal markings and lines. The box was flat and blunt. Just the dial and a handle protruding from steel.

I got down to the level of the dial and turned it. The spindle rotated with no resistance. Just enough play to be accurate and fast. A very fine object. I'd seen movies where safe crackers dialed open the combination lock by listening to the sounds the wheels made as it spun around the numbers. I put my ear close and worked the spindle back and forth, nice and easy. I couldn't hear anything special. Just the sound of perfectly machined steel whirring against perfectly machined steel. So it wasn't going to be like in the movies.

And then I heard breathing, turned, and saw that the library door was slightly open. I'd had my ear to the dial, hadn't noticed.

I waited. Nothing happened, no sound, no movement. The door was to my left, so I pulled it towards me, and looked around it. Gilles Vaugeois was hanging on to the door jamb. He was looking haggard, like climbing the steps to the second floor had taken out whatever juice he had left in him. And now he was even more of a scarecrow than before. He was dressed in thin cotton pajamas that hung badly from his body.

I put my arms around his narrow waist and lifted him off the ground and then shouldered him. I softened the impact when I took his weight, but I could still hear the whoosh of air from his lungs as he came to rest. I carried him, his heart beating like a sparrow against my upper arm, and placed the old guy carefully in one of the leather chairs, supporting the back of his neck with my left hand. I allowed his head to lapse against the cushioned backrest. His breathing was shallow but fast.

I closed the library door. The latch snicked into place.

I went back and crouched at his level. His eyes were open, looking right at the safe in the middle of the bookshelf. His eyelids hung loose. I stood aside. He was staring at the safe and breathing hard. I stepped back in front of him and got down.

I said, "What's the combination?"

Nothing. No movement. Not a twitch, not a sign.

I took his head in both of my hands and looked at him. The bones of his skull were just beneath the surface. His skin was velvety smooth and felt like worn paper. I said, "You have to relax now. Just breathe."

Nothing changed on his face, but the breathing slowed down. His eyes were unmoving in their sockets, but they gleamed with life. I put my forehead to his, until we were touching.

"Relax now. Just relax." I felt his head lean into the chair as he allowed himself to be held. His eyes shifted ever so slightly, unfocused. I closed my eyes and counted to thirty. Then I opened my eyes and was looking directly into his from inches away.

They had focused.

"What's the combination?"

Vaugeois' left eye blinked three times in rapid succession.

I said, "Three."

Nothing. No movement. Vaugeois was as still as a lake on a windless day. Then his left eye blinked again. Three times in rapid succession. I retrieved the notepad and pencil from his desk drawer. Came back around and wrote '33' on the top sheet of paper. Then his right eye blinked four times. Then two. I wrote the numbers down on the pad, '33-42'. Vaugeois' eyeballs rolled back into his skull and he trembled. I figured he was working hard. Each wink was costing him, big time. I got back down in front of him.

"Come on buddy, push through."

His left eye blinked, nine times. Then eight.

"33-42-98."

Vaugeois closed his eyes and an involuntary sigh came out of him, like air escaping from an inflated plastic bag.

CHAPTER FORTY

33-42-98.

I spun the dial a couple of times to the left, then a couple of times to the right, to clear the lock. I tried to remember which direction these things usually go. I figured, right, left, right. But then I realized that Vaugeois had used both his left and his right eyelid. Left first, then right, then left.

I turned the tumbler left to 33, right to 42, then left to 98.

And it didn't open.

Then I tried left to 33, right all the way past 33 again until it hit 42 for the second time, then left to 98.

No dice.

I'd done it before, with other locks. Regular combination locks in the army, for lockers. I reached back and summoned the old muscle memory. Three times to the right, stopped at 33. Left once, did a complete turn past 33 and hit 42. Left again, straight on to 98. It made sense, in a muscle memory kind of way.

Nothing.

Then I did exactly the same thing, but the other way.

Left three times to 33. Right once, past 33 to 42. Left directly to 98.

Bingo. The catch released, steel whispered on perfectly machined steel. I turned the handle and the safe opened.

The interior was matte white. There was an object inside, smack in the middle. A thick volume. It had a plain cover of cream-colored card. I carried it over to the desk and set it down. I lifted the front cover to take a look, but Vaugeois was moaning. He was agitated in his chair, staring at the safe. His eyes were bulging. Froth was forming on the edges of his mouth. I looked in the safe. I had thought it was empty but it wasn't. At the bottom was a metal lock-box with a handle, the same width and color as the safe's interior. It had blended in and I hadn't noticed. The lock-box was made of steel and painted white, with a small key hole in the front of it.

Vaugeois was making noises. He was agitated. I took out the box and showed it to him.

"This. You want me to open it."

He made gurgling sounds. His eyes were rolling back in his head again and his lips were distorting into a frantic grimace. I remembered the skeleton key in the back of the cutlery drawer.

I said, "The key. I'm going to get it." He collapsed into a pile on the chair. Breathing heavily, but relieved. His eyes closed.

I crept down to the drawing room, stepping on the outside edges of the stairs. Removed the heavy cutlery drawer, set it down and recovered the small skeleton key from the strip of duct tape stuck to the back. I pocketed the key and put the drawer back.

Up in the library, I eased the door shut again. Vaugeois was conscious. He was as alert as I had ever seen him. I showed him the key. "I've got you, old buddy. I'm going to open this up for you."

He moaned and blinked both of his eyes twice, nice and steadily. I said, "Two."

He made a moaning sound and his eyes bulged. I said, "Not two."

He blinked both eyes again, steadily. "B?"

He was calm, which I figured meant yes. I wrote on the pad, 'B'.

I looked at him. He blinked his eyes twenty one times in a row. I wrote on the pad, 'U'.

He blinked his eyes eighteen times in a row. I wrote 'R'.

He blinked his eyes fourteen times in a row. I wrote 'N'.

I said, "You want me to burn it. Whatever it is in the box."

Vaugeois looked at me with no expression. His face was entirely slack, like he had nothing left to give. No strength at all. I said, "You speak English." Up until this point we had been using French. His mouth curled up into a crooked smile.

I put the key into the box and opened it.

There were five or six photographs. They were pictures of a woman, taken a long time before. She was young, in her thirties and very beautiful. It wasn't Simone Vaugeois, but someone else. Maybe from the islands or some French colony. No idea, I was just guessing. In one of the pictures she was looking directly into the camera. Her face was so beautiful that it was easy to miss the fact that she was naked and covering herself with the bed sheet. Gilles had taken that photograph. He had been there with his lover. He wanted me to burn the photos so that Simone would never find them. He knew that unless the photographs were burned she would eventually open the box and find them. He was protecting her from the knowledge of an infidelity.

I didn't judge. I found a box of fancy matches in the cigar drawer. I took the office garbage can and put it on the desk. Then one by one I set fire to each of the photographs. Gilles watched as the pictures burned. One by one the images of his beautiful young lover took flame and were consumed until all that was left was a pile of warm ash. As they burned, I dropped the corners into the garbage can.

When I was finished, he looked deflated. Worse than I'd ever seen. It was like from one minute to the next he had aged an extra decade. I picked up the cream-colored volume from the desk and brought it over to the other leather chair. Switched on the reading lamp. Then I sat down and opened up the secret book from Vaugeois' safe.

It was a hand-written and sketched account of the system of caverns, caves, tunnels, and limestone passages hidden under Alencourt and the department surrounding the town. There was a history and an archaeology of the underground city. There were pages and pages of drawings and diagrams showing depth and distance, connecting tunnels and larger caverns. Some tunnels connected, others missed connecting by only several feet of raw stone.

It was a life's work. Gilles Vaugeois' life's work.

I read the whole thing, from beginning to end, and tried my best to understand it. Gilles slept as I read. I had to stand up and consult other volumes in the main bookshelf. Maps of the region that laid out context for the caverns. Surface charts that allowed me to understand the logic of the system. Or as much of it as I could figure. It took all the rest of the night.

Afterwards, I put the volume back in the safe and closed it. Spun the dial to scramble the lock and closed the fake book panel. I memorized the combination and burned the note paper. Then I carried Vaugeois downstairs over my shoulder. And put him to bed next to his quietly snoring wife.

Nazari was asleep, and she had no clothes on. I took mine off and slipped back under the covers, careful not to wake her. But I failed and she woke. Although not entirely. A little bit, but not all the way. Enough to use her sense of touch and smell and maybe other senses that I wouldn't know about first hand because they were all hers. But it was enough to get us started all over again. As if the passage between this time and last time had just been an interlude between movements of a single orchestration. Which in a way it had been. And this time it was all slow and quiet and sleepy, just as good as last time if not much better.

Afterwards we lay on our backs looking up at the ceiling, dark except for a couple of streaking moonlight reflections coming in through the window. They started as thin points of light and spread wider as they crossed the room. We'd neglected to draw the curtains all the way. The blue of dawn was just beginning to show.

Across the room, something buzzed, like a dentist's drill. Light from the burner phone shone through my discarded pants pocket. The phone vibrated a couple more times before I reacted. I stretched out to where I'd dropped my clothes and after fumbling around with it, fished out the burner. I showed the screen to her. *Unknown Number*. She nodded, silently.

I pressed the green button but it was too late, the other side had hung up, or had been redirected to voicemail. The only thing that showed on the screen was the call record.

Unknown Number.

CHAPTER FORTY-ONE

I SLEPT for a couple of hours and woke up hungry. Nazari wasn't in bed.

So I went downstairs, following a trail of breakfast smells. They were good smells. The kind of smell you hoped for, waking up in the morning. Bacon, freshly baked pastries, coffee. Nazari and Madame Vaugeois were in the kitchen. The oven was on and I looked through the glass door. Croissants.

I hadn't had many opportunities to eat croissants as a search and rescue operator. We lived on base most of the time, and there weren't any croissants. Other times we lived outdoors, in a range of climates and locations. No croissants there either. We ate a large portion of our meals out of bags in fact, they call them MREs, meals ready to eat. Ready to eat military meals don't usually feature flaky crusts and hot, soft interiors. Mostly we root around in the bag until we're done, which doesn't take long. Early in my first Afghanistan tour one French ration could be traded for five US MREs. Which is just one reason why I fisted one croissant after another into my mouth with no shame at all. I washed them down with strong black coffee that Nazari had brewed.

Simone was delighted to serve us eggs and bacon after that, and to keep it coming with more coffee. I didn't speak much while we ate but noticed that Nazari wasn't in uniform.

"Not going to work?"

"I called in sick. Today we do leg work on the vehicles."

Nazari fixed up her laptop computer with the internet connection at Brumaire. She said that we would start by doing research on the companies that had registered the cleaner's Ford van and the Chinese refrigerated meat truck.

Then we'd move on to the blue Opel Corsa, and the company it had been rented from. Then we'd see.

We setup Nazari's laptop on the big table in the drawing room. She tapped on the keys for a while and then we both leaned over the screen and read the results. After that we did the same thing again. In the French system, basic corporate information is available to anyone on the internet. So we were able to see that both Argo Enterprises, and Gilbert and Sons were corporations registered in Paris. And that the Paris address for both was the same.

Nazari said, "It's going to be a post office box."

"Can we find out who owns the companies?"

"I'd have to go to Paris and look through the public records. They haven't made everything available online."

"I thought the whole world had been scanned and printed back onto the internet, or whatever they do."

"Not yet, at least I don't think so."

"Anyone you can call?"

She leaned back. "You know they're both going to be owned by another shell company registered in Lichtenstein or Panama."

"And?"

"More leg work. They design shell company structures so that it takes years to track down the basic information."

"They buy time by buying financial advisors."

"Something like that. They hire experts to obscure the traces. The experts use computers and the internet to bury the companies in a bunch of other companies, with different owners and cutouts all over the world, in jurisdictions that don't talk to each other. Across borders. In the end it's all one person, or one group of people that own everything. If we had a team of computer guys we could do it. As it stands, we don't."

Nazari was right. We might find that information from another direction, but at the moment the vehicles were a dead end.

"What about the car rental in Lille? We could track down the Opel instead."

Nazari tapped some keys. The rental agency in Lille wasn't a large global franchise like Avis or Hertz, it was a local company, Pegasus Auto Leasing. She said, "They're not going to tell us who rented the car over the phone. That's confidential information."

I said, "So let's go to Lille, not just over the phone but in real life, in person. I like that way better. I can be very persuasive in person, face to face."

She laughed lightly, as if that were a joke. "What are you going to do when we get there?"

"We'll see."

"Seriously?"

"Yes, seriously. I'll think of something."

"Like what?"

"I don't know yet. We'll improvise."

We hit the road. On the way to Lille I pulled off the highway into a big-box store parking lot. Nazari looked at me curiously but didn't say anything. She stayed in the car. I bought duct tape, a baseball hat, hoodie, new tracksuit pants and a pair of sneakers two sizes too big for me. All of that was in black. She shook her head when I came back to the car, but she was smiling at the same time.

"What's the tape for?"

"There's always a good reason to have duct tape around. I've been missing it, to tell the truth."

My plan was to get access to the computer once we got to the rental agency. I was going to wait until their lunch break, hide in the bathroom. But it didn't work out that way. Pegasus Auto Leasing was not a car rental place, it was a small office with nothing but a guy taking messages for a whole bunch of shell companies. I asked Nazari if we could trace the companies. She said good and persistent investigators could usually find out, but it might take a couple of years.

We were walking out of the office, with nothing to show for the trip. A lot of expectations, but no results. It was disappointing. And then the burner phone in my pocket vibrated again. In the noiseless corridor, the discreet ring sounded like a stone cutting saw going through granite. This time I got the phone out in time and pressed the green button.

CHAPTER FORTY-TWO

I PUT the phone to my ear.

"Keeler."

At first there was only noise. Like helicopter rotors chopping air. It was a muffled noise, as if the phone on the other side wasn't capable of handling the amplitude.

My intelligence officer friend Blomstein spoke. "Keeler. I tried calling before."

"I was busy."

"I've been busy too."

"With the guy's face I hope."

There was a pause. Blomstein trying to decide what to tell me. He settled for something about nothing.

"I didn't run the face yet. I've been busy. But I took a look at the pictures."

"I'm listening."

"That's why I was trying to call you. To tell you what I thought, initially, off the top of my head. Which might be important to you, before I get the face run properly."

"I'm still listening."

Now it was Nazari's turn to listen in on a one-sided conversation. Blomstein hadn't run the Afghan's face, but he'd flipped through the photos that Nazari had taken on her phone. He'd taken one look at the tattoo photo and called me, except I hadn't answered, until now.

Nazari was leaning against the wall and paying attention. I didn't say much. Just a couple of grunts and appreciative noises. Blomstein was full of interesting information. He wasn't reading from a computer or anything. He was improvising from memory, a smart guy.

He talked for quite a while. He told me all kinds of things. Some of which I already knew. Some of which I didn't already know. When he was done I said, "Roger that."

Blomstein said, "I'm going to run your pictures through the computer in four hours."

"Appreciate it, Blomstein."

Then I hung up and Nazari said, "So?"

"Hundred yard rule."

We walked out of the building. Crossed the street and took a right towards the Lilles train station. There was a guy selling pressed sandwiches out of a van. We bought a couple of those and sat on a concrete cube in the middle of the square.

"It was my guy."

"That was fast."

"It's not about the face. He didn't run the face yet. It's about the tattoo, it got his attention. Maybe we'll get something on the face later."

"So what about the tattoo?"

"Iraq. You ever heard of the Ba'ath party?"

"Is that a gentleman's club?"

"It's not how it sounds. It isn't a spa thing, it's a Middle Eastern politics thing. Ba'ath means something related to the Koran, but this isn't a religious thing either. More like a military dictatorship thing. Ba'ath was a political party in Iraq that we put out of business when we went in there in 2003. The Ba'ath party were die-hard Saddam loyalists. They were his people."

"Hold up, Iraq, not Afghanistan."

"Correct. Baathists were the ruling party in Iraq. This has nothing to do with Afghanistan. Guess what the Iraqi Ba'ath party slogan was."

"Unity, Liberty, Socialism."

"Correct. Same as the tattoo."

"So Qayoumi isn't an Afghani asylum seeker, he's Iraqi. And his name's not Qayoumi. The asylum seeker papers are fake?"

"That's what my guy is suggesting."

"And he came to this conclusion based upon a three-word tattoo. What if Qayoumi was just a fan of the Ba'ath party?"

I nodded. That was a valid point, given the information that I had just given her. I tore off a corner of my sandwich and wolfed it down. "Good question, but there's more. The tattoo isn't just the three words. There's a line and three dots on top of it. What my guy was really excited about was the line and the three dots. The words are interesting, the line and three dots put it over the edge. They signify tribe and clan affiliation. And our guy was from the same clan and tribe as Saddam Hussein."

She whistled. "Old-school ruling class."

"Hard core Saddam guy."

"So why is a hard core Saddam loyalist now a dead Afghan asylum seeker in France?"

"We don't know, but if the dead guy was Iraqi ruling class, penny to a dollar he'll feature in a US military database."

We ate the sandwiches. I got us coffee and brownies from another guy in a truck. Brought them back and sat down again.

I said, "I wonder though, about the body in the morgue."

"How so?"

"Let me give you some context."

"Go for it."

"Alright. I got to Iraq for the first time in 2006, and stayed there, for a couple of years. Back in 06 we were dealing with what they called 'the insurgency', basically patriotic Iraqis who didn't want us there, saw us as occupiers or whatever and wanted to kill any American they could find. Pretty much how I would be if the whole thing was flipped around. So our job was to take them out, which we did. One at a time or many at the same time, didn't matter."

"It was war."

"But it wasn't easy to know who was who, and what they were doing before or after the US invasion. So we cast a wide net, took thousands of them in for interrogation, which sometimes lasted years. Top of the list, the first guys we looked at, were Iraqi ex-military and Ba'ath party members. You ever hear of a place called Abu Ghraib?"

"Nope."

"Notorious prison in Iraq. Saddam had fifteen thousand political prisoners in there at the height of his dictatorship. There was routine torture and weekly executions. When we threw Saddam out, we took over the prison. First thing we did was kick every Ba'ath party member we could find out of the military. Then, like I said, we put them into jail.

"A lot of them stayed there for years. Some of them ended up establishing this little club called ISIS that you may have heard of. They called Abu Ghraib a terrorist university. It didn't help that our prison guards were torturing the inmates.

"Anyway, the point is that our man Qayoumi, who is not Qayoumi, if he was a Ba'ath party member from Saddam's tribe and clan, there is almost no chance that he did not pass through a military interrogation at some point. Whatever he became afterwards, over the years, regardless if he is a dentist, a birthday party clown, or a barber, he'd have experience of running away, maybe fighting, definitely hiding."

"Like a veteran prisoner."

"Like a cross between a combat soldier, a hard-timer, and an urban guerrilla fighter, yes."

"So what's your point?"

"What I'm trying to say, is that a purely external examination won't do. Not in this instance."

"You think they should do an internal autopsy, cut him open and look inside? I don't understand what that would bring to the table."

"No saws, no knives, no cutting anyone open. I'm not advocating that."

"What then?"

"Where do guys hide stuff when they're in jail?"

She chewed her sandwich for a second, looking into space. "Where the sun never shines."

"Yup. Where the sun don't shine."

"So you want to go looking in this dead guy's ass."

"I'm afraid so."

She thought about it for a minute and finished her sandwich.

"Ok. We can do that." She stood up, brushing crumbs from her clothing.

The Lille train station had a big old clock built into the steeple piled on top of the yellowing stone structure. The hour hand was at one p.m., not that far from the two.

I said, "There's another thing I want to do first though. Do you know how to get to the migrant camp near Calais? I went there the other day with Father Bousquet and Miriam."

Nazari nodded. "Sure. I can get us there."

"On the way?"

"Not exactly, but only an hour out of the way, give or take traffic." She looked at her phone. "Why do you want to go to the camp?"

"I'll show you when we get there."

CHAPTER FORTY-THREE

I CHANGED out of the big sneakers and threw them in the bag with the duct tape. We decided that I'd drive, and Nazari would navigate with her phone. She said, "Scenic route or the highway. Three or four minute difference."

"What are we talking about, in terms of scenery?"

"I think the choice is between flat fields and more flat fields."

"Let's do the flat field route then."

She laughed. "So many choices."

She was right, the road from Lille to the Calais area was nothing but flat fields in all directions. I held the wheel lightly, scanning the road. Near and far, using my peripheral vision and an intuitive sense of distance and proximity. I felt alert and sharp. No problem. Things were shaping up now, a resolution was vaguely in sight.

I pictured Blomstein in the chopper. Knowing him, he'd insisted on joining a mission. Intelligence officers don't usually go boots down, but Blomstein liked to, whenever he had the chance, which was not often enough for him. The guy looked like a GI Joe action figure, six-five and racked, with cropped blond hair and high cheekbones. He'd chosen to go intel officer because it interested him.

Before transitioning into that he'd done a long stint enlisted with Delta.

I didn't know if we were on the scenic route, or the non-scenic route, but the route was flat, with a heavy dose of yellow rapeseed fields. The oil-bearing flowers were a golden carpet, until Nazari directed me off the highway and the round grassy island of a traffic circle loomed ahead. Like the last time with Miriam and Father Bousquet, we took the second exit, and the rapeseed fields disappeared, replaced by low green crops.

We hit the departmental road until it entered the piney forest, with sandy soil peeping out from under bushes and scrub. I had the windows rolled down and the smell of pine was clear and pleasant, as was the fresh warm breeze. I looked over at Nazari and saw that she too had her face in the wind, enjoying it, letting her hair whip around. She glanced back to me, and it was like I'd caught her in an unguarded moment, but that wasn't a problem. She liked it. She grinned at me and I felt an enormous surge of good feeling and power. Whatever we were facing, bring it on. I grinned back and let out a loud and sustained whoop. She joined me and we howled like wolves, speeding through the pine forest.

Then we started seeing people walking along the road and sobered up. They looked dispossessed, carrying precious items like plastic water containers and wash tubs in primary colors that would have been insignificant, or easily replaceable for most citizens with the right documents. We started seeing tents and then more tents, clustered together in little groups.

"Here we are." She was scanning through the window.

I spotted the wood-framed cabin headquarters of the *Fondation D'Accueil*. I slowed the Peugeot down as we approached. The cabin was closed, with a padlocked door. The fresh water tank was open for business however, a dozen camp dwellers made an orderly line to fill their containers. I said, "Let me just see up ahead."

I was looking for a left turn off the main path, into the forest. I wanted to find the group of tents belonging to those migrants brought here by the *Les Brosses* crew. After a couple hundred yards I gave up and pulled the Peugeot to the side. Nazari looked at me. I switched off the ignition. We got out of the car and locked it up. "C'mon."

I walked into the forest with Nazari following closely. The tents were grouped in clusters. We nodded to folks, who sometimes nodded back, sometimes said hello in French, or sometimes in English. I was scanning up ahead and after a while I saw the road that the Sprinter van had taken, pretty much parallel to the route by which we had entered. When we got to it I was initially uncertain which way to turn, left or right. There was no sign of the cluster of small tents from before.

Those tents had been hiking tents, one or two-man shelters. I turned left intuitively. We walked along the gravel and sand trail for a minute or two. Nazari said, "What are we looking for?"

"A bunch of tents, small ones. One or two-man."

After a while I noticed something red through the woods. We got closer and I saw a red cord strung up between two trees. I recognized it from the other day, when sleeping bags had been hung up to air on it. The tents were gone but they'd left the cord. Probably because it was knotted badly and they hadn't bothered to cut it down. I slowed. "The tents were here but now they're gone."

We stood around looking at nothing. Across the trail and into the forest, in the main part of the camp, a couple of guys were sitting around a small fire outside a semi-circle of tents. They were looking at us. I walked over.

"Speak French or English?"

They were young, in their twenties. They all nodded. The guy in the middle was tall and heavily built, he said, "French, English, Arabic, Swahili. We've got it all covered, friend, you choose."

I spoke in French for Nazari's benefit. "There were some guys camped over there. Do you know where they went?"

The guy clammed up and his buddies looked away from us, avoiding eye contact. I said, "Calm down guys, no trouble. I just wanted to speak with them. Now I see that they're gone and I wondered if you knew anything that could help me. I'm not police."

"So what are you?" The big guy was tapping the fire with a stick. Sparks flew up.

"I'm just a guy, like you're just a guy."

"They left yesterday, for the other side." He indicated the direction of the English Channel.

"All of them at once?"

"That's right. They had money. If I had money I'd be gone, like them."

"So what, they just pay the fare and get across?"

"No problem. You have money you get a ride on the cruise ship, it's no problem. Those guys you're looking for, they were on a guided tour. An all-expenses paid package."

One of the other guys agreed. He swept his hand around, indicating the camp. "All of us here, we're here because we don't have money. That's why we're in this place."

"Did you speak with them, while they were here?"

"Not a word. They kept to themselves. Not a single hello or nothing." He shook his head.

Nazari asked, "Who took them?"

The three guys went silent and shrugged in unison, like a choreographed movement. The big guy in the middle spoke finally. "They were gone when we woke up. People who leave here, usually do so before dawn, if you know what I mean."

I nodded. "Yeah I can understand that. Early wake up, even on cruise ships."

"Why are you interested in those lucky tourists?"

"I wanted to talk with them, ask them some questions."

"You can ask us questions if you like. We're in no rush, we've got all day." He smiled.

The other guys smiled too. "No rush at all. Ask away."

I said, "I'd love to stay and chat, friends, but I need some specific information that only those men would be able to give me. It's not about this place, it's about something else."

The big guy shrugged. "Just trying to help."

"I appreciate that. Thanks, and have a great day."

"We'll do our best."

We walked back to the trail. The red cord was bright against the green and brown forest colors. I heard the sound of snapping twigs behind me, so I turned. The big guy was approaching. He was taller than I had thought. He said, "One thing though, if you want my impression. There was something that stuck out about those guys, more than anything else."

Nazari spoke first. "What's that?"

"They were dusty."

"How do you mean dusty?"

The big guy stepped onto the sand and gravel trail and squatted down. He pointed to the ground. "See that? It hasn't rained for a few days, so you can still see the dust they had on them."

I recalled the migrants emerging from the back of the Mercedes Sprinter van, brushing off dust from their clothing and footwear. The big guy was pointing to a layer of fine, light-colored dust that remained on the surface of the trail. The *Les Brosses* guys must have swept out the van before departing, because there was still quite a lot of it. I figured we were very lucky, because even a small amount of wind would have dispersed the stuff.

I joined the guy and scooped some of it into my hand. It was soft and powdery. I said, "What do you think it is?"

He bobbed his head. "I worked in a quarry back home when I was a kid and we got that stuff all over us. Stone dust." He circled the dust against his fingertips.

I said, "Stone dust, I think you're right about that." I looked up at Nazari. She was staring down at the dust. "It makes sense in a way."

She said, "Stone, like from caves?"

I brushed the stuff off my palm. "That's what I'm thinking. Stone from the caves."

CHAPTER FORTY-FOUR

THIS TIME, Nazari drove.

The Peugeot hummed along, a collection of well machined objects spinning and firing off together, like a good musical ensemble. She said that we'd just about make it to the medical examiner's office before they closed, which was around five. We talked about dust. I told her about my night in Gilles' library, reading through his life's work on the system of stone caverns around Alencourt.

She was fascinated. "So you're thinking there's a connection. Vaugeois, the crew from *Les Brosses*, migrant trafficking and underground caves."

"Yup. Clear connection. Maybe they had the migrants hiding out in one of those caves or something. I don't know. We'll have to see."

"And maybe Vaugeois was caught up in it with them. Was complicit in whatever they were up to with the migrant trafficking. Maybe that's why they attacked him."

"Sure, that's possible. Although I don't think so."

"Why's that?"

"A feeling."

"So you want to go poking around all the caves of Alencourt? You won't make it in a lifetime, there's too much of it."

"Yeah I know. I think I want to go looking around in the basement of Brumaire though." I glanced at Nazari. "Do you remember? The basement door where the Vaugeois' gardener and cleaning lady were arguing."

She blushed. "When we were in Vaugeois' bedroom. And had to wait for Madame Vaugeois' live-in help to leave before coming out, yes." She looked at me. "You think there's a cave down there, or migrants hiding or something?"

"Not sure, but I'd like to take a look."

The medical examiner's office was a regional morgue that served the area including Alencourt. It was situated on the outskirts of a large cemetery, about six miles north-east of town. The building was a two-story cement cube in white. At the front, chrome rails surrounded a ramp that I assumed was used for wheeling bodies in. I guess they wheeled them out afterwards too, unless they had been subjected to an internal autopsy, in which case they might be delivered out in a box.

The medical examiner was a friendly guy with curly black hair and glasses. We met him in his office and Nazari introduced him as Dr. Amin. The two of them were chummy, kidding each other right off the bat. From their banter I deduced that they'd known each other for a while, like a childhood thing. Amin was a couple years older. After the jokes died down, Dr Amin said, "I'm guessing you two are here regarding the dead asylum seeker, the one you called me about."

Nazari coughed. "Right. Can we see the body?"

Dr Amin looked at me, then back at Nazari, peering over round John Lennon glasses. "Really?"

She kept up the confident bluff. "Yes. Really."

He shrugged. "Ok then, follow me. There isn't a hell of a lot to see."

Neither one of us commented. Amin led us down a corridor, past the receptionist, down a stairwell and into the basement. The temperature dropped several degrees. He saw that we were shivering, "Yeah. Cold down here. Should have called ahead, I would have told you to bring a coat."

The morgue was colder yet. It was a large room with an L-shaped stainless steel work area in the middle of it. The work surface looked like a restaurant kitchen counter and sink, except it was made for a different purpose. One side of the L was a flat, rectangular steel plane where the corpse went. The other surface was the same size, except it was divided into a deeper section, and a shallow shelf. I guessed that this was where they placed organs and whatever else they found in the corpses. Two walls were taken up by a desk, the third wall had two square refrigerator doors built in to it.

Dr. Amin wheeled a gurney over to one of the square refrigerator doors. "You sure you want to see this?"

Nazari nodded. Amin opened the door, which made a sucking sound as the seals released. The corpse was in a translucent gray bag made of an expensive-looking polymer. The body was on a shelf that slid out on well-greased bearings to the gurney. Dr Amin rolled the gurney over to us, then went back to close the refrigerator door. I looked at Nazari meaningfully, she looked back at me. Amin saw the look. He wasn't smiling. He said, "What is it?"

Nazari said, "Maybe you and Keeler should step out for a minute and grab a cup of coffee."

Dr Amin's face aged a couple of years. "How's that?"

She didn't say anything, she just looked at him, like staring him down. Whatever the relationship was between these two, it ran deep. I looked at the floor. I studied the tiles and the way they were put together. Meanwhile, I figured there were significant looks and maybe eyebrows raised. Maybe words were mouthed, I wouldn't know. It wasn't my business. There was no sound.

After a while, Dr Amin got moving. Nazari grabbed a pair of latex gloves from a dispenser. I followed the doctor to the coffee machine.

CHAPTER FORTY-FIVE

Dr. Amin walked in front of me, moving with his head down. I caught up with him at the coffee machine. He looked at me with morose eyes. "Want one?"

"Thanks. Black no sugar."

He nodded. "When I was a kid she scared me. Now she's just really impressive. You know that she's going to do the BRI exam."

"She told me, yes."

Dr Amin was looking at me intensely. "She'll ace that. Cecile came in here for three weeks. Watched us work and only puked twice. First and second time she came. After that, all business. Never saw that before. I puked for about six months straight. Almost quit actually." He handed me a cup of coffee.

I took it from him. "You get used to it?"

"Eventually," he agreed. "After a week she was assisting me. That woman knows what she wants."

I switched subjects. "Did you do examinations on the axe murders?"

He nodded. "Houdin family, and now Rigalle. Yes."

"Anything out of the ordinary?"

"Besides the fact that two entire families were hacked to pieces and piled on the living room rug no, nothing out of the ordinary."

"Cause of death?"

"Strangulation in all cases." He let that sit.

"A rope, or cord?"

"Hands and thumbs."

I pictured the guy in the refrigerated truck, strangling his victims in front of their families, then hacking the bodies into pieces. I pictured the two cleaners helping and observing, aiding and abetting.

I said, "Thumbs."

Amin nodded. "Thumbs."

"You mean the perpetrator was looking at them while he strangled them."

"That's the most likely conclusion, yes. He was standing directly in front of them."

"Let me ask you something else."

"Go ahead."

"What was the order of death? Was it the guy first, then the kids, then the woman, or was it the guy last, kids first, then woman?"

"I get the question, we don't know the answer. The deaths were separated by minutes, not hours. We simply can't know. If it were important, the remains could be sent to Paris for more specialized analysis." Dr Amin pulled his coffee cup from the machine and took a sip. "I just hope they get the guy." I didn't say anything, just sipped my coffee. He shook his head gently. "And the world goes on."

Dr. Amin was an optimist, but I guess you'd have to be, in his job.

Nazari came out of the examination room a few minutes later. She addressed the medical examiner. "All done. Thanks."

"As if I had a choice."

She walked up to him and put her hands on his shoulders. "On this one, none whatsoever. See you around." The doctor received a peck on the cheek. We left him standing, bemused, shaking his head, and in my view, head over heels in love.

"Nice guy."

She nodded. "A sweetheart and a pushover. Always was, always will be."

We were walking out of the building, down the ramp where bodies were transported in and out.

Nazari sat at the wheel of her Peugeot, a safe hundred yards away from the morgue. She dug in her jeans and pulled out a resealable polythene zipper bag from the change pocket. She grasped a corner with two fingers and held it up. "Found it inside of another bag. That one wasn't as clean."

I looked closely. Inside the little plastic bag was a tiny SIM card.

I said, "I know what this is, but not the details of how it works."

She was pulling her own phone out of the other pocket. "There are different phone standards around the world. Most countries use GSM, which stands for Global System for Mobile. GSM takes SIM cards. So this SIM goes into a GSM phone, like mine."

I said, "You can change a SIM card and it's like you've got a different phone, as far as the network is concerned."

"Network sees the SIM card, not the big thing with the screen."

"So it's the brain of the phone and you can replace it."

"Yup. It's the brain of the phone and you can also store stuff on it, instead of storing it on the actual phone."

"What kind of stuff?"

"Phone numbers, contacts, call records, and other stuff, like photos, or files, or even documents I guess. Depends on the memory capacity of the SIM card."

"Did the dead guy have a phone on him?"

"Negative. But since pretty much everyone has a phone, it was assumed stolen. Remember, there was the assumption of robbery."

"Right. Keep going."

"So if I'm correct, and this is a phone SIM card, the dead guy would have kept two of these. I'd guess that the one in his stolen phone corresponds to his identity and cover as an Afghan asylum seeker. Matches up to the identity documents that were found on him. So, maybe this SIM card right here corresponds to his real Iraqi identity, if your theory is correct." She flicked the plastic baggie.

"So the assumption is that he had another one of these in his phone when he was murdered. And it got stolen by the murderers."

"I think that's a reasonable assumption."

"What can we do with that thing?"

"I'm going to see what happens if I put it into my phone."

"Is that safe?"

"Might be safe, might not be safe. No idea."

She removed the SIM card from her phone and put it safely in the tray in front of the Peugeot's gear shifter. She took out the dead man's SIM from the little baggie and slotted it in. The card fit perfectly into the smart phone and made a satisfying click to let us know it was safely seated. She looked at me with eyebrows raised. I said, "So far so good."

She restarted the phone. It took maybe a minute for the thing to turn back on, but it seemed like ten. Anticipation was high. The medical examiner's office sat like a bunker against the wooded backdrop of the cemetery. It was a Catholic cemetery with stone crosses and religious figurines, built to last, unlike the occupants.

The phone made a sound. I looked at Nazari and she nodded. It was her phone restarting. We both watched it, waiting for something to happen. There was no magic, the phone just turned back on. I said, "Is it working?"

She looked at the phone and pointed to the top of the screen. "Working. Got signal and everything."

"Can you see what's on the card?"

"Give me a second." She went into the phone's contacts and things were different. There was only one contact saved to the SIM card, 'Office'. Next to the word was a phone number with a +964 prefix. She went into an internet page and searched '+964 phone prefix'. The search page didn't even wait for her to finish tapping in letters before it spit out a line of text, 'Iraq telephone code 964'.

She tapped around in her phone but couldn't find anything else unusual.

"It's an international SIM card I think."

"What makes you think that?"

"It says so on the network information screen."

"So what does that mean?"

"I'm no expert but I guess it means you can use the SIM card in a bunch of different countries. So if the guy bought it in Iraq he'd be able to use it here or in other countries as long as he'd paid credit onto the card."

"So it's like an international burner phone card or something."

"Something like that. Can't be traced to an individual person."

"You haven't found anything else?"

"No. But I haven't checked too hard. You want to look while I drive? We might be able to plug the SIM card into my computer back at the Vaugeois house."

I took the phone from her and started tapping every icon that I could find. One by one. She got the Peugeot going. The streets and trees and houses rolled by. I clicked through her applications. Most of them asked me to sign back in, as if it wasn't Nazari's phone anymore. I tapped my way patiently through three screens filled with icons. Then I tapped on the notes application icon. A box popped up on the screen asking me if I wanted to import notes from the SIM card. I clicked yes. A little wheel turned in the middle of the screen and then flipped to a list of notes with only one note in the list: 'untitled'. I clicked it and it opened up with a little magnifying animation. As if a piece of notebook paper had grown out of the middle of the phone.

Nazari looked over and saw that there was something. "What is it?"

"Names, seven of them."

"Latin alphabet?"

"Yeah."

"Read them."

I read her the list:

Layan Baqir
Yamina al-Zahawi
Safiya Raena Alshaibi
Nejla Ashkouri
Jamila Alasadi
Maryam Al-Ali
Khawlah al-Baghdadi
She was nodding as she drove. I asked, "Why are you nodding?"
"Those are female names. It's all girls."

CHAPTER FORTY-SIX

I LOOKED at the top right of the phone screen. The time was 6:23 p.m.

I figured Blomstein had run the pictures by now. As if on cue the burner phone in my pocket made a little buzzy twitch.

I pulled it out and saw a message: *1/3 Your man is Iraqi ex-Ba'ath military intelligence: Abd al-Karim Qadduri. Not a person of interest at this time.* Before I had time to consider that, the phone made another buzzy twitch, this time in my hand. A second message animated on to the screen, pushing the first down: *2/3 Search threw up a Bogie. Don't know why, as Qadduri is not POI.* Then, a third message dropped down with another buzz pushing the two previous messages to the bottom: *3/3 De Oppresso Liber. - B.*

I looked down at the phone and quickly decoded the messages in my head. It confirmed that the dead Afghan wasn't an Afghan, he was an Iraqi guy called Qadduri. And Qadduri wasn't a person of interest, or POI. But doing the search had thrown up a warning message on the system. *De Oppresso Liber* is a Special Forces motto, something about liberating the oppressed, in Latin. Which meant good luck and goodbye.

Nazari was curious. I said, "It was my guy. We've got the dead man." I read off the screen, "Abd al-Karim Qadduri. Ex-Ba'ath, Iraqi military intelligence." She whistled. I said, "Not a person of interest at this time."

"Meaning?"

"Meaning Qadduri is thought to have moved on from his past as a Ba'ath party guy."

I had a phone in each hand. My left held the burner. In my right hand Nazari's phone was heavier, and still had the SIM card we'd found on the dead guy, whose name was apparently Qadduri. "I'm calling the number."

I tapped on the one and only contact registered on the SIM card. 'Office', the +964 Iraq number. The phone dialed it automatically. Nazari said, "Put it on speaker." I handed her the phone and she tapped something. We heard dial tone. Then, the phone gurgled, as if it were being hooked into another network of phone lines. A new dial tone came on. The first one had been long tones, with silence in between. The new pattern was a series of short tones. Like dots on a page. Five dots and then a blank space, then the five dots again.

Then there was a click. A voice spoke in Arabic. I didn't understand a word. The voice was calm and female. Without understanding anything that she said, I picked up qualities in her voice. Not old, not young. Experienced and fluent. Like a string instrument crafted by a master luthier, tuned and played by a veteran performer. There were miles of road behind that voice.

Nazari said, "That's Iraq. It's voicemail. Should I leave a message?"

I said, "Not you, me."

She held the phone for me. I waited for the beeps.

"My name is Keeler. I'm calling from France about Abd al-Karim Qadduri. Call back on this number."

Nazari hung up the phone and put it away. "Think they'll call?"

"I don't know, but I would, if I was worried about a friend or a colleague. I'd call."

"So I should leave the SIM card in my phone?"

"Do you need your phone otherwise?"

"I don't think so, not at the moment, no."

I shrugged and leaned back in the seat. She drove. I closed my eyes and a familiar vertiginous feeling came over me, like I was in free-fall. Just air around me rushing by and time stood still, like I had plenty of time to think. No worries either, because I'd packed my own chute.

I thought about Blomstein's texts, the second one. *Search threw up a Bogie. Don't know why, as Qadduri not POI.*

Blomstein's search had thrown a Bogie, slang for an alert. But a Bogie is an alert that gets automatically triggered when certain very specific search parameters are entered into the military intelligence query system. For example, if a person of interest were involved in a classified operation, a Bogie could be set that would trigger an alert if a search on that person was made.

But if Qadduri wasn't a POI, why the alert?

It didn't take a genius to figure that by now, whoever brought in the cleaners must have known they'd been taken out of the game. And after the little show I made at the police station, it could be they'd send another team for us. Like a last chance charge before full on panic. Because they'd already sent the cleaners for Nazari, it was reasonable to expect that the next team would be a higher grade of paid killer. So all bets were off and it was time to circle the wagons.

I guess Nazari was feeling it too. She turned and said, "Tom, will they come for us?"

I opened my eyes. I felt very calm and at peace. "Could be that they'll try something. Could be that they'll figure to try it here and now."

She nodded. "There's always the possibility that we were caught on camera going into that office in Lille. Either lobby, hallway, office, or all three."

I hadn't thought of that. "True. Time to prepare."

She drove for a while in silence. I closed my eyes again. Then I looked at her. She was gripping the wheel tightly, head tilted forward, eyes staring at the road. I said, "You alright?"

She nodded. "Fine, yes. I was just thinking." She looked over at me, "You remember the Welcome Foundation? *Fondation D'accueil*."

"Father Bousquet's outfit."

"Right, the fundraiser and all that."

"What about it?"

"They deal with migrant issues all the time. That's their thing. We could run the list of names by Father Bousquet, the ones from the phone card. Maybe he'll recognize one of them."

"That's a good idea. And maybe if he doesn't, Miriam will."

She looked over at me again. "Yes. Maybe Father Bousquet is different, but most people around here couldn't remember an Arabic name if their lives depended on it."

"But Miriam might, even though she's from Afghanistan. Similar sounds, related alphabet. Like a French person reading Italian."

"She might, and maybe I'm wrong about Bousquet."

"Because he's been around enough to start to know the difference. I get the problem, it was the same for our guys in the military. At first they couldn't deal with Arabic language names. But once you get involved it changes. When your life depends upon it."

"You mean to say, people are lazy."

"I don't know about lazy. I heard chess grandmasters can lose ten pounds in a big stressful tournament, just sitting around thinking all day. What does that tell you?"

She laughed. "That people aren't lazy?"

I said, "That thinking is hard. You ever see an animal lose weight by thinking?"

"Can't say I have."

"Right, that's because they don't think the same way, not the same kind of cognition. Thinking is hard and we conserve our energy, that's all. So, where do we find Father Bousquet?"

"We could start with his house."

CHAPTER FORTY-SEVEN

FATHER BOUSQUET LIVED on a quiet street of houses cloistered behind walls. From the road we could see the top floor and the roof. Looked big. Nazari parked out front. She didn't bother with knocking, just opened the gate and we stepped through to a scrappy yard.

The house was big and ugly, not built to please, built to house. There were kids running around, little ones, a couple of chickens and a white cat. The cat was rolling in the grass while the chickens pecked.

I looked at Nazari. "Wouldn't have thought that a cat can get along with chickens."

"No, me either. Weird."

"Maybe the cat's a Christian."

A woman was sitting at an old garden table. She was around thirty, her head wrapped in a twist of bright yellow cotton with some kind of orange motif. A phone was tucked into the head wrap. She was speaking rapidly into it while smoking a cigarette. The woman waved at us pleasantly and continued her conversation in what I figured was an African language with tongue clicks. A chicken squawked. I looked for the cat, who was up on the garden wall stretching. Nazari pushed at the door and a bell tinkled.

It was close to dinner time and smells were coming from the back, which I assumed was the kitchen. Two men and a teenage boy were shucking peas. Nazari asked about Bousquet. The guys said we'd find the father upstairs in his study.

We found Father Bousquet sitting at a large and messy desk in the corner of a large and messy room. He was staring into an ancient computer monitor and stabbing at an old keyboard, the plastic yellowed with age. He noticed us and swiveled ninety degrees. He pushed back in the chair.

"Mister Tom Keeler and Mademoiselle Cecile Nazari. Same time, same place." He said the word *mister* in English with an exaggerated French accent. *Meester*. He turned back to Nazari and wagged his eyebrows. "Interesting." Then turned back to me. "And you. Still here." His eyes looked up as he counted something. "Four days, by my reckoning. A regular Alencourt citizen by now."

I nodded. "Yes, sir. Something like that."

Bousquet looked again from one to the other. "Looks like serious business." He pointed to a set of arm chairs either side of a coffee table. "Come, sit, talk."

We sat down. Father Bousquet wheeled his office chair over to us.

"It's close to dinner time. My life is in danger if I'm late, so you'll have to be brief, or come back after."

I said, "We can do both. Remember that thing with the police?"

"I do."

"Well it isn't finished. And it's going to get worse before it gets better."

Bousquet nodded. "That's an accurate description of many phenomena and their relation to time. Has there been trouble?"

"More than a little."

He spoke to Nazari. "Police matter?"

"Not officially."

"That's not good."

She agreed, "No it's really bad. But as Tom said, there has been trouble."

Bousquet pursed his lips. "And there will be more before this is finished. What's it about, in a nutshell?"

Nazari spoke, "Migrants, most likely females."

Father Bousquet looked sad. "The most vulnerable suffer. We must do all that we can to help them."

She held out her phone with the list of names. "Do you recognize any of these names?"

He took the phone from her and looked at it for a while, reading the names out loud in a soft voice.

"Layan Baqir, Yamina al-Zahawi, Safiya Raena Alshaibi, Nejla Ashkouri, Jamila Alasadi, Maryam Al-Ali, Khawlah al-Baghdadi. Beautiful names." He looked up below those massive eyebrows. "Safiya Alshaibi, that rings some kind of a bell." He kicked the wheeled office chair over to the desk, muttering as he rolled. "Problem is the names all sound the same to me still."

He unleashed a flurry of keyboard stabs, like a man who has had a lot of practice in two-fingered typing. "I'm not very good with this computer stuff, but Miriam showed me how to search my emails."

Nazari said, "Do you want me to help you?"

Father Bousquet waved her away. He triggered another machine gun clatter of key clicks. Bousquet looked into the screen. "I don't think it's right no. I've got Safiya Khaled, Safiya Rahal. No other Safiya." He pushed back in his chair and thought for a moment. "Maybe the alphabetical spellings are wrong. The priest launched himself back to the keyboard and typed furiously, biting his lip. I stood up and looked over his shoulder. He was trying different combinations. S'fiya, Sufiya, Safeya. Nothing was working.

I said, "You may want to try that with all the names. Must be multiple spellings of each in the Latin alphabet."

He nodded, looking at the monitor as if staring at it would force the machine to produce something. "That's a good point. Problem is,

I've had Miriam setting up the system. We might need her help if we are to really do this right."

Bousquet turned back to the monitor and resumed his assault on the keyboard. For a while, the clacking of his fingers on the keys was the only sound in the room. Nazari and I just stayed still, watching. I don't know about her, but I was just hoping that he'd squeeze some kind of a breakthrough out of that machine. But it wasn't to be. The dinner bell rang from downstairs, and Bousquet froze in his chair. He swiveled around. "Can you leave me the list?"

Nazari dictated and Father Bousquet copied the list into his computer. When he was finished he turned around again. "I'll show this to Miriam in the morning. Are you still at the Vaugeois house?"

"Yes."

"I can find you there in that case. Perhaps tomorrow morning then."

"I hope so."

"So do I."

We came downstairs with Father Bousquet. As we were leaving, Bousquet began saying grace. The whole extended family chimed in, like a chorus.

Nazari closed the door behind us, but the invocation was still audible as we crossed the yard. It sounded kind of haunting and ghostly in French.

Aide-moi à Te bénir,
et pour celle qui me déplaît
à la manger avec le sourire!
Seigneur, merci pour tous tes bienfaits
et garde ce monde dans Ta paix!
Amen! Merci! Alléluia!

I could hear the kids' voices real loud, really getting into it. I glanced at Nazari, who was looking at me. I figured the grace sounded ghostly because of the storm that we were facing. A warm wind had risen. The leaves were fluttering and the chickens were calm. I felt thrilled and happy.

I looked straight at her and said, "Bring it on."

Her eyes widened in surprise. She said, "You're crazy."

I nodded at her. "I can go into berserker mode."

She was momentarily confused. She had never before been confronted with the realities of impending extreme violence, but I could tell that she was learning, and liking it. She was summoning her warrior spirit. Her eyes met mine. Something sharp and fierce was concentrating in her; she was going through a baptism of fire.

I thought she was beautiful. We kissed in the car for a while, before heading back to the Vaugeois house.

CHAPTER FORTY-EIGHT

THE GATEKEEPER's house was up on the right. The dark green Renault was neatly backed into its spot, so I figured Daniel would be in.

I wanted to talk to the gardener. Nazari let me out, then continued up the drive and parked. The sky was low and grey, threatening to rain. Leaves were rustling in the trees and a small black bird flitted over the vegetable garden. I walked over to the cottage door and knocked. It was a nice little spot. Tucked into the trees. I looked around the building. There were exterior lights hung where the rafters stuck out from the walls. They looked clean.

The door opened. Daniel wore thick Scandinavian socks in black and white wool. He saw me looking at them. "Christmas present last year."

It was warm out. I couldn't imagine wearing wool Christmas socks. I shrugged, pointed at the lights. "These work?"

He came out holding a tea cup. Maybe he'd been watching television or something. He looked up at the lights hung on the outside of the cottage. "Yes. They work." He ducked in behind the door and flicked them on and off.

I said, "Keep them on for a second." He turned the lights on and stepped out.

They were halogen floodlights, angled to project out and down. I felt a drop of rain on my forehead. Daniel noticed. "Rain tonight."

"Heavy?"

"I hope." He was looking at the vegetable garden.

I stepped back to the cottage. "Can you keep the lights on tonight?"

He made a gesture, hands rising up, shoulders shrugging, like that wouldn't be a problem. "Expecting friends?"

"Might be expecting uninvited guests, yes. Just keep them on for me will you?" I wanted the lights on in part to discourage any intruders from coming this direction. It was better to block off a couple of possibilities. Either that or you had to cover all of them. There was a metal outdoor table and chairs painted in white. I dragged a chair under the corner light, "You mind?"

Daniel said, "Yes sure."

I stood on the chair and angled the light so that it would fully cover the driveway. I put the chair back and dusted my hands off. Daniel was amused. "Anything else?"

"Do you have a weapon?"

He paused to sip from his cup and looked up at me while he swallowed. "For hunting birds, but the season doesn't start until September."

"Show me."

He waved me inside. The front door opened directly to a living room area with a sofa and armchair, where I guessed Daniel spent his down-time. The television was on with the sound turned off. The place was immaculately clean and tidy. From behind a bookcase Daniel pulled a canvas and foam rifle bag. I wanted to look at his weapon because then I'd be able to have an idea of his competence and worthiness as an ally. If he pulled out a filthy old gun with cobwebs in the chamber, that would tell one story, as would an immaculately kept piece.

He glanced at me for a reaction as he drew the weapon out of its case. I made a kind of surprised laugh because the gun was a gorgeous French double barrel shotgun with an oiled walnut stock. It was immaculate, and Daniel was proud of it. "Chapuis double barrel. Artisan model." The double chamber snicked open revealing a truly clean interior. "Three inch chamber, double trigger." That was good. No fumbling around for the second barrel if push came to shove.

"Load?"

Daniel pulled a cartridge belt and threw it at me. I caught it and pulled one out. Zenith cartridges, with a 70mm case, a fiber wad and 32-gram load of No 5 shot. "That'll do."

"Do for what?"

"Just in case hunting season opens early this year," I said. "Keep it near tonight."

"And then?"

"And then we'll see."

He examined the gun. "Should I be having Maria stay with her sister tonight?"

"Your call. I can't really say. I'm not going to alarm them." I indicated the main house. "I'll stay up and keep an eye open, just in case."

"Then it might be better if everyone stays as they are, business as usual, so no one gets nervous. I'm guessing you don't want to scare off the birds either."

That was an insightful comment. Daniel cottoned on quick. As far as I was concerned the sooner this got resolved, the better. If I evacuated the civilians, the enemy might notice and come more prepared. If it was business as usual at Brumaire, that would tell another story. "Yep. Could be." I looked outside. It was still bright and sunny out after six p.m. Late June. "What time does it get dark now?"

"Twenty two hundred hours, give or take."

I grunted. If they came, they'd come at night, in which case the window of opportunity for attack would be relatively short. Four, five hours of darkness. No more. "Might be a good idea to take a nap."

Daniel nodded. "Thanks for the advice."

"My pleasure. I'll come down before ten to tuck you in."

I didn't wait for his response, went out and closed the door behind me. Daniel was solid enough. I walked up towards the house. Boots crunching on gravel. I felt energized. The bare limestone cliff face was a straight drop of around fifteen yards. On top there was brush and small trees, going back into the woods.

Nazari was in the dining room setting the table for three. She told me that Maria was giving Gilles a bath. Apparently he wasn't doing very well. I thought about his exertions the other night and how he had gotten all excited. Probably wasn't good for him to get his blood up.

Simone was in the kitchen washing lettuce in a sink filled with water. When I came in to see her, she began talking about the salad. "You see Tom, we use very cold water, you know why?"

"No, ma'am, why?"

"To keep the salad firm. There is nothing worse to a French person than salad that is not firm."

"That makes a lot of sense. Why would anyone like salad that wasn't firm?"

She looked at me strangely. "Are you making fun of me, Tom?"

"Not at all, ma'am."

"Do you like French cheese?"

"Sure."

"Good. Because I went to the cheese shop today."

I let her speak a little longer and observed her, while engaging when I had to. Madame Vaugeois was dealing with the situation by accepting certain things. She accepted that I was there now, helping to resolve a situation that had begun for her with the attack on Gilles in the winter.

I figured that after the attack on her husband, the world had become a frightening and chaotic place. She must have wondered about the attack, and the why and who of it. The buzzing trail bikes would have been no consolation, only an increase in the chaos. After my arrival a semblance of order was being rapidly restored, and I could see that she appreciated that.

Even as she was speaking about something mundane, like cheese and salad, in her eyes I could see trust, almost devotion. She was scared, but dealing with it, which was about all anyone can do. She was counting on me to get her through the situation, to the other side —from chaos to order. There was a lot of pent-up fear and anxiety hiding behind the good humor she showed. Which was understand-able because she had no training, nothing to prepare her for what was going on.

I began thinking of the end game. If anyone came for us tonight, there would be bodies.

When she had finished cleaning and drying the salad, she put the leaves in a bowl and wiped her hands on a dish towel. I said, "Tell me about the basement ma'am."

"The basement. You mean the cave."

I'd forgotten that the French word for basement was cave. "Yes, the cave. You have one?"

"Oh yes. Gilles and Daniel did a real job on it."

"Can I see it?"

"Of course you can, Tom." She opened a cupboard door. The inside of the door was a key rack. She held up a long skeleton key. "Voila. The light is on the inside of the door. Do you know where that is?"

I said that I did.

CHAPTER FORTY-NINE

I WENT BACK past the stairs to the little door in front of Gilles and Simone Vaugeois' bedroom, where Nazari and I had seen Daniel and Maria arguing. The key turned easily.

I flipped the lights. Hardwired wall sconces lined a limestone corridor, illuminating the pale stone. I figured there'd be a lot of similar projects around these parts. Homeowners getting obsessed with stuff wasn't new. Here in France they had all this ancient limestone to preoccupy them.

Simone was right, the basement was a cave. The corridor was almost horizontal, descending gently in the direction of the cliff face beside the house.

I mapped it mentally, based on what I had seen in Gilles' documents. The cave under Brumaire pushed east into rock. From Gille's diagrams I knew that the first excavated area was around thirty yards in, and I wasn't disappointed. A medium-sized room was dedicated to the wine collection. A few hundred bottles stacked in racks on the south side, resting horizontally so that the residue was settled as the bottles were maintained at a temperature of sixty-five degrees year-round. The corridor continued from there, curving to the north twenty degrees so that now the tunnel was running north-east.

That made sense because in the diagrams, the excavation under Brumaire met up eventually with another system of caverns dug under the woods. If this was correct, then Gilles and Daniel had bored out another thirty or forty yards to link up with a big cavern situated beneath the north-east corner of the garden.

I followed the corridor until it opened to an empty blackness. I located the light switch on the inside to the left. I flicked it on and the magnificent vault ceiling was revealed by a dozen strategically placed spots and floods, casting warm light over the white stone ceiling, cross-hatched and scored by mattock blows. Vaugeois had set anchors into the stone every couple of yards to reinforce the structure. This was set up for festive occasions. On one side of the room were folding tables covered in plastic tarps, stacked close to the wall. The air was cool and humid, and smelled musty.

On the other side I spotted a dark tunnel entrance. From the maps I knew that this was the part of the excavation that would eventually lead up to the forest mound entrance. It hadn't been cleaned up. The old tunnel went on for fifteen unlit yards. Over to my right was yet another dark entrance, bigger, and darker. According to Gilles' maps this one went further and longer. It ran along the river bank and ended at some point. The excavation looked rougher, older and less maintained. I walked through it for a while, but it wasn't long before there was nothing to see, no lights, just pure black darkness.

I retraced my steps and returned to the house, switching off the lights and closing and locking the door behind me. It was warmer up top, the kitchen smells wafted around and I was drawn to it, like a bat to flies.

We didn't speak much at dinner, just ate and drank and made small talk. Simone occupied herself with the logistics of it, with Nazari and me helping whenever something needed to be carried. I didn't want to discuss the evening's plans in front of the madame and she seemed to realize that. She went pretty heavy on the red wine and I figured she was dosing herself for an early night.

When we had finished eating, Nazari and I excused ourselves and thanked Simone for dinner.

"You didn't eat much cheese."

"I wasn't terribly hungry, ma'am, I promise to eat more cheese tomorrow."

Nazari went to the bathroom and I walked around to the other side of the house and entered Gilles' library. I flicked on the light and closed the door. Then went around the big desk and pulled open the drawer. The mini-mag light was there waiting. Exactly where it had been before. The batteries had juice. I pocketed the heavy steel thing.

The two Berettas I'd taken from the cleaners' house were still rolled up in a towel, stuffed into the backpack in our room. Nazari came in and sat on the bed quietly while I was crouched over the bag. I handed her one of the pistols. Then I removed the two boxes of ammunition. Each box contained twenty rounds of Speer gold dot 9mm jacketed hollow points. Police classics, and very reliable. The metal jackets were nickel-plated brass. I said, "I'm sure you've seen these before."

She slipped the magazine and started loading. "Just the two boxes?" She didn't waste time asking where I'd gotten them from.

"Yup."

The Berettas were M9s, which was a good thing. The mags were standard and had a fifteen-round capacity plus one in the chamber. So we'd each get a full mag and four extra rounds clinking around in the pocket just in case. I watched as she loaded her gun. When she racked back the slide she let it go without riding it, which was a good sign. The first round chambered with a satisfying snick, as the spring mechanism did its work. I could see the round was chambered because the external extractor was protruding nicely.

She looked up, caught me watching and smiled. "Checking on me."

I shrugged. "Can't help myself."

The M9 has the same double action trigger press as the Sig-Pro in the French police armory, so she'd be good to go with that. Otherwise it would have been a potential issue for her. Double action means that the trigger pull is divided into two parts. The first part cocks the pistol, the second fires it. But that's only for the first shot, subsequent shots are standard single action, until the safety is set again and the whole process repeats. The idea is that, with the double action trigger, distracted people are less likely to accidentally shoot themselves or each other. The first pull requires around nine pounds of finger muscle.

"You know what? I'd feel better if you dry-fired that a couple times." The issue with a double pull is that the shooter tends to miss with the first shot, because the pull is heavier than expected. Then, when the second shot is lighter than the first, the shooter overcompensates and misses again. It was her turn to shrug. She cleared the gun, aimed it down at the floor and dry-fired a few times.

"Heavy pull?"

"First one's a little heavier than the Sig, yeah."

"Thought it'd be slightly different than you're used to."

"I'll be able to hold it down."

"No doubt."

She dry-fired a few more times and then reloaded. I did the same with the other M9. Then I put the Beretta and the mini-mag flashlight on the bedside table and lay down. She put her pistol next to mine and lay down beside me. We fooled around for a while. After a bit, she propped herself up on her side. I stroked her hip through the jeans. "You ready? Might be a long night."

"I'm ready."

I swung myself into a seated position and picked up the light and the gun. We left our phones in the room.

Downstairs, I led her to the drawing room with the pool table. It was still light out, but twilight blue was coming on. The low cloud made it darker than normal. A few rain drops already streaked the window.

I pointed through the window towards the stone wall about fifty yards across the grass. "See the Hortensia?" I was pointing to a big bush with round and colorful flowers. She nodded. I said, "I'll be in that. It's got a decent one-eighty of the property." I pulled a chair and set it strategically. "You'll be comfortable in this, watching my six with a view of the driveway that I won't have from that position."

"What if I see something?"

I pulled out the mini-mag light and gave it to her. "We'll make it real simple." I sat down in the chair and pointed out areas of the walled garden, from left to right. "One, two and three. Left to right from your spot in the chair. Three zones." I got up and she sat down. "You see something to your left, one flash. Straight ahead and behind me, two. Down towards the driveway, three. Is that clear?"

"Crystal."

"Now the other thing. If anyone enters the house you don't hesitate. Two to the chest, one to the head. Triple tap." I looked at her. She was focused. "You good?"

"I'm good."

"This is going to be your spot. Starting now."

She nodded and sat down in the chair. "Where are you going?"

"I'll go speak to the gardener. Be back in a minute."

I WALKED DOWN to the gatekeeper's house. The floods were on, throwing light in nice round arcs across the driveway and all the way to the fenced-off vegetable plots. I hoped that would be enough to dissuade anyone from using that approach. The cliff face was the other obstacle, which left two directions. North and west. Daniel had seen me coming and was at the door, which was a good sign. We shook hands. The little cottage was quiet, and I wondered where Maria was. He told me that she'd already gone to bed with a book.

That was good too. He already had the lights off inside the house. I figured he'd be sitting back in the shadows with his bird gun.

I said, "You take care then."

He nodded. "I'll be here."

I walked the stone wall perimeter of the estate. The wall ran alongside a narrow road. I stopped at the Hortensia bush. The position was good. Slightly raised, backing up against the wall and facing the house. It was right beside the only part of the wall clear of brush, therefore it might be an attractive entry point for an attacker. I'd have the whole north-south axis covered. The only way intruders could get past without me seeing was by rappelling from the cliff top, which I discounted as improbable. My view of the cliff top was obscured by a tree, which worked the other way too. Anyone sitting up there with a scope would be unable to spot me.

The sun would be down in a few minutes, so I headed back to the house.

The room had grown dim and Nazari had already settled down to wait. She was neutral in the chair, like she could wait for hours without moving. I said, "You okay?"

She spoke calmly and slowly. "I'm fine. It's going to rain out there."

"Which will make it difficult to hear. But that goes two ways."

"Okay."

I went out to the hallway and passed the central staircase. I put my ear to the Vaugeois' bedroom door. Silence. The house was making its evening noises already. A little gurgling of water sloshing around in the pipes. The hum of charged electricity wires in the walls. And I thought that just maybe I could hear the soft snoring of Simone, who had no doubt taken a handful of pills to help her along.

Nazari had brought the bag with the duct tape and sneakers upstairs to the bedroom. I rooted around in my backpack and unwrapped the big sharpened screwdriver that I'd taken from the trail bike. The snake head edge was like a razor. I rolled up my sleeve and fastened the tool to my forearm with a strip of duct tape. Then I pulled the sleeve down. I moved my arm around a little. No problem with freedom of motion. I was wearing the black hoodie I'd bought earlier over my jeans. The hoodie would do nicely for the dark.

Good to go.

CHAPTER FIFTY

I DUG my fingers into the soft dirt near the roots of the Hortensia bush. It was black soil, the kind chewed over endlessly by worms in the shade. Passing through the worm's body, day after day, night after night, until the dirt is like moist powder ejected from a fine-grind espresso machine. I fingered handfuls and then brought them up to smear over my face. The skin produces oils that gleam in the night. I knew operators who had died because of the shine their skin made in the dark. I couldn't bear the thought of a tombstone that read: killed because his skin was too shiny. So I'd do what I could to make sure that didn't happen. I smeared well, pushing the dirt deep into the skin with my fingertips. Then I did the back of my hands, rubbing the dirt in slow little circles, until my exposed skin had no shine, and was a dull matte brown.

For a guy who had to wait all night in the rain, I already felt lucky.

The stone wall had a shelf. One of the slabs protruded a couple of inches and I was able to back myself into the wall and have that narrow shelf take my weight. It was enough for me to feel comfortable and safe. From there I had an excellent view of the house directly ahead. Left and right were clear. There was nothing going on, except for the rain, which wasn't so obviously a case of good luck.

The weather got worse during the first hour. From a couple drops every now and again, to a persistent light drizzle. The rain wasn't good for hearing. I wouldn't be able to rely upon my ears to tell me if something was going on. The patter was constant and masked other sounds that would have been heard otherwise, like boots creeping through the undergrowth. By the second hour of the night, my head and shoulders were wet. So I wasn't lucky with the weather.

But I did feel lucky about the night. Because technically speaking, in late June there is no night. Technically speaking there are three degrees of twilight, but no night. When the sun passes below the horizon, light still refracts off the microscopic particles in the atmosphere. That's called civil twilight, in which you can pretty much see almost as well as during the day. Next up is nautical twilight, in which a guy on a boat can still see pretty far, but a guy in the forest struggles with the shadows. But once the sun slips lower than that, eighteen degrees or so, you are in astronomical twilight, and true night isn't far away. Thing is, because of the way the earth leans in late June to early July, the sun doesn't slip lower than eighteen degrees below the horizon.

Which is to say that I could see just fine. I couldn't see as well as a guy on a boat with the flat calm sea in front of him, but for a guy backed into the shadow of a Hortensia bush in the rain, I could see quite well, without being easily seen myself.

To my left was the gatekeeper's house. The floodlights were illuminated, and I didn't stare too long and hard in that direction. I did think a little about what Daniel might be doing. I pictured him sitting there in a chair waiting. Not looking at anything in particular, just vaguely and unspecifically out the window. Which is pretty much what I thought Nazari would be doing. Maybe she was thinking about her upcoming exam for the BRI. Or maybe she was thinking about the dead Iraqi.

I was thinking about the Bogie.

Blomstein's message said that the search he'd done on Nazari's crime scene photos had thrown up a Bogie. Which meant that by now, it wasn't just between me and Blomstein. Someone else had been alerted to the query. All Blomstein had done was enter Nazari's pictures into a computer program. The computer then chewed on them for a while. Scanning through the pictures, one by one, from top to bottom, impartially. Making connections between this pixel and that pixel. When it was done, the program tied up and packaged those connections into something that it could communicate to other computers.

Then the computer program had called up the big network.

Blomstein's computer was on a desk in a borrowed Royal Air Force base in the UK. But while he sat back and chewed on a pencil, his computer was able to call up reinforcements from millions of other computers all over the United States and allied nations. The call awakened warehouses full of hard drives and computer processing units dotted around the deserts, plains, and forests, each of them several football fields across, packed and humming with air conditioners, cooling fans, and blinking data ports.

The faces in Nazari's photographs would be matched at blistering speeds against every other photograph that had ever been saved onto a United States or allied military hard drive. Which would be something along the lines of four billion facial recognition quality images, give or take, it was difficult to say precisely.

If matches were made, the network would gather up all the information it had, and send it back in a nice and tidy report to Blomstein's computer program, which would then pop up a little window on the screen. Blomstein would quit chewing his pencil and lean into his screen to read off the report. Then he'd call me.

But it hadn't happened like that.

Somewhere on that journey, another program had interfered with Blomstein's original search query. We called the new program a Bogie. The Bogie was like a scavenging predator, a vulture, or a hyena. It hid in the shadows and waited until a search was made, and then it pounced just when results were filtering in.

The Bogie then did two things. First it called foul, and blocked certain search results from getting out. Then, it notified primary stakeholders. People who had set up the Bogie in the first place. People who were permanently worried about information getting into the wrong hands.

The most obvious reason for the Bogie was the dead Iraqi guy. Abd al-Karim Qadduri, ex-Ba'ath party guy, Iraqi military intelligence. All kinds of stuff was still happening in Iraq, most of it with our involvement. There were a couple different possibilities that came to mind. For starters, Qadduri could be working for the new Iraqi intelligence service. While we'd booted the Ba'ath guys out of power in '03, we hadn't exactly found competent allies to replace them. So, from what I'd heard, the CIA were taking some of them back. Although what Qadduri was doing in France was anyone's guess.

Another reason for a Bogie could be because the dead guy had worked for US military intelligence against his old friends, either in the Iraqi Ba'ath party, or the insurgency that came after. He could be under some kind of protection program. That would throw up a Bogie for sure.

I rolled back my memory of the photographs Nazari had taken of the dead guy, like hitting rewind on a movie. She'd tried to cover all the angles and produce a collection of images that would work for an investigator. I figured she'd done that for practice, because of her exam. Because she was into it, hoping to pass and get into the BRI. Not because it was her job as a municipal police officer, or for kicks.

She'd accomplished that goal in spades. But she'd done something else that she might not have intended. Nazari had taken pictures on her phone. So when I'd flipped through them, they had appeared in the same order that they'd been taken. Which is pretty obvious, because that's how all cameras and phones work. But in this case it was different because the order of the photos told a story of the crime scene, a chronological report of the body's discovery by her and Bonnet, and then of the subsequent takeover of the crime scene by the BRI investigators.

Moving through the photos in my mind, I saw a shot of the dead guy—whose real name was Qadduri—curled up around his wound, lying on the sidewalk with his back against a building. Nazari started off her photo series with the whole scene, wide shot of the dead guy in context. Then, she had moved in. The angles changed and she went for close-up shots of the wound. But after that, she had backed up again.

She'd backed out because new characters had arrived. Those new characters started coming into the photos. The investigators had arrived on the scene. Inspector Martaud and Caro. Which added new possibilities for the Bogie. The Bogie could be for the dead guy, or it could be for Inspector Martaud or Caro. Those options then forked logically away from Qadduri.

Waiting's a funny thing. I'm capable of waiting indefinitely, for hours or days. But to do that you shut down parts of your brain. You go into a kind of hibernation. All the muscles relax. Half the mind wanders around groping and probing the stuff of life. The other half remains aware, focused, but it's an animal awareness like a fox or a cat. I heard something, a scraping sound. Half of my mind stopped wandering, the other half was already there.

Nothing happened. The rain trickled down from the hood I was wearing, to my face and neck. I concentrated on hearing. But, the only sound was rain tapping on things, leaves, road, dirt, stone. The smell of wet dirt and vegetation was overwhelming. I was looking straight ahead. The window where Nazari sat was dark. I wasn't worried. My muscles were relaxed and I was breathing evenly through my nose.

Walls are a common issue for operators. You can hide behind one and you can huddle in front of one. I was huddled in front of one. Being on top of a wall isn't a great option because everyone and anyone can see you. So when you go over a wall, you do it fast.

I heard the guy this time.

I didn't hear him walking up from the road. He had probably stayed close to the wall, moving slow and quiet. Then stopped on the opposite side from me. Maybe brushing against the stone, that's what I had heard. Now I heard him again, from the moment his boots pushed into the wet ground, squelched into mud, launching his body to vault over the obstacle. I heard his hands placing on the flat stones above my head. His operator's gloves contacting the stone and following up on the power generated by his legs. Then I heard the various sounds as his clothing brushed once more against the stone. All of that happened over the course of a single second, one sixtieth of a minute. Then he had already dropped down beside me, crouched against the wall.

I couldn't see him, because I wasn't looking. I kept my head still and saw with peripheral vision. A dark shape about a foot away from me, moving, scanning. But he wasn't looking close, he was looking far. He was scanning the house and the trees and things, not looking into the Hortensia bush on his left. He was feeling covered by the bush, hiding with his side leaned against it. Then I heard what I was waiting for, a quick double click on his radio unit. A signal to his team that he was inside the perimeter. I didn't hold my breath. I breathed quietly and easily, and waited for him to make a move.

I heard him repositioning his weapon, which must have been slung for the wall jump. I couldn't see anything clearly, just vague motion at the edge of my right eye. But I knew he was getting a weapon up, I heard him take a deep breath. Then he started to move, pushing off of his back leg, and I exploded out of the bush.

I did two things almost simultaneously, but not quite. First, I jumped on his back by launching myself off the stone wall and into the air. Once I was in the air and on my way to the guy, I stuck out my left leg so that when I landed on him I was already hooking his legs out from under him. That happened in less than a second. Then I was up on his back, my weight bearing down, taking full advantage of the guy's forward momentum to bring him face-first into the dirt.

Once I had the target down, I slipped my right leg over the other side so that I was wrapped around him like a snake. At the same time I was pushing his face into the ground with both hands. He squirmed around vigorously but I held on. I released my right hand and reached into my left sleeve for the sharpened flat-head screwdriver taped to my forearm. It came loose without hassle. I was looking at the back of the guy's head. I slipped the screwdriver in right where the nape of the neck meets the base of the skull, going in from the right side at an upwards angle. That was meant to avoid the spinal cord and drive right at the medulla oblongata.

The tip of the flat-head went in like a needle, it was that sharp. The edge parted the skin without struggle. Three drops of blood welled up from the insertion point; that was it. I'd got it right. No resistance from bone or ligaments. Just a straight drive up through soft tissue and into the brain stem, destroying it. No sigh, no twitching. The guy died instantly.

I wiped the screwdriver on his collar. I was almost jealous. They say that death has no mercy. Show me a more merciful death.

CHAPTER FIFTY-ONE

THE SCREWDRIVER WENT BACK in my sleeve. I pushed the duct tape back into place. Then, I pulled the guy back into the Hortensia bush, and started scavenging.

He was dressed in regular clothing. Jeans and a pull-over windbreaker. Despite that, the guy was well equipped. Tactical vest with Motorola radio and extra magazines for his weapon, which was a Heckler and Koch MP5SD. The MP5 is an excellent close quarters, tactical submachine gun. High-end German machining. Light and handy, easy to use, accurate and quiet. It's the go-to gun for units that can afford it, because it isn't cheap. Typically only the best military units and highest end private contractors get MP5s.

The SD variant takes a regular H&K MP5 and adds an integral suppressor that muffles the sound and muzzle flash. One of the ways it does that is by slowing the bullet down to sub-sonic speeds. Because a supersonic bullet's going to make quite a bang when it breaks the sound barrier. So the MP5SD stops that from happening.

I checked the weapon. Locked and loaded with one in the chamber and twenty-nine rounds left in the mag. The guy had two extra magazines in the vest. Overkill, but reassuring. I put them into my jeans pockets anyway. I thumbed the selector on the MP5 to the second position, which is a three-round burst, palmed back the bolt and then over to lock it down. While my hands were busy doing that from muscle memory, my eyes were up and scanning.

Straight ahead was nothing but rain. To my left, the floodlights were lighting up still more rain. To my right was the north end of the estate, a large field of grass with a big tree smack in the middle of it. The tree was about fifty yards from my position. I saw movement behind it, the tail end of someone's run to get cover behind the tree.

The MP5 can be fired accurately to two hundred yards. That's for a highly trained operator firing a regular MP5 on a nice sunny day, no wind, no rain, no pressure. But a sub-sonic, slow bullet fired out of a suppressed barrel isn't going to pack as much of a punch at two-hundred yards. But at fifty there isn't an issue. At fifty you just lead the guy by an extra half inch.

I held position in the Hortensia bush. Waiting for the guy to get comfortable, and move out from behind the tree. After a minute, he started from the tree towards the house, scurrying like a crab. I took a breath and put him in my sights, leading a little to compensate for the slow speed of the bullet. I triggered a three-round burst, which sounded about as loud as rainfall tinkling on a tin roof. The guy dropped. I held him in the sights and waited for a twenty count. No movement, no nothing. I thumbed the selector to single shot and put a round into his head. *Kaplunk.* The pink mist kicked off in the rain. I got down alongside the stone wall and picked the four ejected casings out of the wet dirt, tucked them into my back pocket.

When I looked up, I saw that something had changed. It wasn't obvious, it was like one of those picture puzzles, where you've got to find what's different in the landscape. It started as a feeling, and then it narrowed down to a certainty. There was a light on in the house that hadn't been on before. It was coming from the doorway of the room where I'd left Nazari.

I looked at the windows of the room where she had been sitting, and besides the new light, all I saw was dark. The rain started coming down hard, and felt great, warm and comfortable. I needed to move and get to the house. To do that, I'd either have to go all the way around, keeping against the cover of the wall, or straight across and risk being out in the open. I chose the fastest route and charged like a maniac across the lawn.

Ten seconds later I was glued to Brumaire's limestone wall, hugging the facade next to the big window on the south side of the house. I figured that she must have seen me crossing over from the stone wall perimeter, so I peeked into the room. Nothing. Dark room, pool table, empty chair. No sign of her. The door to the hallway was open.

The big French windows were vintage classics. These weren't PVC storm windows for hard winters, they were solid wood and glass windows for mild weather, with snow perhaps once per year. The windows were two-piece, single glazed, framed in oak that had withstood rain, wind, heat and cold for thirty, forty years.

The twin window panels were fastened on the inside by vertical iron bars. I forced the sharpened screwdriver straight through the seam between panels. I was able to pretty quickly dig out enough space to push the screwdriver through. Two holes like that and I had some leverage to twist the knob enough that the iron bars eased out of their stone crevices.

I vaulted into the room without making much noise. Whatever sound I did make was covered by the rain. I crouched there for a second and put the screwdriver back in my sleeve. The duct tape binding still had life in it. Then I pulled the window shut and turned the knob to lock it back into place. I got the MP5 up and selected for triple burst. If I was going to have to use it, I'd be going for a tight pattern in the upper chest area. There wasn't much recoil, but the muzzle would be moving vertically upwards over the course of an eighth of a second, so the rounds would stitch a little crooked line.

The room with the pool table opened up towards the back of the house, to another sitting room where the chimney had been fired up a couple nights ago. From there I crept around towards the central staircase. I stopped at the bottom of the stairs and listened. Nazari's voice was coming from the other drawing room, the one with the dining table, where I'd found Gilles with his spilled silverware.

I could hear her speaking in low and smooth tones. Like a hostage negotiator. I figured she'd been reading up on those skills for her exam. She was telling someone that there was nobody else in the house, that she was Gilles Vaugeois' live-in nurse. Then I heard a male voice, gruff and vulgar. He wasn't buying her story.

"I know who you are, you're the hot cop. We've got plans for you."

"What do you mean?" I didn't hear fear in her voice, it had gone cold.

"What I mean is, we've got plans for you. Your American boyfriend is dead. My buddy put two in his head about a minute ago, so he's leaking out in the garden. We'll make a spectacle of the rest, but not before we all take turns with you."

Nazari's voice went cold. "You're going to die."

The guy laughed. "Eventually yes, but I'll die knowing you in all kinds of interesting ways. I'm planning on memorizing you."

Nazari said nothing.

The conversation wasn't going to get any better, so I figured I'd intervene at that point. Nazari wasn't dead yet because of the mundane and revolting stupidity of this mercenary killer. But I was quite certain that he had her in a vulnerable position. Because if he didn't, he'd be dead. Still, it was a tricky situation. Time to calm things down for a second or two. I put the MP5 on safety and lifted it up over my head. Then I stepped around into the drawing room, *not too fast, not too slow.*

The guy was dressed in jeans and a light canvas jacket. He had a tactical vest over that, with twin MP5 mags in the front pouch. He wore a black balaclava, so only his eyes were visible, which made the head look a little stubby on his thick frame. But the eyes were experienced and calm. A chestnut shade of brown. Clear and intelligent. They were the eyes of a man in his late thirties or mid-forties. Not

wild rookie eyes and not the dull eyes of a tired and over the hill operator. They were prime veteran fighting eyes, the eyes of a seasoned
mercenary killer.

The MP5 was slung around his back. He had Nazari's Beretta in
his hand, the barrel brushing her neck. She raised her eyes to me, and
we connected for a fraction of a second. It was a good connection.

Then our eyes were back to business. I spoke softly and slowly.
"Gun's on safety. I'm unarmed. We're good. You can put the gun
down."

CHAPTER FIFTY-TWO

THE GUY DIDN'T WAVER, didn't hesitate, didn't speak, and didn't move an inch. He didn't put his gun down and he didn't look away. The eyes in the balaclava narrowed and the Beretta pushed hard into Nazari's neck muscle. She flinched. I crouched down and made a big show out of laying the MP5 on the ground. Then I used my boot to slide it across the room. I felt my own pistol pressed against the small of my back, held in by the waistband. I spoke again. "No issues, no problem. No reason for anyone to get hurt. Whatever you need you'll get. Is it me you want? Did they tell you to get the American?"

The eyes blinked. Not a slow and convincing blink, more like an unconscious millisecond long twitch that told me I was correct, that I was the target. No doubt they'd kill everyone else in the house, just to be professional about it. But, it was me who had aroused this next-level ferocity. And while I spoke, I didn't stop moving. I crept slowly towards them an inch at a time, narrowing down the angles, closing down the space of possibility for him.

Nazari was looking at me. She had an embarrassed little smile that curled up at the edges of her mouth. A smile that said, 'shit happens'. The corner window was open. The intruder had entered that way, then surprised Nazari and dragged her back to the drawing room, where he felt safer. It was the corner of the house hugging the cliff. Out of sight from where I had been positioned. The guy was looking at me, not at her, and not down at the gun. The Beretta was against her neck, but it wasn't positioned for a kill shot. The barrel rested against her neck. No doubt the guy was a professional and could easily readjust. But he wasn't going to be able to shoot her and then turn it on me. He'd have to choose.

I said, "If you want me, just go for me. You think I care about the nurse? Kill the nurse. You have to decide now. I figure you've got two seconds left, maximum."

By then I was two paces away and piling pressure on the guy. All he needed to do was shift the pistol about fourteen degrees to his right and he'd be dead centered on my body mass. And all I needed was another fraction of a second.

The guy had already waited too long. Because I'd been shifting the screwdriver in my left sleeve down to my hand. While I was waving my arms in a big show of harmlessness, I was getting the sharpened tool loose from the wet duct tape, easing the soft-grip handle into my hand. And at the same time, the guy was making a decision. Getting me in the bag would make him a hero. That was a certainty. Probably a fat bonus had been promised. He knew that if he fired into Nazari's neck she'd be dead. One hundred percent. But, he was experienced enough to know that there was a chance that it would be his last shot.

Operators are confident in their abilities. We're selected and trained for that. So, he'd have some confidence of being able to take Nazari and me both. But I'd seen that twitch when he heard me say I was the American. Which meant that he'd been briefed. So he was aware that I was the danger, aware that there were new odds in play. No statistical certainty, just odds. And with me sliding an H&K over at him, he'd know the odds were pretty good that I'd taken it from one of his buddies.

Taken it without asking.

He made his decision, and swung the gun towards me. Fourteen degrees to go.

I'd calculated wrong of course. There was no way that I'd be able to beat him from two paces away. Screwdriver against Beretta . Beretta's going to win every time. But the guy had also made a miscalculation, because he hadn't accounted for Nazari. All she needed to do was grab his gun arm, which she did, and pulled down hard. Which wouldn't have worked, on its own, because the guy was very strong. However strong Nazari was, he was stronger.

But she wasn't alone, she was with me. We were a team, a unit. And by the time the guy had compensated for the new force pulling at his arm, I had the screwdriver out and ready, slipped into my left palm. While the Beretta swung over, shrinking that space, I was stepping forward. And with each step I was creating more space that he needed to cover. One more step and I shifted my weight to the left. The Beretta kept swiveling toward my body mass but by the second step I was inside his swing and it was all over.

My problem was that the screwdriver was in my left hand and because I was stepping to the left, it was the wrong hand. So as I took that step, away from the Beretta, I tossed the screwdriver from my left hand to my right hand in mid-stride, while my weight was shifting. The right hand caught it in mid-air, around head height. The guy's eyes lost focus trying to track the tool, suddenly so close to him. The momentum of stepping towards him swung my weight forward, and I drove the tip of the screwdriver into his left eye.

It made no sound as it went in, and I pushed it deep, there was a click when the thin bone behind the eye was penetrated and gave way, and then the screwdriver entered his brain. The gun dropped to the ground with a clatter. Nazari stepped clear. By then I was behind the guy, turning to look at his back. She was in front of him. We both watched.

The guy didn't drop. He tottered on his feet like an unstable ice skater. Then, he walked out of the room and through the front door, like he had some really important place to go.

I followed him. The guy was stumbling down the terrace stairs. He was making a strange high-pitched humming sound. Nazari stepped past me. She shot him three times with the Beretta he had taken from her, and then dropped. The first round went in at the middle of the guy's back, the last demolished the vertebrae at the base of his neck. He crumpled face down and silent.

She moved to him and put a single round into the back of his head. She looked back at me. "You okay?"

"Fine, why do you ask?"

She shrugged and pointed to my face. I was painted in dirt and maybe some backsplash. "You've got blood."

"Not mine. Let's go into the house."

I turned the light off in the drawing room, pulled her next to the wall, where the hallway met the front door. She said, "You think there are more?"

"Three down. I figure there's someone waiting in a vehicle."

"Nobody else on the property then."

"Three's a crowd in a van, with the driver. Big guys. Gear. Four with a driver would be too much. I'll go get the guy in the vehicle. You sit tight. Keep the gun and stay away from windows."

"Be careful, Tom." I liked the way she said my name. As if there were an 'e' at the end. Like Tome, or dome.

"I'll be careful. First, let's move the guy you shot."

I took the dead guy's MP5 and handed it to Nazari. She slung it over her head. Then we dragged the body up onto the terrace, pushed him into a dark corner. There would be time later to clean up properly. She went back inside to hold the fort. I heard a whistle from down by the gatekeeper's house.

Daniel was walking up through the trees with his French gun. The rain had stopped. We met halfway. I said, "Three so far, I'm guessing there's a fourth in a vehicle somewhere."

"I didn't hear any engines, so maybe down near the bridge."

"I thought the same."

He nodded. "What next?"

"I'll take care of the vehicle. Then we'll have some cleanup to do. I'm hoping you've got a wheelbarrow."

"Yes. We have two."

"Great, we'll need both. See you in a bit."

I walked the perimeter once, just to make sure. Then I headed into the woods.

CHAPTER FIFTY-THREE

DON'T ENVY the getaway driver.

First, you're stuck in a vehicle without options. Visibility is limited, and everyone knows where you are. Then, the boredom and uncertainty of waiting. By now the radio was dead, with no communications from his team, no response to his attempts at communication. Zero options. The van was pulled in near the bridge, next to the water, below where the forest path met the road.

I came at it from the other side of the bridge, along the river. I had walked down through the wooded path to the water, feeling my way slow and easy in the dark. Then I followed the river's edge until I was under the bridge. From there I could see up the incline and spotted the vehicle. A rectangular shadow lurking among the trees. It was a white Renault van, a model called 'Trafic'. I crept up from the water and stopped around twenty yards from the van, unslung the MP5 and stood behind a tree in the dark to watch.

The Renault's cockpit was dark and without movement. I considered simply stepping over to the forest side window and shooting into the cab with the MP5, quick and dirty. Problem was the windows were up, and I didn't want to break glass because I anticipated driving the van, later on. I could hear the sound from the river down below, now that the rain had stopped. Which meant that I could also hear the creatures, the little nighttime animals that shift and shuffle in the trees and between rocks and scurrying holes.

The forest sounds lulled me into a false sense of security. They made me feel safe, as if the forest had been undisturbed by human beings until I got there. What I didn't anticipate was that the driver might have done the same thing as I did, come out into the forest and get comfortable for a while. I only figured that out when a hammered fist crashed into my right kidney.

A good solid kidney punch is a knock-out blow. The gun fell away and I crumpled to my knees, sucking for air. A totally involuntary reaction. It felt like battery acid was being poured into my side. I couldn't breathe at all for a second, and by then it was too late. Because the guy had already looped a muscular arm around my neck and was pressing with his other arm for a sleeper hold. A part of me couldn't move at all, but another part of me knew that I had maybe four seconds to get out of that hold before I lost consciousness.

The guy's arms felt like steel bars, even though he was still consolidating his hold. It felt like my neck was being squeezed between two I-beams. Oxygen deficit saps the will. It takes training and repetition to get beyond that. I was trained, my will wasn't going to diminish. So I wasn't in despair; I was trying to think.

I needed to make him relinquish the hold, and the only way to do that was to make it absolutely necessary for him to let go with one of his arms. So I tried the first and most obvious thing, which was to reach back and grab the guy's nuts and pull as hard as I could. The only thing I got from that was a grunt. The guy shifted his hips. No relief, no pressure let up. A second and a half wasted. I started seeing stars.

The next thing I tried was improvisation, no thought, just muscle memory. I pushed back against the guy using his body mass as an anchor. Just threw myself backward at him and leveraged his strength and resistance by walking up the tree I had been hiding behind.

When I got more or less horizontal I kicked off, used the muscle power of my quads and calves to explode into him with all my weight. The guy was strong, but no one's that strong, and he went over, stumbling down the incline until we both crashed into the river.

The shock of the fall and the water was enough to loosen his grip, so that I managed to squeeze my chin into my chest and duck out from under his forearm. Then I spun myself around like a wrestler, boots scrambling in the shallow riverbed, and jumped off him. I backed up into a fighting crouch, catching my breath. I could hardly see the guy, just a massive shadow in front of me. The shadow came at me instantly and aggressively. He was about my height, compact and muscular.

The guy came at me with a left cross, so I stepped left and threw a right hook into his nose. It connected and crunched, but that didn't stop him. He followed with an elbow into my ribcage that landed like a sack of bricks. I fought the pain, stepped up and kicked him in the knee, which made the guy stagger a little, giving me the chance to send an elbow to his right temple. That didn't land too solid, just glanced off him. By which time he had grabbed me around the waist and was pulling me into a bear hug.

We were now face to face. Two guys battling in the dark, splashing in the water. I couldn't see his features because it was dark, and he was too close to me, squeezing as hard as he could. My face was pressed into his skull, which was cleanly shaved and smelled like aloe-vera moisturizing lotion. He smelled familiar.

I grabbed his face and thrust thumbs into both of his eyes. I had to go deep before he let go of me. Then I was done fooling around. I scrambled up the incline and found the gun. Got the H&K up and ready. The guy was already coming back at me from the river. I clicked the safety off and he stopped. The guy was a shadow, about four yards from me.

I said, "Grouse."

The guy was breathing hard. He coughed out a laugh. "Yeah. How'd you know."

Everything clicked into place for me then, like a Rubik's cube solving itself or a series of tumblers and cogs clicking in satisfaction. I said, "Your skin care products."

"So what do you want?"

"If you're not a cop, I want to know who you work for."

Grouse spat. "Forget about it."

"Come on up out of there and into the light. I want to get a look at you."

"If you like money, there's plenty of it, believe me."

"Get moving, up to the road."

Grouse moved off toward the road. I tracked him with the H&K, then started walking after him.

I said, "You're a soldier in Martaud's little private army. Who's the client?"

By then, Grouse was close enough to the road for a little residual moonlight to cut through the opening in the tree line. "That's enough. You can stop there and turn around." Grouse turned to face me. His nose was flattened, blood was still pouring out and down his face to a dark stain on his shirt. That made me feel pleased with myself. I said, "Who's the client?"

"Go to hell."

"You look bad, Grouse, you'll look worse dead. Who's the client?"

"Fuck you."

I put a triple burst into the darkest and most solid part of his body mass. The H&K sounded sweet, like a really fast full-metal drum roll. Like chamber music for robots. Efficient and deadly. He went down. I stepped up and put a single round into his shiny head.

Then there was silence. I lay down on the ground and caught my breath. The sky looked lighter. I figured we had entered another version of nautical twilight before the sun came up. After a minute I got to my feet.

I had some cleaning up to do.

The back of the white Renault Trafic had a large roll of polythene sheeting and plenty of duct tape. Grouse was heavy. Not only was he dead, but he was wet. Wet, dead, and large is difficult to get a hold of. I got him into a fireman's lift, staggered under the weight uphill for a while, and threw him into the back of the van.

I drove the van slowly up the drive to Brumaire. I showed myself to Daniel and he walked towards the house while I parked. Neither he, or I, or Nazari said much. We stripped off the weapons and gear from the corpses and loaded them onto wheelbarrows. Then we rolled them into the woods and dumped them next to the cavern entrance mound. Four bodies required two trips with two wheel-barrows.

I stood in the woods with Nazari looking at Grouse's body.

He didn't look at rest, he looked dead. She played the flashlight beam over his face, pale and puffy. "Dirty cops freelancing. You think it's just him?"

"I don't think they're cops freelancing. They aren't cops at all."

"Who are they?"

I shrugged. "I figure Martaud and her crew aren't cops, they're corporate mercenaries. That accounts for the shell companies and weird corporate structures."

"That's a hell of a theory."

"You got that right."

We dug out the tunnel for around an hour before I decided it was enough. Then we rolled the bodies in and piled them up. Daniel had a sack of lime powder for the vegetable garden. He poured it all over the corpses. Nazari said it would reduce their smell. We pushed the rubble over them again. I figured that would do for at least a couple of days. I wasn't expecting a long-term solution. They were dug in deep enough to maintain an even sixty-five degrees Fahrenheit. Which wouldn't stop the processes of putrefaction but wouldn't speed it up either. And the lime might help. I figured we'd have a good forty-eight hours before things started to get ugly.

It was time to make the van disappear.

CHAPTER FIFTY-FOUR

NAZARI KNEW A PLACE.

A golf course under development out of town. The money had run out, or someone hadn't paid someone else. Or maybe an important guy had quit, she wasn't sure, in fact nobody was. Rumors were thick, facts thin. In any case for now it wasn't a golf course, just a big construction site.

She drove her Peugeot, I took the Renault van.

Meanwhile, Daniel was cleaning up at Brumaire. He was taking care of blood spots in the drawing room and whatever loose ends remained. We all agreed that Madame and Monsieur Vaugeois should not be disturbed, in as much as that was going to be possible.

By the time we hit the road it was full-on morning. People were around, going to work, going to school, dropping each other off. They craved coffee, or tea, and vitamin supplements and powders. Still they yawned in their cars. After the rain and cloud, morning brought sunshine. It had been a productive evening and I felt fine.

We drove for something like twenty minutes before she pulled into a secluded picnic spot around a bend. The picnic table was on a grassy hill looking down on a country club. Tennis courts were set into bucolic green areas, bordered by strips of trees. I figured the dream was to pair up the country club with the golf course.

The spot was mid-way up the hill. I rolled the window down. She was out of the Peugeot and pointing. "Keep going up and you'll see it in a minute. I'll wait for you here."

I nodded and gave the van some gas. Crested the hill and the golf course development was right there, stretching out on the plateau. It was a big construction site, an ambitious plan. There were Caterpillar diggers and other machinery, abandoned the way crustaceans abandon their shells. The whole area was torn up. Didn't look anything like a golf course. I scanned for cameras and didn't see any, but I put up the hoodie anyway.

The place was nothing but dirt and piles of rock, sand, and gravel in various gauges. There is a science to making golf courses; I'd stumbled upon an abandoned experiment. Which was perfect for my purpose. I parked the van deep into the development. Sandwiched between a bulldozer and a container half filled with pipes that looked to have been ripped out of the earth. Heavy clotted mud stuck to the galvanized steel. I wiped the Renault down using a rag. Then I locked it and walked away. Buried the keys in a dirt pile on the way out.

Nazari was sitting on the picnic table looking at the view. I joined her. Two couples dressed in white were playing tennis down below, early birds, retirees. She said, "Old rich people living a life of leisure."

"What do you mean leisure? That looks like hard work." It didn't, the tennis players barely moved. She laughed, and I sat down next to her and looked out over the tennis club. I said, "Let's talk about caverns."

She leaned an arm on my shoulder and said, "Ok, talk to me about the caverns."

I had already told her about what I'd found in Gilles Vaugeois' library, the way he had mapped out the system of caverns under Alencourt. On paper the underground map looked like a bunch of cartoon speech bubbles. Tunnels from the surface, opening up to bigger spaces, all over the place, underground. Tunnels connecting caverns and linking up, and so on.

So, I told her what I thought, that Gilles Vaugeois had become a target because of what he knew about the caverns. Which led to a hypothesis, the caper was related to two things. First it was clearly related to migrant trafficking. Second, there were the caverns. Either migrants were being held in caverns or housed in caverns.

Which led us to segue into a discussion of the pale dust from the migrant's feet and clothes. She thought it was because they were being made to work digging the caves. I processed that and added in the dead guy with the Iraqi Ba'ath party tattoo and his SIM card. I said, "There's a third thing."

"What's the third thing?"

"It's gender. Tell me about the gender aspect of the caper."

She thought for a second. "The migrants you spotted up near Calais were all male."

"Correct."

"And the list on the Iraqi's SIM card were all female names."

"Correct again."

"And we haven't seen any female migrants." She looked at me then, hurt in her eyes. Because what we were processing was coming out bad. Nazari had the kind of eyes that change color. More hazel, or more green. Her face was blooming darkly and her eyes were getting real green. She said, "You thinking what I'm thinking?"

"Yeah. I am."

"It's about girls, in the end." She looked away and cursed under her breath.

I said, "We haven't seen any female migrants because they are being kept out of sight. Now we add that third thing to the other two."

"Which is why they are digging. Digging to hide the girls."

"Maybe. We don't know yet, exactly."

"But we can call the Iraqi guy's number. The office."

The Iraqi SIM card was still in Nazari's phone. So she dug it out

of her pocket and started to hunt for the number. I was looking at
something down by the tennis courts. A young guy was setting up a
coffee cabin in front of the tennis courts. It was a little wood-sided
structure with a fold-up counter. He was flipping up the fold-down
windows. I could see pastries in a glass case. I figured, if he was
opening up for the day, he'd have fresh-brewed coffee happening.

I said, "Do you see what I see?"

She looked up and followed the direction of my gaze.

"Coffee."

"Which is something that we should drink, now."

"Most definitely."

"I'll get the coffee. We'll call the Iraqi while we drink it. It'll be
more comfortable that way. No reason to suffer unnecessarily."

"And pastries, of different kinds."

"Hopefully."

"At least two each."

I walked down the hill. We hadn't eaten since the evening before,
and I'd burned a lot of calories. I could feel the jitters telling me I was
craving nutrition. There was a little footpath down the hill and over
the grass to the courts. My eyes hunted the pastries. I thought, two for
me, two for Nazari. Coffee, light and sweet. Plenty of milk, plenty of
sugar. Keep the energy going, at least until we could take a nap.

The coffee hut guy was young, skinny, and blond. When I saw
the way he was staring at me, I realized how scary I looked. My face
smeared with a thin crust of dried dirt, maybe a little blood. I said,
"Digging is hard work, my friend. Hard, hard work."

"Digging?"

"Yes, sir. The garden is a harsh mistress." I smiled broadly.

A smile is infectious, and in France it's uncommon. Smiles in
France are like sunshine in Finland, a treasure to be cherished. So the
guy couldn't stop himself smiling back. "Can I help you?"

I ordered the coffee and the food. While he worked the coffee
machine, I looked at the place. The hut sold coffee, snacks, and tennis
gear, like balls and racket tape and sweat bands for the head and the

wrist. They had a big case of energy drinks and sports supplements. Prices were written on big yellow star tags. A sign said, 'cash only'.

When the order was ready, I paid. The guy handed me a little paper receipt, which I crumpled into my pocket. I hauled the sack of croissants and the to-go cups back to Nazari.

She was watching me as I climbed up the hill. She said, "You must have scared the living shit out of that guy."

"I realized that, then I tried to turn it into a joke. Hopefully he bought it."

"Looks like he got over the scare."

The guy was now sitting out on a chair reading a paperback. We started eating croissants and sipping coffee. The croissants were crunchy and flakey on the outside and soft, warm, and chewy on the inside. Just about perfect. After I'd finished one of them, I was able to breathe again. I said, "Let's call the Iraqi."

She looked her phone. She said, "Right now?"

"Right now."

She tapped on the screen for a while and brought up the 'Office' contact, then tapped for speaker phone. I recognized the French dial tone, long bursts separated by silence. Then the phone gurgled, like it was swallowing something. Then, as before, another kind of dial tone came out of the little speakers. Like the audio equivalent of braille, five dots and then a blank space, then another five dots.

Then there was a click. Unlike the previous time, it was a living person. The atmosphere changed then, between me and Nazari. We stopped chewing and all of our attention got sucked into that little screen. The voice was female again, and in English. "Allo." Which might not have been English exactly, it might have been an international code word for answering the telephone. I leaned forward and spoke into the phone. "It's Keeler. I called before."

There was a short silence, filled with some static from the distant connection. I heard the sound of breathing, and looked at Nazari. The voice said, "I need to call you back. Two minutes."

The phone clicked off.

I handed Nazari another croissant from the bag. We ate in silence, looking out across the landscape. It was pretty out there. A fertile land with fields divided by areas of forest and bush. Well watered and rich. I finished the second croissant about the same time as Nazari.

We both looked at the phone.

It was flat, rectangular and glossy, with a bright screen that showed small squares for each of the applications on it. It looked like an object with special powers, something that people stare at expectantly, as if it could do surprising things. Which it could, depending upon the application loaded on to it. Then it rang, almost silently because Nazari had turned off the ringer, but not quite silently because she'd turned on the buzzer.

The phone's screen had changed. Before, it had displayed the time and date. Now it showed the word 'Office', and below it was a green button for accepting and a red button for rejecting. Nazari touched the green button with the pad of her index finger.

CHAPTER FIFTY-FIVE

"My name is Leila."

The voice was not old, not young. Experienced, like a string instrument that had been played-in enough to have achieved peak qualities. Miles of road behind that voice, but still at the top of its game.

I said, "I'm calling regarding Qadduri."

"Karim. Is he with you?"

"He's dead."

A pause.

"Dead how?"

"Knife. A single stab wound to the heart. He didn't suffer."

"Karim suffered enough, make no mistake about that."

"Are you his wife?"

Another long pause, then, "It's a valid question, under the circumstances. No I am not his wife, I am his boss."

"I see."

Leila said, "I take it you don't know anything really, is that right? I mean, you might as well say."

"Not much, no. I'd be grateful if you could fill me in."

"You've got me on speaker phone, so I assume that there are other people listening."

"Correct. There is one other person listening."

"What are you, police?"

"I'm just a guy, ma'am. Not police."

"An American guy."

"That's right."

The voice cut through the clear air above the tennis club. Leila said, "What's your story?"

"Mixed up with yours. The people who killed your friend tried to kill me first."

"Why would they do that?"

"Mistaken identity."

There was a long pause on the line. Leila said slowly and softly, "After what Americans have done to my country, I'm having a hard time trusting you."

"That's neither here nor there, Leila, your friend Qadduri would have been responsible for his own share of suffering, as a Baath party guy. In fact you could say that what Saddam and the Baath party guys did to their own people puts at least half the responsibility on their own heads."

"So you know about that. You're an educated American."

I didn't say anything. Nazari was holding the phone. Something was bothering her. She flashed me a look, then glanced back to the phone. Which was silent now, just a light field of static, as if Leila were weighing up what to say. Nazari held up a finger to me, like 'wait a second', and launched into a long stream of Arabic that I didn't understand.

When she was done, Leila responded in a quiet voice. An extended bunch of phrases, all in Arabic. I understood nothing. Then Leila switched out of Arabic. "Ok. I'll play."

I reached over and hit the mute button on the phone. I said to Nazari, "What did you tell her?"

"Told her the facts, Keeler, just some of the more pertinent facts.

About you and me, about the situation here. I figured it's better that she trusts us, we might get some cooperation."

"Ok." I hit the mute button. "Leila, we're just trying to figure out what your friend was doing."

"Do you know anything about Iraq?"

"More than a little, yes."

"Then you know what we've been through. What we are going through. Here, the past and present are so terrible that we've got nothing but the future."

"I get what you're saying. Some monumental events have been taking place in your part of the world."

"That's right. Problem is, when monumental events take place, they usually end up being violent events. People end up moving around, mostly against their will. People try and get away from the violence, and if they can't, they try and send their family members to other, safer places. For the future."

"So what happened?"

"What happened is, the girls started disappearing."

"Disappearing from where?"

Leila said, "You already know that Karim had been a Baath party member. More than that, he was a member of the security services. After the American invasion, the party members were ejected from military and security roles, so Karim, like others, went private."

"Like a mercenary?"

"No, the war changed him. He made the decision to switch, to work for good. He wouldn't turn mercenary or help the Americans, or the Iranians, or anything else political. Karim was done with politics. He joined my outfit."

"What's that?"

"We help people who have lost loved ones."

"Like a private investigator?"

"Yes, like a private investigator. Difference is, I don't do infidelity, or digging up dirt, or any of the other bullshit that goes on between unsatisfied people in the world. I focus on one thing, and one thing only. Finding missing people who've been lost since the war. I focus on bringing closure to families and loved ones, so that they can move on and start concentrating on the future."

I said, "And you're all by yourself, now that Qadduri's gone?"

"I've got fifteen investigators working with me in the Baghdad office. We're a small outfit, but we are professional."

Nazari cut in, "The girls."

"That's right, it all started with the girls."

I said, "So tell us about the girls."

"Let me start by painting you a picture. I think that will be helpful, for the context."

"Ok."

"Think of two phases. Phase one was the American invasion. What the American invasion really did was kick off a civil war in Iraq. We went at each other's throats. One side against the other, roughly along religious lines. Shiite versus Sunni, with the Americans stuck in the middle, clueless pretty much. Problem was that before the invasion, both sides had lived in the same neighborhoods, so that got all pulled apart. People had to up and leave at a moment's notice, or risk being killed by their neighbors. A very real risk, and they started to go missing. Phase one was all about us killing each other, and people going missing internally. You following me?"

"I'm with you."

"Phase two kicked off a couple of years ago. Phase two was all about people fleeing the country for Europe. Exile and emigration, making a new life in a better place with better options. In phase two the young people got sent first, in the hopes that they'd be more resilient than the older folks. Fact is that those migration routes are tough. First you have to make it out of Iraq, which isn't a given, since you have to pass through areas that are controlled by some very bad people. Next you have to choose between two evils, getting through Turkey, or swinging down through Jordan, and into Africa, then Libya, which has its own particular horrors. After that, you go by boat and try and get yourself washed up in Europe somehow."

I said, "Ok, so what about the girls?"

"Those are the two phases, and we're now talking about phase two. Most people take the second option, down through Jordan and through the desert. That way, you've got a better chance of making it to Europe and not getting hung up in Turkey. It started with one or two reports. Parents contacting us, concerned about their girls. Which happens all the time, half of what we do, find sons and daughters, mothers, fathers, grandparents and uncles and cousins. By and large, it's only family who are willing to spend money and time looking for the missing. But Karim noticed a pattern, and started doing the leg work."

Nazari said, "What was the pattern?"

"We get requests about people missing along migration routes quite often. If we are able to trace them, the usual thing is to find that they've drowned crossing the Mediterranean. That's our normal expectation. This is the case seventy-five percent of the time. A lot of people die crossing. The other twenty-five percent usually turn up somewhere, Europe, Turkey, sometimes they make it to the UK. Mostly they don't."

I said, "How do you track them?"

Leila said, "Usually the only way to track people along those routes is by their mobile phone connections. Often they send pictures to family and friends, from borrowed phones, or phones they manage to get hold of along the way. From the pictures we can do forensic analysis and find the location."

Nazari asked, "How do you do that?"

"Shadow analysis for time of day, matched up to metadata on the image file, usually JPEG. We can often triangulate the location using open source intelligence."

"So Qadduri found a pattern."

"That's right. Karim was methodical. He worked with spreadsheets and began to analyze the data. He built up a data set and ran simple algorithms over it, matching data and sorting it. So at some point he was able to put it together. The girls were disappearing at the same place, more or less. From our point of view it was like a black hole was opening up somewhere in Northern France." Nazari and I looked at each other. Leila said, "Our girls were falling into that black hole. You can imagine how we felt about it."

I said, "And Qadduri came out here to find them."

"Eventually. First, Karim activated his network here in Baghdad, ex-security people who were now in the private sector or worse."

"What do you mean by worse?"

Leila chuckled. "You've heard of a group called ISIS, or DAESH? That's what I mean by worse. Many of the leaders are ex-Baath party military people."

"Okay."

"But what I'm getting at, is that he didn't just go out there on his own, he was invited."

Nazari flashed me a look and said, "Invited by whom?"

"As far as I know, Karim made contact with the local security forces."

Nazari said, "You mean the police?"

"That's right. The local police."

Nazari and I looked at each other again. I said, "So, he came with his Iraqi passport, all out in the open and above board?"

Leila paused a beat and I heard the sharp inhalation of a smoker. She said, "No. He was not a stupid man, Keeler. He would never walk straight in like that. I'm sure you had to do some investigating to uncover his real identity."

Nazari said, "Deep investigation, yes."

Leila laughed, and coughed. "Yes, indeed. He was a character, I'll tell you that. I loved the man. Not romantically mind you. Loved him for his courage. But he wasn't stupid. Karim hedged his bets. He made a double approach. One approach through the official channels, the police, and another approach through the unofficial channels."

"Such as?"

"Such as the criminal networks. The migrant traffickers."

"So I guess his approach was compromised."

"It looks that way. Compromised, most likely from the beginning. Most likely both ways."

I said, "So is that it? We've got the list of names, those are the girls in question?"

"From our side, yes. Those are the ones that we have identified, who fit the pattern. I'm guessing that there are more."

"Anything recent from them?"

"Nothing, they've just disappeared."

I said, "The black hole. Do you have a precise location?"

"We have an area of interest. A set of coordinate triangulations. The girl's phones went dark in different locations, but there is a pattern. Like an epicenter. I can send that through after we talk."

"Ok. So what's next?"

Leila said nothing for a while. Then she spoke quietly, "What's next is, I ask you what you're going to do about it?"

I said, "We'll get them back if we can. That's what we're going to do."

Leila said, "Good. Do I need to come?"

Nazari's eyes got wide.

I said, "You'll come too late, Leila. It's all going to happen right now."

"I'm just wondering if you'll finish the job, or if I'll have to do it for you."

"How do you mean?"

"You said you'll get them back. I said, 'good', but that's only half the job."

I said, "What's the other half?"

"To make sure that justice is done. That nothing remains to be corrected."

Nazari spoke, "We'll take care of that."

"I hear you, but from what I can see, it's no better there than over here. And over here there are no guarantees that justice gets done. You've got to make damn sure yourself."

I said, "Roger that. We'll take care of it."

Leila said, "Good." The call disconnected.

Sixty seconds later, a text message came through. It was a set of GPS map coordinates. Nazari tapped on the phone. She brought up a map, which zoomed out to reveal the whole of France. She tapped a couple more times, and then one final tap. The map zoomed in and went blank. I looked at her. She said, "It's processing."

We watched the screen for around thirty seconds.

I said, "It's slow."

She said nothing. A few seconds later, the blank screen began to be filled in by the graphic lines and place names of a map. A few seconds after that, red pins began to populate the map, around a dozen of them. She said, "That's it."

"What is it?"

"The black hole."

"I don't see a black hole, just a bunch of pins in a map."

Nazari futzed with the phone. She said, "The pins are where the cell phones went dead. I'm just trying to see if there's a pattern."

I said, "Do you recognize where that is?"

Nazari used her fingers to pinch and un-pinch, trying to get the map so that she could figure out where it was. She said, "It's here."

"What do you mean 'here'?"

"Alencourt. The central point is an area near the river." I heard a little involuntary 'oh'. She said, "I know where that is."

"Great. Where?"

She looked at me, surprise written all over her face. "The middle of the circle. I think it's the mayor's house."

"It's that precise?"

"No but it's either his house or the Vaugeois. Only two properties in that area."

I said, "Which would explain the attack on Gilles."

She looked at me, "How so?"

"I'll show you when we're back at the house."

CHAPTER FIFTY-SIX

WE DROVE BACK FEELING LUCKY.

The sky was pale blue, but not just one shade of blue. It went from light blue, almost white on the edge, to deeper blue. Reminded me of a Blue jay, the bird, not the baseball team. I'd spent a winter training in New Hampshire. Up in the White Mountains. It was a cold weather survival course. The last week was a solo. Which meant that they dumped me blindfolded and bound on a trail somewhere, threw a bucket of water over me, kicked me in the balls and took off. They left a purple smoke grenade in case I wanted to tap out.

I didn't tap out. I almost froze to death in the first few hours, but I figured it out and ended up having a pretty good time. First and foremost, I cheated. Before getting in the back of the truck, I'd stuck a little cigarette lighter where the sun don't shine, which proved useful when making a fire to cook the beavers I trapped. Second, I made the most of my body temperature, which meant digging in the snow and staying there, using my body as a heater and the snow as insulation.

So, I never learned how to make a fire by rubbing sticks together, but I got a taste for roasted beaver tail. And every morning I'd wake up to the blue mountain sky, and the same old Blue jay would land on the same branch and just look at me and caw. The bird's colors ran from white to deep sky blue. Just like the sky over Alencourt France.

But we didn't need to make a fire in Alencourt, the day was heating up all by itself. Mostly because the sun was out and it was late June. We had the windows rolled down and Nazari turned the knob on the Peugeot's radio. Luckily it wasn't French music, which might have been an issue, but the Rolling Stones. One of my favorite songs, 100 Years Ago, off Goat's Head Soup.

We were feeling lucky, so she cranked the volume. She was laughing and dancing and playing air guitar while she drove. I'm not much of a dancer so I just nodded my head to the beat.

We were coming up on the bridge towards the house. She was looking at me and I was looking at her. She mouthed my name, "Tom", and even though I couldn't hear her voice over the music, I heard it anyway, in my head. Her hair was out and wild, blowing around with the wind coming through the window. And through her hair I caught a quick flash of sunlight glancing off a reflective surface, like a window, or a pair of glasses, or a rifle scope.

WITHOUT EVEN THINKING or knowing about it, I was moving across towards Nazari, who was cluelessly bopping around and having a great time listening to the Stones. My hands were flailing out like autonomous grapplers, looking for any part of her that they could bring down. They were ruthless. At the same time, but separately, my eyes were tracking the source of that reflection, and I saw the muzzle flash long before I heard it.

I grabbed at Nazari's hair and pulled her head down quick. It was vicious and unkind in one way, and loving and helpful in another. It might have been unpleasant, but not as unpleasant as being shot in the head.

That all happened in a fraction of a second. Then, I had her down on the seat, and I was flattening myself over her. I wasn't paying any attention to the car, likely to crash soon. A car crash was the least of our worries. Half a second after the initial reflection, the bullet passed through the air over our heads. A .50 caliber bullet will make a supersonic shock wave that mulches anything soft into pink mist within twelve inches of its path. Which is why I was flattening us down and hoping for the best.

The projectile rifled through the driver's side window, came through the cockpit with a wicked hiss, and then shot out through the passenger side. A split second later I heard an enormous boom, as the sound of the rifle fire finally arrived. That was no normal sniper rifle. The bullet stopped eventually, that's for sure, but on the way it might have taken out a small tree, or vaporized a family of squirrels, you never really know.

I was not conscious of unclipping the seat belt, it just happened. First hers, then mine. The car went off the road, bumping to the left, over the edge and onto the incline. The same side of the road as the shooter. I pulled the hand brake, which didn't totally stop the car, but softened the impact. We hit a tree on the way down. Lucky again, because the Peugeot hadn't built up extra speed. I kicked open my door and pulled Nazari out the passenger side. By then she was aware, vaguely, of crisis. She scrambled over. I said, "Get behind the engine block and keep your head down".

Two rounds slammed into the car in quick sequence, followed by the sound of fast burning powder exploding. One of the supersonic bullets ripped through the Peugeot, and exploded out the other side, about a foot away from me, leaving shredded metal. The other was stopped by the engine block. The gun was so powerful that the impact rocked the car. It felt like a huge angry robot was punching the Peugeot with a sledgehammer. Definitely .50 caliber antimateriel.

The shot had come from the woods near the river. The shooter was up on a hill in the forest. I risked putting my head up and looking over the hood. An anti-materiel sniper rifle is a big deal. It is noisy and raises a hell of a lot of dust. But the woods weren't dusty, because of last night's rain, and I couldn't see much through the leaves. The shots were still echoing off the hill.

Another round smacked into the car's hood, destroying the front end and tearing off a piece of the bumper. I hunkered down with Nazari, willing myself to disappear. The Peugeot's not a big car, but the engine weighs about three hundred fifty pounds, so it's a decent thing to have between your body and the barrel of a monster gun. I looked at Nazari. She was curled up behind the wheel well, beside what I figured was the position of the engine block. She yelled out, "What the hell is that?"

"I guess they really want us to go away forever."

"Yes. But what is it?"

"Sniper rifle."

"Shit, I liked my car."

I put my head out again and took a more careful look. Either my head was coming off, or I would get a clue. Either one was better than being huddled in terror. I saw movement up in the forest. I reached into the back seat of the Peugeot and pulled the MP5 from where I'd stashed it under the front seat. I chambered a round and flicked the switch to triple. Fifteen rounds in the clip and one in the chamber. Sixteen rounds total.

I stretched out my foot to drag in the torn-off piece of car bumper, raised it up above the car. Another shot boomed and the shock wave from the round rippled across the skin of my hand, missing the piece of car bumper by a couple inches. I stood up, laid the H&K over the roof and fired two triple bursts more or less randomly in the general direction of the shooter. Then I saw someone coming up the road from the bridge. It was another shooter, not a friendly. I put a quick triple in his direction before ducking down behind the engine block.

Nine rounds gone, seven to go. At least two active shooters. Not good.

I risked another look. The guy on the road had taken cover, which was good. At least it delayed him. Maybe the sniper was doing the same, after I'd put a couple of bullets his way. I didn't even consider the possibility he'd been hit. My shots were way off target, suppression fire.

She said, "What's the plan?"

I didn't know. It wasn't a good situation. We were stuck on an incline from the road into the forest, towards Brumaire. The only cover we had was the engine block. We were being squeezed from the flank by the guy coming off the bridge. Nowhere to run, nowhere to hide. Then I heard the tinkling of submachine gun fire from a suppressed barrel, followed by the sound of bullets peppering the Peugeot. The guy on the bridge was armed with the same gun as me. Which made a lot of sense, since we both had the same supplier.

I figured it was now or never. I'd go for the guy on the bridge. A dash of several seconds, firing on the run. Get to cover on the other side of the road. Then, I'd put down covering fire for Nazari to join me. I started to sprint towards the shooter. Number one thing to do when you're ambushed, close them down, fast as possible.

Another monster .50 cal round ripped past me, took out a chunk of the road. The boom came a fraction of a second later. By then I had the MP5 up and was tracking through the sights as I ran. I saw the guy, who was huddled besides the concrete barrier on the bridge walkway. I put a burst towards him while on the run. Came close, but not close enough. The rounds kicked up dust from the concrete bridge paving.

Four rounds left. Make em count.

Then, from behind the guy, a neat white Volkswagen roared over the bridge. The little car was being pushed to its maximum acceleration, which wasn't that fast, but fast enough. Miriam was behind the wheel. The shooter was focused on me, for good reason, I was a deadly threat with a gun. He looked over his shoulder eventually, but by then it was too late.

I caught a glimpse of Miriam's face, a mask of grim determination. No emotion, just concentration, nostrils flaring, eyes wide and raging. Beside her was Father Bousquet. I could make out the distinctive bush of white hair.

That was like a frozen frame in a movie. Then, the movie kept playing and Father Bousquet's Volks nailed the guy straight on at around fifty miles per hour. Miriam had the killer instinct. The white car's bumper made contact at hip level. The guy's hip moved weirdly, but his head and legs stayed. I heard the pop and crack of broken vertebrae and spine.

The impact flung the guy toward me, like a teddy bear thrown across the room by a raging child. The limbs were askew and loose, doing things that a living human being's limbs would never do. Dead on arrival. The whiplash from impact must have broken his neck straight away.

I was yelling to Miriam, not words really, more like incoherent brutal sounds. What I wanted to tell her was to get to cover and off the elevated road. I ran like hell and pointed madly towards the other side of the road. Father Bousquet was looking wildly around, at the dead guy, then at me, then at the dead guy again. I was screaming like a crazy person, trying to get Miriam to move.

But of course, she had no way of knowing about a sniper up on the hill. Her face was flushed red.

It was too late. I saw the flash out of the corner of my eye. The .50 cal round entered through the rear window, passed through Bousquet's head and out through the windshield, like a stone dropped in a pond. Bousquet's head ceased to exist and the windshield blew out. Then there was the terrifying delayed boom of the gun. The Volks veered off road and disappeared on the other side.

I didn't reflect or think, just ran, sprinting directly towards the big gun. No time to pick up the dead guy's ammo. No time to think. I needed to close them down, fast as possible. Eyes up and scanning. I saw something through the trees. The shooter was moving, which meant that he wouldn't be in a good position to aim the beast of a gun he was carrying. I ran toward a mound of earth on the way to the river. I felt another shock wave as a projectile passed, then heard the sonic boom. I dove against the mound, took a breath and ran down to the river, thinking that I'd come around to the shooter's flank.

When I got down to the water, underneath the bridge, I heard the whine of a ten horsepower engine. The small boat was three hundred yards up river. At that distance, the figures were silhouettes. The surviving shooter splashed into the water and clambered in. Looked like the guy with the beard, Grouse's friend. Another guy stood in the back and hit the engine throttle bar. He spotted me.

I took a knee and got the MP5 up and sighted. I squeezed off a triple burst and the standing guy dropped. The boat started to spin. But then the bearded guy was up, seated and steering. I sprinted forward and braced against a tree. Took a breath and released it, steadying my hands. Then I saw movement on the river bank behind the boat. I lowered the H&K and watched the boat move off downstream.

One round left in the chamber.

On the other side of the river a couple of old guys were setting up their gear for a day of fishing. A dog was running around happily. They must have heard the shooting, at least the .50 cal. But they were clueless, as if they hadn't noticed a thing. Lucky them.

CHAPTER FIFTY-SEVEN

I GOT BACK to the road. The tarmac was littered with windshield glass fragments. Little shiny cubes catching the light, crunching under my boots. Miriam was crouched by the road looking at the wreckage of Father Bousquet's white Volkswagen. I could see that she was shivering. Not from the cold, but from the adrenaline surge. She looked up at me as I came over the rise.

I said, "You found something, with the names?" Her teeth were chattering, she was trying to speak. I crouched down next to her and put a hand on her shoulder. "It's an adrenaline dump. Got to give it time. Close your eyes and concentrate on my voice." I kept the physical contact and counted down from twenty, nice and slow, encouraging her to breathe as deep as she could. After that she was better.

She opened her eyes and engaged mine. "The girls' names. I found them as soon as Father Bousquet gave me the list. I was organizing the database, that's why he didn't have them on his computer. He wasn't good at that stuff."

"Ok good. What about them?"

Nazari's voice came up in an angry shout. "Help me!" She was trying to pull the priest's body out of the wreckage. The corpse was headless and soaking with blood and gore. She was having a hard time getting the legs free from the wreckage. The front end had crumpled on impact with a big tree, no doubt Father Bousquet's feet were trapped.

I yelled down at her, "Forget it. We don't have time for that." Miriam looked at me darkly. "We'll be back for him later."

She didn't look happy. "You can't leave him like that."

I said, "He's dead. Get over it." I squeezed her shoulder. "About the girls. Keep going."

Miriam blinked twice and looked away. "Remember what I told you, about the selection for the foundation."

"I remember. They were selected?"

She shook her head. "No. They were not selected. What they had in common was not being selected."

"They all appeared in front of the panel of foundation board members, but didn't make it?"

Miriam said, "That's right."

I nodded. "And the mayor was on the panel each time."

"Always."

"And that's how he made his special selection."

Nazari came up to the road. "Did you get the shooter?"

"There was a boat with a driver. The shooter got away. But we'll get him. No worries."

"How do we do that?"

I said, "Come on up to the house. I'll show you."

The H&K felt light, which reminded me. I walked over the road to the remains of Nazari's Peugeot. The car had seen happier days. The extra magazine for the MP5 was under the passenger seat. I stuffed it into my back pocket. When I came up to the road again, a Municipal Police car was rolling slowly off the bridge, over the busted glass. Acting Police Chief Antoine Bonnet had his window down and was staring at the chaotic scene. He pulled the cop car over to the side and Nazari walked up to meet it.

By the time I made it over to them, Bonnet was out of the car and he and Nazari were in an animated conversation. Bonnet turned when I approached. He looked terrible. Shocked and stressed and covered in black soot, as if he'd been burned alive. He smelled strongly of smoke. I said, "You smell like an out of control barbecue."

Bonnet ignored the joke. "The police station's on fire. I think there are several dead."

I said, "So what are you doing here?"

"There was nothing to do there, the firemen are on it. I came to make sure Cecile is okay. Do you think this is connected?"

Nazari laughed bitterly. "Damn right it's connected. Those assholes from Amiens aren't cops, they're imposters. Private mercenaries working for the mayor."

I said, "Looks like someone triggered an exit strategy."

Bonnet said, "I don't understand."

"How'd you know Nazari was here?"

He looked at her. Nazari said, "He doesn't know my first name."

I said, "I do but for some reason I think of you as Nazari more than Cecile."

Bonnet looked from me to her. He said, "Cecile told me you were both here."

She said, "I sent him a message. He's a friend, Keeler."

"Ok." I smiled at him coldly. "Sent him a message when?"

She said, "When we came here after what happened. Day before yesterday."

Bonnet said, "She messaged me after the Rigalle family were killed. You remember when I saw you outside the station. I was with the mayor, and the investigators."

"The fake BRI investigators."

"I guess so." Bonnet looked exhausted. "She messaged me after that. So tell me what's going on."

I said, "Tell me about the fire first."

"I was home and got a call. When I got to the station it was already well underway."

Nazari said, "When did the fire start?"

"Early this morning. Before the first shift at least."

I shared a look with Nazari. They must have fired up the police station when they knew that last night's raid on Brumaire had failed. I pictured the scene at the police station. Big fire, every resource mobilized to tackle it. Good tactics. I said, "Ok. So the game is on for real now. The fire's a diversion. All in all it's a good thing. Everything's coming out in the open."

Bonnet snorted, "A good thing! That's rich. There are dead cops now."

"Which is why we need to go up to the house and regroup."

"Who put you in charge? I'm acting chief so we'll do as I say." Bonnet looked uncertainly at the gunman's body, sprawled like a puppet on the edge of the road.

I made eye contact with Bonnet and didn't break it. At the same time, I lifted the H&K and popped the last round out of the chamber. The bullet flew up in the air and I caught it without looking, and put it between my teeth. I pulled the empty mag out and traded it for the fresh one from my back pocket. Once the new mag was properly seated I slipped in the extra round and closed the bolt.

I said, "Far as I'm concerned you're not acting chief of anything."

Bonnet was looking at me like a hypnotized lobster. Nazari said, "Tom's right. Looks like that creep mayor Marbot is behind this. If he put you in charge, it wasn't for any of the right reasons. We've done the leg work, so you'd be better off cooperating."

Bonnet was wavering. "I should go back."

I said, "This is the priority, right here and now. Believe me. We're going to end it."

"From the house?"

"Yes."

Miriam was listening. She said, "Quit wasting time."

Miriam helped me drag the guy's body off the road and behind Nazari's Peugeot. I retrieved his weapon and ammunition. Then we all went up to the house.

CHAPTER FIFTY-EIGHT

DANIEL WAS up on the terrace in the rocking chair. The Chapuis double barrel was cradled in his lap. He hadn't fired it, yet. When we came up he said, "Breakfast in the kitchen if you want it." We wanted it.

Madame Vaugeois had put together egg sandwiches with bacon and cheese. She said that it was a special recipe for when her husband Gilles went out hunting. I asked her what was special and she pointed at Maria. "Maria's bread."

Maria was pulling rolls out of the oven. Smelled real good. Maria said, "Busy night deserves a wholesome breakfast."

I would have agreed verbally, but I was already occupied with an egg sandwich. Bacon, egg, bread, cheese, grease, everything a body might need. Nazari had also fallen mute, devouring one of those beautiful hot things. Neither Miriam nor Bonnet had eaten yet, so we all sat at the table focusing for a minute on nutrition. The coffee was hot and black and kept on coming.

Once I had eaten and put down four cups of coffee, I felt the energy flowing through me again, full bore. So I went outside to breathe some air. The day had turned out clear and crisp. Not too

hot, not too cold. Just a perfect day. Which is why I was paying attention to something tugging at a corner of my mind like a bird dog who's
gotten a scent. Something was bothering me and I couldn't put my
finger on it. Far as I could make out, we were on track to make a
straight shot through to the other side and finish this thing. But my
gut was telling me otherwise, and I always listen to my gut, even
when I don't know what it's saying.

Whatever it was, it wasn't coming through just yet. So I figured it
was best to carry on. The problem would reveal itself when it was
ready. I just had to trust my intuition. I put those thoughts behind me
and gathered everyone in the drawing room around the big dining
table.

I went up to Gilles' office and returned downstairs with an
armful of maps. I spread out a big one on the table. It was a map of
Brumaire and its immediate surroundings, maybe a two mile radius
around the house. I pointed out the salient features. Cliff face, terrace
of the house and the direction it was facing, gatekeeper's cottage, the
road, the bridge, the river.

I traced my finger along the river bank to the next house over.
"This map shows the surface features of the area. You all recognize
what this is?"

Simone said, "Mayor Marbot's villa."

"That's right. The only two significant properties this side of the
river."

Marbot's house was represented in the same detail as Brumaire.
It too had a terrace and a couple of outbuildings, a barn, and access to
the river. A bridge across the river connected the house to the road on
the other side, which was its main access. The two houses dominated
that part of the river bank. Madame Vaugeois said that this was
because both houses once operated adjacent apple and pear orchards,
which had now turned to forest.

I unfolded another large map and spread it over the first. The
map was mostly blank. What it did show were large irregular shapes,
like cartoon speech bubbles drawn in thin, squiggly lines.

I said, "This map shows what there is beneath the surface. You see those big shapes?"

I looked around at the others. Everyone was deeply concentrated. Nazari saw me looking and nodded at me. "Yes."

"Those are the bigger caverns. The excavations. You see the squiggly lines that taper off?"

She nodded again. "Go on, yes."

"Those are entry points to the system." I traced a finger along the edge of a large cavern shape. "If you look close you can see that there are actually two systems represented on the map."

The others leaned over. What they were looking at was a boundary edge, the thin borderline between neighboring cave systems that came close to each other, but didn't connect.

I turned to Simone. "I believe that's the reason for the trouble and the attack on your husband. He got too close to what the mayor was doing, and the mayor became paranoid."

Vaugeois was struggling to make sense of the map. She said, "I don't understand how you can draw that conclusion from this. It just looks like a bunch of crooked lines drawn on a piece of paper."

"Watch." I squared the two maps, one on top of the other, corner to corner. Same size paper. I fastened the big sheets together with a bunch of foldback paper clips from Gilles' desk drawer. Daniel took one end, I took the other. We moved over to the big window and held the maps up to the light.

The white paper sheets became transparent with the backlight, like tracing paper. Only the drawn lines were visible. We were now able to see the surface map overlaid with the underground map. Like a single unified truth.

I said, "Look where the cavern entrance tapers in." I was pointing to a part of Brumaire. The cavern shape clearly narrowed to the corridor right in front of Gilles and Simones' bedroom. The location corresponded perfectly to the entrance to the cave from the house.

Simone inhaled sharply. "*Mon dieu.*" She was at my shoulder and clutching my arm. "But, Tom, why was the mayor worried about what Gilles might know? What is he doing with his cave?"

"Nothing good, ma'am, that's for damn sure."

Nazari said, "That's what we're going to find out."

I looked at Bonnet. He said nothing. I said, "What do you think, Bonnet?"

He licked his lips. "Did you think it might be a good idea to call the police?" He turned to Nazari. "Did you think about including me?"

She said, "There were good reasons not to trust our colleagues, and that included you. It's all happened fast."

I said, "Don't dwell on the past, Bonnet. The mission happens here and now. We have no time to call backup because they are activating an exit strategy as we speak. Now listen up and I'll tell you what we're going to do."

Bonnet shrugged and held his hands up, body language for, 'okay, no problem.'

I said, "The plan isn't complicated, it's simple. We're going to bust through the Vaugeois cavern wall, and into the Marbot cave system. Then it's a straight shot up through to the mayor's house. Cleaning up whatever we find on the way."

Nazari said, "Bust through how?"

Daniel was in the back, sitting on a chair with his bird gun. He spoke quietly, "We'll use a sledge hammer."

I said, "That's correct. Two things to prepare first, the precise entry point, and weapons."

Daniel fetched a couple of tacks and pinned up the maps so we didn't have to hold them. The double sheets hung at the window, making the room feel like a command center. I thought it improved the look. A sense of *deja vu* was nagging me. But I'd seen a whole bunch of maps hanging on walls in my service career, no big deal.

Gilles had used graph paper sheets for the surface map. He had made a little map key at the bottom, which showed scale. Since we were in France they counted in meters, and each square on the graph represented five of them. I counted out the squares, from the cave entrance over by the Vaugeois' bedroom, to the part of the cavern adjacent to Marbot's cave system.

The excavation closest to Marbot's was a section of tunnel. It was the long, old and dark tunnel I'd seen before. Counting along the right-hand wall, the best access point would be sixty-two and a half squares from the door. That was three hundred and twelve odd meters, give or take. A meter is like an extended yard. Like taking a really big step instead of just a big one. I'd need to go deep in there.

Daniel had a click wheel for measuring off garden areas. We'd use that. I figured that the measurements could not be incredibly precise. We would have to wing it to some extent.

I turned to the weapons. We had four H&K MP5s and the two Beretta M9s. Bonnet had his Sig-Pro, and Daniel had his Chapuis bird gun. I put the H&Ks and the Berettas on the table. I wanted Nazari and Daniel to strip the weapons and clean them. We had rags and cotton swabs and coat hanger wire, but we had no gun oil in the house. Daniel had some for his double barrel, so he went down to the gatekeeper's house to get it. He slung the Chapuis over his shoulder. Didn't need cleaning because he had not used it.

Meanwhile I took a tactical vest and crammed as much ammo as I could into it, plus the roll of duct tape. I looked around the room. Maria and Madame Vaugeois had gone to rest. Nazari was showing Miriam how to use the Beretta M9. Bonnet brushed past me, and out the door. I figured he was using the head. In the corner of my eye the white maps waved in the breeze coming through the old window.

Then something clicked in my mind, like a marble dropping into a chain-reaction machine.

The nagging problem, the intuition that something was not quite right. It was the white pieces of map paper. One on top of the other. I looked at Nazari. She was already looking at me. We were tuned up, on the same wavelength.

I said, "The fact-pattern."

"What about it?"

"I think I can make an addition."

"How so?"

I pulled the paper receipt that I'd got for the coffee and croissants out of my pocket and handed it to her. "Hold that. It's the receipt from the tennis club coffee hut." Then I put my fingers into the little change pocket of my jeans and pulled out the crumpled receipt I'd found way back, when I was searching the Woodcutter's empty office. I held it up. "Remember this?" She nodded. I examined the older receipt, then handed it to her. "Looks the same."

There was electronic printing in dark violet against the white paper. Five items. No words on the receipt, just numbers, prices and codes. The top right side had a seven-digit computer printed code. Nazari looked at it, looked at the new one from the coffee hut. Two white pieces of paper, one next to the other.

She said, "It is the same. See the numbers up top?"

I looked at the numbers up top, which were the same.

She said, "It's the retail identifier. Same retailer."

"Same place."

She looked down at the receipts, then up at me. "The tennis club. Everyone goes there."

"Who's everyone?"

"The rich guys. Rigalle went there, the mayor, Antoine goes there. It's the spot. Bonnet goes there as well of course."

I said, "But not everyone had a reason to be visiting the Woodcutter."

"Yes, that must narrow things down some."

And then the marble dropped again, like a definitive click.

"And there's another thing."

"What's that?"

"Tennis balls."

She looked at me as if I were making a joke. But I guess my face didn't look so funny, because she just examined my eyes, like she was searching for something there, rationally and with curiosity. She wanted the facts. "What about tennis balls, Keeler?"

"Take a look at the receipt I found in the Woodcutter's office. There are five items listed. Three of them are the same price, five sixty-nine. Then you've got a couple of higher ticket items. Is that right?"

She examined the receipt. "Correct. Three for five sixty-nine and then thirteen twenty-eight, and another for thirty-two eighty-seven."

"And guess how much a can of tennis balls costs?"

"Five sixty-nine."

"Bingo. Five sixty-nine. Written on a big star-shaped tag down there in the coffee hut. That's for the good balls, the expensive ones in a gold can."

"So the Woodcutter was a tennis player? I don't get it."

"That's enough."

Nazari and I turned. Bonnet was standing in the doorway. He had his Sig-Pro up and pointed at me.

Nazari said, "Antoine, what are you doing? Put that down."

He said, "I think Keeler was about to explain something." He gestured to me, "Go on."

Bonnet was walking into the room. I walked slowly away from the dining table, putting distance between myself and the other two, drawing him with me.

I spoke to Nazari. "When you brought me into the police station, after we realized there was a crooked cop, I had a little chat with your friend here, the new interim director of municipal police, Antoine Bonnet. Everyone says that Bonnet's a great tennis player. Isn't that so, Bonnet?"

He had a slight grin on his face, like he was proud. "That's what they say."

I turned to Nazari again. "So, on his desk he had three brand new cans of tennis balls, which would make sense since he's a big tennis guy."

Nazari looked as though she'd been punched in the gut. She turned to Bonnet. "Antoine?"

I said, "The cans on his desk were gold. The expensive kind. Only the best for the new police chief."

Bonnet shrugged at her. "It's complicated."

I turned and backed toward the wall. I was trying to position Bonnet so he'd be framed in the other big window. He was keeping his gun on me, but trying not to lose sight of Miriam and Nazari. The weapons on the table were useless because they'd been disassembled. I was patting the air with my hand, the kind of gesture that says, 'slow it down'. Nazari wasn't following, she was concentrated on Bonnet. Behind her, Miriam was using Nazari's body as a shield. She was trying to assemble one of the Berettas, but failing. She looked up at me and I shook my head slightly.

Nazari was also shaking her head. Not as if she didn't believe what I was saying, but because she was pissed off. She ignored Bonnet. "What about the other items, the bigger ticket prices."

Bonnet waved the Sig-Pro at me. "Go on, Keeler. What about them?"

I said, "I've thought about that. Does thirty-two eighty-seven sound like the kind of price you might pay to have a tennis racket restrung? Those tennis guys break strings all the time, or at least that's what I've heard."

Bonnet said, "I'll give you credit, Keeler. It's a reasonable assumption."

I was playing for time. "He had his racket there in the office. As if he'd just picked it up from the club and bought a couple of cans of balls, the good kind."

Bonnet shrugged. "The good kind are worth the extra expense."

I said, "One thing I don't get. Why did you go to see the Wood-cutter and take the risk? Why not just use the burner phones and keep the communications safe?"

Bonnet said, "It was getting messy. Sometimes you need to have a face to face conversation." Bonnet turned to Nazari. "It isn't too late for you to join us. This guy's dead within the next minute or two."

I said, "Actually it's the other way around. You'll be dead in ten seconds."

Bonnet laughed abruptly. "How's that, Keeler, I've got the weapon, it's loaded. Full metal jacket."

"Five seconds."

Even though he held the gun, I could see the confidence waning. He'd become pale. A sweat had broken out under his perfect hairline.

"Three seconds."

Bonnet said, "What? Three seconds for what?"

Behind him, through the window, Daniel was mouthing the count. He had the big Chapuis double barrel up. Two, one, I dropped to the floor. Both barrels fired. I was thinking, 32-gram load of No 5 shot. That's an average of about a hundred and seventy pellets per cartridge. Daniel fired two cartridges simultaneously. The spread was tight and flat. Bonnet's head separated from his body, but both fell in a pile where he had been standing.

I lay curled up on the floor, peppered with tiny pieces of window and Bonnet. I was painted with blood, as if I'd stepped into a custom spray shop. Daniel stepped through the window with his gun. I picked myself off the floor and wiped my eyes carefully with a sleeve.

I nodded to him in approval. "Okay, the gun works."

CHAPTER FIFTY-NINE

Nazari wasn't happy, but I figured it was best if she and Daniel stayed up in the house as a rear guard. We had no way of knowing if there was a plan to come back at us. I doubted it, which wasn't any kind of a guarantee. *Hope for the best, prepare for the worst.* Miriam and I loaded up. We each slung an H&K over tactical vests crammed with ammo. Not that there was an endless supply. We had two extra magazines each. I had one of the M9s with spare rounds in a pocket, the roll of duct tape, and a flashlight. The sledgehammer went over my shoulder. Good to go.

Daniel stayed up on the terrace. Through the open door he had line of sight on Nazari, in a chair by the stairs. From there she was close enough to the cavern entrance. I told Daniel to keep back against the house. No reason to make an easy target of himself. Once in the caverns there wouldn't be any communication between us, which is why I wanted them to hold the fort and guard my rear.

I turned the knob on the Vaugeois' bedroom door and opened it a crack. Gilles was asleep. The curtains half drawn, letting in soft light. The oxygen pump in the corner wheezed with each labored breath. I figured Madame was upstairs napping. I pulled the door closed and turned to Miriam, who had already opened the door to the cavern entrance.

Miriam was quiet and eager. She went first with Daniel's click wheel and started measuring from the door, straight through the alcove with the wine collection, into the big cave. I was close behind her. We hugged the right side wall. I dragged a hand along it. The scored stone was cold and pale. The wheel clicked every meter, and each time it did that, a little display ticked over a new number. At the end of the big cavern the wheel clicked to one hundred and fifty.

Beyond that the tunnel entrance extended into darkness.

I unslung the H&K and tore off five strips of duct tape. Three went on my tactical vest just in case, the other two secured the mini-mag light under the H&K's barrel. I looked at Miriam, she looked back. Her eyes were clear and confident beneath the ruler-straight brow line. She looked positively dangerous. The mini-mag from Vaugeois' desk drawer spread light in a cone. The click wheel ticked rhythmically as we chased after the light, pushing into the black. Took us a couple of minutes walking before the wheel ticked over and Miriam whispered, "Three hundred and twelve." I raised a finger to my lips, we were close to the Marbot caves. I gave it another half meter and ran a hand along the wall. It felt solid, but we'd see just how solid it was real soon.

I exchanged weapons with Miriam, and pointed to the spot on the wall. She backed up against the other side of the tunnel and took a knee, aiming the light to give me a nice big circle for a target. I made a gesture with my gun, and Miriam nodded. She got the short code, no fuss, no problem, and slipped the H&K safety off and the selector to triple burst, just like I'd showed her. I set the other MP5 against the cavern wall. The sledgehammer felt good in my hands. The wooden handle was old and I figured it had been impregnated with the sweat of working people like Daniel, their callused hands smoothing down the oak until there it was now, in my fists, tight-grained, dark with use, ready.

I swung the steel head in a long horizontal arc. The entire motion was a force multiplier, transferring the mechanical work into kinetic energy gathering in the steel head. The steel hit stone with a thick thwack that echoed in the confined tunnel. I'd hit the sweet spot, deep and hard. I reset immediately and swung again. Same thing. Steel cracked against the limestone wall. The seventh strike penetrated. The hammer head got stuck in and I had to pull it out with a violent tug. I made two more hits in quick succession, and we had a hole.

Seven big hits, two secondary. I'd made some noise. So it was a gamble going through.

I tossed the sledgehammer aside and picked up the H&K. When I looked up, Miriam was already in, a fast mover. The hole was a good size for her, not so good for me. I lost sight of her, which wasn't a good thing. But then she was looking back at me. I got through the narrow opening and she shone her light around.

We had passed through a thick membrane of limestone, into a large space shaped like an egg sliced lengthwise. The other half of the egg was blocked off by a man-made wall. The cave we were in had higher ceilings than the tunnel we'd taken from the Vaugeois cavern. Mineral deposits rose up from the floor in spikes, other spiky stone formations hung from the ceiling. This was a natural cave, not excavated by hand. But the wall wasn't natural, it was made of cinder blocks, and around fifteen feet high, by twenty feet wide.

I whispered, "We'll have to put a hole in that, but it'll attract attention on the other side."

Miriam whispered back, "Can you break through in one shot?"

"Not one shot, more like five. Problem is, that wall was built as a sound barrier."

"How's that?"

"Most effective sound insulation is air, we're standing in an air pocket between Marbot's caves and the Vaugeois system." I walked over to the cinder block wall and inspected it for faults. A spider web crack ran from floor to ceiling. I whispered, "That's where I'll go in. I figure the bulk of their cavern is to our left." I pointed. "So you get in position to the right side, back from the wall."

Miriam got in place. I retrieved the sledgehammer.

I got the sledgehammer ready. Miriam was in position, crouched with her H&K up.

The hammer went through the block like it was a china plate. I didn't wait for the result, just went right into the next swing. It hammered home about half a second after the first. Two blocks gone. A black space had opened up. I was mid-way into my third swing, eyes focused on the target, when I saw a movement in the darkness on the other side. Nothing clear, a flitting shape in the dark. I didn't think, just reacted instinctively. Thirty-four years of struggle, failure, and hard-won success translated into an awkward improvisation. In mid-swing, I changed the plan and adjusted the sledgehammer to poke through the hole instead of slamming into a third block. The hammer head went all the way in, sticking through into the other space.

I heard a surprised grunt.

CHAPTER SIXTY

I LOOKED QUICKLY through the gap. Because I hadn't felt any contact I swung three more times, demolishing cinder blocks, until there was a big enough hole to get Miriam through. She whipped in like a ghost. I heard scurrying movements as I ditched the sledgehammer and picked up the H&K.

There was a gunshot, then two more. Not close, not far. Maybe thirty yards away. Not Miriam, someone with a semi-automatic pistol. I needed to get through the hole fast. A triple burst tinkled from Miriam's suppressed H&K. I squeezed through the hole. Miriam was crouched, waiting. Her mini-mag lit up a narrow tunnel. She pointed down the hole. The mini-mag has an impressive throw, something like a hundred and fifty yards. But the darkness had been made gloomy from the dust I'd raised.

Miriam suddenly sprinted into the gloom. She was gone in about two seconds flat. I heard another pistol shot. I ran into the darkness, weapon up and tracking. Straight through and came up against a stone wall. Pitch black now that Miriam was gone with the light. No vision whatsoever. I quickly traced the stone to my right and found a corner, kept going and did a u-turn. I'd missed another tunnel entrance. The faint tinkle of suppressed 9mm fire came through and I accelerated. My lead hand found the lip of an entrance, and I was through.

The new tunnel curved round in a bend. I could make out a light outlining a silhouette. I ran up to Miriam and tapped her shoulder. She looked at me quickly and gestured forward. About ten yards down, through the gloom, I could make out another light source. Looked like it was on the ground, which might mean that Miriam had hit her target.

I ran down the tunnel, bent at the waist. Weapon up and ready. I approached the shape of a person, sprawled out on the tunnel floor. It was a guy. He was alive. He was trying to figure out what had happened to him. What had happened was a tight pattern of 9mm parabelum rounds stitching up from the belly to the chest. A Glock 17 lay by his hip. I kicked it away. He looked up at me in confusion. I thumbed for single and put a round into his face, then flipped back to triple burst. I picked up his flashlight. Two strips of duct tape torn off my tactical vest secured the light to my gun. Better.

Miriam was right behind me. I turned and gently pushed her against the wall. Spoke quietly, with respect. "Don't do that again."

"Do what?"

"Run away without me. That was dangerous."

A man's voice called out questioningly, from up ahead around a curve, "Sam?"

I switched off the light and crab-walked towards the voice. Looked back and Miriam had done the same. She was just off my right shoulder. The guy called out again, "Sami, you ok?" The tunnel turned slightly and the guy was visible, standing at a door, half open to a dimly lit room. Low lighting for a room, bright as day in a cave. Beginning at the other side of that door, the tunnel was lit with wall sconces distributed down its length.

The guy was a silhouette in the doorway. "Sami, stop fucking around."

From behind him there was laughter. Another male said, "Look at this."

To which a third guy responded, "You're an idiot."

The first guy was still looking into the dark for his friend. I raised the pitch of my voice some and said, "Come here."

The guy took a step. "Sami?"

Soon as he stepped out of the door I put three rounds into his chest.

I was there before he hit the ground, guiding the body down. I stepped over him, and into the doorway. The room looked like a computer graphics studio, but carved out of solid limestone. Desks lined three walls, with big screens and discreet lighting drawing attention to the stone walls, like some form of interior decoration. These guys were artistic types, sensitive to the way things looked.

Two men in their late twenties, early thirties were leaning back in ergonomic chairs. They looked up at me in surprise as I came through. I shot the first one in the face. Three rounds made a tight triangular pattern where his nose and mouth met. Brains, blood, teeth fragments, and pieces of his skull went all over the computer screen, keyboard, and fancy trackball thing. Not to mention the wall, the desk, and partly his buddy, who sucked in once and began hyperventilating.

I said, "What's all this?" Although I could already see from the picture up on the screen. The guy couldn't speak, could only attempt to breathe, sucking the air for oxygen like a drowning fish. I said, "Take your time."

The guy was getting closer to being able to say something, but Miriam had seen the screens, and her H&K got there first. She put two bursts into him, one after the other, like a parade ground drum roll. The guy's muscular skeletal system collapsed, slumping him off the chair and onto the floor. I looked at Miriam. She was looking at one of the screens.

She said, "Pigs."

The screen was a big professional graphics monitor. Something that a guy like Blomstein might use for monitoring data feeds. But, here they weren't using their high tech gear for intelligence.

The screen real estate was divided into boxes, seemed like what a video editing interface should look like. One of the boxes showed an image of a young girl in a fancy-looking bedroom. The furniture looked old, like from the Middle Ages of knights and princesses, aristocratic and expensive. Above the bed was an open window looking out on green hills and forests with a river valley snaking off into the distance. The girl was naked except for a black hood, which wasn't very aristocratic. Her arms were tied and attached to the ceiling, braced in what looked like a very uncomfortable position. And that didn't account for other aspects of the position, which left her even more vulnerable. Miriam stepped up and pressed a button on the keyboard. The video started playing. For a couple of beats, the girl was just there, kind of swinging from the ceiling, shifting uncomfortably under the strain. Then two men entered the frame. They were dressed in long robes and wore white masks with large hooked bird beaks.

I said, "What's with the masks?"

Miriam said, "They're dressed as plague doctors. I don't know why."

"Plague doctor, how do you know that?"

"I read a book about it."

One of the plague doctors began unwrapping what looked like a canvas roll containing medical instruments. Strange and ancient tools that looked like no fun at all for the patient. The other guy just watched the girl. Then they started doing things to the girl. They used instruments and hands and other parts. She struggled and strained at the rope, but it was no use. The guys in robes were abusing their power, that was for damn sure. The video was a grim mix of pornography and pure, unforgivable sadism, not the fun kind that people pay to endure. We both stood there and watched until the end, like it was a chore we needed to complete. The girl survived, exhausted, violated, and betrayed. For her there was no happy ending.

Miriam and I looked at each other. She said, "No mercy."

It wasn't a question, and I wasn't arguing.

Miriam got involved with the computer. There were more videos, hundreds of them, all kinds of scenarios. Medieval looked popular, but there were modern ones as well. Each of them featured young women and girls in vulnerable situations, being abused. She said, "They're selling these on the internet. Like a subscription service for psychopaths."

"Not anymore they're not."

"This is disgusting, people send in scenarios, and these guys make them. Like customized torture."

I said, "Let's shut it down."

We went back out to the tunnel and continued moving. Despite the twists and turns, I was oriented. The tunnel was running along an east-west axis. We were underground and heading toward the river, and ultimately, Mayor Marbot's house. The excavation was clean and thorough, the result of significant work over at least a year if not more. There were doors neatly spaced out all along the left-hand side of the tunnel. The right side was limestone, wall sconces were pegged into the stone, scored like the other caverns I'd seen around Alencourt.

The first door was open. I stepped up and I pointed my light in. It was the film set from the most recent video, the same fancy-looking bedroom. Above the bed, the window we'd seen in the video swung open. Except, there was nothing there but a stone wall painted green. The room was empty of people, filled with tripods and lighting gear on one side, all turned off and silent. The bed and furniture were on the other side, empty and haunted. We kept on going. More rooms, all empty of people, all setup for filming various degrading and violent scenes. Some were bigger than others.

Up ahead, someone walked around the corner. I was moving in a crab-walk with the H&K up. Before he could blink I'd put three rounds down the hole, the suppressed muzzle purred. Ten seconds later we arrived at another body. This time the guy wasn't moving. He got tapped regardless. Better safe than sorry.

I took a moment to examine the corpse. He was young, maybe twenty max. The guy wore a navy tracksuit with a stripe down the side. He had on fashionable sneakers. Footsoldiers. Young enough to be brave, dumb enough to die for it.

The guy had walked out of a toilet. About fifteen feet further on was a door. Closed. I looked at Miriam. Her face was flushed and she was breathing hard. Her eyes shone and the pupils were pins in the half light. We approached the door. As we got closer, I began to notice a growing humming noise. Miriam moved into a covering position. She had good tactical instincts. She nodded at me, like she was ready. I shrugged, and tried the handle. Locked.

I nodded to the dead guy in the tracksuit. Miriam was closer. I mimicked putting my hands in pockets. She saw my meaning and hustled over to the body. The second jacket pocket was a score. Miriam came up with keys and tossed them at me underhand. I caught them in a clenched fist. First one didn't fit. Second one didn't either. Third one went right into the lock.

The handle turned and I opened the door.

CHAPTER SIXTY-ONE

A LAUNDRY ROOM.

Three washing machines, no dryers, no people. One door to the left, a dark opening in the cavern to the right.

One of the washing machines was spinning, fast. Whirring at breakneck speed. Off to the right was an opening in the stone, beyond it was darkness. I aimed the H&K into the dark cavern and the light cone from the mini-mag picked out rows of clothing hung on thin line. They'd run the clothesline through hooks screwed into the rock. The cave didn't give out to any tunnels, or other rooms, a dead end.

The washing machine made a loud click and started to spin down. The high-pitched rattle and hum had covered our entry but we were about to lose that cover. I pointed towards the other door out of the laundry room. "Let's go."

I flattened my back against the wall, right side of the door. The H&K was slung across my chest. I had the M9 Beretta in my right hand. I turned the handle slow with my left and let the door swing open a few inches. There wasn't a whole lot to be seen, through that crack, at that angle. A stone wall, and something on the floor, textile or foam, like a mattress.

The machine spun down for good and made a beeping sound. I waited until that was finished. Then listened. Miriam was to my left, waiting with me. Patient. A minute later there was no sound coming from anywhere. Quite the opposite, the silence was deafening. I pushed the door open a couple more inches, swiveled my head around and took a good look.

The look revealed a dormitory, which explained the clothes. But it wasn't a dormitory like something out of basic training, which was my only reference. The dorms at Lackland Air Force Base had contained beds in organized rows, with two files of personal lockers on the other side of the room. In San Antonio the floors had been cleaned twice daily, with eager recruits on their knees, scrubbing away with toothbrushes. The floors there positively shone. Here it was different, there was no floor, just rock and dust.

We went through.

The dorm was a large cavern with a high ceiling. As far as housing went, the place was a dump. The limestone walls were lined with squalid mattresses, barely covered by thin sheets and insubstantial blankets. Instead of pillows, meager piles of clothing were being used. The smell of damp textiles and cooking oil impregnated the place. In the middle of the room was a food preparation area, which consisted of a camping stove on a foldable table. Bulk supplies of basic stuff, rice, beans, oil, and various bottles were set in open cardboard boxes, surrounded by a couple of upside-down crates to sit on. A big pack of drinking water bottles was mostly depleted. A pile of cooking utensils sat submerged in an orange plastic wash basin, half filled with dirty water. Two naked bulbs hung in the center of the room, too high up to give out much light. I scanned and counted fifteen mattresses.

And then I noticed the girls.

At first glance the beds had been empty. The room looked like it had been vacated in a hurry. Discarded foam mattresses with crumpled sheets and blankets. But something moved in my peripheral vision. I zoned in on the movement, advanced with the H&K up and ready. Someone was under the sheets, lying down. A pale yellow forehead was visible, dark greasy hair stuck out from the covers. The girl had dark circles around glazed eyes. The eyes were green, and glinted in the light of the exposed bulb. The girl saw me, that was for sure. But she avoided looking at my face, as if she'd made that mistake before and suffered consequences. A moaning sound came out of her mouth and she turned away, curling protectively into a fetal position.

I looked around at the other beds. They were inhabited. Miriam approached one of the mattresses and caught my eye. She cursed. We covered the room and checked each mattress. More than half of the beds were occupied by limp but live bodies under dirty sheets. The blankets were thin fleece, at best. I walked over to another mattress. The girl had dark curly hair. She might have been sixteen years old or less.

I touched the back of my hand to the girl's cheek. "Cold." I whispered to Miriam.

She nodded. "Drugged, obviously." At the far end of the room was another door. This one looked more substantial. Miriam said, "We need to get them out of here."

I said, "Correct, and quick."

Miriam crouched above one of the mattresses and turned the girl's chin towards her. The girl was barely responsive, a waxen face in a mound of curling black hair. Miriam slapped her cheek hard and the girl made a sound. Miriam turned to me. "I don't know if we can get them up and moving."

Then the girl on the mattress focused her eyes on Miriam. The girl spoke in French. "Who are you?"

Miriam said, "We're the ones who are going to save you. Can you get up?"

The girl sat up in the bed. "Where will you take us?"

"Somewhere safe. Out of here."

The girl looked at me "And him?"

I said, "I'm not coming with you. I'm going the other way."

"They'll kill you."

"They can try." The girl's eyeballs shifted in an immobile head. First to Miriam, then at me. I said, "What did they give you, pills?"

The girl nodded mutely, then pointed up towards the wall.

A half dome with a wicked little camera eye. Electric cable ran through conduit pipe and disappeared into the limestone wall. I reached up and grabbed the camera. Pulled it out of the wall and crushed it with my boot heel.

Miriam said, "They've seen us now."

I said, "Not necessarily. They've only seen us if someone's watching."

"What are the chances?"

"Slim to none. But let's get going anyway."

The girl began to rise unsteadily, managing to prop herself up on all fours. Miriam helped her.

The girl said, "The others are afraid of you, it's why they're pretending."

Miriam said, "Pretending what?"

"To be asleep." She stood up, leaning on Miriam and spoke in Arabic. Immediately there was shuffling of bodies.

"What did you say?"

The girl shrugged. "I told them we've got nothing left to lose."

I went to the locked door and listened. Nothing. Thick steel no handle. No keyhole either, just a steel plate. Looked like we were getting somewhere important, given that security was increasing.

I said, "What happens when you pound on the door?"

Another girl spoke, from a closer mattress. This one had dirty blonde hair. Her voice was hoarse, "Bad things happen when they come."

Miriam and the first girl were helping the others up. They began whispering to each other. Too far gone to be excited, but mobilizing anyway. Brave and motivated. The girls looked bad. Like the undead. They staggered and lurched, thin and sallow. Malnourished and beaten down. Despite what they had been through, the girls were supporting each other and putting on socks and a sorry assortment of domestic footwear. They still had hope, which made me confident that they'd pull through in the end.

Miriam said, "How are we going to get them all out? It's too dark and the way back is too complicated. It's a labyrinth. We're going to lose some of them."

I said, "You'll get lost, not me. Because I'm not coming."

"What do you mean, you're not coming?"

I pointed to the locked door. "I'm going the other way."

"Suicidal."

"No, more like homicidal at the moment."

Miriam shrugged. "Your call. So what do you suggest?"

"I suggest that you avoid getting lost." She gave me an exasperated look. I said, "Come with me."

We went back through the laundry room. I stepped into the clothes drying cave. The clothes were hanging on thin line. I held it in my fingers, it was braided fishing line.

"This is improvised. It's not the usual stuff people hang clothing on."

"So?"

"So, maybe there's more of it lying around somewhere. Nobody uses fishing line for laundry unless it happens to be lying around."

I pushed through the hanging laundry to the back of the cave. There was a bunch of old cardboard boxes piled up, just as I'd figured. The spool of fishing line was resting in the first box, exactly where it had been thrown after use. The box was full of fishing gear. Bait and tackle boxes, spools of line. An old French clasp knife with a wood handle. It was a big spool, the label said twelve hundred meters. I figured they'd used about thirty to hang the washing. I picked it up and turned to Miriam.

"You're going to let this run out behind you. I'll have the other end."

"What's that going to do?"

"Two things. The girls will go after you in single file, running the line through their hands as they go. They'll stay in touch and organized. Second thing, if I find the others, I can send them down the line to you."

"What others?"

"There are empty beds."

She nodded. "How do I find my way back?"

"You've got a light, you'll have to figure it out."

Miriam said, "Is that enough line?"

"It'll do." She looked up at me, fierce and determined. I said, "Good to go?"

"Good to go."

I looped the spool of braided line through a strap on the back of Miriam's tactical vest, and tested it. The line spun off without any issues. I tied the end to the clasp knife. The knife was an Opinel, famous French brand with a signature wooden handle and locking mechanism. I threaded the closed knife through the belt loop on my pants, and stuck it in the back pocket. That way, I'd stay in touch, and the Opinel wasn't going to fall out of my pocket. And if the line got stuck, I'd use the knife to cut it. Miriam went out the door, back the way we'd come. The girls formed in a single file after her, each one of them holding loosely to the braided line, letting it run through their hands. The last one out the door looked back at me for a moment. I leaned against the wall and counted two minutes in my head.

Then, I turned to the locked security door and pounded on it for thirty seconds straight. I figured that would get someone's attention.

CHAPTER SIXTY-TWO

For a while, nothing happened. I stopped pounding on the door, and the deep subterranean silence returned, fast. Then a mechanism inside the fancy steel plate snicked. A second later, the door swung in about an inch. I gripped the edge with my fingers and pulled it open. On the other side was another room, about the same size as the dormitory. But very different, and very empty.

The room was something out of a French royal pleasure palace. A place where it wasn't difficult to imagine Marie Antoinette eating a slice of strawberry shortcake, helped down with a coupe of champagne. Or worse, Mayor Marbot dressed like Louis XVI, which was a distinct possibility. The big room was divided into four circles. Each one more than ten yards across. Each circle had a domed ceiling, painted with a sky motif, edged with ornate ceiling cornices in gold leaf. Below each dome was a massive circular red velvet sofa banquette. The carpeting was blue and gold. It looked like an even fancier version of one of Madame Vaugeois' Hermes scarves. The four circles formed the organizing principle of the room. From there, the interior designers had been inspired to include all manner of antique furniture. Two and three-person love seats, pillowed plat-

forms with seats gathered round for observers, footstools, and uphol-
stered chairs. Large tables held candelabras. The walls were papered
in red and gold arabesque. I guess they'd gone for the expensive look
and succeeded.

This wasn't a movie set, it was the real thing. Marbot and his
friends had been hosting parties here. Parties that featured the
captive girls. The videos were one thing, shocking enough. But this
was on another level entirely. I've seen bad things, very bad things.
But this was brazen, an evil and cynical abuse of power.

I was turning in a long circle, trying to take it all in. I'd thought I
was alone, but as I finished the three-sixty I found out that I wasn't. I
might have heard the movement through the air, before I saw the
flashing motion in my peripheral vision. Whatever, that didn't matter
much, just a little bit. It was the little bit that saved me. Because a fist
the size of my head was coming at me fast. Instead of flinching away,
which would have been useless, I flinched into it and twisted at the
last minute. The punch didn't hit me straight on, my last minute twist
made it a glancing blow. Which was enough to knock me flat on the
ground, given the size of the fist and the muscle behind it.

I saw stars, literally. The ceiling above me was a night sky motif.
A nymph was entwined around a half-moon. Then the giant Caro
stepped in and looked down at me. I pulled the Beretta from my
tactical vest. He swatted it away. He reached down with a massive
paw and pulled away the H&K, handed it over to someone else. I
started to get up, but a female voice said, "Not just yet."

It was Martaud, or Inspector Martaud, as she'd called herself.

She was holding the H&K up and trained on me. "I'm really not
happy with you, Keeler." Her steel gray hair was up in a chignon. She
looked sharp.

I said, "You're happy with yourself? Helping these people get
away with their crimes?"

"I don't give a shit what they get away with, as long as they pay.
Now you've scared off my clients, and they're not going to be
paying anymore. So yes, I'm really rather displeased. It isn't easy

finding clients these days. The market has become a lot more competitive. There are a lot of people relying on me for their livelihoods, Keeler."

Martaud nodded to Caro. He picked me up by my neck with one hand and gut punched me with the other. The punch threw me a couple of feet. My head slammed into the cushioned side of a sofa. I took the pain and rode it out. Then I looked up at him and spoke calmly. "That's it, you beast. Anymore and you die badly, in terror, rather than cleanly, in surprise."

Martaud coughed out a weird laugh. "What I'm going to do is let Caro tear you to pieces. That will be your punishment."

Caro wasn't laughing, he looked deranged, like he was under the influence, which I figured he was. The giant was twitching with barely contained violence. His blond hair was swept back and unkempt. I noticed that Caro's fists were clenching and loosening, in a looping, involuntary spasm.

I said to Martaud, "What are you ex-French intelligence, DGSE?"

She laughed. "Can't fault your detective skills. Not that it'll do you any good."

That accounted for Blomstein's Bogie.

I flipped back to the photographs Nazari had taken. They told the story of how Qadduri's body had been found, and then the crime scene taken over by Martaud's team of imposters. Obviously to stifle any actual investigation of the knife murder. That was slick. Ordering a murder, then suppressing its investigation. There had been a shot of Martaud standing over the body, with Caro. Bonnet had been in the picture, looking at Martaud. I'd overlooked the complicity between them. Maybe it had been impossible to judge at the time, given the information available to me.

An ex-spook turned mercenary. I indicated the giant Caro. "But he isn't ex-anything, at least not anything interesting. Where'd you find this monster?"

Martaud looked reflective. "Found him when I set up my private practice. I think he was killing people for free, just because he liked it. Now I pay him. Caro is very useful and loyal."

Caro was hulking, glowering, red-faced and psychotic. His fists were clenching harder, pulsating with muscle.

I said, "That other guy, Grouse, he didn't end up being very brave. What makes you think you can count on this monster?"

"I'm not counting on him." She racked the slide back on the MP5 and let it snick into place. "I'm counting on Heckler and Koch." Martaud sat down on a cushioned velvet divan. "Now I'll watch you die." She spoke to Caro. "Slowly, and make sure to tear off pieces."

During that exchange, I'd been on my ass, where I'd landed from Caro's sucker punch. Right up against the sofa. Behind my back I'd been using hidden fingers to remove the Opinel from my back pocket, thread it back through the belt loop. Then I flicked it behind me, wrapping the knife handle once around a sofa leg with the line. Taking out the knife wouldn't be a good idea, since Martaud had an automatic weapon. I needed to go through with her little charade, at least to some extent. I didn't have any intention of dying, but I wasn't stupid enough to think staying alive would be easy.

Caro advanced on me, arms out, fingers splayed. Each finger was the size of a Cuban cigar. I figured the main issue was going to be avoiding getting gripped by those hands. I counted my assets. Brains, training, speed, versus pure strength and size. Brains and speed can be overvalued, because brute force can be powerful. Training helps. I got up into a fighting crouch. Arms out just like Caro. But I had no intention of engaging in a fair fight, just needed to find a way of cheating. Caro wasn't going to circle round and think this through, he was going to come at me all in a rush. So, I waited for the signs.

In unarmed hand-to-hand combat, you look at two things, the guy's back leg and the place where his throat meets his chest, that little hollow spot. Back leg because it's what he pushes off from, hollow of the throat because that's his center mass. Both can give you a fractional advantage in knowing what the other guy is about to do.

Caro pushed off his back leg. He pushed hard, lunging at me in a grab with his right hand. I slipped in below the grab and landed my fist into his throat as hard as I could. I held my position for the follow through, then spun across his body like basketball player spinning off a pick. Ended up behind him, watching as the big guy staggered, coughed and spat. I moved in and got a pair of brutal hooks into his kidneys. The punches sounded impressive, like sledgehammers on a side of beef. But they didn't seem to do anything.

Caro came around, glowering at me. He advanced again, slowly. I went first. Jabbed twice to his face and caught him with the second jab in the nose. He shook that off easy. I committed a straight right, which was a mistake. Because Caro was coming up with an uppercut. If that landed I'd be a goner. I switched up halfway through the punch, twisted my body in motion, so I could take the blow somewhere else. Anywhere but the chin, which would have put me out for sure. The clenched fist caught me on the chest, and raised me up in the air, flying like in free fall.

I landed on the cushioned sofa. For a second I didn't think I'd get up again. My brain was saying 'move', and my muscles were saying 'hell no'. Caro was grabbing me around the middle. If that giant managed to pick me up, there was nothing stopping him from hurling me down on something and I'd break for sure. The human body is frail, compared to the floor, or a rock, or the edge of a table. So, I got an elbow up and hit him in the eye. A lucky strike. Caro rocked back, like an annoyed grizzly. No one likes to be hit in the eye. Even a bug can hurt there.

I was hanging down off the sofa where he'd dropped me. The Opinel knife was right in front of my eyes. I unwrapped the wooden handle from around the sofa leg, and clenched it in my fist, like a roll of quarters. I'd found a way to cheat. A solid object clenched in your fist acts like brass knuckles. It isn't a question of weight, but of structure. I rolled off the sofa and came up swinging. My reinforced fist smashed into the side of Caro's head. He staggered sideways.

I was done screwing around and was on him in a flash, looping the braided fishing line around his neck. Then I swung behind him and pulled, quick, before he got his fingers in there. The line dug into his flesh, making an angry white line in red-corded muscle and popping veins.

He was staggering around like a wounded bull. I was riding him, legs wrapped around and holding on for dear life. He was flailing with his arms, trying to get me off. But I was persistent, keeping tight to his body, hugging myself in where he couldn't reach. I had the Opinel handle in my right hand, while the left forearm braced against the nape of his neck. I was holding the line taut but stable enough to restrict the air flow. The beast was shuddering and snorting. He was trying to get oxygen to the brain, I was trying to prevent that. Problem was, I couldn't put immense pressure on the line, or it would break.

So I held the tension, enough that Caro wasn't able to get a real breath in, just a quarter breath maybe. When I felt him sucking wind, I'd twist harder and apply an extra ten or fifteen pounds of pressure. Careful to keep the oxygen flow restricted.

I had promised him terror, and that's what I was delivering. Somewhere in Caro's brain was the knowledge that he was going to die now. At the same time, he was slowly starving of oxygen, so the brain was ceasing to function. Slowly, in terror. I figured that while Caro's thought process was limited, he was a human being after all. Like me, like Martaud. He'd have an instinct to survive. But that wasn't going to help him.

After a minute or two of staggering around, trying to brush me off against the walls and furniture, Caro burst into a furious attempt to shake me. He went all in and put every ounce of remaining energy into a backwards run towards the wall. It might have worked, but I wasn't going to wait and find out. I wrenched his neck to the left. The beast veered to the left and lost his legs. We went over and ended up on one of the love seats. I was underneath the giant, choking him out while he twitched, gasping on top of me. I flashed a look at Martaud. She was watching in fascination with a little curling smile on her face. Eventually Caro quit twitching. I held on tight for another minute, ignoring the pain of something hard sticking into my ribs. No movement, no breathing. I released the line. My hands were throbbing.

It took a while to get my breath back. By then, Martaud was standing over the love seat, pointing the H&K at me. There was nowhere to hide, I was stuck under Caro's corpse. My ribs throbbed, and I realized why. It was Caro's weapon, holstered at his back. I pulled the gun behind his back. Martaud was breathing heavily, excited by the blood lust. Then she looked angry, like I'd broken her toy. I was watching her trigger hand. She thumbed off the safety and selected for single. Her eyes were red. Maybe she'd loved the monster after all? I watched her finger start to squeeze the trigger. And I shot her in the face through Caro's armpit.

Martaud dropped like a sack of rocks, leaving Nazari framed in the doorway, out of breath and holding an H&K MP5S up and ready. I said, "Better late than never."

CHAPTER SIXTY-THREE

I ROLLED out from under Caro's corpse.

Nazari was in shock, looking around at the pleasure palace room. "This is the most evil thing I've ever seen."

I said, "Let's go. There are a couple of girls missing from that room." I picked up the H&K Martaud had dropped. I checked the chamber and closed the bolt. "Everything okay up top?"

"The girls are in bad shape."

"They're young, they'll recover."

We threaded between the sofas and chairs, and across the room. On the other side was a set of double oak doors, like some kind of a grand entrance. I pushed one of them open with my toe. Through the doors was a carpeted ramp. Red carpet with oak-paneled walls. The ramp was steep and extended maybe thirty feet. At the other end was a fat security door. Blank. No handle, no keyhole, nothing. A blunt fingerprint scanner was set into the wall on the left side. An even higher level of security. I figured it meant we were near the end.

I said, "Wait here."

The Opinel is a useful tool. It severed Martaud's right index finger at the knuckle as easily as separating drumstick from thigh. I figured there was a three in ten chance that the severed finger would work. That's because fingerprint sensors are capacitive. Dead tissue is no good. The sensor looks for an electric circuit. The heart sends out signals that make a circuit throughout the body. Once the heart stops beating, the electric signal fades off. That happens in a matter of minutes.

I sprinted back up with Martaud's finger. It felt light and unsubstantial, like a piece of high-end technology. Except it was bleeding flesh and bone. I held it to the sensor. The door clicked and swung back towards us, revealing a white wall with a picture frame. The frame was simple wood. Inside was an oil painting of a stormy sea. A shard of light cut through the clouds to light up a crashing wave. Below the painting were wooden floorboards. A corridor. Then the door opened wider, revealing the bearded guy seated on a bench to the left of the painting. An H&K was resting on the seat next to him. To the left of the bench was a big rifle leaned up against the wall. It was a Hécate II, standard issue French anti-materiel sniper rifle. The guy looked up, probably startled to see that it wasn't Martaud and her beast. I flicked Martaud's finger at him and he caught it instinctively, then dropped it in a panic. Nazari had her H&K up and in his face. He opened his hands and held them out wide.

I said, "Where's everyone else?"

The bearded guy swallowed, like his throat had gone dry. He coughed, then shook his head, as if that would wake him from the nightmare. "He's upstairs, with the girls."

"The mayor, Marbot?"

The bearded guy nodded.

"Who else?"

"There's nobody else."

I spoke to Nazari. "This is the guy who killed Father Bousquet and totaled your Peugeot."

The bearded guy started to protest, but she pulled the trigger before he could get a word out. A triple burst of 9mm bullets stitched upward from his chest to his neck. The gun barrel tinkled, and the rounds thudded into the wall behind him. Light smoke hung in the air, mingling with shredded cotton from where the bearded guy's shirt had caught lead.

We were inside Marbot's fancy house. The bearded guy's corpse was slumped against the wall. Above him, stairs rose to the second floor. The house was quiet. For a moment it felt empty. Then we heard a shuffling sound from upstairs. I signaled to Nazari and we went around to the staircase entrance. It was an old house, like Brumaire, but bigger and fancier. The stairs were polished wood. They creaked as we went up. I whispered to Nazari, "Been here before?" She shook her head.

We got up to the landing. The corridor ran perpendicular to the stairs. We had to choose, left, or right. I chose right. The old floorboards ground against the joists, so there wasn't much point trying to be quiet. I guess Marbot felt the same way, because he cried out from behind one of the closed doors.

"If you come any closer, I'll kill them all!"

The mayor's voice was a shrill shriek, like he was in a state of high tension. I looked at Nazari. Her eyes were narrowed and serious. I continued down the corridor, making no attempt to disguise my footsteps. The mayor's room was at the end. On the way I passed a full-length mirror and saw myself. My face and upper body were covered in blood and grit. Armed, with the tactical vest. I looked like a demon from hell. The mayor shouted again, "I'm going to kill them all!"

I made a running start and kicked in the door. The jamb shattered. Wood splinters exploded out and the door flung open leaving an empty rectangle for me to fly through.

The room was large and filled with light. The walls were yellow. I scanned quickly. On one side was a big four-poster bed. Three girls huddled together trembling. Mayor Marbot sat at a computer desk in the other corner. When I burst through the door, he looked up in shock. He was twisted around from his position at the computer keyboard, like he'd been real busy with something on the screen. The girls had their heads down, not looking up, whimpering in horror and shame. Marbot was dressed in pajamas. White flannel with thin vertical blue stripes. His bulky frame dominated the antique arm chair. A Glock 19 sat next to his keyboard. The mayor picked it up in a hurry, as if it had just occurred to him, like an afterthought. I grabbed the barrel and pulled it out of his hand.

Nazari was right behind me.

Marbot looked like he'd been having a bad morning. He summoned up that old phony charisma. "There's a lot of money. You can have it. I don't care anymore. It was never about the money."

Nazari stepped closer to look at the computer screen. The mayor held up one hand. "First we deal. If you come any closer, I'll press this little button and all the money disappears, forever. First we deal."

He had a finger hovering above the delete key.

I said, "I've never heard of disappearing money."

Nazari was reading the screen from around fifteen feet. Outstanding vision. She said, "It's crypto, it can disappear alright. Why should we care?"

The mayor said, "You should care because of the amount. It's a life-changing sum of money."

I said, "How's that going to disappear if I shoot you in the head right now?"

The guy was a politician. He thought that he'd save his neck by talking his way out of it. "This is a wallet address and private key, you imbecile. It's the only copy. If I press this button, even accidentally, as a muscle reflex, the address disappears and ten million turns to dust."

I'd heard of crypto currency, but I'd never been interested. Some kind of computer money, is all I knew. I said, "Address for what?"

Nazari said, "Crypto currency address. It's a unique record of the funds, like a code for an anonymous Swiss bank account. Don't worry about the technical details, the scumbag's right."

"You learned that in the BRI course too?"

She nodded. "Yup."

I said to Marbot, "So, you're sitting there looking at your money and we're supposed to be impressed?"

He went for an authoritative tone. "No, you fool. I've been consolidating the information and the funds in one place. I'm ready to cooperate now."

"You mean you're ripping off your partners, now that they're dead."

Marbot laughed. "Partners. More like puppets. The puppets were all very happy with the money and the girls, very happy indeed. Then, one by one they began having moral qualms. Hypocrites." The mayor was nodding like a crazy person, eyes wide, face red and fleshy jowls bouncing. "Bonnet, Rigalle, Houdin, you think of a name that means anything in this town and they were involved."

Nazari said, "What about Vaugeois?"

"That idiot? He was just a pretentious old fart who got in the way. I'll tell you everything. I've got dirt that goes all the way up to Paris if they want that."

She said, "In exchange for what?"

Marbot spit out an arrogant laugh. "Immunity of course. For what I've got, they'll give me a deal. They'll hush it up. They always do."

I looked at Nazari. "Think that's true?"

She shook her head. "I don't know, it's possible. It's above my pay grade, that's for sure."

He shouted, "Possible? The deal's already done. Just call my police chief, he's an experienced professional. Why the fuck do you think I brought him on the force in the first place?"

It made me think about Bonnet. Last time I'd seen him, Daniel's shotgun had cut him in half. I wondered which half the mayor wanted to say hello to. I said, "You want to be reunited with Bonnet?"

The mayor nodded greedily. "Bring him, yes!"

I shot him in the head.

The bullet entered just under the right eye, which flipped up in its socket, like a spun pinball. There was a momentary pause before the mayor's body slumped into death. I took advantage of that moment by kicking him off the chair. So, the unique crypto codes didn't get deleted. They stayed right there, highlighted and blinking on the screen.

On the other side of the room, the girls were not huddled with their heads down anymore. We had their full attention. Eyes wide and staring at the mayor's body. They looked relieved and excited.

I said to them, "You can rest easy now, this is over. You're going to be fine." I looked at Nazari. "Crypto currency. I've heard of it, never seen it."

"Me too. I know what it is, in theory."

"So, in theory there's no bank, no nothing right?"

"Nothing, just that code right there."

We both stepped closer. Ten million. Didn't matter if it was ten million bucks, dollars, euros, pounds. Ten million of anything is a lot. There were two strings of gibberish. A long mix of numbers, and lower and upper case letters. One string of numbers and letters was longer than the other.

I said, "So that nonsense gets you ten million bucks."

"I guess so, there are ways of checking how much exactly."

I looked over at Marbot's body, slumped awkwardly on the floor. "No reason to doubt him though."

"Not really, given who he was, and what he's done."

I said, "So what happens to the money when the real BRI gets to it?"

Nazari was looking at the computer screen, like it was something powerful and magnetic, which I guess it was. She shrugged. "I'm not sure exactly. I don't think many people know what this stuff is. They'll probably accidentally delete it. If not, they'll call up a bunch of experts, who will swarm around the computer, blocking it off with sheets of plastic maybe. Then, best case it'd go through a long process. Could take years. Most of the money would get absorbed by the process. Like any kind of government thing."

"Like taxes."

"Yeah, it'd just drip out endlessly into different budgets. Maybe some officials would fight over it. That'd probably cost a bunch in legal fees on top of everything else, which would subtract even more of the funds. The politicians would tug at both ends before any kind of resolution was arrived at. So the ten million would be more like three before they actually did anything with it."

"And then it's liable to disappear into some politician's pet project."

"That's a likely outcome, yes. Or a compromise of three different projects. I could imagine a local or regional politician successfully claiming a portion of it."

I said, "So there are no guarantees of justice."

"No guarantees, nope."

"But you could guarantee justice. I'd trust you."

She shrugged. "Thanks for the vote of confidence. That's a heavy responsibility."

I said, "And if we delete that code on the screen, nobody gets it?"

She said, "Sounds crazy, but I think that's the way it is, yes. It might actually cease to exist in any useable form."

"But, with a Swiss bank account, the bank gets the money, until someone claims it."

"But that's not how crypto works. Here, there's no bank. The money's just up there on the internet, floating around."

I said, "So that's what money looks like in the future."

She shrugged. "I guess we're already in the future."

"I still trust you, in the future."

We looked at each other. I raised my eyebrows, she raised hers.

She took a pen and a notepad from the mayor's desk. I read the string of numbers and letters off the screen, dictating as she wrote onto a piece of paper. We did that again just to be sure. Then, she ripped the page out of the notebook, and put it in her pants pocket. She nodded to me, and I pressed the delete key on Marbot's computer keyboard.

The two lines of expensive gibberish disappeared and only a cursor was left blinking alone on the screen.

CHAPTER SIXTY-FOUR

AFTER THAT THINGS GOT BUSY.

The affair blew up and became a scandal. A proper investigation was conducted, by serious professionals with bullet-proof resumes. Thousands of hours of testimony were taken, recorded, transcribed, printed, and bound into heavy volumes. For months, France woke up to over-excited reports. Some of them were official, others leaked from the investigation. At least a third of it was true.

The town itself was invaded by outsiders, journalists for the most part, but also teams from the BRI, and busloads of civil servants sent there to sort out what had happened, and to write up white papers of lessons to be learned. The media frenzy lasted a couple of weeks before it died down. Once it was pretty much over, the president of the republic held a press conference. Grave and stern statements were made, about how terrible and unprecedented the whole thing was, and how such things could never, ever, be allowed to happen again. A couple of laws were proposed, then ran into difficulties in parliament, and eventually got watered down and adjusted over the course of endless negotiations. Of course, that all took time. Politicians will be politicians, and the motto is, crisis equals opportunity.

Luckily there was no one left to punish, no living body to remind the country of the affair. The perpetrators were all dead. Mayor Marbot got his fifteen minutes of fame as a posthumous villain.

Nazari came out of it the heroine. She was the young police-woman who had gone against the grain. When she'd realized the extent of corruption on the force, she had stood firm. She had exhibited astounding bravery when faced with a clear and present danger to her life. While she wasn't the kind of person to bask in acclaim, she recognized the opportunity for change and reform. There were institutions to reconstruct and trust to rebuild. She took ownership of the situation and rose to the challenge, allowing herself to become a kind of poster girl for a new generation of law enforcement and civic service. She was definitely going places.

But I wasn't there to see any of that.

Back in the mayor's bedroom, the three girls needed to be taken out. I looked at Nazari and she looked at me. Nothing really needed saying, we were both on the same page, looking at each other in relief. I said it anyway, to avoid any misunderstandings that might turn into misgivings.

"That's it then."

Nazari said, "Looks like it, yeah."

"You okay?"

She smiled. "Never been better."

I nodded. "Euphoria after action, normal. Come here." We embraced once, hard. I said, "You did real good."

"Thanks."

"It was great knowing you. No regrets right?"

"Zero."

"I won't forget you."

She said, "I know you won't."

I said, "I guess I could still catch a train today."

"Still pretty early. Spain?"

"Whatever, I'll decide at the train station."

She stayed back in the mayor's house. Someone had to call in the external authorities and begin dealing with the aftermath. I took the girls back through the caverns to the Vaugeois house. Once they were safe and being cared for, I had a long, hot shower, alone. I still had the brown shirt from Fanny's place, relatively clean.

By the time I cleaned up and came downstairs, the house was busy. Emergency care workers had begun to arrive. Madame Vaugeois and Maria were overwhelmed. Miriam was coordinating. I shouldered my backpack and walked out of there. Daniel was digging in the garden. He looked up at me and nodded. I nodded back and came down the driveway next to the vegetable garden. I turned right at the road. Father Bousquet's white Volkswagen and Nazari's Peugeot hadn't been moved yet, but Bousquet's body was being taken care of by a team of firemen. They were cutting it out of the wreckage. I walked past them and over the bridge, past Fanny's Friperie, and into town.

The train station was busy for a Wednesday afternoon. I looked up at the departures board, and matched destination names with locations on the map. I bought a ticket to the city of Tours. From there I could catch an overnight train into the Iberian Peninsula, or maybe cut the other way, down through the south of France toward Italy. The Mediterranean suddenly sounded pretty good.

Whatever, I'd take it one step at a time.

The train was waiting patiently at the platform. Passengers were already getting comfortable in their seats. There were groups of travelers chatting excitedly, solo travelers reading books, or immersed in their own world, cocooned in headphones. After a while I came to the rail car at the back, the one that had the old style seating. I walked by several compartments that had already been taken and found an empty one. The curtains drew closed and I found a seat facing forward. I leaned my head against my backpack and closed my eyes. I got that old familiar feeling, free falling through a cloudless blue sky. Nothing but air around me. Down below an incredible and remote landscape. I'd get there, eventually, but not yet.

When I opened my eyes again, the train was moving at speed.

Chugging down the line through open fields. The sun was up and it was a glorious day. I wasn't alone in the compartment. There were five of us. Directly in front of me was a young woman. She was in her twenties, strawberry blonde hair, long nose, high cheekbones, slim and attractive. She was looking at me as if she knew me. Then I recognized her, the librarian in the floral print dress. She wasn't wearing the same dress. She was in jeans and a light cream-colored sweater. She smiled and leaned forward. I leaned forward, and we met in the middle.

She spoke quietly. "You remember me."

I nodded. "I do. From the library."

She smiled. "You never came back to see me. I was waiting for you."

"Things got busy I guess, I'm sorry about that."

"No big deal. That happens all the time. I don't take it personally."

I said, "I'm sorry just the same. I ended up finding my mother's relatives. That's why I didn't come back to see you."

The librarian's face turned red all of a sudden, her mouth formed into a worried shape. "Oh."

"What, did you find something?" She was embarrassed. I said, "You can tell me."

"Well, actually I did. But, let me ask you, did your relatives recognize your mother? Did they know her?"

"Not personally, but they found her in the family history, the link was there."

She nodded. "Yeah, that's misleading. The tricky part is in the last name. Your mother's name is Delphine Vaugeois, right?"

"Was Delphine Vaugeois, yes."

"Sorry, was. In town, we have a Vaugeois family. Simone and Gilles. I assume that's who you found. They're prominent."

I nodded. "That's right."

"Thing is, wait ... Stop me if you don't want to be disappointed."

I said, "No, go on."

She said, "Thing is the local family aren't Vaugeois. Simone's maiden name is Blanchett, Simone Blanchett. She married Gilles fifteen years ago, a second marriage for both of them. Before that, there's no trace of a Vaugeois living in Alencourt. Nothing. So, it's possible that Gilles is somehow related to your mother, tangentially, loosely, whatever. But it's unlikely that your genetic relation to Gilles Vaugeois is closer than your relation to any random person, in this train carriage for example."

I looked around at the people curled up into their seats. "So, Gilles and Simone are not my cousins, and there's no trace of my mother's family in Alencourt."

The librarian smiled. "They aren't more your cousins than I am. Although all human beings are related somewhere down the line, way back."

I nodded, absorbing this information. She dug into her backpack and pulled out a Tupperware box. She opened the lid. Two sandwiches sat side by side, plump and attractive. "Do you want one?"

I bit into the sandwich, I was suddenly extremely hungry. The train hurtled down the track, gunning southwest, into the late afternoon sun. The librarian smiled and looked out the window. I followed her gaze and settled in for the ride.

AN EXTRACT FROM
BREACHER

CHAPTER ONE

I was crossing the street, noticing the cross-walk lines on the road, freshly painted, and the foot gear choices of the cruise ship tourists. It looked as if trail walking was high up on the list. New and newish hiking boots, adventure sandals, low-top trail shoes. Then I raised my eyes and caught the guy's reflection in the window of a drug store.

He was walking behind me. Not too close, but close enough. It was a guy I'd seen before.

Specifically, I had seen him during the third bite of my burger, which was about twenty minutes earlier and memorable. I had looked up and there he was at a deuce by the window, looking right at me. Eye contact. An athletic blond man in his late twenties with a trimmed beard. He was drinking from a mug with a string coming out of it. It took me a moment to realize it was a hot beverage called tea. By that point he had looked away. Besides the tea, the other thing was the beard.

In Port Morris, Alaska, beards are not memorable. They are commonplace, but a well-trimmed beard less so. Most beards I'd seen in the last four months working on a fishing boat had been either untrimmed or badly trimmed, but this guy's beard was well-trimmed. Like he had access to a good mirror and good light. Maybe a mirror with lights on it, like in a hotel with a star rating. Good mirror and good light, two things definitely missing in the sleeping quarters of a fishing boat, which tend to be dimly lit mirrorless cavities behind the engine room.

I stopped and pretended to look at something in the window display. The guy swerved, slowed up, and started thumbing through a postcard rack outside of the tourist gift store. His left hand was bandaged, so he was thumbing through the cards with his right hand. I scanned in the reflection for other watchers. Another man was posted by the door to the diner. I hadn't seen him before. He was leaning against the wall, below the stairs. Baseball hat and light blue button-down Oxford. I started walking again, nice and slow this time.

The next intersection was catty corner to a bank with an angled window. I glanced at the reflection before crossing the street. The guy with the well-trimmed beard was moving, now around forty feet behind me. I upped the pace from casual to brisk. Walked a couple of minutes without looking behind me. If there was a team tailing me, that might string them out and break their formation.

I cut left over a footbridge, crossing the creek to go up Lake Road. There was overflow from a bar. Fishermen taking a smoke break from drinking their salmon money. All beards were either badly trimmed, or untrimmed. I asked one for a cigarette, using the interaction to turn and glance down the road. The well-trimmed beard guy was on the bridge, both hands on the worn railing, looking down at the fish running up the creek from the Pacific toward the sweet water spawning grounds.

At the intersection, I saw a crowd of tourists from the cruise ship. Around forty of them packed together like fish in a net, spanning the street and sidewalk. They were coming down Bryant Street, headed back to the boat after a tour of the salmon creeks. I let myself be absorbed by the crowd. Threaded my way in and amongst them, keeping my head low. I dropped down as if to tie my shoe, screened by geriatric vacationers. It only took a couple of gestures and a shrug to pull off my backpack and jacket. I had a ball cap in the bag. I turned the jacket inside out and wrapped it around the backpack. When I stood up again, I wasn't a bareheaded guy wearing a forest green Gore-Tex jacket and a backpack, I was a guy wearing a t-shirt and a black cap and holding a tan package under my arm.

I reversed direction to join the flow of tourists as the group shuffled downhill toward the dock. I smiled at an older lady pulling on the arm of her partner. I said, "Are you with the boat?" She nodded and I turned away. From the hill I could see the cruise ship below. In fact, it was visible from almost anywhere in town. I moved down the street, going with the flow. Like a paper boat in a rain-swollen gutter. I didn't see the first guy from the diner. He was probably still searching for me further up the hill.

A minute later we passed the guy with the Oxford shirt. He was walking uphill, looking like a kid who had lost his teddy bear. I broke out of the crowd below him and stepped into the shadow of a chartered trips office.

I was now a few buildings up from the diner where I'd had that burger, like a full circle. I stayed there for a minute, observing. My baseball cap was pulled low and I figured with the beard I looked just like any other fisherman in Port Morris. Mid-thirties, tall, and jacked from pulling on ropes all season. I hadn't been in shape like that since pararescue indoctrination.

I recognized the girl standing on the other side of the road. She hadn't made me. She was blonde, wearing a tourist bucket hat with a Port Morris logo, and carrying a bag from the souvenir store. Like she was just another tourist. But I was pretty sure that she wasn't just a tourist.

I had met her the night before.

GET A FREE NOVELLA

Building a relationship with my readers is the best thing about writing. I send the occasional newsletter with details on writing, new releases, and other news related to the adventures of Tom Keeler.

And if you register for my Reader Group I'll send you a copy of Switch Back, a Tom Keeler Novella.

Get your free copy of Switch Back by signing up at my website. jacklively.com

See you there.

JL

ENJOY THIS BOOK?

You can make a big difference.

Reviews are the most powerful tools in my arsenal when it comes getting attention for my books. Much as I'd like to, I don't have the financial muscle of a New York publisher. I can't take out full page ads in the newspaper or put posters on the subway.

(Not yet, anyway).

But I hope to have something much more powerful and effective than that, and it's something that those publishers would kill to get their hands on.

A committed and loyal bunch of readers.

Honest reviews of my books help bring them to the attention of other readers.

If you've enjoyed this book I would be very grateful if you could spend just five minutes leaving a review (it can be as short as you like).

Thank you very much.

JL

ALSO BY JACK LIVELY

Tom Keeler Novels

Breacher

Novella

Switch Back

ABOUT THE AUTHOR

Jack Lively was born in Sheffield, in the UK. He grew up in the United States of America. He has worked as a fisherman, an ice cream truck driver, underwater cinematographer, gas station attendant, and outboard engine repairman. The other thing about Jack is that since he grew up without a TV, before the internet, he was always reading. And later on, Jack started writing. All through those long years working odd jobs and traveling around, Jack wrote. He'd write in bars and cafes, on boats and trains and even on long haul bus trips.

Eventually Jack finished a book and figured he might as well see if anyone wanted to read it.

Tom Keeler is a veteran combat medic who served in a special tactics unit of United States Air Force. The series begins when Keeler receives his discharge from the military. Keeler just wants to roam free. But stuff happens, and Keeler's not the kind of guy who just walks away.

Jack Lively lives in London with his family.

Made in the USA
Las Vegas, NV
19 June 2025

23805039R00215